GONE

IN SECONDS

GONE
IN SECONDS

A.J. CROSS

First published in Great Britain in 2012 by Orion Books,
an imprint of The Orion Publishing Group Ltd
Orion House, 5 Upper Saint Martin's Lane
London WC2H 9EA

An Hachette UK Company

1 3 5 7 9 10 8 6 4 2

A CIP catalogue record for this book
is available from the British Library.

ISBN (Hardback) 978 1 4091 4267 6
ISBN (Trade Paperback) 978 1 4091 4268 3
ISBN (ebook) 978 1 4091 4269 0

Typeset at The Spartan Press Ltd,
Lymington, Hants

Printed and bound by CPI Group (UK) Ltd,
Croydon, CR0 4YY

The Orion Publishing Group's policy is to use papers
that are natural, renewable and recyclable products and
made from wood grown in sustainable forests. The logging
and manufacturing processes are expected to conform to
the environmental regulations of the country of origin.

www.orionbooks.co.uk

Gone in Seconds is dedicated to the following very special people:
Martyn, Kathy, Hope, Evan, and Brian, my husband and best friend.

A hot summer's day during a time of innocence, years before, two small girls walking along a familiar road; a man cycles past, waves, then disappears between nearby park gates. The girls do not know him. They're thinking of ice cream. Minutes later they follow his route into the park, cones in their hands. Laughing. Licking.

The man is there, leaning on his bicycle, close to a densely wooded copse, watching, waiting. He understands little girls; quickly identifies and intuitively rejects the bossy one, in favour of her small friend. He studies her, absorbing the tumbling hair, the short-sleeved T-shirt revealing rounded tanned arms, the small striped skirt lifting on the light breeze, exposing pink pants as she frolics with her friend.

It takes a single, soft call from the man to get her to come to him, as his hand increases its rhythmic action. He looks into her eyes, sees her face mesmerised by his movement. Then he seizes the rich hair as she falls backwards, mouthing a silent 'O'. His throat releases a guttural sound, the curls slipping from his slick grasp.

Times change. But people don't. There's always a predator, ready to create a victim. A young woman, her blonde hair tied with a red bandanna, a heart-shaped purse and her father's letters in her hand, walks away from her home and into a void.

Four years later another young woman strolls through a shopping mall, laughing with friends. She too is lost and the world spins on.

The years slide by, the predator blends, but the girl in the bandanna has left a tiny legacy, concealed in a crack in a cement floor, where it waits for anyone who cares enough to look.

CHAPTER ONE

Dr Kate Hanson walked quietly through the rear door concealed by a curtain to one side of the auditorium. The only person she'd anticipated being there had already arrived: Julian Devenish, her very able student helper, who was frowning into a textbook, wiry frame sprawled on a canvas chair. He got to his feet as she entered.

'Hi, Kate, Dr Hanson. Everything's ready to go,' he said, itemising what he was saying with a finger. 'Sound checks are done, I've adjusted the lighting like you asked, and the PowerPoint is on stand-by. I've put copies of the research notes on the table, ready for students to take at the end. If anything goes wrong – which it won't – I'll sort it. All you need to do when you go on is tap—'

Kate smiled up at the tall, long-haired student's earnest face and nodded, voice low and reassuring. 'Thank you, Julian. I really appreciate your help. Please – carry on with your reading. I'm sure everything will work out perfectly.'

Propping herself on the edge of a nearby table, she glanced at her watch – 1.55 p.m., Wednesday afternoon. She could hear the sound of the auditorium filling and an accompanying buzz of talk. In another five minutes she would begin her first lecture of this academic year. Closing her eyes, she took a series of deep breaths, then opened them.

Julian was holding out a note to her. Leaning forward, Kate took it from him and glanced at it as she riffled through her bag to locate her phone. Checking its screen, she frowned. No evidence of the call she had been expecting. She transferred her full attention back to the note. *Phone DS Watts, Rose Road. ASAP.* She scrolled through to his listed number and waited. No reply. She cut the call, then switched off her phone. No one seemed to want to talk to her today. Another glance at her watch. One minute.

Standing, she smoothed the narrowly tailored black Armani skirt over her hips and adjusted its matching jacket. Noting a glance and a nod from Julian, she breathed deeply, flipped her thick dark-auburn hair behind her shoulders, readjusted the jacket and walked out on to the platform amid an expectant hush, one hundred and fifty pairs of eyes tracking her movement.

Tapping a key on the waiting laptop, she turned to the ranks of young faces. Some she recognised from university interviews. One or two she knew well, including a surprise attendee sitting at the back of the cool auditorium, fair-haired, pristine white shirt reflecting the light. She sent a small smile in his direction, but he didn't pick it up. Too far away.

'Welcome to my introductory lecture for Criminology Year I, Module 1, "Psychology, Crime and Criminal Justice". Anyone misplaced or not interested might consider leaving now.' She waited. Heads turned. No one moved. 'Good,' she said quietly. 'A captive audience. Let's go!'

Another tap filled the huge screen with head-and-shoulders photographs. All female, approximately two-thirds white, some with dated hairstyles, young, smiling and guileless. Others with more 'used' faces. Quiet murmurs drifted from the audience.

Kate glanced at the screen, then out into the auditorium, voice quietly authoritative. 'An extensive picture gallery, isn't it?' She laser-pointed. 'These eight females are connected. These seven are another skein . . . as are these fourteen.'

Her audience gazed at the images. She monitored them with peripheral vision. 'I suspect that most of you won't recognise these faces, but I'm hoping they're part of the reason you've chosen criminology as your field of study and future career. In my view, they need to be.'

Kate walked slowly to the front of the stage and faced her silent audience, lowering her voice to make the first key point of her lecture. 'Twenty-nine females. Mostly young. British, Italian, German, American, Canadian, Australian. No geographical boundaries. I could have shown you many, many more.' A few seconds' pause. 'They and the twenty-nine young women on the screen are waiting. For those working in criminology to give them something.'

Knowing that her audience was listening intently, Kate returned to the laptop. 'What happened to these young women that made them into victims is that their paths crossed with those of individuals –' a decisive tap – 'such as *these*.'

The screen changed to an array of male faces. Gasps and murmurs of recognition drifted down to her.

'You may not recognise all of them, but I'm willing to bet there isn't a single person in this lecture theatre who can't name at least five.' She waited.

Silence.

'I win,' she said quietly. 'Odd, isn't it, that we're more familiar with individuals who commit cruel acts than we are with those who suffer at their hands?' She nodded, observing small, embarrassed smiles on a number of faces.

Kate laser-pointed the head-and-shoulders photographs. 'All of these men are, or were, predators. If still alive and given the opportunity, they would commit further violent offences, similar to those that led to their incarceration.'

She looked up at the pictures, then back to her audience.

'There's no reason to blame ourselves if it's the predator's face rather than that of his victim that triggers recognition and stimulates our interest. Much of the responsibility for that lies with the media. In all its forms.'

Kate paused for a couple of seconds. 'Before you begin your studies with me, I have some advice for you. It's this. Forget the fictionalised crime that books, television or Hollywood have shown you. Forget what passes for theory about repeat murder, whereby a killer's activity is presented as rigidly focused on the same victim type, never deviating from a pattern.'

Another pause.

'Sexual predators have their preferences, but they don't necessarily display the exact same stereotypical behaviours towards all of their victims. That they always do so has, unfortunately, been a cliché for the last two decades, because it makes for appealing books, TV, films. But that's all. We need to be wary of making lazy assumptions based on unreliable science.'

Kate scanned her audience. 'Predators are not as rigid as we might be led to believe.' She took a few steps towards them. 'Why not?' She lowered her voice. 'Because these men's fantasies *change*. And, like you and me, they *adapt*. They *learn*.' Adding even more softly, 'Which I'm hoping is something that's going to happen here in the coming weeks.'

The sound of the Chamberlain Tower bell drifted across the lush, unseasonably hot late-September campus and into the auditorium. No one in the audience moved.

'I said that the young women whose photographs I showed you earlier are waiting for something. From you and from me. What is it they want?'

She heard the several one-word responses and nodded, gratified. 'Yes. If and when you become workers in criminology, there will be other victims. You'll need to be clear-sighted and use reliable theory to give them the justice they're waiting for.'

Kate scanned her audience again, before emphasising her next key statement. 'These men *never stop*,' she said quietly. 'Because their behaviour is driven by deep psychological need. It's not unknown for them to *rest*. For a year. Or more.' A pause. 'But never doubt it. Eventually they return.'

In the heavy silence of the auditorium, a single hand was tentatively raised.

'Yes?' asked Kate.

'Why? Why do they . . . rest?'

She smiled at the puzzled-looking student. 'For a criminologist, "why" is one of the most powerful words there is.'

She returned to the front of the platform. 'Why *do* they rest? Research suggests that this may occur when repeaters experience some positive change in their lives. Something new that provides them with satisfaction, soothes the compulsive need. Maybe a change of job, or a new relationship, which carries reward sufficient to distract them from deviant patterns of thinking and behaviour.'

The students watched as Kate paced, then turned, emphasising her words with an adamant hand. 'But inevitably a point is reached where the new-found satisfaction is not sufficiently strong to suppress the urgency of fantasy and the thrill of re-enactment. Once he's taken his "sabbatical", he'll be back.'

With a small smile, Kate laser-pointed the photographs still displayed on the screen, her eyes on the young people gazing at her. 'A final plea, particularly to the females in the audience. Take a really good look. Ordinary males? Some quite attractive?'

Grins appeared on many faces.

After a few seconds her own face became serious. 'For the young women I showed you, one of these faces may have been the last they ever saw. One of those men may have been nightmare personified. *Never* underestimate such a man. He's not just an actor.' She paused. 'In the theatre of repeat murder, he's the director.'

The words hung on the still air of the auditorium.

Kate anticipated that maybe a handful of her audience would recognise the real-life predator in the description she was about to offer. 'So. Next time a nice-looking man with his arm in a sling drops his books at your feet and asks you to help him load them into his little Volkswagen Beetle, *please* tell him, "Sorry, I'd love to help, but I *really* don't know you."'

The auditorium lights came up as she finished, tension dissipating as her audience burst into spontaneous applause. She smiled and gave a small wave, then walked quickly towards the end of the platform and disappeared from view.

CHAPTER TWO

Against the hubbub of tilting seats and raised voices, Kate collected her bag and files, aware of her up-tempo pulse. Not an unusual experience, she'd found, after the long summer vacation.

Julian loped past her in denim cut-offs to retrieve equipment from the platform, 'Grateful' in red on the front of his black tee, 'Dead' on the back. When he returned carrying the laptop and laser pointer, Kate gave him a warm smile.

'Thank you for being here today, Julian. It frees me to focus on my presentation without getting distracted by technology and whether it'll screw up what I'm doing.'

'No problemo, Kate.'

Not the kind to stand on her dignity or demand deference, Kate allowed informality outside of lectures, particularly as Julian was also her junior colleague in the work she intermittently did with the West Midlands Police.

Seeing that she was ready to leave, Julian waved a hand. 'See you at the next tutorial.'

'That you will.'

Kate left the auditorium and went out into the afternoon heat. She walked purposefully along the hot asphalt path edged with ragged brown grass, past motionless campus trees burdened still with summer leaves, although some were beginning to flame and fall.

Looking ahead, she caught sight of an athletic figure in white shirt and jeans, a holdall on one shoulder. The unexpected member of her audience. She hurried after him.

'Harry! Hey, Harry! Wait.'

No response. She tried again, louder this time. He stopped, pulled out earpieces and turned, face closed and dour as students surged either side of him. Kate recalled Harry's liking for Mahler and Wagner. Those two could darken anybody's outlook.

On seeing Kate, Harry's face cleared, then broke into a wide grin as she quickly covered the distance between them. Reaching him, perspiration oozing on to her forehead and chest, Kate pushed her sunglasses further up her nose and passed her briefcase from one hand to the other.

'Didn't expect to see *you* in my lecture this morning.'

Harry Creed managed the forensic scenes-of-crime team based at West Midlands Police Headquarters, known to its familiars as Rose Road. Kate's role there as consulting psychologist to the Unsolved Crime Unit had brought her into occasional contact with Harry and his colleagues during the last eighteen months. She felt indebted to him for agreeing during the previous academic year to allow Julian to shadow the scenes-of-crime team, thus allowing the student to add an additional module to his studies. Aside from this, she found forty-ish Harry likeable.

'Hi, Kate. Thought I'd come and see how the fortunate few among us pass the time in academia.'

She smiled, knowing that Harry, a forensic graduate, coveted a part-time lectureship in the university's psychology department.

'So. What do you think? Did you like what you saw?'

He nodded enthusiastically. 'Definitely. I can see myself being a part of it. The students are keen, and in lectures you're master of your own universe – or "mistress" in your case.'

Kate laughed as they walked side by side. 'Yes, well . . . sometimes.'

They'd gone a few steps in silence when she glanced at him. 'What did Professor Bennett have to say when you went to see him?' Aiden Bennett was Birmingham University's Professor in Criminological Psychology, and Kate had agreed to mention to him Harry's interest in an academic position. She'd been happy to do so, aware of Harry's ability to connect with students, which she'd observed from his inter-actions with Julian. Her understanding was that Harry had arranged an appointment with Professor Bennett to discuss the possibility of his providing, as a first step, the occasional unpaid talk based on his forensic work.

'I haven't met him yet.'

'I thought you'd agreed a date?' said Kate, surprised.

Harry shook his head. 'No. But I will. Definitely. I want to prepare properly for when I do see him. Make him aware of my dedication to the education of young minds and—'

'Why not just go along for an informal chat? See how the land lies?' asked Kate.

'I want to present my strengths and commitment to him as clearly as I can . . .' Kate glanced at Harry, seeing keenness in his face but sensing from his voice that there was a problem. 'But there're a few distractions at the minute. Donald's future's uncertain. He's on a fixed contract, and with the cutbacks, he might have to contemplate a move.' Silence fell between them. Kate was aware that Harry had a partner. 'And my mom and dad's health isn't the best. I've been staying at their place for a few days.'

Kate nodded her understanding. Shortly after she had started work at Rose Road, Harry had come into UCU, where she was trying to get acquainted with some of the police procedures that might be relevant to her in her new role. They'd talked easily for a while. Kate had spoken a little about herself, and Harry had told her about his situation, particularly his parents' support of his relationship with Donald. Kate had been heartened by what she'd heard.

She was about to offer a sympathetic comment but Harry's face had already brightened. 'It'll all sort itself out, and I *will* phone and arrange that meeting with Professor Bennett. I'll let you know how I get on. I'm really grateful to you for putting in a good word for me, Kate.'

Kate smiled. 'All I did was mention you, but Aiden did seem interested.'

They had reached the short path leading to the multi-storey car park.

'Got your car, or do you need a lift?' asked Kate, eyeing the lower floor of the car park, not her favourite parking choice.

Her gaze moved rapidly over the deeply shadowed car-filled area, her caution a legacy of her theoretical knowledge as senior lecturer in forensic psychology, plus the work she did for the criminal courts evaluating offenders prior to sentencing or release. The questions asked of her as part of that were many and varied, but the gist was the same: would she comment on the risk of this person committing sexual and/or violent acts in the future? The work brought her into contact with a mix of problematic individuals, including the opportunistic, the mean and the vicious, and occasionally she was required to defend her opinions in court.

'I'm on foot, today. Want me to walk you to your car?' asked Harry, seeing Kate's face and aware of her personal caution. Unsurprised by his chivalrous offer, she declined.

'Thanks, Harry, but I'm fine.' If it had been midnight she might have taken him up on his offer, but three thirty on a sunny afternoon?

She gave a small wave as Harry walked away towards the main exit road, then hurried into the multi-storey and directly to the black Audi TT parked in the shadowy dimness. She scanned the floor of parked vehicles as she reached the little car. At this stage in the term the campus was extra busy. When she'd arrived earlier, lecture imminent, she'd needed to be certain of finding a parking place. This had been the only option available.

Scanning her more immediate surroundings, Kate deactivated the TT's alarm and unlocked the car. *So I'm paranoid. I'm also alive.* Dumping her belongings in the boot and adding her jacket, she opened the driver's door and got into the car. One benefit of parking here: your car wasn't a furnace when you returned.

Operating the central locking and checking her watch, she tapped for the numbers list on her phone and selected one. It rang out. Frowning, she tried again. This time she left a brief message. Recalling the note Julian had given her earlier, she tapped that number too. No luck there either. Sighing, she dropped the phone into the small-change compartment, turning on ignition then air conditioning.

Guiding the Audi out of the multi-storey and towards the main exit of the university campus, she scrutinised the red-brick building opposite. King Edward VI High School for Girls. The destination of one of the messages she'd left. With some brief drumming of fingers on steering wheel, she crossed the flow of mid-afternoon traffic and followed the curved drive to the wide-open doors of the school, scanning the small groups of young pupils and lone stragglers meandering away.

Stopping the car, she peered through the doors – above them the school motto, 'Trouthe Schall Delyvere' – to the wood-panelled entrance hall with its cool marble floor. Deserted. Everyone gone. Checking her watch again, she followed the drive back to the road and rejoined the traffic.

CHAPTER THREE

Mother and daughter were engaged in a face-off in the large square kitchen, cooling now that the massive floor-to-ceiling folding doors were opened on to the extensive garden. Dressed in dark-green combat trousers and charcoal agnès b. T-shirt, Kate was unpacking shopping, crossing and recrossing the pale ceramic floor to disperse cartons and packets to various cherrywood cupboards as she spoke.

'We *agreed* that you would ring me during the morning or at the end of your lunch break, so I would know what time to pick you up. You *didn't* ring,' she finished irritably, closing one of the cupboard doors firmly to emphasise the point, feeling the metal bracelet of her watch slide loosely against her wrist. *Must get that fixed*.

Since her tenth birthday, Maisie had consistently pressured Kate to allow her to have a mobile phone, pressure Kate had resisted for around eighteen months. Since then she'd been anticipating a demand from Maisie for Facebook access. Surprisingly, so far none had come. If it did, Kate determined, there would be *no* Facebook, unless Maisie demonstrated by use of her mobile phone that she was trustworthy and reliable.

A muted pain started up behind her eyes. *Don't fight battles before they start*. She pulled open the twin doors of the tall aluminium fridge freezer, depositing items and removing others, closing the doors with a foot and an elbow.

Seated at the large scrubbed-wood table, head supported by one hand, Maisie glared at her mother and rolled her large blue eyes, heart-shaped face defiant, tawny skin flushed beneath a mass of thick curls.

'Because I knew you were busy with freshers this morning so there wouldn't be any point! What's *wrong* with catching the bus, anyway?'

Maisie got up and mooched to the biscuit jar sitting on one of the black granite work surfaces.

Kate didn't yet have an answer prepared for that question, so she ignored it, reluctant to communicate directly to Maisie her own fears around personal safety. 'You know very well that you could have left a message if I didn't answer. You and I must agree ground rules, Maisie, for when you are out of this house, and then we have to stick to—'

A sudden pounding on the solid oak front door reverberated across the wide hall and into the kitchen. 'Who's *that*?'

'How should I know!' groused Maisie, dropping back on to her chair and nibbling a biscuit.

Kate heard the vacuum cleaner upstairs fall silent, followed by heavy footsteps coming downwards. Still annoyed with Maisie, she quit the confrontational atmosphere of the kitchen and walked into the hall, to see her housekeeper, Phyllis, beating a path to the front door. Kate slowed, watching Phyllis move, a galleon under full sail, bust an impressive bolster, hair a mix of bleach-blonde and grey. Phyllis had begun working for Kate way back, when Kate had an erring husband and a plump, puce-faced Maisie in her arms. The two women understood each other. Phyllis had reached the door and now heaved it open.

Standing on the wide porch, in white shirtsleeves, arms folded across his barrel chest, was a man who would not see fifty again. Greying hair plastered to his scalp by heat, face flushed, his eyes sharp beneath impressive eyebrows, he grinned, showing the small gap between his two front teeth, which added to the louche look.

'Afternoon, darling, is your mother in?'

As Phyllis turned away in disgust, there was a distant snigger from the kitchen.

Kate acknowledged her visitor. 'Oh, it's *you*. Come in.' She turned and headed back to the kitchen. 'It's okay, Phyllis.'

'Afternoon to you too,' responded Detective Sergeant Bernard Watts of West Midlands Police Headquarters, following her inside.

Kate and Bernie Watts had met around eighteen months before, when the plan to establish an Unsolved Crime Unit for the re-investigation of cold cases of sexual attack and murder was first mooted by West Midlands Police. Her working relationship with Watts and her other colleagues in the unit had evolved into an easy camaraderie, despite her initial wariness of his abruptness and sarcasm, his broad Birmingham accent and his allusions, historical and local, which she'd found difficult to follow at times. Black humour and banter had also been a part of her early induction into the ways of the Force. She now recognised both as necessary coping mechanisms.

Kate entered the kitchen to find Maisie perched on the kitchen table, a calculating expression on her face. Giving her daughter a meaningful glance, Kate walked past her and on to one of the work surfaces to construct a sandwich, talking over one shoulder.

'We haven't finished this discussion, Maisie, but it'll keep for now.' Her daughter responded with a theatrical sigh.

Their visitor took a seat at the table, grinning at Maisie. 'What you been up to, bab?'

Maisie pouted. 'Nothing! That's the point! I'm not allowed to *do* anything and every move I make is questioned. Who? When? What? Why? Where?' She sighed again. 'I don't have a private life,' she finished, watching her mother keenly from beneath long lashes.

Kate turned wearily, butter knife in hand, knowing she should quit the back-and-forth. 'Maisie, you're too young to have a "private life". You are twelve years old, and while . . .'

'Thirteen in eighteen-point-five weeks *actually*, Mother.'

'. . . you are young and in my care, you and I have to agree ground rules. I must know where you are when you aren't in this house.'

Scowling and muttering, Maisie jumped down from the table and headed for the door.

'What did she say?' demanded Kate, watching her daughter's back as it disappeared in the direction of the stairs. 'And those shorts are too . . . *short*!'

After a few seconds' silence, a door on the upper floor slammed. Kate sighed, putting the plate she was holding down on the table.

'She said something about "No wonder my dad left",' Bernie responded helpfully. He reached for Maisie's uneaten sandwich as Kate dragged a tall plastic container of skimmed milk from the refrigerator. 'Some advice for you, Doc. Forget it. Life's hard enough.'

'Coffee to go with that?' Kate asked. 'The trouble is, she knows how to get me going. I understand she's at an age when she thinks she can be out there making her own decisions. Obviously she can't. So this is all we do at the moment. I set rules and guidelines, she ignores them or argues, I rise to what she says . . . It's a constant merry-go-round. Compared to the aggravation I get here, my working life is – yes, I *know*. I've forgotten it. See?' She displayed even white teeth in a phoney smile and put the container down on the table.

'Got any decent milk in this house?'

Kate massaged her temples. 'Don't *you* start. Why're you here anyway? I got your message. I rang you. Twice. No reply.'

Bernie wiped thick fingers on kitchen paper and reached into an inside pocket as Kate got busy with the cafetiere.

'It's possible UCU's got another cold case. Remains found off the Halesowen Bypass. Got a likely name already, would you believe. Have a look.'

He pulled a flat manila envelope from his pocket and tossed it on to the table. Kate came to pick it up, looked inside, then withdrew a single ten-by-eight photograph.

'Who is she?'

Bernie leaned forward and tapped it with a finger. Kate read the name from the gold necklace around the girl's neck. ' "Molly." '

'If it *is* her, her full name's Molly Elizabeth James. Eighteen. Disappeared from Touchwood shopping mall in Solihull in 2002.' There followed a brief silence while he ate. 'You know that Joe's back?'

Kate took the remaining half-sandwich, giving it her complete attention. 'So I heard,' she said lightly.

'He's meeting me here in about ten minutes,' he said.

Kate's heart executed a small back-flip.

Bernie continued: 'We're going over to have a look at the scene. Connie's been there since early this morning.'

Kate noted the involuntary movement of Bernie's hand to his hair as he mentioned the name of Rose Road's attractive pathologist. She placed coffee beside him, poured one for herself and sat down opposite.

'How about it, Doc? Be useful to have you there as well. Want a ride in my car?' The eyebrows rose and fell.

Kate looked at her watch, then nodded. 'Definitely, despite Mummy's caution against that kind of invitation.'

Bernie finished the sandwich and scanned the table. As Kate rose, there was a commotion on the other side of the kitchen door and Phyllis appeared, lugging the vacuum cleaner. She and Bernie eyed each other warily. They shared a history of sorts, both having grown up in the same tight-knit working-class area of Birmingham, which Bernie invariably referred to as 'the Old End'. Kate wasn't entirely sure where this was located or even if it still existed, given Birmingham's extensive urban regeneration over the last forty-something years.

Many months before, on learning of Kate's professional involvement with the police at Rose Road, and more specifically with Detective Sergeant Bernard Watts, Phyllis had delivered a quick foundation course on the ways of 1950s working-class Birmingham and Bernie's place in it.

'*Detective Sergeant?* Ha! His mother had seven kids, you know. All in steps.' Phyllis had raised a flattened hand in a step-wise manner to demonstrate the close, regular production of the Watts progeny. 'She was a real tartar. Used to stand on the corner of their street screaming the kids' names – "*Chrissie! Josie! Malky!*" – and they'd all come running from different directions. *He* was the youngest. Everybody in the area knew that family. My mother said they were common.' Phyllis had closed her mouth at this, opening it to add, 'We had a television. *And* a car.'

Kate now turned to her housekeeper. 'Phyllis, I told you to call me and I'd carry the Hoover down. Would you like coffee?'

Phyllis bustled past. 'Yes, ta. What's he after?' she muttered.

Bernie adjusted his face to bland. 'The Doc's helpin' the police with their inquiries.' He looked at Kate. 'The Arse is raising the case at headquarters' meeting tomorrow.'

Kate nodded at the reference to Inspector Roger Furman and to indicate that she could be at the meeting. Her university timetable for the term hadn't fully begun. She heard Phyllis tut, probably at the word 'arse', as she shoved the vacuum cleaner into its cupboard.

'She's got enough on her plate without you bringing her more to do. She's got that girl to raise single-handed, she's up at that university all hours and in court—'

Bernie lowered the eyebrows at Kate. 'You been at the shoplifting again?'

'It's okay, Phyllis. I'm fine.'

Phyllis was now at the table and on a roll.

'What she *doesn't* need is you or that other one coming round here with murders and . . .' Here she dropped her voice, mouthing the word 'sex'. 'And I don't know what else. She could do with an 'oliday.'

Phyllis shifted her attention back to Kate. 'Did I tell you, Avis has just got back from the Republico Domingo? She said it was fantastic!'

16

Kate offered Bernie another sandwich and a repressive glance as Phyllis exited the kitchen.

He shook his head, grinning. 'She's worth every quid you pay her, just for the comedy value.'

'*Sshhh*,' hissed Kate. 'If Phyllis ever gives notice, I'll be in a real mess.'

There was a sudden knock on the front door, followed by Phyllis's heavy footsteps, more muttering and the sound of the door being opened. Kate heard a deep, resonant voice and her heart picked up its beat. In seconds Phyllis was back in the kitchen.

'It's the other one. The Yank. I told him to wait. Shall I let him in?'

'Of course, Phyllis!'

Kate leaned sideways, taking in the details of the tall, broad-shouldered arrival as he walked across the hall and entered the kitchen. He was wearing a blue shirt the colour of his eyes, jeans and brown Frye work boots. His hair was longer than it had been when Kate last saw him, brushed back from his tanned face, sun-streaked and reaching his collar at the back. He also had a small beard, brown flecked with grey. Seeing all of this, Kate was oddly perturbed at the changes eight or so weeks had brought. She glanced at him again, guessing that he was as oblivious to his physical impact right now as he had been when he joined the Force at Rose Road more than a year earlier, his arrival causing a stir among its female officers and civilian workers.

Kate left the table with the cafetiere, in search of an extra cup.

Joe Corrigan. Kate knew that the Birmingham police had seized the opportunity to offer a secondment to the highly trained firearms officer from Boston, Massachusetts, at a time when all police forces in the UK were having to deal with the threat of internal terrorism and the consequent need to skill up their armed response teams.

She felt her spirits lift as she heard the soft 'Hi', and smiled up at him as he took the coffee she offered. He thanked her with a tired grin.

Within another two minutes, Bernie stood, adjusting generous trousers. 'Right. Time we was gone.'

Kate walked with them into the hall, calling upstairs: 'Phyllis? Can you stay until I get back? Then I'll give you a lift home. I'm going with Bernie and Joe.'

Getting what sounded like a positive response, she turned to follow her colleagues as Maisie appeared on the half-landing, lolling against the banister, watching them as they crossed the hall.

Bernie looked up at her and winked. 'Stop giving your mother an 'ard time.'

Joe acknowledged her with a grin. 'Hi, Cat's-whiskers. How's the math?' he asked, referring to Maisie's prodigious mathematical talent, towards which Kate felt a marked dissonance: pleased for Maisie, but also worried that it might set her apart from her peers. So far that hadn't happened. Maisie wore her gift lightly.

Maisie returned the grin. 'Easy,' she said, matter-of-fact. Recalling her 'put-upon' role, she grimaced and tossed her curls, giving her mother a quick glance. 'I'm going to Chelsey's house. Could you drop me in Hamilton Avenue, Bernie?'

Bernie eyed Kate, who gave him an imperceptible nod.

'Can do. You ready?' Bernie said.

Maisie bounded up the few stairs and reappeared in seconds with her backpack. Kate followed her as they stepped outside the house.

'Seven thirty, Maisie. *Don't* forget. And I told you not to have your name embroidered on that.' She pointed at the pink backpack. 'It's an unnecessary risk to advertise your personal details.'

'Stop being so tetchy. It's only a *name*,' muttered Maisie, as a small black-and-white cat darted past their ankles and through the open door.

'Phyllis?' Kate called into the hallway. 'Mugger's home!'

They walked across the drive in leaden afternoon heat and climbed into Bernie's four-by-four. Sitting with Maisie in the back as they moved forward, Kate asked Joe about his return journey to the UK.

'Did you have a good flight?'

He nodded. 'Fine. But I've got a *real* bad case of let-jag. There. See?'

Maisie giggled. With a glance in her mother's direction, she leaned forward and spoke directly to Joe.

'Would you like to come and have dinner with us again, Joe? Mom could make a curry.' Her tone became reassuring. 'Don't worry. It'll be okay. She makes it from a kit—'

'Maisie!'

Within five minutes Bernie slowed as they neared a sprawling mock-Tudor residence with black wrought-iron gates at its entrance. Maisie quickly opened the car door and leapt out.

'Seven thirty sharp, Maisie. *Don't* be late.'

With an open-mouthed shake of the head and a 'yeah-yeah' response, Maisie ran to the gates and pressed the button on the intercom. She spoke into it and one of the wide gates glided silently open. Bernie released his handbrake and started to roll forward.

'Not *yet*,' commanded Kate.

He applied the brakes sharply. 'You born bossy, or did you have to work at it?'

Kate watched as Maisie ran the length of the drive and reached the front door, which opened almost immediately, revealing a tall, shapely blonde who waved to them. Chelsey's mother.

Getting an okay from Kate, Bernie pulled away from the house, and within a few minutes they were into their journey along the teeming dual carriageway of the Hagley Road, one of the main arteries leading out of the city.

CHAPTER FOUR

Now that they were on their way to the scene, Kate's increasing anticipation acquired a sudden frisson of tension. She hadn't seen any human remains in the months she'd been a member of UCU. Was it the girl whose picture Bernie had brought? As if reading her thoughts, Bernie looked at her in the driving mirror.

'We've got the necklace, but it might not be this girl, Doc. Her details are on the PNC "MisPer" database, but *you* know how many people disappear in a decade.'

Kate nodded and gazed out of the window at the open country now racing past them. Coming as she did from the south-east, Kate was often surprised even after several years of living here at how quickly one could leave the UK's densely built second city and be in rural surroundings. Even from its centre, it only took minutes. Theoretically. Add half an hour to that for congestion.

Several more minutes of following the traffic stream and Joe's voice broke through Kate's thoughts. 'We're almost there.'

She looked up to find his blue eyes on her face, before he turned back to the road. Pulse quickening, Kate leaned forward between her two colleagues, looking to where Joe was pointing. A knot of parked police vehicles some way ahead, traffic slowing as it passed.

Reducing his own speed, Bernie activated his left-hand signal and executed a gradual turn, close to a red-faced young officer in regulation short-sleeved shirt who was energetically waving on gawking drivers as they neared the police activity beyond the roadside. Kate recognised the young officer. Whittaker. From the reception desk at Rose Road. He directed Bernie to an open area running alongside the dense, tree-lined expanse beyond the road. They came to a stop beside a black estate vehicle with tinted glass, half a dozen blue-and-yellow squared 'Battenberg' Vauxhall Astra police cars, plus two similarly marked transit vans.

Stepping out of Bernie's vehicle, they swapped air conditioning for sudden heat, despite the hour. Kate caught a glimpse of white through the press of surrounding trees, and her pulse accelerated again.

Bernie showed ID to another officer, who took their names and added them to a sheet attached to a clipboard, writing Kate's under the heading 'Civilian'. Issuing each of them with a roomy white jumpsuit, into which they struggled, he directed them towards a narrow pathway worn into the thick undergrowth.

They walked in single file, Joe in the lead, Bernie following, flapping his hands against insects, a red baseball cap now on his head.

'That's a bad look, Bernie, if you don't mind my saying so,' Kate murmured.

'Julian give it me. It's medicinal. My scalp's sensitive.'

As they followed the path over the bone-dry ground, Kate eyed the cross-hatching of grasses and tiny dark-blue flowers whose name she didn't know. She saw evidence of a fire and a litter of cans off to one side. They walked on in silence, past silver-grey saplings, beneath bowed mature trees, their lower branches spread like open hands, leaves lit by the sun. She reflected that in different circumstances the area might be a pleasant place to ramble.

How did anyone manage to navigate a way through here from the road, burdened with a dead weight?

Or was she made to walk?

She.

Molly Elizabeth James.

Perhaps the area was less overgrown so many years ago.

Kate shivered as the direct heat was momentarily blocked by heavy foliage. Another minute's walk and they reached a clearing. Added to the natural sounds of birdsong and the hum of distant traffic were the harsh, disembodied voices from the Communications Centre, breaking intermittently from receivers attached to various uniformed officers. Off to one side forensic scenes-of-crime specialists in blue jumpsuits were using pegs and narrow yellow tape to mark out a grid. Others pushed latexed hands into earthy thoroughfares made by animals or worked in twos sieving earth, the bone-dry topsoil cascading around covered feet.

Kate caught a glimpse of Harry Creed, blue-suited, pointing and instructing as he moved around the site. With him was one of his team, Matt Prentiss, a surly expression on his long face as he followed, attending to what Harry was saying.

A technician was busily photographing every feature of the site. Despite his mask and coveralls, Kate recognised the dark hair and wire-framed glasses of Jake Brown, crime-scene photographer, and nodded to him. No response. Back when Kate joined UCU, he had invited her out for dinner. She'd politely declined. He hadn't asked again. Or even acknowledged her, as far as she could recall. A 'mature' man who couldn't handle minor rejection? She'd got *that* one right.

Kate suddenly caught sight of a slim figure in white, beyond quivering *Do Not Cross* tape. She gave a small wave and got a positive response. On reaching the tape they stopped. Bernie, now hatless, smoothed his hair.

Connie Chong, Home Office pathologist, approached them carrying her plastic face-shield in one hand, face flushed. 'I was expecting you, UCU! Come under the tape and follow me.'

Kate and her colleagues did as bid, following her towards the white tent. Kate felt Matt Prentiss's eyes on them as they passed. No one acknowledged him, knowing from experience that Prentiss rarely responded to overtures.

As she walked through the tent's entrance, Connie pulled on the hood of her jumpsuit and repositioned the face-shield.

'Okay, UCU. Hoods up and come forward . . . forward and . . . *stop.*' She held up a hand and they stood side by side inside the mouth of the tent as she proceeded beyond them.

A wall of heat and earthiness rose to greet them. Kate gazed uneasily at the stark rectangle of raw earth surrounded by green-yellow grasses. More tiny blue flowers quivered at its edge.

Connie was now on the opposite side of the rectangle. Crouching, she pointed a small gloved hand towards what looked to Kate to be little more than undulations in the raw earth, then gazed up at them.

'Two Forestry Commission workers were out here early yesterday. They noticed a marked increase in vegetation in this particular area.' She gestured at the patch immediately in front of her. 'They trowelled it briefly and came up with part of the gold necklace you know about.

Adding two and two, they rang Rose Road.' Connie stood and flexed her legs.

'Nobody tells you how hard pathology can be on the knee joints. Anyway, this is as far as we've got in our excavation, but it's clearly human remains. Almost certainly female.' She crouched again, pointing. 'See? Head this end. Feet there. I can't be categorical about her age or how long she's been lying here. I'll let you know when I've had a chance to get the bones under UV light and measure the nitrogen content.' She scanned the barely visible remains, then looked up at each of them in turn. 'My *guess* is that she's been here at least five years.'

Interest piqued, Kate stared down at the newly worked earth. She now recognised the undulations as human remains; could make out the lines of long bones, the dome of a skull and the tiny pebble-like features of a hand. She considered the timescale Connie had just indicated.

It fitted Molly James, who disappeared in 2002.

Might fit any number of others . . .

Connie gestured towards the area immediately outside the tent. 'The technicians are looking for any remains that might have been dug up and carried away by small animals in the past.'

Kate and her colleagues now crouched, studying the excavation and the poorly defined skeleton.

Joe glanced at Connie. 'Got any guesses as to age?'

Connie smiled at him. 'Push, push! Okay, I'm guessing young. Late teenage years possibly.'

Another fit with Molly James.

'I'll have an informed opinion when I get her back to Rose Road, do the bones and take a look inside the mouth. Right now I can't even confirm if the jaws are fully intact. If they are, it'll still be only an estimate. The DNA samples I've collected from her may be degraded, but I'm hoping to rely on familial DNA for identification.'

They waited as Connie gently dislodged red-brown earth from around the skull with what looked like a very fine trowel. 'I took a look at what's on the system for Molly James before I left this morning.' She sat back on her heels. 'Some far-sighted type from the Bradford Street forensic team that worked the initial investigation requested DNA samples off her mother shortly after the daughter was reported missing. The samples from our girl were sent to the lab early this morning. Being processed as I speak.'

Kate wiggled fingers at Connie. 'What happens next?'

'We carry on freeing the remains, sufficient to move them without causing damage.' Connie stood and walked over to Kate, removing her face-shield, face damp with perspiration. She ruffled her hair with her other hand. 'Which I reckon might take us into the early evening. We've got scene lights, but any later than that and my job gets difficult. I prefer to work in daylight. Once the remains are freed, they go back with me to Rose Road for a thorough examination. The scenes team will stay. To make sure we've got everything there is to get.'

Kate and her colleagues straightened, Bernie with a grunt.

'What about debris around the general area?' asked Kate, pointing. 'There's remains of a fire back there, plus some drinks cans.'

Connie looked at her, head on one side. 'What's your thinking, Katie? Our girl's been here at least half a decade. The stuff you're referring to is probably recent partying.'

Kate lifted her shoulders. 'I thought it might be worth salvaging. Depending on whoever killed this young woman, he *might* have returned since. For some . . . recreational purpose.' She was referring to the predilection of some killers for spending masturbatory time with their victims.

There was a huff of disgust from Bernie. He'd learned a lot from Kate in the short time they'd been colleagues. Most of it he'd have preferred not to know.

Connie gazed at Kate for some seconds, then grinned, with a shake of her head. 'Yours is a dark art, Katie. Okay. I'll instruct the scenes technicians to snap-and-bag.'

Kate nodded her thanks.

Bernie had not spoken up to then. Now he looked away from them, squinting at the woodland scene. 'Bloody waste. Whoever's done this, if you want my opinion, he wants stringing up—'

'Once incarcerated, such offenders can make a useful contribution to theory,' intervened Kate, knowing all too well Bernie's hang-'em-and-flog-'em sentiments.

'Yeah, yeah. You've said. And give 'em all a plasma screen and therapy and everybody's happy, according to you.'

Kate left it. 'Any ideas at *all* as to cause of death?' she asked Connie.

Connie shook her head emphatically. 'None. Even when I've got her back to Rose Road, I still might not be able to establish cause, given her condition and the time lapse.'

Joe quietly thanked Connie and turned to retrace their careful route back to the road, boots striding over the dried vegetation.

Bernie gave Connie a terse nod and walked in the same direction. He liked the pathologist. He liked the small stature and the neatness of her. Like Kate, but without the attitude and the quick mouth. He never minded getting just a 'yes' or a 'no' from Connie.

His phone rang. Furman. Wanting to know what was happening.

Kate hung back to watch as Connie deftly worked around the contours of the remains with the little trowel-like implement, perspiration sheening her face. Inside the Protech forensic suit, the fine hairs on Kate's forearms suddenly stood to attention. She hugged herself, wondering how and why the destroyer of this young woman, whoever she was, had brought her to this.

Maybe he was a boyfriend and they'd argued?

He killed her in a fury of – jealousy?

Or maybe he was a stranger?

If so, how did he accomplish what they were now seeing?

A sudden blitz attack, or something more subtle?

An opening gambit?

Hello! Can you direct me to . . . ?

Kate's thoughts took a darker turn.

Hello, darling. Looking for business?

She looked again at the remains that might be all that was left of a young woman named Molly James. She considered what might reasonably be deduced about the doer – the killer – known or stranger.

Had to be mobile.

Familiar with the area.

. . . And that was it.

UCU would have a lot to do in the coming weeks if it was their case.

Kate shivered despite the heat, pondering the enduring daily risk to females, thoughts of Maisie whispering around the edges of her thinking. She suddenly found herself hoping it wasn't the young woman whose photograph she'd seen.

Without looking up, Connie spoke quietly. 'If you want to know when to come and talk, and assuming I get her back to Rose Road

25

later today, I'd say your best bet is really early on Friday morning. It'll be quiet then. Just Igor and me there.'

With a last glance at the remains, Kate left the tent, her mind still full of questions. Removing the white suit and dropping it into the large paper sack held by a gloved officer at the entrance to the scene, she joined her colleagues inside Bernie's vehicle and began to order her thoughts.

Length of time fits.

Gender fits.

And most significant of all – the 'Molly' necklace found with the remains.

She shook her head. They needed to wait for Connie. Still . . .

The question now: why was this young woman's life ended?

Establishing the why would lead them to consideration of the bigger question.

Who?

Kate was finally on top of her outstanding work and prepared for the new term ahead. She tidied the desk in her downstairs study, thinking not for the first time that her post as senior lecturer at the university was enough work for anyone, without taking on the extra demands associated with criminal cases.

Shaking her head, she recalled the telephone call she'd had early in the summer vacation from a firm of solicitors, asking if she would be willing to see their client, currently on remand in Birmingham Prison, assess him, and report on her opinion as to his future capacity for violence. She had allowed herself to be drawn in by a mix of professional flattery and detail about the client's deviant history.

Now she glanced at the hefty addressed envelope sitting on the corner of her desk. Report completed. The solicitor wouldn't like it. Neither would his client, who, in Kate's opinion, was a tightly coiled spring of impulsivity and resentment, ready for activation at the slightest provocation. Somewhere down the line she would probably be directed to attend court to defend what she'd written about him.

She had decided she wouldn't take on any more such work. What she did at the university, plus the hours she now gave to UCU when needed, was enough. She walked out of the study and closed the door firmly.

*

Professional life under control and Maisie eating dinner at Chelsey's, Kate was now revelling in the quiet of the old house, watching a rerun of *Inspector Morse*. With a faint tinkling sound Mugger padded across the sitting room, leapt on to the sofa and circled several times before draping himself over Kate's legs. The case was defying Morse, who was becoming increasingly grumpy, despite having one eye on a beer and the other on his well-built leading lady.

Kate repositioned the sofa cushion, half-closed eyes on the screen. She hadn't a clue who'd done it and cared even less. Her thoughts turned to Maisie and the friction between them earlier in the day. A small frown appeared at the top of her nose. Maisie knew she was expected to return home from Chelsey's house at seven thirty. But would she? As Kate watched the mellow collegiate scenes play out, she felt torn between her reluctance to allow her daughter out alone and the need for Maisie to learn how to keep herself safe whilst becoming increasingly independent. Kate knew that the forensic nature of her profession, combined with her innate circumspection, resulted in a marked personal caution. Did she really want the same for Maisie?

She put the strains of single parenthood firmly to the back of her mind and let her thoughts drift to Joe. Their working relationship was characterised in the main by light-hearted banter, and there was a lot she didn't know about him.

How old? At a guess, early forties . . .

Old enough to have a significant other tucked away in Boston?

Her thoughts moved on to UCU's new case. What was it her old and beloved PhD supervisor had said to her several years ago?

Work with the police if you feel you must, Kate. But be warned. Do well and they'll take all the credit. Make a mess of things and they'll hang you out to dry.

A loud advertisement for car insurance dragged her back to full consciousness. Dislodging the cat, she walked from the sitting room across the spacious hall to the kitchen in search of the envelope left by Bernie earlier in the day. Returning to the sitting room and the sofa, she opened it and shook the colour photograph on to the low table in front of her. It came to rest face up.

Kate studied its subject.

Young, female, sweet smile, long fair hair. A hint of spiritedness in the eyes. She touched the photograph gently. It felt slightly warm, from the residual heat of the kitchen. Peering into the envelope again, she noticed a sheet of paper. Extracting it, she read the name 'Molly Elizabeth James', plus a reference to an ex-boyfriend of Molly's, aged twenty-eight at the time the girl went missing.

Mmm . . . Bet that didn't please her mother.

She replaced the sheet and the photograph in their envelope. Morse had reappeared. In a pub. The cat stopped arching and circling and rearranged itself on her legs.

Kate stared in the direction of the television screen, now robbed of relaxation by her second viewing of the photograph of Molly Elizabeth James. She thought about tomorrow's meeting at Rose Road. She disliked that kind of formality. Just as she had managed to recreate a more relaxed mindset, the front door opened, then slammed closed almost immediately.

'Hi, Mom! I'm home. Dead on time!'

Kate heaved herself to standing, leaving a small, disgruntled cat alone on the sofa.

CHAPTER FIVE

Molly James gazed from the free-standing glass screen inside the spacious square office of the Unsolved Crime Unit, located on the ground floor of the massive modern red-brick building that housed West Midlands Police Headquarters.

It was early Thursday morning, and Kate and two of her colleagues were already at work at the extensive table in the centre of the room. Near one wall stood a computer workstation, the curved desk supporting various manuals, textbooks, Caffè Nero cups, an opened crisp packet and another packet in similar condition containing M&Ms. Julian's domain. The office was carpeted in dark green, its walls a pale toning green. Hung with vertical cream blinds, the wide windows looked out on to smart little terraced houses beyond the black metal railings and brick pillars of the car park.

'We need to get some ducks in a row, quick, if what we've seen is the James girl,' said Bernie. 'You know what'll happen at the meeting. Furman'll be going on about finances and he'll see to it that the minimum's spent and we won't get enough time to reinvestigate properly.' He gestured to a box labelled 'James'. 'Any road up, on the strength of what we know so far, I fetched this from the evidence store.'

The phone suddenly rang and Joe lifted it. Today he was wearing a formal dark grey suit. The long hair and beard were still in place.

Kate watched as he listened and occasionally nodded.

He hung up and looked from Kate to Bernie. 'Connie's started the post-mortem. Short length of gold chain found within the bypass remains matches the rest of the necklace found at the scene. In case we're still in doubt, the DNA checks out. It's Molly Elizabeth James lying downstairs.'

Kate breathed in. They'd expected it. Now they knew for sure.

The door suddenly opened and Julian walked in dressed in Lycra shorts and carrying a cycling helmet.

'Afternoon, Devenish,' murmured Bernie.

The youngest member of UCU turned to him, looking surprised. 'It's only eight fifteen!'

Kate smiled at the young newcomer. 'Hi, Julian.'

Bernie placed a hand each side of his substantial waist. 'If I can carry on? The stuff in this box is all we've got on the James girl's disappearance.'

He flipped the lid and lifted out what looked to be a motley collection of loose A4 sheets and plastic envelopes, which he placed on the table, proceeding to divide them into two approximately equal piles. He passed one of these to Kate.

'Here you go, Doc, you and Devenish have them. Me and Corrigan'll take the rest. By the way, have you heard what he's up to?'

'Dread to think,' responded Kate with a wary glance at Joe as she prepared a page in her notebook to receive the day's information, and Julian left the room carrying his backpack.

'Corrigan's got himself a mountain bike. Easy Rider comes to Harborne.'

Kate gave the relaxed American a mock-severe look. 'Hope you've bought a helmet as well. Wouldn't want a scraped nose.'

'I'm improvising. With half a watermelon.' Kate laughed and he gave her a grin, head on one side. 'Sounds like you care about my well-being, Hanson.'

Kate looked up quickly, straight into the blue eyes. 'Actually, I only have to care for people under fourteen,' she huffed, cursing as she listened to herself, uptight and humourless.

As if reading her thoughts, Joe grinned again, brows raised. 'Have to take your laughs where you can get 'em, Red.'

'More Boston-Irish philosophy?' she snapped. 'And I've told you not to call me that,' she added stiffly, at a loss as to why she'd become so snippy and wondering how to recover the usual lightness between them.

'Probably. But still true,' he said.

Kate gave her attention to the small heap of papers Bernie had handed her. Within a few minutes Julian had returned, showered and wearing jeans. Leaving his backpack near the computer, he took the chair next to Kate. She looked up as Joe stood, watching him as he walked to the glass screen and picked up a black marker.

'How about we get some background information up here for quick reference?'

Mind back on the job, Kate read the notes he was making, including some verbal contributions from Bernie. There wasn't much. Molly Elizabeth James, aged eighteen, disappeared from Touchwood shopping mall, Solihull, in July 2002. The ensuing local investigation was followed by a request to West Midlands Headquarters here at Rose Road for assistance. The investigation into Molly James's disappearance officially ceased in early 2003. Kate considered the timing of that decision. Probably financial in part, plus the impingement of newer, equally serious investigative demands.

'Why aren't these cases better recorded? Why aren't they on some detailed system of missing—'

'They would if they weren't "old and cold",' interrupted Bernie. 'There's no money to include them on the COMPACT system that's now up and running. This force is no different to any of the others. It's cash-strapped.'

Joe pointed to some yellowed newspaper cuttings on the table. 'Molly was eighteen, five-seven tall, long fair-to-blonde hair. The day she disappeared she was wearing a pale-blue polo shirt, cream casual trousers, brown suede loafers, gold necklace, carrying a navy-blue backpack with white trim and Ellesse logo. Reports from Birmingham's own newspaper, the *Post*, and one or two nationals, including *The Times*, indicated that she was regarded as a cool, on-the-ball kind of young woman. Not the type to go anywhere with a guy she didn't know. Consensus from the adults in her life was that she was responsible. Sensible.'

Julian's head shot up. 'Why wouldn't she be? She was eighteen, man.'

'Listen and learn, lad.' Bernie snorted. 'I've got a daughter older than you.'

'You got suits older than him, my friend,' Joe murmured, scanning what he'd just written.

'All I'm saying is most of 'em *seem* sensible but generally they're mad as herrings,' Bernie responded indistinctly, pen in his mouth acting as surrogate cigarette.

Kate sighed, looking ceilingwards. 'Holding *that* thought for now,

31

do we know who from Rose Road was actually involved in the original investigation?'

'Let's see . . .' Bernie riffled A4 sheets. Kate watched patiently as he read through information, mouth moving silently. At last he spoke. 'Rose Road was called in very early on . . . after the first couple of weeks, by the look of it. I remember there was talk of local officers struggling and needing Headquarters expertise.' He turned more sheets. 'Names of six officers from Upstairs . . . none of them still here . . . Bradford Street nick provided the forensic scene specialists.' He looked up. 'Rose Road didn't have its own Forensics back then. Let's see who the senior investigating officer was from here . . . Oh, you'll love this. It was the Arse. *Sergeant* Roger Furman, as he was then.'

Julian was leaning on his forearms studying the press cuttings. Kate looked from him to the two senior colleagues.

'How do you think he'll view our reinvestigation of the case, given that it was once his?' As she asked this, she experienced a quick jab of dislike for Furman, now an inspector. Joe raised his shoulders slightly in response, his limited experience of Furman more or less matching hers.

Bernie walked heavy-footed towards the glass screen, talking over his shoulder. 'I've known the Arse a few years now, Doc. He don't like or support *nothing* that isn't in his own interests. But I'll tell you one thing that'll happen now: as it was originally his case, he'll be interfering with everything we do.'

He scanned the written-up information, clearly finding it deficient. 'This girl . . .'

'Molly,' prompted Kate.

'Yeah, she leaves home, walks the mile or so to the shopping mall, and *zap!* Good night, Vienna. What we've got to find are the names of persons of interest from the original investigation.' He pointed at the papers on the table. 'They'll be in that lot. Then we get 'em into a list.' He turned to the screen and wrote Molly James's name and 'Persons of Interest' in large letters, which he underlined twice.

Within ten minutes they had five names.

Kate watched as Bernie completed the last entry on the list, then pointed to the first. 'John Cranham – I've heard that name. Why? How?' she demanded.

'You would, if you've ever had a Mercedes. A right posh git from what I recall of the talk here at the time. His family owns one of the biggest dealerships in the country. In Solihull. I'd really be interested in him as one of our persons, but according to his statement, which I've just read, he was out of the country when she went missing.'

'So he had an alibi?' queried Kate.

Bernie held up a wide hand. 'Not so fast, Doc. All this needs rechecking. And there's something else here that could use our attention. According to the press cuttings, Cranham's dad offered a twenty-thousand-pound reward a couple of weeks after the girl went missing, "for information leading to the whereabouts of Molly James". *That* could indicate a link to Posh Git.'

Kate frowned at him, palms up. 'So, Cranham Senior's a wealthy local businessman? Maybe he wanted to be seen to be doing his civic duty, by encouraging the search efforts?'

Bernie gave her a look. 'The point I'm making is what might've been *behind* the reward angle.'

Kate eyed him. 'How about altruism?'

He shook his large head and one thick finger. 'No, no, Doc. You need to start thinking outside of the box.'

'I'll do my best,' she said drily.

'How about this for a theory. Maybe Cranham Senior had an idea that Number One Son *knew* this young girl – yeah, yeah, Molly. She lived close to his place of work, don't forget. He could've seen her out and about. Maybe the reward angle was his dad's way of diverting attention from Posh Git being involved in her disappearance?'

'Right. By drawing nationwide attention to the family? I see your thinking,' responded Kate, rolling her eyes.

Bernie continued, unabashed. 'Reverse psychology. You should know about that. What I'm saying is, all the persons of interest need another good look, right?'

'What about Person of Interest Number Two, George Colley?' asked Kate, pointing at the glass screen. 'Who's he?'

'I know him *and* the next one,' Bernie replied. 'First, Colley. He's a sex type who was living close to the mall at the time. Says here he was in a bail hostel. A nuisance in the area for years. A flasher.'

'Exhibitionist,' corrected Kate.

'Wha'ever. There's a lot else he's done. We'll definitely have him in if he's still about. Now, Alan Malins, our third POI, he was working at Molly James's mother's house at the time Molly disappeared – *and* he's one of the Lads.'

Kate looked thoughtful. 'What was he doing there?' she asked, recognising the police euphemism for known criminal.

'Local building contractor. With sidelines in domestic violence, GBH and fraud. He was landscaping the Jameses' front garden at the time Molly disappeared, which is very promising for us.' Bernie rubbed his hands together.

Julian looked up at Bernie, frowning. 'Why's this photographer guy, George Brannigan, a person of interest? He was working at the shopping mall taking pictures that day. He had a legitimate reason for being there.'

Joe turned to him. 'Probably for that very reason, Jules. He would've been regarded as a potential witness.'

Bernie jabbed a finger at the list. 'POI Number Five – Jason Fairley. *That's* the boyfriend. And not much of a boy at the time, neither.'

Julian looked at Molly's photograph, then at Kate. 'What do you think might have happened to her?' he asked quietly.

'I could only guess, Julian, until we know the results from the post-mortem.'

'You listening, Devenish?' Bernie transferred his gaze to Kate. 'Sex, Doc. It's *always* about sex.'

Kate nodded. 'Often true.' She stood and paced slowly towards the window, thinking of what they'd seen at the bypass, then turned. 'It seems to me that we need to focus this reinvestigation quickly.' She avoided looking in Bernie's direction. 'But, we need to be careful not to make any assumptions. The remains are a key source of information for us.' She paced some more. 'When we get Connie's findings, they might help us establish whether Molly was killed by someone in whom she evoked strong personal feelings. Maybe someone who was angry with or about her. Perhaps that person was jealous, or frustrated by some incident or situation involving her. Emotions so strong, directed at her as an individual, that he – and it probably was a he – killed her. Obviously that would mean that he *knew* her. It would signify his having an *emotional* connection to Molly and a personal motivation for what he did to her.'

Joe stood and walked to the glass screen, where he wrote two of Kate's words, ending with a question mark. Kate continued as they listened, Julian busily note-taking.

'The other possibility is that she was abducted by someone who didn't know her at all. A total stranger. Motivated by some unknown agenda or need in him that he felt compelled to express . . . and he used Molly as a vehicle for that self-expression.' There was a brief silence. 'If she was killed by a stranger, our reinvestigation is obviously going to be much more difficult.'

'That'd make it a sex murder, what you just said? Like *I* said, sex.' Bernie nodded sagely.

'Probably. It would also signify that Molly's abduction was *instrumental*. She was a means to an end that only the doer knows and understands.'

In the following small silence, Joe wrote another of Kate's words, again adding a question mark, as Bernie looked at Kate, eyebrows together.

'So say, just for example, it turned out be somebody like this photographer who done it, somebody who didn't know her – that'd be your . . . instrumental type, right?'

'Possibly,' nodded Kate.

Bernie shook his head, looking vexed. Never expect a straight yes or no from the Doc.

The door opened suddenly and they all watched, silent, as Inspector Roger Furman crossed the room. He was wearing a well-tailored suit, light-brown hair faultlessly brushed, his usual air of arrogance evident in the set of his shoulders and his facial expression, Bernie's epithet for which was 'Arse-about-face'.

'Forget them,' said Furman, jabbing a finger at the list on the glass screen. 'They were exhaustively checked out as part of the original investigation. After this morning's meeting I'll brief you on time-scales. I'll see you upstairs in ten minutes. I've got an important document to look through.' He headed for the door and disappeared back through it.

Bernie watched him go. 'He means his Blockbusters catalogue's come in the post.'

With a last look at Molly James's face staring from the glass screen, Kate adjusted the fitted white shirt over slim caramel trousers and followed her colleagues out of UCU and upstairs to Meeting Room One.

CHAPTER SIX

As UCU's personnel walked into Rose Road's largest meeting room, they were subjected to a barrage of greetings and comments from the officers already present, a group known collectively as 'Upstairs', due to the location of their extensive office.

'Hey, Wattsie! Got yourself a cushy cold case investigation? Here's a tip for you – it was the butler that done it.' This from Detective Sergeant Alan Rand, a sharp-eyed officer whom Kate knew as one of Joe's armed-response trainees.

'Ta for that, Randy. I'd write it down if I was interested.'

Randy transferred his attention to Joe. 'Hey, boss, can I be there when the Arse sees the hair? And the beard?' Joe grinned, and Randy continued: 'When's the next range practice? I've been watching *The Wire* and I'm gonna humble you.' Following this, Randy and his two colleagues, 'Newt' Newton and 'Sticky' Hemmings, began a tuneful rendition of 'A-Hunting We Will Go', as they executed small side-by-side steps, arms rolling, fist over fist, fingers pointing in unison.

Joe gave a sideways glance at Randy. 'All in the game, boy, and I'm gonna whup yo' ass.' This elicited laughter from all three officers.

Newt grinned at Bernie, then looked to Kate and back again. 'See you still got your shrink, Wattsie. She sorted your little problem out yet?' He took a bite of the doughnut he was holding, followed immediately by a mouthful of coffee.

As Kate and her colleagues took seats at the expansive meeting table, Newt rested his considerable backside on its edge and Sticky slid into the chair next to Kate.

'Hey, Kate,' he said softly, but sufficiently loud for the others to hear. 'You started reading our minds yet?' He grinned at her, one eyebrow raised.

'Sticky, I'd be reading yours right now, if you had one,' she said with an answering grin.

'Ooo-ers' and laughter drifted around the room. 'Word of advice, Stick,' called Randy. 'Kate's way out of your league, my son. Brain the size of a small planet, which well outranks your walnut.' There was more good-natured laughter.

Kate thought back to her initial experience of scenes like this and the difficulty she'd had at the time in identifying her own responses, given that she was used to the politically correct social discourse of the university. Now that she knew what to expect in terms of Force humour and repartee, she was a match. Which didn't stop her tackling Bernie whenever she considered something he said to be inappropriate.

Female inconsistency? And why not.

The door suddenly swung open and several people filed inside, Connie Chong among them. Kate raised her eyebrows in Connie's direction and the pathologist responded with a small smile. The atmosphere had now changed in the room. This was what Kate didn't like. The formal meeting. Everyone quietly took seats as Kate gazed around at the newcomers.

Chief Superintendent Gander was seated at the head of the table, a heavyweight with ruddy jowls spreading over his shirt collar. He sat, hands clasped together, rhythmically tapping the surface in front of him. To his left was Superintendent of Operations Al Bowen, heavy-set northerner and sometime golfing partner of Gander, and next to him, Superintendent CID Gus Stirling, mild-mannered, courtly, known to don the kilt at Headquarters celebrations. Kate had had some limited contact with the three men during the time she had been part of UCU. They all belonged Upstairs.

The door opened again, this time to admit members of the various forensic departments Kate had seen at the bypass, including Matt Prentiss, Scenes of Crime Operations, looking older than the late thirties Kate knew him to be. He took a seat, his gaze not shifting from the middle distance, his usual sour expression in place. Next to him was Jake Brown, Kate's would-be date, whose glance skimmed the top of her head, and Dr Wes Jacobs, the short, scholarly scientist responsible for forensic testing. Kate had never seen him dressed in anything other than his white lab coat. Harry Creed, in a cream-coloured shirt and black linen jacket, grinned across the table at Kate.

37

He was looking tired, and she was aware that he, along with Matt and others in the Scenes department, was working long hours at the bypass.

Kate's contact with Upstairs was renewed only when a cold case was identified for reinvestigation. So. Here she was again, keen to pursue the new case, grateful that the Vice Chancellor had slightly reduced her university workload for this academic year to enable her to pursue her additional role with UCU.

Gander quickly opened the meeting by thanking them all for attending, then officially informed everyone of the resurrection of the Molly James case. Connie briefly and efficiently communicated her limited findings from the remains so far, in similar terms to those she had already used with Kate and her colleagues.

Furman seized the opportunity to keep the limelight on UCU, which Kate knew he regarded as his personal fiefdom. She focused on the table as he turned to her and her colleagues. It was Joe he singled out.

'Lieutenant Corrigan. Familiarise the meeting with the facts of the case,' he directed.

Joe calmly outlined the basic information about Molly James's disappearance. As there was little to say at this point, he switched to describing the unit's ideas for working the case.

'We've already got some names, persons of interest from the original investigation who we'll be following up.'

Kate flicked a look at Furman to see how he was receiving this. The vein in his right temple was now just visible. He took back control of the meeting.

'Chief Superintendent Gander and I have agreed that I'll be SIO of this reinvestigation, given that I had that role in the original investigation.' Kate sighed inwardly. Furman as senior investigating officer of UCU's cold case. That hadn't happened before. Did that mean he'd be micromanaging them every step of the way? She retuned. 'There was no evidence at the time that this girl was even abducted, let alone murdered. She could have been one of hundreds of people of all ages who walk away from their lives every year.'

Kate studied him closely. *Self-aggrandising dolt.*

There was restlessness at the head of the table, followed by Gander's voice: 'Inspector Furman and I have agreed that UCU shall have—'

Furman swiftly cut him off. 'I've arranged a meeting in UCU

immediately after this, sir, when I'll inform personnel of agreed time-scales. I can reassure this meeting that, given the financial constraints all departments are under, this reinvestigation will involve a limited, controlled expenditure to establish that nothing was overlooked by the original investigation.'

Kate analysed Furman's words. They provided her with further confirmation of his considerable self-regard. *Budgets. Regulations. Initiatives. All serve to keep you centre stage. The most important person in the room. Or so you think.*

Bernie's face was stone. Joe was doodling on a pad. Seeing that neither of her colleagues was about to make a response, Kate broke the small silence.

'I thought that reinvestigation was exactly that – a further *full* investigation. Not an exercise merely to confirm what was done previously.'

Gander looked benignly at Kate, then frowned at Furman, who was now smirking in her direction, vein pulsing.

'Your problem is you've been too long in academia. Or watching too much TV crime, if you don't mind my saying . . . Dr Hanson.' Furman gazed round the table, getting one or two weak smiles in response, one of them from Jake Brown.

'I do,' she said.

He swivelled back, frowning. 'What?'

'Mind. I *do* mind.'

Gander jumped quickly into the silence, jowls quivering as he spoke. 'Okay. I think we can move on . . .'

Kate occupied herself with monitoring her breathing. Gander was still speaking, and she gave his voice her full attention.

'. . . to Matt Prentiss. Matt has a brief statement on experimental work currently being conducted at the Facility.'

Kate and the others turned to the sour-looking Prentiss. Kate glanced at her student helper's smooth, seemingly untroubled face and experienced the usual twinge of concern she had about Julian's contact with Prentiss. She knew that at times it was Prentiss, rather than Harry, who directed Julian's forensic-scenes training, and she had some doubts about his ability to do it with sufficient patience and insight. Although she was Julian's senior supervisor, she hadn't yet raised the issue with him, not wishing to influence his perceptions. She thought now that it was time she discussed it with him, and began a quick note in her diary. As she wrote, she recalled the reason for Julian being assigned to UCU. Eighteen months before, he'd hacked into the university main computer and got into its financial records. He'd done nothing other than that, and the Vice Chancellor had prevailed on Kate to request that Julian be given a small role in UCU in which he might legitimately apply his computer skills. Gander had agreed. It was working fine, and Kate wanted it to stay that way, for Julian's sake.

Prentiss talked on about work being done at the Facility, a Home Office-funded forensic service occupying a large tract of land at the edge of the university campus upon which sat a substantial property, Winterton, surrounded by high razor-wire fences and 'Keep Out' notices. Forensics was allowed to have up to five donated bodies buried or otherwise concealed there for research purposes.

Prentiss was now well into his monotone discourse. 'We're currently investigating the effects, if any, of a purposeful increase in the arachnid population . . .'

Kate paused in her writing, aware that Furman's eyes were on her again.

'. . . on two recently placed remains, one hypothesis being that a purposeful increase of arachnids would impact on the availability of flies and other organisms, which in turn might impact on rates of putrefaction and thus the estimates of times of death . . .'

Now it was Kate's face that was stone.

Furman smirked as he leaned towards her, eyes drilling into hers. 'A little anxiety?' he whispered.

Bernie gave him a scowl and Kate a wink. Bernie was catcher-in-chief in UCU, as and when required. She looked Furman in the eye, face serious, tone matter-of-fact.

'No. Actually, it's a phobia.'

Furman quickly withdrew, having spotted Gander's mouth beginning to open. As Prentiss finished, Furman promptly intervened in order to exercise his voice further. 'The usual reminder to each department. Nobody, but *nobody*, mentions the Facility outside the walls of Headquarters. This is an area of expensive housing. Residents round here are Nimby as hell. If they get even an *idea* that the Facility exists, that remains are being used for research purposes, there'll be a hell of a stink.'

Harry Creed shook his head slightly and grinned at Kate, crossing his eyes in response to Furman's unintentional joke.

It was now Harry's turn to address the meeting.

'The Facility is continuing to prove its value in providing us with opportunities to study human decomposition. Inspector Furman's reminder about confidentiality is appreciated by all the forensic services at Rose Road.'

Kate listened as Harry spoke about the work being done at the Facility, aware of visits he'd made to law enforcement in Virginia and New York State a few years previously as part of his commitment to the Facility's early development. Following a couple of other, unrelated reports from Upstairs, Gander brought the meeting to a close.

Five minutes later, Kate pushed open the door of UCU, causing it to hit the wall with a low thud. Julian started to speak, but stopped after a warning look from Joe. Bernie followed them inside, walking directly to the drinks-making corner, known as the Refreshment Lounge.

After a few minutes, furnished with coffee and a muffin, Kate had calmed down. Slightly. She looked from one to another of her colleagues.

'*How* do you do it?' she demanded. 'How do you sit in a meeting with that . . . that . . .' She flailed both arms, frustrated at her lack of descriptors.

'Imbecile?' suggested Joe.

Kate smoothed her hair from her face, twisting it more securely behind her head, and sipped her coffee.

Joe turned in his chair to face her. 'Like I said before, Red, we all know he's a dope. That means we pretend to listen while we think of other things.'

'Like *what*?' snapped Kate.

He shrugged. 'Beer, women, soccer . . . women . . . beer. You might want to work on your own list—'

Julian grinned and Kate sighed as Furman thrust open the door. He walked casually into the room, glancing at each of them in turn.

'Given the Chief Super's insistence that you're a part of this unit, I want *you* –' this with a finger-point towards Julian – 'to be responsible for entering into the system data from any new statements in this reinvestigation, marking any anomalies and raising them with Lieutenant Corrigan. You did a more or less reasonable job of it last

41

time,' he added grudgingly. 'Lieutenant Corrigan and . . . you, Watts, can focus on information-gathering.' He hadn't mentioned Kate. No one said anything. 'Chief Superintendent Gander and I have had a discussion and agreed a time limit of four weeks,' Furman continued. 'That's from today. After one month, if there's no real progress, no new persons of interest worthy of further investigation, the James case is closed again. Clear?'

Kate stared at him in the ensuing silence, suddenly very fed up. She shook her head. 'It isn't possible to do a thorough reinvestigation in four weeks.'

Furman hardly acknowledged her directly. 'Instead of querying management decisions, this unit needs to get started on its task.' He gave Kate a sideways glance. 'Which means you could get on with "entering the mind of the killer" or whatever it is you—'

Kate had had as much of him as she could take this morning. 'I don't do that,' she said coldly.

He glanced at her. 'I'd assumed from last—'

'Don't make any assumptions about me, please.'

There was a brief silence before Furman responded. 'I sense you have some kind of problem with the parameters I'm laying down.'

'This isn't about parameters,' responded Kate, knowing very well that it was. Mostly. He glared in her direction but slightly beyond her, his mouth a lopsided sneer.

'Whilst this unit continues to be in existence, as its superior officer, what happens here is—'

Mindful of Julian's presence, Kate tried for a stance of positive assertiveness. 'Actually, you're not my superior,' she said evenly, sticking to facts. 'I'm a civilian. Managed by my professional body and my university.'

'*Yes* I am.' Furman looked directly at Kate for the first time. 'This unit is *my* responsibility, and anybody working in it is, by definition, managed by me.'

Tension thickened the warm air. No one spoke. Kate was aware of the ticking of the clock on the wall. Furman broke the silence.

'I want a progress report seven days from now.' He picked up the keys and files he'd laid on the table earlier, strolled to the door and left.

Kate was the first to speak. 'I take it we all see what he's doing? Setting up UCU to do a superficial job. He's a vain, self-centred idiot with all the management skills of a house brick and *zero* interest in this case.'

'Attagirl, Red. Don't hold back.'

Kate scowled at him. 'I've told you not to call me that.'

Bernie gave Kate a close look. 'Your trouble, Doc, is you take him on. You don't gain nothing by taking on the likes of Furman. Here's some advice – take the indirect route, like me. When I'm around Furman, I'm like a lynx—'

'You don't say. That'd be one of the *missing* links, would it?' snapped Kate.

Julian lowered his head to the computer keys, shoulders shaking.

'What's amusing him?' Bernie threw down his pen cigarette and rubbed his face. 'I got a funny feeling that if we don't sort this case, he'll try to make some changes to personnel in here. That means I'm history. Or PBI.'

Kate frowned.

'Poor bloody infantry,' supplied Joe.

'I'd jack the lot in anyway, before I'd go back on the beat or get desked. I could find plenty to do at home . . .'

Kate's attention was snagged by Julian's now serious face.

'Something wrong?'

He shrugged. 'What about me if what Bernie said is true? I like it here. I'm doing this cool forensic stuff with Harry and his team. Harry's got plans for the team and he wants me to be part of it. He says I've got real aptitude.' This elicited a grunt from Bernie. 'A year ago I didn't have a clue what I wanted to do. Now I do. Something forensic, something with psychology. If I'm chucked out of the unit, my dad'll have a fit. He'll *never* believe it wasn't my fault. He'll probably pull his financial support and that's me finished at uni, *and* I'll never get to work on the projects Harry's told me he's got planned.'

Kate reflected on what she knew of Julian's background. No mother. A father who divided his time between business interests in London, Europe and Canada. Home for Julian, when he went there and could find anyone in it, was a modern tenth-floor apartment overlooking Imperial Wharf in Chelsea. A privileged background? Kate thought not.

'Hey, don't start catastrophising just yet,' soothed Kate.

'Don't worry, lad. You know what they say – nothing's finished till the fat bird has her turn. Any road up, Furman's not the chief round here, Goosey is,' added Bernie, using the chief superintendent's Rose Road nickname. 'And he supports this unit.' He turned to Kate. 'Furman really has got *you* in his sights.'

'Why?'

'Who knows, but he ain't bothering to hide it.'

Kate huffed. 'He's probably worried that we'll expose his hopeless investigation of Molly James's disappearance. Surprising as it may be to Furman, this isn't about *him*. It's about Molly James and her family.'

'Your problem, Doc, is you expect a fair world. I got news for you. It isn't,' responded Bernie, getting up from the table.

'What I expect is that people do their damn jobs,' snapped Kate, still riled.

At that moment Harry strolled in, giving each of them a quick acknowledgement before turning to Julian.

'Julian, my man! Here's your graded assignments, as promised. Good work on the modules I set for you. Have a look at the grades.'

A mix of emotions on his face, Julian took the folder Harry offered him, looked quickly through it to the end, then flushed with pleasure.

Watching the brief exchange, Kate smiled. Couldn't have come at a better time.

She turned her attention back to the table, reminding herself that she had a well-paid and valued job as senior lecturer and had chosen to put herself in UCU. She began replacing papers in the box.

'At least we know where we stand. We know what we're up against.' She pointed at Molly James's face gazing out from the glass screen. 'Furman doesn't care what happened to Molly. His main focus is his own advancement, and if he can further that by concealing any ineptitude, he will. *So.* We're going to solve this case.'

'Jeez, I love it when you get dominant,' murmured Joe, studying the list of POIs they'd generated earlier. 'I'll go over to Fairley's office for a chat. I'd like to hear what Molly's ex-boyfriend has to say. Then I'll go and make a brief call on John Cranham at his place of work. That okay with y'all?' he asked, using a vernacular he sometimes parodied.

Bernie nodded as he gathered together evidence sheets and dropped them into the box. 'Molly James's family's got to be told

ASAP about the DNA confirmation, before the press gets wind of it. I'm going to see the mother this morning.'

'Shall I come with you, Bernie?' asked Kate.

'No, you're all right, Doc. No telling how it might go, coming out of the blue after so many years. I'll be taking somebody from Victim Support.' He reached for the phone.

Harry walked past making a 'Drink?' signal to Kate. She nodded, mouthing, 'Coffee.'

From her handbag, her mobile started to ring. Digging inside, she pulled it out and answered.

'Maisie?'

'Mom, my extra maths class at school is cancelled. Chelsey's got a dance lesson at four, but her mom can drop me at home.'

Kate paused, rubbing her forehead, then glanced at her watch. Phyllis was leaving early today. 'Why don't you ask Candice to drop you here at Rose Road and I'll take you home?'

Ending the call, she calculated that Maisie wouldn't be at Rose Road for another three hours at least.

'How about I phone Brannigan and see if he's available for a visit?' she suggested.

Getting no dissent, she lifted UCU's phone as Bernie replaced it and started to make the call.

CHAPTER SEVEN

To the accompaniment of John Coltrane, Kate manoeuvred the Audi through the heavy Broad Street traffic, past clubs and bars and the vast grey-white Symphony Hall, its reflection gleaming in the blue glass slab of the Hyatt on the opposite side of the road. Although not native to Birmingham, she knew enough local history to appreciate the vast changes that had occurred here in the last forty or so years. The city was now home to a first-rate theatre, renowned orchestra and the Sadler's Wells Ballet. It was difficult to comprehend that it had once been the blackened industrial heart of the country.

Kate felt her spirits rise as she drove past clean-lined buildings and litter-free kerbs, before turning left over a small bridge spanning one of the city's many reclaimed canals. Turning right into a wide drive-way, she parked in an area designated for 'Visitors to Symphony Court Only'.

Retrieving her bag from the boot and securing the car, she walked into the main entrance hall and pressed one of the numbered buttons beside the lift as George Brannigan had instructed on the phone. While she waited, her thoughts turned to the small number of initial questions she'd identified for Brannigan. She hadn't written them down. After years of devising schedules of key questions to ask during time-limited, once-only prison visits as part of her criminal caseload, knowing what to ask came almost as easily as breathing, and was the reason Gander had sanctioned Kate being involved in UCU's interview process.

After some seconds a male voice boomed through the small grille, followed by the arrival of a lift, which conveyed her swiftly to the second floor.

Exiting the lift, Kate located Apartment 20, rang and waited. Noting the small aperture set in the door, she adopted a relaxed friendly face. Within a few more seconds, the door was opened by a tall heavyset man in his mid-fifties, dressed in a white cotton shirt, ubiquitous little polo player on the chest, casual trousers and leather sandals on otherwise bare feet. He politely motioned Kate inside, then made a phone gesture and disappeared, giving her a chance to evaluate her surroundings.

The sitting room was huge. Kate walked towards the expanse of window and peered down at the nearby canal, where tubs and hanging baskets of flowers lined the towpath. There are worse places to live than right here in the city, she thought. But with Maisie? And the cat?

Turning from the window, she gave her attention to the room itself. Three massive abstract canvases occupied much of one wall. Natural-coloured linen window blinds; engineered-wood floor, upon which pale rugs and two long sofas upholstered in coral linen were the only other furnishings. Kate noted Bang & Olufsen sound equipment mounted on another wall. All tasteful. *Just* this side of extravagant.

She returned to the window, musing on Brannigan's professional work. On young women who might be flattered to have their photographs taken. Or even dazzled by the promise of an exciting career.

Oh, yes! Click. *Hold it there!* Click.

You're a natural, darling! Have you thought of becoming a—

'Sorry about that. I've got a job at the airport. UB40 are due in this afternoon to do a concert. I've been commissioned by their agents to get some shots, so –' Brannigan glanced at the steel Tag Heuer on his wrist – 'I have to leave in fifteen minutes at the latest.'

'Thank you for agreeing to see me, Mr Brannigan. As I said on the phone, UCU is reinvestigating the disappearance of Molly James in 2002 from Touchwood mall.'

'That was a real shame, what happened there,' he said with a head shake, sounding like he meant it.

'Can you tell me what you remember of that day at the mall, Mr Brannigan?'

'Of course,' he responded, waving Kate to a seat on one of the sofas and taking one himself opposite her. 'There was a fashion show that day and I'd been commissioned by John Lewis to do some marketing pictures. I got there just after one. Yes, a real shame,' he repeated, running a hand through his thick grey-black hair.

'Did the police speak to you at all?'

Brannigan nodded. 'They came to see me about three days afterwards. After they knew she was missing.'

Kate stopped writing and looked at him, brows raised.

'When they knew she was gone, the police put out an appeal for witnesses, for anybody who was at the mall on that day to come forward.' Brannigan gave a small shrug. 'I was working over in Solihull again, so I dropped in at Touchwood and gave my details. Couple of days later I got a visit at the office I had then.'

'Can you remember who came to see you?'

Brannigan blew air between his teeth, looking thoughtful. 'Let's think . . . There were two of them . . .' He frowned in concentration, one flexed arm resting on the back of the sofa, hand supporting his head. He nodded. 'Yeah, that's right. One was a tall, fair-haired chap, the other one was shorter, dark, with glasses. I don't remember their names.'

The first one would probably have been Furman. Kate was unable to place the other, from the minimal detail Brannigan had given.

Brannigan spoke again, unprompted. 'I remember their description of her. The girl. Eighteen, long blonde hair, pale-blue polo top and light trousers . . . and . . . an Ellesse backpack.'

Kate studied him. 'Extremely good recall, Mr Brannigan, after so many years.'

He smiled openly. 'I'm a details man. Goes with the job. That's how I can be pretty sure that I didn't notice anybody matching that description. I never saw her.'

He glanced again at the Tag.

'Did you take many photographs while you were at the shopping mall, Mr Brannigan?'

'Quite a few, yes.' He gave Kate a direct look and a small shake of the head. 'Sorry, I can see where you're probably heading and I'm going to disappoint you. They asked me the same thing at the time. The police. I told them I took only runway shots. The models. None of the shopping crowd.'

Kate made a few quick strokes of her pen. The MacBook she'd had for months was in her study at home. She preferred the shorthand she'd learned years ago. Closing the notebook, she gazed around the room. 'Thank you for your time, Mr Brannigan, especially as you're so busy.'

She stood and moved slowly towards the door. 'This is a lovely apartment. I can see you're doing well.'

Brannigan looked keenly at her as he walked with her to the door, then laughed loudly but pleasantly, raising heavy shoulders. 'And it's not from porn, if *that's* what you're thinking.'

She was. Years of forensic experience had created in Kate a useful mix of scepticism and cynicism. Not merely useful. A professional necessity for dealing with the devious.

'Here are my contact details, Mr Brannigan,' she said, handing him a card. 'If you think of *anything* else, I'd appreciate it if you'd ring me at UCU.'

He took the card and slipped it in his pocket as they walked to the apartment's small hallway. Beside the front door Kate noticed a narrow wall filled with framed eight-by-ten black-and-white studies. She gave them a close look. Without any knowledge of photography, she could appreciate the evident technical know-how and flair. She turned to Brannigan, who was looking distracted but amiable still.

'I can see you enjoy your job.'

He nodded. 'The years I've been doing it, it's lucky that I do.' He offered his hand and Kate accepted the firm grip.

'If I need to see you again, Mr Brannigan . . .'

'Just ring me. Any time. You've got my number.' He waited until Kate reached the lift, then, with a brief wave of his hand, he disappeared, closing the apartment door.

Back at UCU, Kate was sitting on the team table, feet on a chair, listening to Bernie's account of his visit to Molly James's mother.

'I tell you, Doc, it's a real shame to see somebody like that.'

The phone rang and Kate leaned across to pick up.

'Kate, it's Joe. I'm about to leave Fairley's building at Five Ways. I should be back in about fifteen minutes.'

'How did it go?' Kate asked.

'Not much to tell. He came across as cut up about Molly, but he didn't show the curiosity about our investigation I'd have expected. If Bernie's there, can you ask him if he's arranged for Colley to come in?'

Kate relayed the question to Bernie, then returned to the phone conversation.

'Yes. In half an hour.'

'Thanks, Red. See you in fifteen.' Kate opened her mouth but he was gone.

Replacing the phone, she scanned the glass screen for information relating to Fairley. An age gap of ten years might not be a big deal later in life, but it raised queries for Kate, given that Molly was said to have been barely sixteen when she and Fairley first met. She'd got as far as adding a fourth query to her notebook when Joe walked through the door.

'Was Fairley Molly's boyfriend at the time she disappeared?' she asked immediately.

Joe grinned at her, shaking his head slightly. 'Hello, Joe! How ya doin'? Nice to see ya.'

She pulled a face at him.

'He said not. They were "just good friends". And it seems that Cranham *was* out of the country the day Molly disappeared. Most of it, anyway. He didn't fly into Birmingham until around midnight that day.'

Bernie looked vexed. 'Anything of interest to give us about Fairley?'

Joe sat, leaning back on his chair, fingers laced behind his head. 'Like I told Kate on the phone, I expected him to show some curiosity about the reinvestigation. He didn't. That's as far as I'll go right now. He stays on the list.'

The phone rang and Bernie snatched it up and listened, giving Joe a thumbs-up sign. Kate stared moodily at the glass screen as Joe handed her a professional-looking leaflet relating to Jason Fairley's company. It included a photograph of Fairley, managing director, with impressively white teeth. The prose reassured her that his company was capable of servicing all her software needs.

Bernie stood and walked to the door. 'Let's get moving, Corrigan.' He turned to Kate. 'The sex pest's cooling his heels down the hall. Want to observe?'

Kate seized her notebook and followed him and Joe out of UCU.

CHAPTER EIGHT

Kate watched through one-way glass as her two colleagues entered the interview room, where their reluctant interviewee was waiting. As soon as they were seated, Bernie took the lead, his initial setting on 'bonhomie'. The little man opposite him was mono-browed, narrow face wary, lank hair hanging over his sweating forehead and grimy shirt collar.

'So you found us, Mr Colley. But then you've been to Rose Road before, haven't you?'

Colley made no eye contact. 'That was years back,' he muttered.

Bernie nodded, his face benign. 'Well, we're grateful to you for agreeing to this informal little chat. I'm Sergeant Watts, but you and me know each other already. This here's my colleague, Lieutenant Corrigan. We need to talk to you about July 2002. We think you might be able to help us as a witness to something that happened back then. Any idea what that was?'

Colley looked from Bernie to Joe and back. 'No,' he said, almost inaudible, his eyes dropping to inspect the room's skirting boards.

Kate saw a trickle of perspiration slide down the side of Colley's face. As he fingered it away with a dirty-nailed hand, she leaned towards the microphone in front of her.

'He's way more nervous than I would have expected, even with his history. Offer him some water. Try some nurture,' she said into the tiny earpieces her colleagues were wearing.

Bernie lounged back on his chair, forearms folded across his wide chest. Kate watched his face growing increasingly disdainful and beginning to heat up as he glared at Colley. She knew that what she'd said about nurture was akin to suggesting to Bernie that he walk on water. She shook her head. He couldn't do it, given what he knew of Colley's criminal antecedents.

Joe stood, and Kate tracked him as he walked deliberately to the water cooler, filled a paper cup and returned, gently placing the cup on the table near to Colley before regaining his seat. Sighing, Kate pushed her hair off her face.

'We had you collected in an air-conditioned police limo, Mr Colley, and this building is good to work in,' Joe said conversationally. 'Air con, all floors. And yet you're looking *real* hot. Care to tell us about that? Got something on your mind?'

'Huh? I . . . There ain't *nothing* on my mind. Just tell me why you wanted me here, ask me whatever it is you want to know, so I can go,' muttered Colley.

'We're interested in a young woman by the name of Molly James. She disappeared in July 2002. From the shopping mall not a mile from the bail hostel where you were residing at the time.'

They waited. This got no verbal response from Colley, but he lifted his gaze from the skirting board, eyes darting from Joe to Bernie and back. Bernie stared at him for several seconds without speaking, massive forearms still folded. Colley fidgeted under the unwavering gaze and became interested in the wall to one side of the room.

Bernie pushed his heavy upper body forward, causing Colley to shrink back with a quick intake of breath.

'You've got *form*, Colley. Years of sexual nuisance towards women and a conviction for sex offences against your own stepdaughter!'

Colley's sweat-covered face darkened. 'I ain't no sex offender!'

Bernie looked at him with unconcealed loathing. 'Don't you give me *that*. And don't you dare tell me she come into your bed in the night and you confused her with her mother. I've heard *that* one already. More than once.'

Colley persisted. 'I tell you, I ain't a sex offender! That was consensual incest, that was. It was a *relationship* and she was as keen—'

Kate glanced at Bernie, who was now almost apoplectic. 'She was *seven* years old, you f—'

Kate sighed, shaking her head, aware that even exhibitionists and paedophiles needed to hang on to some semblance of self-regard along with their cognitive distortions. Bernie subsided in disgust, leaving Joe to continue.

'Okay, Mr Colley,' he said evenly. 'Let's get right down to what we want from you. You were interviewed by the police in July 2002. Tell us about that.'

Colley looked furtively from one man to the other, running the tip of his tongue over parched lips. 'Can't remember. What would that've been about, exactly?'

Bernie shifted irritably, pointing a finger at Colley's face, his patience at its limit. 'Listen to me, Colley. You're really starting to piss me off now. You know the way this works – we ask *you* questions and you tell *us* what we want to know. Right? Try it again. Police interviewed you in 2002. Tell us!' he barked.

Colley nodded vigorously, lank hair flopping, but still said nothing. Kate glanced from him to Bernie, whose face was now a pale rust colour, although he was clearly making an effort to stay in control. 'You were interviewed about Molly James, the girl who went missing from the Touchwood mall. Tell us about it *now*.'

Kate noted Colley's hands shaking as he reached for the water cup.

'All that time ago, how'm I supposed to rem—'

'*Stop* trying to be clever. You ain't built for it.' A pause as Bernie skewered Colley with a look. 'Tell us what you remember and then you can sod off.'

Colley resorted to a whine. 'Look, Mr Watts, I can't tell you nothing. *Honest!* I told 'em, I never seen that girl, whatever her name was. I was only picked up because I was at Longmore Hostel. I was never even in that shopping place!'

Bernie glared at him across the table. 'Funny how I get extra suspicious as soon as the likes of you use the word "honest".'

Kate leaned towards the microphone. 'Ask him how he spent his days back then.'

Bernie was back to lounging, glaring at the hapless Colley. After a few seconds he continued.

'Nice place, Solihull. Cracking shopping mall, that Touchwood. Plenty to look at, for somebody like you with nothing better to do. Every kind of shop you could want. Department stores, speciality shops for –' Colley was nodding energetically at this – 'chocolates, perfume, ladies' underwear . . .'

'Yeah, Mr Watts, you're . . . Wha'? No, *no*. Hang on! You're trying to mix me up here.'

Joe rejoined the process, speaking politely, his deep voice measured. 'Thing is, Mr Colley, we could sure use your help. The girl, Molly, went missing at the time you were living in the neighbourhood. If you

53

think you might've seen her, please tell us, so we can get an idea how she spent her last hours.'

Kate smiled to herself. Joe was such a good 'good cop'. His gentle demeanour, and the voice, which could lull even the most hardened criminal . . . She refocused as Colley's voice became a squeal.

'For God's sake, I never seen her. Wouldn't know her from a hole in the floor. It's the truth!' He looked frantically from Joe to Bernie. 'It's always the bloody same. Put a foot a bit out of line and you lot are all over and never let up. I'm *telling* you, I never went in that place. *Never!* Too posh. Full o' women with expensive hair and skinny tarts showing off clothes. Not my kind of place.'

Kate's heart constricted. She watched as her two colleagues became very still, and Colley suddenly noticed how quiet the room had become.

CHAPTER NINE

Colley looked frantically from one officer to the other.
  'Wha'? *What!*' he bleated.

Bernie was quick on the uptake, even before Kate could suggest it. 'We're all ears now, Colley. Tell us about the "skinny tarts showing off clothes".'

Colley's eyes flicked between the two men, and his tongue darted out again in a vain attempt to moisten his lips. 'Figure o' speech, innit?'

Joe leaned forward, his voice low. 'You were there, weren't you, George? When the fashion show was on.'

All of Colley's limbs started shaking. 'I'm telling you, I was never there. Never! Everybody knows they have fashion shows in them places.'

Bernie watched him intently as he slammed his meaty palms on the table.

'Cut the crap. *Now.*'

Colley gyrated on his chair, then subsided, sulkily eyeing both officers from under his brows. Trying to gauge what they knew. They waited. And waited some more.

'Okay. Okay! So I was in there. I just popped in, like, to look around. Wasn't no more than ten minutes. Then I cleared off sharpish. It's a free country,' he added mutinously.

Bernie glared at him. 'Why sharpish?' he hissed. Seeing Colley's mouth open, he jabbed a thick warning finger at him. 'Don't you *dare* tell me it's another figure of speech.'

Colley closed his mouth quickly, eyes shifting, then, 'Had an appointment. Probation officer. She rung the hostel that morning.'

Kate watched Colley as she wrote, noting the meagre content of what he'd just said and the style of its delivery.

Bernie looked at him with disgust.

An officer had entered the room in response to a covert signal from Joe.

Bernie glared at Colley, speaking slowly and deliberately. 'Listen! I want you to go with this nice lady officer. WPC Sharma's going to take you to another room to make a full statement about the day we've been talking about. Tell her everything you remember about it. *Everything*, mind. None of this "don't remember" crap.'

He glanced at Rita Sharma, who nodded, then back to Colley. 'When she's finished taking down your particulars, and *if* you've behaved yourself, she *might* give you a cuppa. When we've read your statement we'll be in touch again. Now *hoppit*,' he roared.

A grey-faced Colley hopped it, followed by WPC Sharma.

Three minutes later they were back in UCU, Julian hanging on their every word.

'He was there, the little runt,' fumed Bernie. 'Inside the mall. How come the original investigation never— *What* am I saying? With the Arse in charge, it's a miracle there's *anything* to work with.'

'Which is why we'll be doing a damned thorough job this time,' said Kate quietly, scouring her written notes.

Joe leaned back, hands linked behind his head. 'Tough talking, Red.'

Kate shook her head. 'But if you want my opinion of Colley, he didn't have anything to do with Molly James's disappearance.'

'Even allowing for the really interesting lie?' asked Joe.

He meant the reference to an appointment with a probation officer. Kate had doubted it herself, on hearing Colley's clipped responses and lack of self-reference, and given the dubious likelihood of a probation officer phoning with an appointment that same day. She nodded at Joe. How does he manage it? she wondered. The interviewing skills, the psychological know-how. And Bernie was often right there with him.

She glanced at Bernie, whose face was now that of a bulldog with dental problems, knowing she was about to worsen his mood.

'Even allowing for his deviousness, Colley didn't abduct Molly James.'

Bernie glared at her, arms folded. 'Here we go again. Just slacken your suspenders, yeah? I know you're already up Theory Alley, but it's too early to say that.'

She sighed. Bernie was no fool. A politically incorrect nightmare, yes, but no fool. Colley probably did require further checking for thoroughness, but all her theoretical knowledge of sexual offenders had confirmed for Kate that he was not the abductor and killer of Molly James. She shook her head.

'There's unlikely to be anything of real interest in his statement.'

'Listen, Doc, he might be from the bottom of the gene pool and look like he's off *Sesame Street*, but he's a sex offender and *now* we can place him inside the mall. You know Colley's type, or you should do. He's tri-sexual – try anything. Bear *that* in mind.'

Joe grinned at Kate as she rolled her eyes. Bernie's problem was that he didn't operate within a theoretical framework but responded on a gut level. Kate was aware of Colley's past form for various sexual offences. She also appreciated that his physical appearance in interview suggested he'd come direct from Central Casting. It wasn't enough.

Bernie sighed, waiting. 'All right. Get on with it. Tell us why he's no good.'

Kate directed her comments to both officers, as Julian resumed writing.

'Think of Molly,' she suggested. 'What can we assume about her? Educated. Almost certainly eloquent, confident, socially cool. No way would she give an individual such as Colley the time of day. Colley is a picture of low self-esteem, low confidence and poor social skills. Chronically under-assertive. A girl like Molly would intimidate the hell out of him. Which is partly why his preferred age group is a lot younger.' She paused, shaking her head. 'No. Whoever took Molly James, if it was someone unknown to her, is a very different personality from Colley. Somebody who was able to plan an audacious abduction and successfully implement it. *And* in broad daylight, don't forget. This was an intelligent young woman. To do what he did required somebody with the ability to manipulate and the confidence to control.'

Joe stretched his arms upwards briefly, then let them drop.

Kate glanced from him to Bernie. Neither spoke. She turned her attention to the glass screen and the photograph of the young woman who went to the mall with her friends and never came home. Molly stared back at Kate across the warm afternoon dimness of the room.

57

Kate wondered how many sexual crimes went unpunished. Undetected, even. She looked directly into Molly's eyes, thinking of the news this young woman's mother had just been given. That her daughter had lain for ten years no more than an hour from their home

Have patience. We'll do whatever it takes.

Please.

Give us a chance.

Kate's mobile phone rang. Startled, she reached for it.

'Kate Hanson.'

'Kate, it's—'

'Kevin?' She immediately lowered her voice. 'What do you want?'

Leaving the table, she went to stand near one of the wide windows as her colleagues started to tidy paperwork, Bernie harassing Julian towards the kettle. Kate massaged her forehead as she listened to the voice in her ear.

'I need to talk to you, Kate.'

When she said nothing he continued. 'I know I'm scheduled to have Maisie at my place from tomorrow afternoon, but something's come up—'

Kate spoke into the phone, quiet but firm. 'No buts, Kevin. We have an arrangement. You, Maisie and I agreed that she has overnight stays at your place every second Friday. You've already changed it this month. What's going on?'

'Situations change, Kate. Stop making an issue of everything. It's just one weekend.'

'This is not good for Maisie, Kevin. She needs to maintain a relationship with you. To do that, she has to have a regular routine of contact—'

'Cut the lecture, Kate. How often do *you* find yourself putting your precious career before—'

Kate's face flushed. 'I'm not giving you a lecture, and I work for lots of reasons, one of them being to support our daughter.' She leaned on the windowsill, one foot tapping against the leg of a nearby chair as Kevin's voice floated into her ear.

'I'll call in at the house on my way back from court. Maybe we can have a civilised conversation then.'

After a deep breath, Kate answered. 'Fine. I'll see you later and we'll talk about it some more.' She mentally reviewed Maisie's commitments. Cornet practice at five forty-five at her music teacher's house. 'Come after six o'clock. I don't want Maisie to hear our discussion.'

She cut the call and walked back to the table, avoiding Joe's glance as UCU's phone rang. She answered it. It was Whittaker from Reception.

'Hi, Dr Hanson. Just to let you know, your daughter's here.'

'Thank you,' said Kate sharply, still irked by the interruption of the previous call. *Why're you irritated?* she asked herself. *This is Kevin being Kevin.*

CHAPTER TEN

Kate silently placed coffee and home-made biscuits on the kitchen table near her visitor, then returned to what she'd been doing before he arrived. She'd decided to let him do the talking. To begin with.

The case. Already she had so many questions. She resumed her listing, aware of Kevin's biscuit-crunching. Strange how small cues like that had the power to propel a person back in time. In Kate's case, to a time she preferred not to think about. Although not all of it had been bad.

'Like these,' he said, watching her.

'Maisie made them.' Feeling his eyes on her, she looked up from her writing at the man she'd been married to for seven years. Medium-brown curly hair, beginning to thin at the crown; average height and stocky. She noted the broad, clean-shaven face, the sensual mouth. Kevin Osbourne. Hotshot barrister. Lousy husband.

He gazed at her, swallowing coffee. 'Ever thought, Kate, that if there had been only one profession in our marriage, it might have worked?'

Kate put down her pen and watched him take another of Maisie's biscuits. 'I see your point, Kevin,' she said easily. 'You the house husband and me the working professional.'

Kevin gave a small grin. 'Very good, Kate, but you know there's a truth there somewhere.' He looked across the table at her, echoing her own earlier thought. 'It wasn't all bad. I can remember some good times . . .'

Kate dredged up memories. 'Probably when I was at home with Maisie and you were at the office getting "acquainted" with Dolores.'

Kevin shook his head. 'Why're you raking up old issues? That was a difficult time for me – for *us*,' he added quickly.

60

Kate gazed at him. 'Mmm . . . I remember how surprised you were to discover that babies needed time and care.' She sighed and changed tack. 'How was court?'

'Just finished a case today. Client accused of sexual abuse of his partner's nine-year-old daughter, his accuser being the partner, from whom there'd been a vitriolic separation. No physical evidence and the only witness the girl herself.' He shrugged as he uttered the last few words.

'And that's relevant? How many intrafamilial sex offence cases include witnesses?'

Kevin examined the ceiling. 'The jury made its call, Kate. They found him not guilty.'

'So, you're still doing the amoral thing? Helping the guilty go free.'

'Change the record,' he snorted. 'You don't *know* that he was guilty. Plus, you know as well as I do how the system works. Or you should do, given that your own father was a part of it.'

Kate's father had also been a barrister. A fact Kevin brought up whenever they had these kinds of discussions. Her chair scraped floor tiles as she stood and walked towards the cafetiere, past the square black briefcase and dark-blue drawstring bag emblazoned with Kevin's initials beside his chair. She spoke over her shoulder.

'I know the system. One that sanctions the roughing-up of victims and allows professionals like you to— By the way, how terrified of you *was* the nine-year-old witness while you cross-examined her?'

He looked exasperated. 'Oh, come *on*, Kate! She wasn't even in court. She gave her evidence via live video link—'

'*That's* all right, then,' said Kate, removing his plate from the table and shoving it into the DishDrawer. She turned, leaned against the granite work surface and folded her arms. He watched her, shaking his head.

'Stop being so bloody idealistic. I'm not expected or paid to put my personal values and attitudes on the line. The legal system isn't about *principles.* Your trouble is you think there's a truth out there. There isn't! It's relative.'

'Yeah, right. Whatever,' Kate said, aware that she sounded like Maisie.

'I see you're still using the vox pop. Trying to rewrite your

61

middle-class roots. Or is it the influence of that coarse yob of a police officer you're working with?'

Ignoring the jibe about Bernie Watts, Kate looked at Kevin. 'What a grey world you live in.'

'Oh, *zip* it,' he muttered irritably.

'Ah, vox pop does it for you too?'

'As far as professional work is concerned, I'll leave the moral high ground to you, Kate, and we'll see where it gets you. You're taking a risk working with the police, d'you know that?'

This was how it tended to be whenever they were together. In fact, it was how they'd been when married, though less vitriolic back then.

A short silence. Kate transferred her gaze from the garden beyond the expanse of kitchen doors. 'You said you want to cancel Maisie's sleepover. What's going on, Kevin? Why the change of arrangement?'

He replaced his coffee cup carefully on its saucer. 'Why would you assume something's going on?'

'Experience,' she responded.

And insight, which protects me from getting caught up in old emotions.

Kevin watched her. 'I don't *want* to cancel, but things are a bit . . . complicated right now.'

'Kevin, I told you on the phone. Maisie needs to have regular contact with you. She lives with me and I care for her seven days a week, except for the times when you—'

'And still managing your university post and working with the Force. Busy-busy,' he mocked.

She waited, looking down at him, at his hands, still surprised after all these years at the absence of a wedding ring. The one she'd given him, a lifetime or two ago. She watched his face as he spoke again, not meeting her gaze.

'I've been thinking that sometime in the near future I might want to increase my involvement with Maisie. She's reaching a difficult age, you know.'

'She's been there for a while.'

'Don't be tart, Kate. It isn't attractive. I was thinking that she might benefit from spending *bigger* blocks of time with me.'

Kate's chest tightened as she walked back to the table.

'Kevin, you've cancelled two of Maisie's weekend stays in the last three months. Now we're on to a third. It's totally illogical to break our arrangement, which means Maisie is seeing *less* of you, and then come here saying you're thinking of an increase in contact.'

He'd stood as she approached. She gave him a close look. And suddenly she got it.

'Ah. Let me *guess*. The liaison of a lifetime, with Stella, has ended. You're feeling lonely. At a loose end. But also feeling the need to put yourself out there again. So Fridays involving Maisie are suddenly inconvenient, because you're looking—'

He picked up the briefcase and drawstring bag and moved towards the kitchen door. 'I'll talk to you another time. When you're in a better mood.'

'There's nothing wrong with my mood.'

He turned to face her, unruffled. 'One of these days, Maisie will be able to make her own choices. When she does, I'll be there.'

'That'll be a first.'

'Take my advice, Kate. Drop the bitterness. Not becoming in a woman your age.'

She glared up at him.

So bugger off.

Get searching for another twenty-something love interest.

She watched in silence as he headed across the hall. Listened as the front door closed.

After he'd gone, she reprised the conversation in her head. He hadn't asked after Maisie. Not even enquired where she was. Absently she ran her fingers over a clutch of seldom-used recipe books, amongst them a small, well-thumbed volume, *Kids First: What Kids Want Grown-ups to Know About Separation and Divorce*. She lifted it out.

She thought back over the last seven years of single parenthood. Single because Kevin's focus was easily diverted. None of his serial relationships to date had been with women sufficiently mature or amenable to welcome a bright, assertive child into the duo. Kate knew she was far luckier than many single mothers. But the bottom line was that for the foreseeable future, she was it. Maisie's well-being would be entirely her responsibility.

Her thoughts took a darker turn.

What if Kevin stepped up the female age range at some point in the next two or three years?

What if he found someone with no objection to the presence of a teenager in the relationship and the household?

Kate's dark thoughts drifted forward.

What then?

CHAPTER ELEVEN

At 7.45 on Friday morning, after a night of disturbed sleep, Kate left Maisie in Phyllis's capable hands and was the first into UCU.

Opening the tall cupboard on one side of the Refreshment Lounge, she peered in the mirror on the back of the door and evaluated her appearance. 'What a mess!' she muttered. Attempting to curb her hair's enthusiasm, she inspected her face closely, sighing as she did so. 'Like something Mugger dragged in.' She began to root around in the small cosmetics bag that was sitting on the draining board.

'Tea or coffee?'

Kate vaulted sideways with a squeak, then whirled. 'Jesus H. *Christ.* When did you arrive?' she yelled, clutching a hand to her chest.

Joe was standing there grinning at her, a tea bag between the index finger and thumb of one raised hand, coffee jar in the other.

'Seems like hours ago. Waiting to see if the soliloquy was likely to morph into a conversation any time soon.'

Kate detected something suspiciously like sympathy behind the grin and bridled.

'*Idiot.* Didn't your mother ever tell you not to creep up on unsuspecting females?' she demanded, her hair suddenly collapsing on to her shoulders.

'Nope. She missed out that advice. Along with a lot else.'

Kate closed the cupboard door hard, stowed cosmetics and comb in her bag and then took the drink he was offering.

'Thanks. I'd have preferred tea.'

Bernie barrelled into UCU, a grease-stained paper bag in one hand.

'Well done, Corrigan! Tea for me. Three and a bit sugars. Let the tea bag stand a good few minutes.'

Kate carried her coffee to the table. As she sat, the phone rang. Joe came over and lifted the receiver. He listened, replaced it and looked at his watch, then at his two colleagues.

'I have mandatory firearms practice this morning, but Connie's ready to give you both the benefit of her extensive skills.'

Ten minutes later, accompanied by Bernie, Kate was tapping on the green-glazed door of the post-mortem suite. Through a small circle of clear glass she glimpsed Igor, Connie's pathology assistant, approaching. His real name was Tony, or something equally prosaic. He unlocked the door and let Kate and Bernie inside. They went to the dispensers on the right-hand wall and each took a plastic apron, face mask and latex gloves.

Applying these, Kate studied the smooth, cold surfaces inside the PM suite, thinking how different Connie's job was from her own. Although both of them worked with people, for Connie, it was people without a voice, while Kate's working days were occupied with either the young and curious, eager for knowledge and full of questions, or those who had transgressed societal rules, often in horrific ways, and were full of negative emotion they couldn't wait to express – hate, fear, anger, denial. Only *very* occasionally guilt. But one aspect of Connie's and Kate's respective professions united them. They were both directed – or maybe it was more accurate to say distanced – by theory.

As they approached Connie at the examination table, Kate detected a reluctance in Bernie, and guessed that he was regretting an earlier enthusiastic patronage of the 'breakfast club' run by one of the coffee shops in Harborne.

Bernie was listening to the powerful fans whirring quietly. He sampled the air. Chemicals. And something else. Glancing at Connie, he clamped his mask to his face and stood next to Kate, his stomach giving a sudden quiver.

Dressed in white rubber boots and coveralls, Connie eyed Bernie for a few seconds, then grinned at him.

'Compared with many of my guests, there's hardly *any* smell. Just earthiness,' she said.

Bernie received this information but continued to hold the mask in position.

Shaking her head, Connie returned her attention to the examination table, its surface covered in heavy-duty white cartridge paper. Laid out on it were the stark remains from the bypass.

Guided only by a distant A-level in human biology, Kate surveyed what appeared to her to be a more or less complete skeleton, the bones stained a rich red-brown by the clay soil that had held them for at least five years. The jaws were separated.

She moved up the table for a closer look. Beside the remains lay a longish length of something that looked like fine rope, one soiled end unravelled. She switched her attention, attempting to mentally super-impose Molly's photographed face on to the skull.

Connie's voice broke into her concentration. 'Forensics are still at the site making totally sure we've not missed anything, but these remains are complete. I'll give you what I know so far, and have I got some goodies for you two?' she murmured.

Kate was avid for information but knew that what occurred down here was in the order and at a pace decreed by Connie. As she prepared to listen, she was aware of Bernie lurking somewhere behind her.

'Definitely female,' said Connie. 'I like to say "definitely" wherever possible. It doesn't happen that often, contrary to televised portrayals of pathology. Age estimate, based on presence of wisdom teeth, eighteen-plus. Indications from the long bones of the arm suggest incomplete bone growth, so she was not more than twenty-five years old when she died. By my rough calculation so far, she was ap-proximately five-seven or -eight tall.' She eyed Bernie, whose jowls were now grey. 'Her hair was blonde-brown in colour.'

She indicated the long item Kate had noticed. 'Looks as though it was plaited. It became detached as part of the normal decomposition process,' she continued, with a glance at Kate, who was busy writing. 'No clothing present, *but –*' Connie gestured with a latexed finger for them to follow her along the table – 'there's something here I think might really interest you particularly, Kate.'

Kate looked to where the pathologist was pointing at the rib section of the remains. 'What is it?'

Connie pulled a free-standing lamp closer to the table, to supple-ment the overhead source. 'Minimal tissue on the side of the body, which has endured in places instead of decomposing because of the presence of something of *real* interest.'

Using a long-bladed scalpel, she directed their attention to a particular section of the bony hoops. Kate moved closer, aware of a rising mustiness as she gazed intently at the undulating area.

She looked up at Connie. 'Duct tape?'

'Ten out of ten, Katie. I found more fragments of it around here.' Connie pointed to the left upper arm bones, then walked to a work surface, returning with a metal dish.

Kate peered inside. Short brown-stained lengths of duct tape, around seven or eight centimetres wide. She nodded, scribbling shorthand notes, then glanced upwards at Connie and Bernie.

'Looks the same. Question is, was it part of her killer's MO? To keep her subdued? Or was it an unnecessary behaviour the killer included because it met a psychological need?'

She examined the tape a second time. 'I can't see how this would have severely restricted her movements,' she mused. 'Looks to me like the purpose of it was fantasy-driven bondage.' She caught the sounds of muttering from Bernie, still somewhere behind her.

Connie smiled at her. 'If Igor ever quits on me, you're my first choice. All I can tell you about it is it's eight-centimetre-wide duct tape. No unusual characteristics found so far.'

Connie returned to the work surface, deposited the dish containing the tape, picked up another item and returned. 'Now have a look at this. Found on the facial area of the skull.'

Kate watched as Connie gently lifted an item from a flat stainless-steel bowl and held it aloft, suspended from scissors with rounded, flattened blades. A largish oval piece of cloth, possibly once white or pale in colour, now stained and foul, a small hole on each side.

'A gag?' The significance of the small holes and the dimensions of the cloth dawned on Kate. The fine hairs on her arms were at attention. 'A full-face covering of some kind. Home-made.'

Connie returned it gently to the bowl. 'Whatever held it in place has long since perished. Any theory come to mind?'

Kate nodded. 'According to my *Bumper Book of Sexual Deviance*, "Any treatment of or activity with a body during the commission of a homicide that is not strictly related to causing the death of or disabling the subject is deemed a signature."' She frowned slightly. 'Actually I'm open-minded about signatures, Connie. There's some theoretical doubt about killers leaving calling cards. The rare exception, when it does occur, is when the killer poses or displays a victim in order to shock the public or the police. It represents a kind of "up yours" gesture, and is almost always done by repeaters.'

Kate peered again at the duct tape on the remains, picking up peripheral sounds of squeaky rubber boots as Igor went about his tasks. 'Both the tape and the cloth *could* be signatures. Whoever this handiwork belongs to, what I *can* say about him – and I'm using "him" for convenience as well as likelihood,' she added, 'is that he's into bondage. Big time. From that and the fact that he appears to have interacted with this young woman prior to killing her, in order to put these "personal" touches in place, he almost certainly has sadistic tendencies. He planned this. It was – is – an expression of his very elaborate fantasy life.'

Connie walked away from them, returning with an item suspended from the long scalpel. 'So this won't come as any surprise to you?'

Kate studied the rusted metal object swinging gently from the scalpel.

'No. Where?'

'Around the long bones of the left arm. Near the wrist.'

Kate looked at Bernie as she nodded at the remains. 'Whoever killed this young woman was intent on objectifying and controlling her whilst she was still alive. And I doubt the killer was someone for whom she had an emotional relevance or attachment.'

Poor Molly.

'Bastard,' muttered Bernie, looking anywhere but at the examination table.

Kate glanced at Connie. 'Was she killed where she was found?'

'No.'

'So, Molly James was abducted and taken to a place by her killer where he kept her for some unknown period of time so that he could do what we can see . . . and who knows what else,' Kate finished quietly.

Connie nodded silent agreement. Bernie's eyes skimmed the bones again.

'Did he leave anything else?' he asked.

'Not in the sense you mean.'

Bernie shook his head and walked a few paces away from the examination table. 'Just for once, just for one case, I'd like to live in *CSI* Land.'

Connie nodded again. 'Know what you mean. A wealth of offender DNA, plus fibres, plant spores and footprints. Wouldn't we all? Back on the planet we currently live on, I've gone over the remains very carefully. Nothing that belonged to anyone else.'

She glanced at each of them. 'I can't identify a likely cause of death from these remains. But before you leave, there's one more item I need to show you, which possibly connects with what you said, Kate, about calling cards.'

She walked to the nearby work surface and returned with a small item lying on a sheet of absorbent paper. When it was placed on the examination table, Kate and Bernie pressed nearer to examine it.

CHAPTER TWELVE

It was a squarish remnant no more than a few centimetres across and heavily discoloured in places. Connie angled one of the lights as Kate leaned forward. Bernie did the same. They stared hard at the small scrap.

'Would you turn it over, Connie, so we can see the other side?'

Connie nodded and did as Kate asked, using slim tweezers. Kate stared at the scrap until her eyes prickled. After a few seconds she straightened.

'I can't see anything on that side. Can you, Bernie?'

Now wearing his glasses, Bernie leaned closer. 'Nothing there as far as I can make out.'

Kate looked at Connie. 'Is it possible for us to get a better view?'

Connie delved into a pocket and handed Kate a magnifying glass. 'Here. Let me turn it back to what I think is the key side.'

Kate looked through the magnifier, then handed it to Bernie. He shook his head and they stared at each other, confused.

Kate broke the silence. 'It looks like a fragment of some kind of heavy-duty card, but card wouldn't have survived so long, surely?'

Connie shrugged. 'I've 'scoped it. It's essentially of paper construction, but *very* robust. Extra thick. It originally had a shiny protective surface, now more or less degraded. But what do you think of what's on it?'

Two heads came together again. Bernie passed the magnifier back to Kate.

'The material itself looks like it was once very light in colour. But there's a patch of something among the discoloration. Just there.' Kate pointed.

Bernie moved away slightly, stomach undulating at Kate's reference to discoloration.

'Looks to be a brownish-red mark,' continued Kate. She looked up at Connie. 'Obviously caused by something that's happened to it while it's been buried. A bloodstain? Or . . . is it part of the card itself?'

Bernie looked at Connie, stomach continuing its undulations. 'Where'd you find it?'

She smiled at him and made a clapping movement with her small hands. 'A key question, Bernard.'

Bernard. Kate saw his jowls regain slight colour.

'I can tell you exactly where.' They waited. 'It was lying directly on the skull. On the face.'

Kate's eyes widened. 'So what're you saying, Connie? That this, whatever it is, was *placed* there, prior to the body being buried?'

Connie lifted her shoulders. 'Can't be that categorical, but that's how it looks.'

'And the face covering, mask, was on top of it?'

'That's how I found it,' said Connie carefully.

Kate paced a few steps from the table then returned to look at the remains and the small item. 'So the card was *under* the mask at the time he buried her?'

Connie raised her hands in a steadying gesture. 'Like I said, Kate, that's how it was when I examined her *in situ*. Can't say more than that.' She pointed at the card. 'The marking you've noticed, we can only guess at the original colour. But it would probably have been strong, primary, to have remained visible so long. Looking at it, I'd say red's a good guess.'

Kate stared at the scrap, a small frown above her nose.

'Why? To what purpose?' she murmured to herself.

Connie picked up the fragment and returned it to its place on the work surface, talking over her shoulder. 'I'll be sending it for testing. As to your last two questions, Katie, that is for you and your colleagues to work out.'

Bernie led the way out of the suite and up the stairs to UCU. Kate watched as he walked directly to the refreshment area, took a glass, filled it with water and drank. Continuing on across the room, she lifted the phone and dialled.

'I think it might be time well spent this morning if I make a visit to see Dianne James. I need to know more about Molly.'

As the number rang out, she noticed a pink message slip lying in the basket on the table. From Reception. She read it and looked up.

'John Cranham's phoned us. His workplace is nearby. I'll do both—'

Kate's call was picked up.

CHAPTER THIRTEEN

Standing at the front door of the detached house, the heat of the day on her back, Kate drew a deep breath and pressed the bell, waiting as the sound of it drifted through the silent house beyond the door. Nothing. Kate frowned.

Maybe Mrs James had gone out? But she was expecting—

The door slowly opened. Framed within it was Dianne James. Mother of Molly Elizabeth James.

Kate knew instantly, from every angle of the woman's body and every plane of her face, that years of desperate hope were gone. The finding of the gold necklace, followed by Bernie's confirmation of identification, had ended them.

Kate opened her mouth to introduce herself but got no further.

'Come in.'

Dianne James turned away from the door and walked slowly away, leaving Kate on the doorstep. Kate stepped inside and closed the door, aware of the heavy air and the silence of the house. She followed the long hall into a light, spacious kitchen, overheated in the absence of open windows. Dianne James was now sitting. Kate assumed this was where she'd been when she rang the bell. She glanced at the ashtray at the woman's elbow, noticing the smell of cigarette smoke for the first time. No book or magazine. No radio. Just sitting. Smoking.

Kate briefly introduced herself and accepted the offer of tea. Dianne James got up and left the table. Taking a seat, Kate looked around the kitchen. A pleasant room, done in tones of yellow and orange-red with touches of pale green that seemed to draw the brightly planted garden into it. She switched her attention back to the rigid figure moving slowly nearby.

74

Who maintained this house and garden? Surely not this woman? Bernie said there was no Mr James—

'Biscuits?'

'No. Thank you.' The silence was oppressive. 'This is a lovely room – I like the colours and—'

Dianne James came to the table carrying china cups and saucers. 'I did it. I used to dabble in interior design. Only in a small way. For people I knew . . .' She placed the china on the table, looking critically around the kitchen as if for the first time. 'It needs doing again. I finished it a month before Molly went.'

The words lay on the heavy air. Kate felt tension settling into her own shoulders. Sympathetic as she was, she wanted to be away from this woman and the sorrow exuding from every aspect of her.

'Mrs James? Is it all right with you if I take a look at Molly's bedroom?' she asked quietly.

'Help yourself. First on the left.' No question as to why.

Kate stood and returned to the hall, climbed the wide staircase off it and slowly pushed open the door of Molly James's room, feeling intrusive. Taking her notebook and a pen from her bag, she stepped noiselessly inside.

The room was stifling but immaculate. No dust. Everything scrupulously neat, as though waiting for its owner's return. Stuffed animals on a shelf, the bed covered by a pink and white duvet, gauzy material draped either side of a white-painted metal headboard. Several framed photographs of young females. Kate recognised Molly in all of them. Soft, smooth face framed by blonde hair flowing freely or tied back. One photograph brought her to a halt and she crouched on her heels for a closer examination. Younger, yes, but still clearly him, from what she recalled of the leaflet photograph she'd recently seen. Did teenage girls keep photographs of their ex-boyfriends?

Her thoughts flitted to her own house. Photographs of Kevin. Two of them. One in the sitting room, a move she'd made years ago, following the divorce, its presence an assurance to Maisie that her father was still a relevant member of the family. And another that Maisie had subsequently requested and that was now on her bedside table. Which hadn't pleased Kate, although she would never have admitted it.

Leaving the photograph, Kate stood and walked slowly to the small desk supporting the outmoded computer. Without touching any of

75

the several items there, she bent, arms folded at her waist, notebook in hand, to examine what appeared to be Molly's college work. Sheets of paper aligned one on top of the other so that the beautifully illuminated manuscript-style writing was visible.

Rage at the dying of the light, she read, recognising Dylan Thomas. An essay, 'The Role of the Shepherd in Virgil'. Another sheet bore a hastily scribbled note. Using her pen, Kate gently lifted the essay by one corner to read it: *Hi, Mol. Go and see what's on offer. J.* No date, no signature. She made a copy of it in her notebook.

She scanned the walls of Molly's room, examining the mass-produced posters and others, home-made but done with flair and computer know-how, gaining a sense of the young woman who had worked and dreamed and prepared herself here for her last day. Given the scant information so far provided by Dianne James, it seemed that mother and daughter had had creative interests in common. She looked down at the small dressing table, at the cosmetics, the electric hair curler, and recalled Molly James lying in the post-mortem suite at Rose Road, unable to come home.

Crossing to the window, Kate thought of Molly's carefree foray with her friends to the shopping mall. A trip that had almost certainly ended in terror and pain for Molly, taped, cuffed, her face masked.

She put her forehead against the warm glass. Not *with* her friends. They came home. She gazed down at the neatly paved front garden. Who had Bernie said was the contractor who worked here? Alan Malins.

Kate imagined a scene during that long-ago summer. Perhaps Molly had had this window open, listening to the contractor and his employees talking and joke-telling as they worked? Perhaps she had leaned out and spoken to them? Young men, laughing, browned by the sun, their employer—

'Tea.' Dianne James's voice drifted from below.

With a final glance around the room, Kate went downstairs and into the kitchen. Dianne was back at the kitchen table. She'd resumed smoking. As Kate took a seat and lifted her cup, the other woman spoke with such unexpected vehemence, Kate spilled her drink.

'After all these years, I *still* can't get past it. She was *warned* and *warned* from when she was a little girl – "Don't go off with anybody you don't know. Don't go off with *anybody*, no matter what they say."' She looked across at Kate. 'I know what you're thinking, but I'm telling you, Dr Hanson, my daughter, my Molly, *wouldn't* have gone with a stranger. No matter how smooth he might be.' She pressed her lips together and fell silent.

Kate wanted to respond. To say how easy it could be to turn someone, anyone into a victim. She didn't. One glance at Dianne James's face indicated the futility of reasoning on the issue.

'Most parents want to know where . . . and what happened, don't they?' Dianne asked softly, looking towards the window. 'I never did. Because it meant that I'd have to handle what had been done . . . when I wasn't even handling her going.' Her eyes drifted slowly to Kate's face. 'Is that wrong?'

Kate resolutely closed a door on the remains in the post-mortem suite.

'No. It's not wrong,' she said quietly. In the ensuing small silence, she glanced at her notebook, keeping to factual issues. 'Mrs James, can you give me the names of the two friends Molly went with to the mall?'

Dianne refocused on Kate. 'Jessica Barnes and Samantha . . .' She stopped. Kate looked up to see a mix of emotions playing across the other woman's face. She waited. After several seconds, Dianne continued: '. . . Wellings. Saying those names reminded me of that day. The last day. Molly was happy. A bit fed up of being a student, having no money, the usual thing.' There was more heavy silence, then: 'I suppose you'd like their phone numbers?'

Kate nodded, and Dianne stood and walked from the kitchen into the hall, returning with a small address book.

'These are their parents' phone numbers. Where they lived at the time . . . I haven't heard from Jessica or Sam for quite a while, so the numbers could be out of date.'

She read out the details. Kate quickly wrote them down, then looked hesitantly across the table.

'Did you have any . . . suspicions at the time Molly disappeared as to what might have happened?'

The older woman blew smoke from her mouth, then crushed her cigarette in the ashtray before responding, voice quiet: 'No. The sights you see nowadays, here and in Birmingham . . . young women out and about at night with next to nothing on . . . that wasn't my Molly. She was a nice girl. Respectable. But she still went. In daylight. I can't accept it.' She was silent for a few seconds, then: 'I never liked

Jason Fairley. Molly knew it. So did he. Too worldly for my liking. But then I probably wouldn't have been keen on anybody Molly liked at that age. She was still young.' Silence. 'Now, she always will be, won't she?'

Hearing those words, Kate felt unable to ask about the nature of Molly's relationship with Jason Fairley. This woman's devastation and anger was too palpable.

Kate left Dianne James's house, ashamed of her need to escape to the warmth and sounds of life outside. Sitting inside her car, a hand on her forehead, she sighed. Not her finest professional hour. She'd carried with her the other woman's final words:

'You tell me, Dr Hanson, why any man thinks he's got a right to take somebody's daughter, put her somewhere so she can't come home, and make her family's life hell because they miss her and can't stop wondering what happened to her.'

Kate knew she had nothing to offer that would satisfy Dianne James. Or anyone else. She hadn't tried to convey the ease with which someone committed to destruction might turn innocent quarry into powerless victim.

CHAPTER FOURTEEN

Kate drove a relatively short distance from the James house and was soon parking in front of the edifice of Mercedes-Cranham, the pink note she'd found in UCU on the dashboard. She glanced at her watch.

So geographically close to Molly's home.

She stepped out of the car into oppressive heat and locked it.

As she entered the cool glass-and-steel showroom, she was instantly aware of the leathery new-car smell. A prosperous company in difficult times.

She approached the reception desk. 'I'm Dr Kate Hanson from the Unsolved Crime Unit, Police Headquarters. I have an appointment . . .'

'Mr Cranham's expecting you.' The young blonde woman behind the reception desk nodded, stretched violent-red lips and tapped the buttons of the phone in front of her with splayed fingertips, gazing up at Kate.

'Hi, John! Mmm . . .' She giggled into the phone. 'Anyway, Dr Hanson's here from the police. Shall I send her up? . . . Okay, bye.'

The blonde replaced the receiver, looked up at Kate and pointed. 'He said to go up. Take the stairs over in the corner. First office you come to.'

Kate followed the directions. As she reached the top of the stairs, she saw a dark-haired man, late thirties, walking slowly towards her. Within five seconds, she had summed him up as someone who projected the persona of a man at ease with himself. A man who felt confident that he knew and understood women. She recognised this so quickly because she had been married to someone just like him.

His voice was low and pleasantly modulated. 'Dr Hanson. Welcome to Mercedes-Cranham. Come this way, please.'

He held out an immaculate hand and led her into the first-floor office, furnished in glass, chrome and black leather. Tediously predictable, thought Kate. Another thought nudged her subconscious. Something Dianne James had said. *No matter how smooth.*

Once they were both seated, she appraised John Cranham further. He was most definitely not tedious. He was extremely attractive. And he knew it. Tanned face, thick dark hair, silk tie, dazzling white shirt topped by a suit Kate estimated to have cost several hundred pounds.

'Tea? Coffee?'

Kate declined both. She didn't intend this to be a lengthy visit if she could avoid it.

'My colleague Lieutenant Corrigan met with you yesterday, Mr Cranham . . .'

'Please. John. Yes, the American officer.'

'. . . to clarify your whereabouts at the time a young woman named Molly James disappeared from very near here in 2002.' Kate gave a slight nod towards the Touchwood mall, just visible from Cranham's office window.

Cranham steepled his fingers. Wedding ring. He gazed directly into Kate's eyes and smiled.

'The TT. A nice little car. But if you ever feel the need for a change . . .' He leaned forward, taking a business card from a silver box on the desk. 'I'm sure we could find something that would suit you. Something with a little more . . . *gravitas*, as well as flair. Something more in accord with your professional standing.'

Kate took the card. What was it Bernie had called him?

'You rang to say you have something to add to what you've already told Lieutenant Corrigan.'

He looked at her for a few seconds, then nodded, becoming businesslike. 'Actually, I feel rather a fool.' Kate doubted it. 'I promised your colleague some paperwork to confirm where I was at the time this girl disappeared. So I had our accounts department do a search. It seems I made an error. A small error. I hope it hasn't caused you or your colleagues any difficulties or unnecessary work.'

As if on cue, a woman of indeterminate age wearing a business suit entered the office, handed Cranham a folder, glanced at Kate, then exited. He extracted a single sheet from the folder and handed it to Kate, who read it quickly. It confirmed that John Cranham returned to the UK on the same day Molly disappeared. But much earlier than he had indicated to Joe. And presumably to the original investigation.

Kate started her car, looking back at the showroom, the gleaming vehicles inside it, the well-presented staff. And their boss. Sleek, like the vehicles he sold. Wealthy. Something else Dianne James had said came into her mind: Molly James had been short of money.

Joe was on the phone as Kate walked into UCU. He covered the receiver.

'How was Molly's mom?'

Kate dumped her belongings on the table, shook her head and passed him the printed information Cranham had given her.

'She's currently clinically depressed. Cranham, on the other hand, is arrogant and always will be. He was making a charm offensive and trying to sell me a car. He failed on both. He *was* in the UK when Molly went missing. He arrived at Birmingham airport at six *a.m.*, not in the late evening as he told you and the original investigation.' She walked towards the Refreshment Lounge, still talking. 'He could have emailed that information – or faxed it. No. He wanted one of us over there so that he could give it to us personally, perhaps disarm us before we found it ourselves.'

Joe raised a hand and turned to talk on the phone.

'Mr Fairley? Joe Corrigan, Unsolved Crime Unit. Since my call on you, I've been thinking – about your coming into Rose Road some time. We're not far from Five Ways . . . No, no, a casual chat.' Silence, then: 'Any time to suit you.' Joe mentioned a date and time and raised his eyebrows at Kate, pointing to a day in his open diary. She came to the table, peered and nodded. 'Yes, that'd be fine. See you then.' He hung up as Bernie arrived. 'Jason Fairley's agreed to a meeting here.'

'When?' asked Bernie.

'Next Tuesday.'

'Why're you getting him in?' asked Kate.

Joe raised his shoulders. 'Partly because I'd like to see if he becomes any more curious about our reinvestigation.'

Bernie dropped on to a chair at the table, face red, hair damp. 'I called in on Malins, just as he was leaving for a few days' holiday. Crete. According to him, while him and his lads was doing building work at Molly James's house he never spoke to her, and he knows nothing. Got him coming in next Friday afternoon. He's away till then. He's not best pleased.'

Kate gave Bernie coffee and the information from Cranham.

'Very interesting. The Git stops in the frame.'

Kate nodded. 'What I want to know is, was it an oversight, an innocent mistake? Or was it a lie by omission?'

CHAPTER FIFTEEN

An hour later, Whittaker powered into UCU with a brown internal envelope, flipped it on to the table and left in the same manner. Kate opened the envelope. Colley's single-sheet statement.

Within five minutes she had read what Colley had had to say to WPC Sharma and she gave the gist to Bernie and Joe. 'He says he went to the mall, saw that there was a fashion show on, but was in there no more than ten minutes because he spotted a couple of people in there he didn't want trouble with . . . so he left.' She passed the statement to her colleagues to read for themselves.

'So who were these two people he saw, d'you think?' she asked.

Bernie shrugged. 'You know yourself, Doc, sex types ain't your most popular members of the community. They was probably local people in the know about what he'd done. That kind of news travels. It can cause a lot of aggro.'

Kate picked up Colley's statement, slipped it into the box on Julian's workstation and started writing up her notes from her visits. They needed to contact Molly's friends, Jessica Barnes and Samantha Wellings.

Bernie and Joe were discussing Malins's Police National Computer check, left for them by Julian, when the door flew open and Furman strode into the room.

'Give me a quick update,' he said, without preamble.

Joe provided details of what was now known about the remains, which he'd learned from Bernie, plus the arrangements made to see Malins and Fairley.

Kate had decided not to voice her own thoughts about Molly James's remains. Not yet. Not to Furman.

He glanced in her direction and she described her own activities. 'I went to see Dianne James this morning, and then John Cranham.'

He wheeled and glared at her. 'I said to leave him alone.'

Kate frowned. 'No you didn't.'

Had he?

'Yes I *did*.'

Kate willed herself calm. 'Actually, he phoned *us* and requested the visit.'

Furman looked momentarily wrong-footed, but quickly recovered. 'His family is wealthy. It could mean trouble for the Force if not handled right. Focus on finding some new POIs. Do some door-to-door inquiries.'

Idiot.

Kate watched him, waiting. When he didn't continue, she asked, her tone patient, 'Would you like to know what Mr Cranham had to say?'

In response to a terse nod, she shared Cranham's latest information. Furman shot her a suspicious look as she finished, then transferred his attention to Bernie and Joe.

'Sounds to me like he made a simple error. Like I said, watch what you're doing with Cranham.' He turned to Joe. 'Lieutenant Corrigan, you can handle any future contact with him.' He walked to the door, then turned back to them. 'The press has got a sense of what's going on. Probably saw Headquarters vehicles coming and going. Nobody from this unit knows anything, got it? *I'll* handle the media, if necessary.'

'Why don't we tell them what's going on? Get them on side? Maybe they could help. The least we could do is make people aware, warn—'

'*No.*' Furman looked at Kate, one corner of his mouth raised. 'That's typical civilian thinking. We *don't* disclose—'

'But—'

'*Listen*. This is the Force line – "following up a number of lines of inquiry in relation to" whatever it is that's happened. That's how it's going to stay. *Got* it?'

Kate stared after Furman as he went through the door, then sat for a while mulling over what else he'd said. *Find some new POIs.* She thought again about what Connie had shown them. The 'goodies', as the pathologist called them. She'd been preoccupied with the visits she'd made, and Dianne James's grief and unhappiness, and hadn't yet given her colleagues any indication as to the clear implications of the items lying in the post-mortem lab.

She looked across the table at Bernie's florid face. He wasn't going to like it, as and when she shared her thinking. She glanced at the label on the file he and Joe were studying: 'Malins, A.' Deep in thought, Kate inventoried the items Connie had shown them. The duct tape, the handcuff, the home-produced mask and the as yet unidentified scrap of card. Of one thing Kate was sure. They were dealing with a very committed killer.

Kate threw open the massive folding doors that made up almost the whole of the end wall of the kitchen. One eyebrow raised, she held aloft a bottle in Joe's direction. He was sitting at the table, eyeing the small book of advice to separated and divorced parents.

He looked up and nodded. 'It's Friday. We know it makes sense.'

Kate took a corkscrew from a drawer. 'It seems to me that Furman wants to keep us away from Cranham. Why would he want to do that, do you think?'

Joe took the glass she offered, sipped and placed it on the table. 'Furman's a career officer. A self-promoter who defines every situation in terms of his own professional progress and future and other people in terms of their money, power and influence. He's afraid of upsetting a rich clan.' He looked directly at Kate. 'I can't take the guy.'

Kate grinned. 'I had a vague impression he's not on your Christmas list.'

A word Joe had just used set up a small resonance inside Kate's head. *Money.*

Suddenly the front door opened and they heard voices. Maisie. And Kevin. What was he doing here again? Maisie erupted into the kitchen, followed by her father.

'Hi, Mom! Hi, Joe! Look who just arrived. Daddy said he's going to take me to Disneyland and—'

'Whoa! Steady on, Maisie Mouse. I *said* it depended on my workload and whether I can get enough free time.' He looked fleetingly at Kate, who was keeping a pleasant face. He and Joe nodded at each other.

'Florida,' said Kevin. 'Your neck of the woods.'

Joe stood, drained his glass and set it down on the kitchen counter. 'Give or take a thousand miles.'

'Joe's from Boston, Daddy. I *told* you.'

'Here for long?' Kevin asked casually, eyeing Kate.

'Uncertain,' responded Joe. Equally casual.

Kate walked with Joe to the door, thinking about names and money. The note on Molly's desk. *J.* She thought of the Js in the case thus far:

J for John Cranham?

Or J for Jason Fairley?

J for Julian. Hardly.

J . . . for Joe.

CHAPTER SIXTEEN

By seven o'clock on Saturday morning, Kate was ready to action a plan she'd thought of the previous evening.

After Kevin had left, she'd spent an hour in her study, completing student grade sheets, then checked through the notes for one of the coming week's lectures. She wanted to spend some time this weekend with Maisie.

Now that Molly James's remains had been identified, however, she couldn't stop the case from dominating her thoughts. Before she raised her ideas about the nature of Molly's murderer with Joe or Bernie she wanted to give them more consideration, including exploration of the killer's behaviour. Which would in turn give an indication of his thinking.

Running lightly up the stairs, she checked on Maisie, who was sleeping soundly. She'd told Maisie last night that she had to go out early this morning. Turning from the room, she hurried downstairs, seized her keys and left the house.

The mileage counter read 5.7 miles when Kate left the road and parked close to where Bernie had parked a few days ago. As the traffic pounded past behind her, she stared ahead through tinted windows towards the bypass site, beyond the press of trees, unmoving in the early morning sunlight. Getting out of the car, she closed the door quietly, locked it and started walking along the same small path.

She passed by the remains of the fire and on to the clearing. To where the forensic tent had stood. She stopped uncertainly, looking around the site. Some markers remained in place, along with the yellow-and-black *Do Not Enter* tape. She slipped under it, surprised that there was no one here. No one guarding the site. Cutbacks?

She walked over the uneven ground, mindful even now not to step beyond Matt Prentiss's carefully placed tapes and pegs. The area had been thoroughly gone over. Perhaps that was why no one was here. They'd got all there was to get, as Connie would say—

'Dr Hanson?'

Kate whirled at the voice and the sound of her name. It was Whittaker. How had he got here? She'd seen no car. Where was he when she'd arrived just now?

He walked towards her.

'Sorry if I scared you. I had to . . . you know.' His young face coloured as he gestured to some trees at a distance from where they were standing.

Kate nodded. 'I thought it was odd – no one about.'

Whittaker grinned. 'I was dropped here at six this morning, when the others went off. I'm here till the next shift come back on at nine.' He glanced at his watch.

'Is it okay if I walk on a bit further? I'll stay within the lines.'

Whittaker frowned, then nodded. 'Gander wants the site watched so members of the public don't get on to it. But you're okay.'

With a small smile at the constable, Kate walked on, away from him. Within minutes she had reached the far edge of the clearing. She was now approximately twenty-five yards past where the remains were found. The trees here were older, the saplings a little heftier and the grasses more lush. She looked ahead, towards a shaded area of woodland, trying to decide if anything might be gained by going further.

Hands in the pockets of her jeans, Kate gazed at the surrounding sweep of trees and vegetation, some of it now bathed in bright early-morning sunlight. She couldn't see the road from here. Nor Whittaker. Neither could she see her car. Leaning against a tree, gazing to one side, unseeing, she let her thoughts roam.

How many people thundering past this spot in their cars knew what was beyond the screen of trees along the road's edge? How many knew that behind what appeared from the roadside to be a densely wooded area there were open spaces?

She hadn't known. Yet the area was familiar to her and close to home.

She toed the dry earth with one Timberland boot.

Once a car was driven off the bypass and a person slipped into the shadows, no one would know what was happening behind these trees.

Five-point-seven miles from the south-west side of the city. Plenty of opportunity for anonymity.

He'd needed a place to leave Molly. A lonely place. Concealed.

He had to have known the area well. He'd selected it on the basis of known characteristics – lonely and concealed, with small areas of accessible soil under which a body could be buried.

Because it wasn't easy to bury a body.

He'd been here before.

Before he killed Molly.

This site was a place he knew very well. He'd already found it . . . ideal?

Reaching into her jeans pocket for her phone, she dialled Bernie's number.

He responded after two rings. 'Watts.'

'Bernie. It's me, I'm at the bypass and—'

'What you up to now?'

'Coming here's helped me to think. About how unlikely it is that whoever abducted Molly and left her here did it only once.'

Silence. 'He's a repeater, Bernie.'

She listened to Bernie's anticipated sigh and his verbal response.

'Must be something I've done in a past life. How sure are you?'

'I'm sure. He planned. He went to a lot of trouble. At the time he abducted Molly, he already knew what it was like here, off the road, behind the trees. You know what that means, Bernie. This site needs extending.'

She heard another sigh. 'Doc, we do the cases that the Arse gives us . . .'

'I know, but trust me on this, Bernie. Molly isn't the only one. It makes no sense for him to put such effort into a single killing. Think of what we know of his methods. The lack of clothes. The handcuff and the duct tape. They all say "repeater". This area must be searched for more remains. And we need another search of the MisPer database for young women missing from the Greater West Midlands area.'

Bernie's voice exploded in her ear. 'D'you have any idea how many names we're likely to dredge up? Names of girls who've left home for any number of reasons, girls who believed a city bigger than Birming-ham might offer them . . .' His voice faded.

'What?' asked Kate.

'Nothing. I give up. The Arse'll go mental when he hears about this. We'll tell him on Monday. Or perhaps not . . .'

Kate was about to respond when the call suddenly ended. Frowning at her phone, she saw the 'Battery Low' message.

With a sigh, she shoved it back into her pocket, conscious once more of her surroundings. A small breeze whipped through nearby trees, creating a dry rustling. Kate eyed the swaying branches, then looked quickly to her left, where she was sure she'd just heard the crisp snap of dried twigs. Whittaker?

Steadying her breathing, feeling her heart rate starting to climb, she began walking in the direction she'd originally come from. She didn't want to be here a moment longer. She wanted traffic noise, the smell of petrol fumes, the presence of people. She wanted to see her car. She wanted to be inside it.

Twenty minutes later, in the weekend silence of UCU, Kate stood at the glass screen. She'd added the word 'REPEATER' in stark capitals above Molly's name.

She gazed around the empty room, then turned back to the glass, feeling suddenly lonely. Forcing herself to concentrate, she looked again at the screen, reminding herself of the information it already held.

Connected to Molly's name by arrowed lines were those of her two friends. And their telephone numbers. Information that needed following up. Saturday morning. Not a work day. Picking up the office phone, she tried both numbers. No reply from either.

A series of quick thumps from the stairs and Maisie suddenly appeared in the sitting room.

Kate was on the sofa, propped up by a large cushion. After arriving home, she'd stripped off the clothes she'd worn in that terrible place and walked into her shower, to stand under cooling rods of water, grateful that she and Maisie were together in this house. She'd spent time on her hair, which now lay glossy and heavy on her shoulders. She'd put on a loose-knit white cotton sweater and yellow knee-length shorts. Her tanned feet were bare, now set off by bright, shiny orange toenails. She'd needed to do all of this.

She turned the page of the textbook and made another note. There was always work to be done. And as far as Kate was concerned, that was fine. She now felt equal to it.

'Hi, Mommy Bear!'

Kate looked up, then looked again, taking in Maisie's ensemble, particularly the knot of silky blue fabric holding back the sumptuous curls. It looked suspiciously like Kate's favourite Ralph Lauren scarf. Her glance drifted over the short lace-trimmed yellow petticoat, to which Maisie had added white knee-length leggings and a blue midi-top. If there was such a thing as a 'picture of health', Maisie was it.

'Hello, Baby Bear,' Kate responded cautiously, lifting her feet off the sofa.

It had been quite a while since Maisie had tolerated the one-time habitual exchange. Kate casually rearranged her notes. Sharp as always, Maisie intuited her mother's intent.

'Mom, I *know* what you do. I don't need protecting from it.' She plumped down on the sofa next to Kate, tucking brown toes under her mother's thigh. Kate continued her writing.

'You know your problem, Mom?'

'No. But I've a sneaky feeling you're about to let me in on it.'

Maisie squirmed on the sofa, reaching for stray notes, mostly those Kate had made as they came to her, when there was no access to her notebook. Kate gathered them together and returned them to her bag.

Maisie continued. 'Well, my theory is *this*. You think you know everything, right? I mean, like, what's going to happen, and what people might do, because all the people you work with are seriously weird – not Bernie and Joe, I mean the others, the risky ones you write reports about for the old judges to read. So *you* think that everybody out there is weird and plotting horrible stuff.' She took a breath. 'That's what I think. Phyllis is right. You need to relax, chill out. Mostly, people are okay.'

Kate glanced at her daughter's face. The smooth tawny skin, the two fans of lashes and the tiny, almost imperceptible fringe of red blonde along the hairline. She knew of sexual offenders who would give . . .

'How about Pizza Express later?'

'Cool!' In one smooth movement Maisie leapt off the sofa and headed for the hall.

Halfway up the stairs she yelled, 'Hey, Mom, I forgot, Joe phoned. Said he'd drop in later. He can come with us!'

91

Kate reached for her notes again. Was it her imagination or had Maisie become noisier lately? She needed to have a word with her about banging the garage door. Old Mrs Hetherington next door had complained again.

CHAPTER SEVENTEEN

Elated, the young woman joined the early Monday lunchtime crowd inside the city-centre coffee shop and waited to be served. As she waited she people-watched, mood expansive due to the incredible opportunity she'd been handed at work just one hour earlier.

Smiling benevolently at the tired-looking barista, she took her order and change from him and scanned the busy scene. She saw a nearby window table about to become vacant and walked swiftly to it. Another sign that this really was her day! Life was on her side.

Smiling to herself, she set down the tray and sat, becoming aware that she was now the object of keen male interest. Feigning aloofness, she casually gave him the benefit of her profile, confident that he was on her 'best side'. She ran her fingers lightly through smooth blonde hair and gently tugged the cream Prada skirt and honey cashmere top to good effect.

Raising the latte to her lips, she took a small sip, then put it down and forked a tiny morsel of the celebratory chocolate muffin, a much smaller mouthful than she might have done if she weren't conscious of being observed. She stole a quick sideways glance, and he gave her a brief smile of acknowledgement before returning his attention to his newspaper. Mmm . . . Very presentable. Late thirties? After Craig's buffoonery, indications of male maturity would be a definite plus.

Listen to yourself! A perfect stranger smiles at you in a coffee shop and you're rating him as potential partner material. She grinned and forked a larger mouthful of muffin.

Through narrowed eyes he watched the little pantomime intently. Saw the private smile. Noted the single strand of graduated pearls, probably her mother's, the soft leather bag she'd dropped carelessly on the chair next to her, the black Gucci loafers.

He knew she was pleased about something this Monday lunch hour. He glanced at the smooth, well-manicured hands. No indication of a fiancé. Expensive to run. Clothes for a modern office. The kind with automatic doors, thick carpets. He had it. An organisation with a career structure.

He continued to watch, absorbing more of her as she removed a silver-coloured phone from her bag. The lightly tanned arm, the slim wrist encircled by a narrow gold bracelet, the pale-gold skin of the hand, each tapered finger tipped with a buffed pink nail. When her attention returned to him, he picked up his coffee cup and made a small acknowledging movement in her direction. He saw the light flush on the cheek, the lowered lashes and the small smile.

Nice, very nice – breathe and relax . . . breathe and . . . ree-lax.

Whilst he'd consumed her appearance he was inside his own head. Thinking. About how she would look when he eventually removed her face with his best little X-Acto blade.

CHAPTER EIGHTEEN

Kate was in her office at the university when the call came from Bernie. The further excavation of the bypass site that UCU had requested was under way, sanctioned by Chief Superintendent Gander. A second set of remains had been unearthed in the small clearing where Kate had stood two days before. A human femur had also been located, some distance away from the second burial site.

'Connie's there now. She's asked me to go over. Which means she'll have something worth looking at or knowing about. I'm on my way. How about it, Doc? Can you meet us there?'

Kate scanned a page of her diary and checked her watch: 3.10 p.m. 'Yes. Has Connie said anything to you about what's been found?'

'You know Connie. Cautious to the last. But it looks like we're in business again.'

The call ended and Kate reviewed the brief exchange. Typical Bernie. No *Hey, Doc, you were right!* or anything approaching an apology for his attitude when she rang him on Saturday. She recognised the call as the nearest he would ever come to such sentiments.

Forty minutes later, Kate was at the bypass site, which was once again a hum of forensic activity. The white tent was back, west of where Molly was found. She looked around and saw Joe and Bernie away to one side, talking to Harry, who was handing them white coveralls. As she approached, she called out:

'Hi, Harry, you two. Know anything yet?'

Bernie grunted his way into the protective suit and Joe shook his head. Kate saw anticipation on Harry's face as he handed her a similar garment. She knew he loved his job.

'Okay, let's go and see Connie,' she said quietly.

They left Harry and walked together in the direction of the forensic tent. Ahead Kate could see Matt Prentiss, brows low, face thunderous as he watched them approach.

'Mind where you're putting your feet, will you? Hey, you!' He pointed at Bernie. 'Keep within the tapes. There could be evidence anywhere around here.'

'Bloody Nazi,' fumed Bernie under his breath as he followed the tape, ignoring Kate's disapproving look.

With a shared feeling of déjà vu, they made their way carefully over the uneven, grass-covered terrain to the tent and stood just inside. Connie glanced up at them, then pointed to the rectangle of ground by which she was crouching. 'It's a rerun of what we got last time,' she said quietly. 'Come and have a look.'

They drew nearer and looked down. It did look very similar, once Connie had pointed out the position of the remains.

'Any characteristics that might be of particular interest to us?' asked Joe.

Connie nodded. 'As before. Female, young – under twenty-five. Been here five-plus years.' She moved to the long side of the rectangle, then gazed up at her receptive audience. 'There's more.' She pointed to bony arches already exposed. 'See?' she said quietly, indicating the remains of what looked to be strips of material encircling some of them. Kate nodded. Duct tape.

Was this it?

Whoever killed these two young women is duct-taping his signature? His mark?

Proclaiming his handiwork.

'The femur we found this morning was lying over there.' Connie pointed to a taped-off area a couple of metres beyond the forensic tent. 'We know that Molly James has her full complement of femurs. I don't yet know about these remains. Ask me tomorrow.'

The four colleagues glanced solemnly at each other.

Kate and Joe trailed back to their vehicles in the heat. Waiting for Bernie to join them, Kate felt both saddened and exhilarated by this development. The remains were clear confirmation.

They now had evidence of a repeater at work in the twenty-first century.

Late that evening Kate was home, showered and in pyjamas, spending a quiet evening in front of the television, Maisie curled up beside her, similarly attired. She put her arm around her daughter and drew her closer. Maisie had her eyes on Sandra Bullock's smooth face.

'Mom?'

'Mmmm?'

'Would you ever have Botox? Or a facelift?'

Kate looked down at her daughter, up at the screen, then down again.

'Depends on how much aggravation I'm likely to get in the next few years.'

Maisie grinned. A couple of minutes of silence drifted by.

'Mom?'

'Mmm . . . ?'

'Can I borrow your Abercrombie top?'

Kate did a quick mental review of the garment in question. Not low-cut. Not tight. Not see-through.

'Yes. *Don't* wreck it.'

Maisie snuggled, wondering how receptive her mother might be if she told her that she wanted to dye her hair. Black. Like Sandra Bullock's. She watched the screen action. Wow! How cool was that!

Kate's thoughts were also drifting. To the likelihood of other victims.

And the 'graduation' of offenders.

CHAPTER NINETEEN

Kate was up and dressed by seven o'clock and tapping on Maisie's bedroom door.

'Maisie?' She opened the door and stepped inside the room, noting the semi-chaos on the floor. 'Are you awake?'

'Go 'way,' responded Maisie from beneath riotous curls and body-moulded duvet.

'Maisie, listen to me, please. I'm going in to the university early. Phyllis will be here at eight, yes? I'll leave a note reminding her to remind *you* to tidy up this room before you leave for school.'

No response.

'Who's coming for you for school?'

Still no response.

'*Maisie.*'

'Wha'!'

'I said who—'

'Che'sey's mom.'

Kate sighed and looked at her watch, experiencing a pang of guilt. She must agree some kind of rota for taking the girls to school. She'd phone Chelsey's mother later. She scanned the room a second time and sighed.

Show me a working mother, single or otherwise, and I'll tell you her middle name – beginning with G.

Which stands for 'Guilt'.

'It's time you were up. I'm going in ten minutes.'

Quitting the room, Kate went downstairs and wrote a hurried note to Phyllis, involving one or two heavily underlined words. She had no concerns about her housekeeper's ability to handle Maisie. Phyllis had raised two sons and two daughters using the tough-love approach.

*

Kate surveyed the ranks of students, waiting for them to finish their note-taking. She'd set up the PowerPoint presentation herself, and was happy to do so given that Julian's absence meant that at this moment he was in UCU, searching the PNC MisPer database for other young women missing from the area in the last ten years.

Closing the Tuesday-morning lecture, Kate invited her young audience to disregard the language and ideas of Hollywood's characterisation of the predatory killer.

'They're based on an approach to repeat crime that isn't supported by quality research. I would truly love the "serial killer" tag and the "organised" and "disorganised" categorisations of crime scenes to disappear. They've become banal terms with which we're now much too comfortable, because cinema and television have done them to death. Excuse the pun. We ought not to be comfortable with the language of repeat murder.'

She looked around the auditorium, particularly at the female members of her audience. 'One of the problems with murder as entertainment is that we're so familiar with it, it has little to no influence on how we live our lives. Watching a film that features serial-killer activities doesn't lead to our living our lives more cautiously. It's just entertainment, right? We continue as usual, never seriously questioning our own safety. Why would we, when we're distanced by television or cinema screens? Or by our choice to finish the story, close the book? But the reality of the threat *is* there. Operating quietly in the background.'

Searching the faces of her audience, most of them of similar age to Molly, she delivered the key message, culled from her own research, that the police often failed to alert the media, and thus the public, to repeat sexual crimes.

'We don't live cautiously because the media is sometimes as unaware as we are of an existing threat. Law enforcement tends not to warn of a predator operating, saying little beyond that it is following up lines of inquiry. Not until a predator's activities become *very* evident, perhaps due to the number of his victims, is there even an official admission of his existence. Mostly, there is nothing from the police until the first press reports emerge – an arrest, a garden being dug up in Gloucester.'

She scanned the faces. Young as they were, they got the history. 'We all need to be aware of and take responsibility for our own protection.' She dropped her voice. 'The kind of repeater or doer of interest to you in your future careers is *smart*. Not necessarily a great intellect, but sufficiently people-wise to repeat on the scale of the men on the screen.'

Kate changed direction, to what was known about the predatory male, his ability to superficially charm the naïve or unwary. 'However, contrary to popular myth, he's no Einstein. For insightful, mature people, he might wear a little thin fairly quickly.'

A pause before she delivered another key point. 'But be sure of one thing. He's capable of fooling *all* of us. His manipulative abilities, his flair for mimicking an emotionally developed person and conning us – that's what gets him what he wants. His focus is always on what *he* wants and how *he's* going to make that happen.' Her audience was gripped.

'As professional workers in criminology, we need to be able to recognise him for what he is, in order to stop him creating more victims. We need to develop a quick awareness that he's operating and not be misled by false beliefs about him. If you want to know more about those false beliefs, you'll find them in this,' she added, holding up three A4 sheets. 'You're welcome to take a copy from the table by the door as you leave.'

The sheets exposed further myths of repeat crime, including one for the would-be police officers among her students: that repeaters are not generally caught via DNA evidence or by-the-book detection.

Kate was back at the front of the platform. 'The predator devotes time to perfecting his craft. *Creating* the situation, *scripting* the *scene*. Remind you of any job or profession?'

A few tentative hands were raised and a one-word answer floated towards the platform.

Kate nodded. 'And as an actor, he can mimic anyone he chooses – use a different look, a new name, a fresh con.'

And like all of you watching me, thought Kate, he progresses.

To graduation.

Thirty minutes later, Kate was inside UCU. Julian was also there.

'Inspector Furman was on my case earlier for the information from the visits and other stuff, but I'm getting into MisPers now to start the search you want, Kate.'

100

When Bernie arrived a minute later, it was to find Kate writing on the glass screen. He gave her a suspicious glance.

' "Graduation," ' he read. 'What's that mean for our cases?'

Kate looked at him. 'It sums up the criminal trajectory of the repeater.'

'Meaning? They start out small, with petty thieving, say, then move on to killing?'

Kate shook her head. 'Not quite. Okay, they might start with low-level dishonesty, but what graduation commonly means is that foundation offences are essentially the same type as the later, more serious ones. In our case, it means he probably committed comparatively minor sexual offences to begin with. Over time, that behaviour becomes increasingly serious and deviant until it involves the sexual death of a victim.'

Bernie nodded. 'Got you.'

Julian took sheets from the printer and handed them to Kate. She took them to the table and glanced through them, then began constructing a separate list in her notebook. Bernie was making drinks as Joe arrived.

'Hi y'all. I see heavy-duty industry. What gives?'

Kate waited for him to be seated.

'I asked Julian to print off details of females reported missing in the West Midlands area between the mid-nineties and now. I specified the mid-nineties on the assumption that Molly wasn't the first to be left at the bypass. We need to avoid being swamped with "missings", so I suggested to Julian that he key in specific characteristics – age range: sixteen to twenty-two; physical appearance: over five foot six, long-haired. I also added "educated". We don't know at this stage if any of these individual characteristics is essential for the doer –' Kate shrugged – 'but we have to start somewhere.' She glanced at Julian. 'Talk us through the cases you've found, please. I'll write them up on the board as an aide-memoire.'

Julian left his computer to stand in front of the glass screen. Kate joined him as he began.

'The search generated five names, including Molly James's. The others are Janine Walker, eighteen, missing since July 1998, from Blakedown –' Julian lifted his eyes from the list – 'which is geographically close to the bypass.'

He continued. 'Vanessa Miles, twenty-two, missing since January

101

2000, from Walsall. Leah Wilson, twenty, missing since September 2001, from Halesowen . . .' He halted the dismal roll-call for a couple of seconds. 'And the last one – Amy Brown, nineteen, missing from Bromsgrove since February 2003.'

He frowned down at his list then turned to look at Kate. 'So . . . how come nobody's looked at these names and linked them before?'

'What matters right now is that *we* have,' said Kate quietly, then turned to properly address Julian's question. 'It's a sad fact that hundreds of people go missing every year. Many of them young and female, with no indication that they didn't go willingly. We need the dental and medical records of these girls in case any of them are at the bypass. Can you do that?'

Julian nodded. 'Chief Superintendent Gander will countersign the requests.'

No one spoke for some seconds. The phone rang and Joe lifted it, listened, then hung up.

'Hey, kids. Ready to be benefited some more by Connie?'

Kate put down the marker pen and went to collect her notebook. Leaving Julian in UCU, they walked downstairs.

In response to Kate's light tap on the frosted door, Igor let them inside the post-mortem suite. Connie was already forensically kitted out and working carefully at one of the tables. They went to the dispensers to collect plastic aprons, face masks and latex gloves, then, suitably attired, they approached Connie. She raised a hand when she judged they were near enough and looked at each of them keenly.

'You're ready to know what we have here? The second set of bypass remains. She's young. At a guess, of similar age to Molly James – *don't* quote me on that yet – and her skeletal structure is complete.' The pathologist's eyes met theirs, each of them thinking about the lone femur.

Connie returned to the remains in front of them. 'I have more little gifts for you, UCU. Look.' She pointed to the duct tape around the ribs that they'd seen at the bypass site. 'Same dimensions. Same characteristics. Now take a look at this.'

Kate looked to where Connie was pointing, then moved up the table for a closer examination.

'It's hair,' said Connie. 'But this time it's been cut. Probably with scissors, not necessarily new, but sharp. Regular scissors. Nothing fancy.'

Leaning down and to one side, her face level with and almost touching the table, Kate gazed at the poor ruined hair: probably blonde to mid-brown in life. As she continued her examination, a tiny beetle came careening out of the ruin, a determined little tank, up-down, up-down over the clumps and tendrils. Within the mass, something else snagged Kate's attention.

'What's this, Connie?' She bent closer to the material, which was stained by decomposition, small clods of earth stuck to its surface. Connie's voice broke into her concentration.

'Appears to be some kind of small hair tie or scarf. Cotton construction. Not sure of the colour yet. Possibly red, with a lighter spot pattern of some kind. *But*, take a look at something else I have for you.'

They looked down at the item in the shallow metal tray in Connie's hand. It was virtually a rerun of Molly. An oval of dirty cloth, holes at either side. Kate felt a shiver of recognition and dread. She glanced up at Joe. His handsome face was solemn. Bernie had his lips pressed together, arms folded across his girth.

Kate moved away from the table and tapped her phone for the contacts list.

'UCU.'

'Hi, Julian. Can you do something for me when you have a minute? Go through the MisPer reports on the girls you've got from your search and take a look at the clothes they were said to be wearing on the day they disappeared. We're particularly interested in hair ties and scarves.'

'Will do. Call you back.'

Kate ended the call and turned back to the PM suite.

'And the final item –' Connie walked to the nearby work surface, picked up a pad of absorbent paper and returned to the table – 'is *this*.'

They pressed closer. A scrap of thick card. Similar to the one found with Molly James's remains. Kate leaned again, her face as close to the item as she knew Connie would permit.

'There are marks . . . there and here. See?' She stepped back to allow her two colleagues to view it.

After some seconds: 'What do you think?'

Joe looked at Kate, then at the card.

'Letters? Writing?'

Bernie put on his glasses and bent closer to the little item, hands on knees, arms braced.

'Yep. A round shape, then another one that looks the same, ending with a long downstroke just there.' He straightened with a low grunt.

Kate scanned faces as they stood around the table. 'What I said at the outset of the case – about classification of murder into emotional and instrumental?' She glanced down. 'This is further confirmation of instrumental murder-by-stranger.'

Connie looked in silence at the remains, then at each of them. 'Because she has her full complement of femurs, the logic is that there's another body still out there.'

Kate pressed her lips together, nodding. 'Connie, we need that whole area to be excavated.'

'Being done as we speak, Kate.'

Kate's phone jangled in her hand. She responded to the call, listened, thanked her caller, then glanced at the faces around the table.

'That was Julian. Janine Walker disappeared in July 1998 wearing a red cotton bandanna with a white heart-shaped design and carrying a small red heart-shaped purse.'

Amid the heavy silence of the PM suite, Kate walked slowly along the table to the mass of hair and peered down at the spoiled item within it. She looked up at Connie.

'I'm assuming there was no purse?'

Connie slowly shook her head. Kate closed her eyes momentarily.

What's the likelihood he took the purse?

As a fantasy aid

Where is it now?

CHAPTER TWENTY

By 6.30 on Tuesday evening, Joe and Bernie were searching the MisPer information for details of clothing worn by all of the young missing women on the day they were last seen. Kate had left at five o'clock with some persuasion from Joe, after he'd heard her phone home twice within the previous hour to check on Maisie.

In the quiet of UCU, Bernie left the table and strode to the glass screen, glancing at Joe as he passed by.

'Here's the complete picture for Janine Walker, Corrigan,' he murmured, holding up a single sheet then starting to write on the board as he spoke. 'MisPer indicates she was last seen wearing a short-sleeved white linen shirt, black jeans, flat black leather sandals. Hair held back by a red cotton bandanna. Carrying two letters for posting and one heart-shaped red purse.'

Joe looked up quickly as he searched the sheets in front of him. 'What I've confirmed for Molly James is . . . pale-blue polo shirt and cream trousers. Plus the gold necklace.' He glanced at his watch, up at the glass screen, then stood and walked over to it, tracing a finger down information put there by Kate.

'Fancy a ride?'

Bernie looked at him. 'Where?'

Joe gave a 'wait' gesture, returned to the table and lifted the phone. After a few seconds, 'Mrs Barnes?'

'Yes?'

'Lieutenant Corrigan here, West Midlands Police, Rose Road, Harborne. We're reinvestigating the abduction of a young woman named Molly James.'

He heard a note of gratified concern in the answering voice: 'Really? I didn't know the police were opening the case again. I'm really glad, but what's—'

'Is Jessica there?'

'You're in luck. She's here on a visit. Why?'

'How do you feel about me dropping by with a colleague to ask her a few questions?'

Silence. Then, 'Well, yes, if it's—'

'Say, in half an hour from now?' Another small silence. 'It's okay, Mrs Barnes, we just want to ask your daughter some basic questions about the day Molly disappeared.'

'Of course. Do you have our address?'

Joe hung up the phone and looked at Bernie. 'Let's go.'

Within the hour they were putting their questions to a young woman in her mid twenties holding a sleeping infant.

'Tell us about Molly the day she disappeared,' Joe said.

The young woman's eyebrows slid together. She looked uncertain.

'If it helps, start by describing how she looked,' he suggested.

Jessica patted the infant as she gazed into the middle distance.

'It's such a long time ago. I need to think . . . She had her hair loose, like long and straight, and she was wearing a light-blue polo top. Cream trousers. She had her Ellesse bag with her. That surprised me, actually. We were just going for a walk around the mall. I couldn't see why she needed it.'

The young woman shook her head. 'That's all I remember. No, wait. She was wearing her name necklace. You know, the kind that spells out your name. Gold. But she always wore that. It was a present from her boyfriend.'

'Which boyfriend was that?'

'Well, he wasn't her boyfriend at that time. Jason Fairley.'

'Can you tell us anything about Molly's mood that day, love?' asked Bernie.

The young woman looked at him, puzzled. 'Her *mood*?' She shrugged very slightly, careful not to disturb the sleeping infant. 'She was as she always was, you know . . . chatty.'

She glanced from Bernie to Joe then back. 'Now I think about it, she was a *bit* quieter than usual, but I put that down to not having any money. Molly and her mom often argued about that. Molly wanted to get a job. There were loads of jobs back then, in bars and shops, that kind of thing, but her mom wouldn't have it. I think I assumed at the time that they'd argued again.'

Joe nodded encouragement. 'That's really helpful, Jessica. The job Molly would have liked – did she have any bar or shop in mind?'

Jessica gave him a smile and a head-shake. 'She didn't actually say anything about what she was doing to get a job. She didn't go to bars or pubs herself very much. I only remember her going into one or two coffee shops in the mall. Bit expensive.'

'Any one in particular?' asked Bernie.

She was silent for a few seconds. 'Sorry, but I have to think about this. It's such a long time ago.' A little more silence, then, 'She liked one in particular called the Coffee Lounge.' She suddenly smiled, causing Joe to give her a close look.

'You went there with her?'

'No, but I've just thought of her telling us about it. She went there a few times to do college work – you know, reading – and there was this guy there who . . .' Both officers listened intently. 'Molly said he was coming on to her. No, no. I don't mean anything weird.' Jessica laughed quietly. 'It was just a bit funny.' She looked from one officer to the other. 'Look, she never said it was anything creepy. It was kind of, I don't know how to put it . . . old-fashioned. For a start, she said he was a bit older than her and I don't think they ever spoke to each other. She didn't even know his name.'

A frown had settled on Jessica's face as she glanced from Joe to Bernie. 'Don't get the idea it was anything . . . Molly just *laughed* about it, saying how they would kind of give a little wave or smile to each other. She mentioned it because she thought it was . . . nice.'

Joe nodded with a sidelong glance at Bernie.

'Molly have a boyfriend at that time, love?' Bernie asked.

'Not really. She'd already finished with Jason.'

'Do you know why?' asked Joe.

The baby stirred and snuffled. Jessica rocked it gently in her arms. 'He was too old for Molly. Spent a lot of time working. The police knew all of this at the time. The thing is, he was an adult, whereas Molly, all of us, we were just teenagers. So they split up.' She gave an imperceptible shrug. 'Let's face it, we were immature. Jason Fairley was, well, a man. But they were still good friends after that. Like I told you, he bought Molly the necklace.'

'So, the older guy. The one in the coffee shop. Was he about the same age as Jason Fairley? Or maybe older?'

107

Jessica frowned and shook her head. 'Sorry. I don't know. As I said, I never saw him.'

'Jason Fairley still looked out for Molly? Helped her out, even after they broke up?'

Jessica glanced at Bernie. 'When you say "helped her out" . . . he didn't give her money or anything like that, but yes, he looked out for her. Because they were still friends.'

Joe nodded slowly to indicate understanding. 'Do you see much of Samantha Wellings now?'

Jessica looked surprised. '*Samantha?* Good grief, no. She, her whole family moved and went to live in – Bristol, I think it was.'

They were in Joe's car en route to Rose Road.

'Don't know about you, Corrigan,' muttered Bernie, 'but I'm getting interested in the old-fashioned cove in the coffee shop.'

CHAPTER TWENTY-ONE

Later that Tuesday evening, Kate was helping Maisie make cupcakes for a fund-raising sale for flood relief that her school was holding the following day. Maisie had remembered it only half an hour before. Because of her own lateness home, Kate hadn't complained. She lined up the little fluted pink cases and Maisie dropped cake mix into them.

Mugger was standing with his front paws on the leg of the kitchen table, his head tracking Maisie's movements backwards and forwards.

She giggled. 'Look at Mugsy, Mom. You silly cat! You like salmon and chicken and . . . what else does he like?'

Kate responded as she separated more little pink paper cases: 'He likes most things. But he has his favourites.'

Maisie put the tip of a finger into the remaining cake mix, peered over the side of the table and offered it to Mugger. He licked enthusiastically. Maisie laughed again.

'Aagghhh! His tongue's like sandpaper!'

'Here we go, Maisie. Let's get these into the oven. They won't take long.'

Mother and daughter each carried a baking sheet across the kitchen. Kate set the oven timer as Maisie returned to the table and the mixing bowl.

'Hands, Maisie.'

Tutting quietly, Maisie went to the sink, ran water quickly over her hands, then dried them. Sorting through a drawer, she returned to the mixing bowl with a spatula.

'Mom?'

'Mmm?'

'How has Mugger decided what he likes? How does he know that he's supposed to chase birds and eat mice and stuff?'

'I doubt it's a decision he makes.'

Maisie persisted. 'But he knows, doesn't he? How come he knows?'

Kate took the scraped-out mixing bowl to the DishDrawer for washing. 'It's what he's born to do. Cats have always done it and Mugger isn't any different.' She caught sight of Mugger crunching a sliver of biscuit. 'Don't give him any more, Maisie. They're bad for his teeth.'

'But he likes them, don't you, Mugsy? D'you think he's a slow learner? Special needs? Maybe he missed out on the lesson "Cats Do Not Like Biscuits",' Maisie intoned, then laughed as she stroked the little cat.

Leaning against the table, Kate watched them, smiling. 'He would have learned a lot of what he does from his mother. Or any other adult cat. But it's not only about learning. It's also about what Mugger *is*. It's instinctive. It's his *nature*. He's hard-wired to chase after small animals, catch them and kill them.'

Maisie frowned, taking a jelly sweet from a small mound on the table and popping it into her mouth.

'So – the people you work with. The ones who've done bad things . . . Are they hard-wired?'

Kate glanced at her young daughter as she handed her a small packet of icing mix.

'That's a good question, Maisie. A really good question.'

'So, what's the answer?'

The house phone shrilled. 'That'll be Chelsey, about the trip tomorrow afternoon!' Maisie jumped off the table and dashed for the phone, leaving Kate in the kitchen thinking about what her daughter had asked.

Hard-wiring and learning. For animals. And people?

She walked slowly to the end of the kitchen to check that the doors were locked, then stood, gazing out at the darkened garden.

A good question.

But it doesn't really help us find who took Janine and Molly.

And whoever else, by the time we're finished.

Kate heard the doorbell. That would be Joe. She'd invited him round for a glass of wine.

A shout from Maisie. 'Mom, Joe's at the door! I have to get my stuff together.'

110

'I've got it,' said Kate, as she walked across the hall and opened the front door. 'Hi, come in,' she said, taking in Joe's faded jeans and the *Go Red Sox!* sweatshirt.

Her attention was caught by movement on the stairs and she glanced upwards, aware of a continuous, faint sound from the kitchen. 'You won't need all of that, Maisie. It's only one night. Come in Joe – oh, the cakes!'

Kate sprinted into the kitchen, Joe following her at a leisurely pace as Maisie reached the hall.

'Hi, Cat's-whiskers. You moving out? Going to university already?'

Maisie giggled. 'We're selling cakes at school tomorrow morning, first thing, to raise money for people made homeless by the floods, and *then* we're going straight to the Lickey Hills by coach for a sponsored orienteering exercise, which is *so* cool.' Maisie paused for breath. 'I'm leader of our team. Will you sponsor me, Joe? Here!' She whipped a sponsorship form from beneath the heap of clothes in her arms.

Joe grinned at her, taking the form. In the kitchen, Kate placed cupcakes on cooling racks and transferred them to one of the granite work surfaces.

'Maisie, you need to mix up the icing and—'

'Mom, I've got all this to pack – oh, *all right*. Where's the icing packet gone?'

'At a guess, under those clothes you don't need.'

'Mom, just listen, will you. Lauren Downell is taking a *suitcase,* I swear. What do you think, Joe? It's one night plus the whole of the next day and we're staying in this hostel thingy and there *might* be some boys.' Maisie took the icing and jelly sweets over to where Kate had left the little cakes, looking back at him earnestly.

Joe considered the heap of belongings on the table, his face serious.

'Well, I never take fewer than three pairs of jeans, four tees, pink PJs and . . . a jar of marmalade when I skip town.'

Kate smiled and handed him a glass. 'So, what've you been up to since I left UCU?' she asked quietly.

'We went over to see Molly's pal, Jessica Barnes,' Joe answered, equally quiet, as they watched Maisie exit the kitchen.

Kate nodded. 'Was it helpful?'

'Uh-huh. Nice to see that the people Molly left behind are doing okay.' He noticed Kate bite her lip. '*And* it seems that Molly may have been the object of some "older male" interest.'

'Tell me,' said Kate.

CHAPTER TWENTY-TWO

By Thursday morning, the most recently found remains had been formally identified via dental records obtained by Julian. Joe pressed the photograph of eighteen-year-old Janine Walker to the glass screen, alongside that of Molly.

Kate studied it. The blonde hair falling straight behind her shoulders, eyes cool, smile subdued as she gazed ahead, as though her photographer had made a not-so-funny joke.

Kate recalled what she'd said about the unlikelihood of Colley as the doer. And here was another poised, intelligent young woman. Colley would have run a mile if she'd given him one disdainful look. Two found, plus the femur. Kate thought of Vanessa, Leah and Amy, girls whom Julian's search had identified as also missing. Did the femur belong to one of them? How long would it be before they were in a position to know?

Kate glanced at Bernie, who was muttering to himself.

'What're you doing?'

'Writing up me notes from our visit to this friend of Molly's to give to Julian.' He shook his head irritably. 'She's told us about this bloke that was giving Molly the eye in some coffee bar before she disappeared. Did she mention it to the original investigation? *No.* She didn't. You just *can't* rely on members of the public in this job.'

'Maybe she didn't make any connection between the man and Molly's disappearance because—'

'It don't seem like rocket science to me! Friend talks about a funny bloke. Friend disappears. You'd have thought she'd have mentioned it.'

'No. Not necessarily.'

Bernie glanced up at Kate from his note-writing, then down again.

'Come on then, clever-clogs. Put me right.'

Kate sat on the edge of the table, drawing her hair into a ponytail before winding it and securing it behind her head. 'It wouldn't be unusual, you know, not to make a connection. Think about it. The funny-bloke bit could've been a while before Molly disappeared. I bet the girls laughed about it. Then she goes missing, which is absolutely tragic and upsets everybody. Two occurrences, separated in time. One very minor. Light-hearted. The other . . . well, tragic, like I said. It doesn't surprise me the two were never connected.'

'I'd like to be like you, Doc. Not surprised by nothing,' said Bernie, looking fed up.

Joe lifted his jacket, glancing at Kate. 'Want a ride to the Walkers' house in Blakedown?'

Kate gazed up at him, uncertain. 'Are they okay about it?'

'I phoned them late yesterday. They have no problem with our visiting.'

Twenty-five minutes later, Kate and Joe had reached the home of Janine's parents, having driven past the bypass site on the journey there. Both had seen the continuing activity but neither had referred to it.

Joe parked the car at the side of the quiet road. Prior to calling at the house, he and Kate walked in bright sun to a nearby corner. According to investigative records, Janine Walker was said to have turned this corner on the day of her disappearance, but hadn't been seen by a man working in his garden in the neighbouring road. Joe studied the road through Ray-Bans, shaking his head slightly.

'What?' Kate demanded, looking up at him.

'If she came along here, surely the gardening guy would've noticed? Do you remember his house number?'

Kate consulted her notebook. 'Sixty-four.'

They walked on, side by side amid residential quiet. The area was clearly pretty much a dormitory for commuters to Birmingham. Ahead of them, standing near the kerbside, was a tall, cylindrical red postbox. Kate and Joe glanced at each other. Janine had carried letters with her to oblivion.

Passing it in silence, they continued on until they reached number 64, the unremarkable semi-detached home of the gardening neighbour.

Kate looked back the way they had come. She pointed. '*Look*, Joe.

114

The road curves before it reaches here.' They studied the view. The postbox was no longer visible.

'Got any ideas as to what happened here?' she asked.

He nodded. 'Yep. Whatever the detail, Janine Walker's abduction was very quiet and controlled. She just . . . went with him.' He stared at the ground near their feet. 'Maybe he disabled her. Maybe he had an electroshock device. Taser. Stun gun.'

In silence, they retraced their steps along the still-deserted road to the Walker home, wide-fronted and well maintained, surrounded by tubs of bright geraniums, the front door glossy red. Standing at the door, Kate glanced around, musing on the tragedy behind the bright facade, as Joe rang the doorbell. She didn't want to be here.

The ring had scarcely faded when the door was opened and they were greeted by both of Janine Walker's parents, invited inside and led into a huge conservatory running the width of the rear of the house. It was pleasantly cool inside, windows open, roof blinds drawn, two large ceiling fans oscillating the leaves of a tall indoor palm. Music was quietly playing somewhere. Kate recognised an orchestral arrangement of 'Eleanor Rigby'.

She took the seat offered and gave her attention to the Walkers, unobtrusively studying them as they went about the business of welcoming her and Joe to their home.

'Would you like some coffee, Lieutenant, Dr Hanson? Or maybe a cold drink? Juice?'

'Coffee would be fine for me, ma'am, thank you,' said Joe with a smile.

Kate watched the social exchange, the seemingly light-hearted eagerness of both Mr and Mrs Walker, finding it odd and unsettling given her recent experience at the home of Molly James.

Mr Walker was probably in his early sixties, with the look of a man who spent a lot of time outdoors, the short-sleeved white shirt and sand-coloured shorts setting off his tan. His wife looked somewhat younger, also tanned, wearing a pink linen sundress, her ash-blonde hair in a bob. Kate could see now from where Janine inherited the facial features shown in her photograph. To her keen eye, the couple looked, if not happy, then relieved. She suddenly got it. Their focus was now entirely on UCU's reinvestigation of their daughter's death.

As they drank coffee, Mr Walker spoke about Janine's disappearance, indicating a willingness to provide any information UCU might need. Coffee finished, he invited them to view the small bedroom that had been converted into an office dedicated to their own search for their daughter.

Kate and Joe followed Mr and Mrs Walker upstairs. As they reached the landing, Kate quietly asked if she could look at Janine's bedroom. Mrs Walker readily agreed.

Again with the feeling of being an interloper, Kate slowly opened the door of Janine's room and walked inside. It was a large room looking out to the rear of the house. As she gazed through the window at the distant roofs of houses visible between trees, her thoughts returned to the road down which she and Joe had walked earlier.

Those roofs belong to the houses in that road.

Where the man was gardening on the day Janine disappeared.

She spun a few possibilities in her head, one of which was that the windows of the upper floors of those houses also had a view of this one. And of Janine's bedroom. She studied the view for a few seconds, then shook her head. Too far away. If she couldn't see any interior detail of those houses from here, it was logical to suppose that anyone looking from them to the Walker home would have a similarly limited view.

In the middle of the room, Kate turned very slowly, studying its decoration and furniture. A sophisticated room, one wall painted cream, the others a pale yellow. A warm room, because the house had full sun on its back elevation in the morning. Oatmeal carpet. No soft toys. A large kilim rug at the foot of the bed, on which stood a stripped-pine chest. She walked to the chest and, after a few seconds' hesitation, lifted its lid. Books. She read some titles. Textbooks. A few works of fiction. She took out her notebook and wrote down some of the titles, then closed the chest and moved to the large mahogany desk to the right of the window.

As in Molly's room, Kate had a sense of time having stopped. On the desk was a copy of *Private Eye*. She skimmed it. An article mocking Mohamed Al Fayed's 'conspiracy theory'. Another about the G8 Summit held in Birmingham, with slights and jokes at the city's expense. Kate looked for the date. June 1998. All now outdated social and political comment.

Above the desk was a wall planner. Kate leaned across to read its notations. Some family birthdays. A day in late September 1998 on which, according to the few words there, Janine anticipated being

116

inducted into her University of Sheffield course. A couple of hair appointments in May, neatly crossed through, presumably kept. Dates marked with times and, perhaps because of a lack of space, the initials of people Janine was maybe planning to meet. She copied them down.

Kate's thoughts turned to Molly's friends. Would UCU need to trace the Wellings family in Bristol before this reinvestigation was finished? She returned her full attention to the wall planner, noting now a regular date annotated for each month. She immediately grasped their significance.

So many experiences Janine and her family would never share.

She walked slowly from the room, deep into her analysis of what it had indicated of Janine's personality. Crossing the landing, she quietly entered the home office, where Mr Walker was talking to Joe.

'. . . and we still get a few hits. Nothing like in the early years, of course, but it can vary, say if a newspaper or magazine runs the story again. Because of the new development, your reinvestigation, we're anticipating a bit of a surge. Janine was a very compelling young woman.'

Kate caught the words, thinking that he and Janine's mother were so much more positive than she herself could ever imagine being if she were in their situation. Mrs Walker nodded her agreement.

'Janine was special.' She looked from Joe to Kate. 'Everyone says that about their child, don't they? But she was. You see, she was given everything. Not by us. By . . . life. She was beautiful, clever, full of plans, full of . . . life itself. She had so much to offer.' Kate and Joe listened, silent. There was nothing for them to say.

The small room in which they were standing was a testament to the Walkers' determined search for their lost daughter. Kate took in the 'Missing' posters bearing Janine's photograph, publicity details for various fund-raising events aimed at keeping Janine's name in the public consciousness. Many were faded, their dates going back several years. A cork-surfaced noticeboard held layers of cuttings relating to televised appeals and programmes about the missing teen. Kate was thinking of the emotional commitment underlying those years. The personal toll.

In response to a question from Joe, both parents confirmed that at the time Janine disappeared she had no boyfriend. Her focus was on her departure for Sheffield and her future studies. She had no known worries about anything or anyone and was full of hopes and plans.

117

Mr Walker looked at Kate then at Joe. 'We always knew our daughter had been abducted,' he said, matter-of-fact, as his wife moved quietly to his side. 'We don't want to sound . . . critical of the police. Especially now. But at the time Janine disappeared, there was a reluctance to accept that that was what had happened to her. They kept asking whether she had a boyfriend . . . she didn't.'

Kate looked at him, feeling a hot flare of anger towards Furman.

'Janine walked out of our lives. I watched her go. Josh, her little dog at the time, ran after her. She didn't want to take him so I went and fetched him, waved to her as she turned the corner . . .'

The room was silent for a few seconds, Mr Walker himself breaking the silence to ask if they would like more coffee. Before they left the room, Joe asked him about the identity of the man living in the road nearby who had denied seeing Janine.

'Howard Kingsley.'

'Does he still live . . .' Joe's question faded as Mr Walker shook his head.

'No. He died about three years ago.' Mr Walker seemed to intuit Kate's next question. 'He wasn't all that old. About seventy. A stroke.'

'Mr Kingsley wasn't able to give the police any help at the time?'

'No. He was adamant he never saw Janine that day. He thought he *might* have heard the sound of a car nearby, but he wasn't really sure. We visited everyone we could in that road, you know. We went from house to house. Asking if anyone had seen or heard anything. No one had. Many of the residents were at work the day she went, and it was also the holiday season, so quite a few of the houses were empty at the time. It's a very quiet area anyway.'

Kate nodded, a sudden thought occurring to her. One on which the investigation records were silent.

'Mr Walker, we know that Janine was carrying a small red purse and some letters of yours that day. Were those letters . . . ?'

Both parents looked at each other and Mr Walker replied. 'The letters were posted in the box just round the corner and received the next day. But by the time the police checked that out, the envelopes had been destroyed, so that didn't provide any leads. They sent some people to look at the postbox itself, but . . .' He shrugged.

Mrs Walker continued where her husband had left off. 'Janine's purse was never found. There was no indication she went to the local shop. You haven't . . . ?'

Kate and Joe shook their heads and Kate gave her colleague a meaningful glance. After the two men had gone downstairs, she followed Mrs Walker into Janine's room, watching as she smoothed the bedspread and straightened the curtains, wondering how to introduce what was on her mind.

In a conversational tone as she looked out of the window she asked, 'What was Janine going to study at Sheffield?'

'Both our children were good at languages. Nick, our eldest, still is, of course. He's working for the European Commission in Brussels.'

Kate nodded, inwardly angry at the lack of background data available about the Walker family from the original investigation. There was no reference to a sibling in the information Bernie had carried up from the basement. Her anger was again directed at Furman, for what now appeared to have been the very superficial job he'd done all those years ago, but she kept her face and voice casual.

'Would you describe Janine as a very organised young woman?' Seeing a slight frown on Mrs Walker's face, she added, 'Her wall planner. Appointments and so on, all filled in.'

Mrs Walker's face cleared. 'Yes, you're right. She was a very orderly kind of person. Not like Nick! But then, I don't see why we should expect our children to be the same, do you?'

Mrs Walker's next comment brought Kate's thoughts crashing to a standstill.

'You'll have seen her diary. He took it, the officer who was in charge of the original investigation. Janine wrote in it every day, just before bed. I never read it, of course, but I think she found it a useful thing to do.'

This was the first Kate had heard of a diary. No one else in UCU had mentioned one. Her thoughts surged, mind racing back to UCU. There had been no diary when she'd looked through the box that had come up from the basement. No diary in which Janine might have written—

Mrs Walker was still talking. 'Janine was a modern young woman. Independent. Self-reliant. She didn't seem to want or need to discuss things. She liked to work things out for herself. I think she did that by writing down her thoughts. I believe her independence, her ability to analyse, would have helped her get the kind of job she wanted.' Kate

119

nodded as Mrs Walker continued. 'She had ambitions to work for the UN. She'd set her sights on America.'

Kate nodded again. It fitted with the books she'd seen in the chest, which included fictional accounts of the CIA. Janine seemed to have had wide-ranging political interests.

Kate had another thought, hard on that one. The Walkers had been willing to leave their daughter's diary in the hands of the police for several years, no doubt hoping that it might help the investigation at some point. Now that Janine had been found, they'd want it returned to them.

What could she say if either of the parents asked for it?

Today.

Pushing the thought aside, she asked, 'Mrs Walker, I noticed that when your husband was talking to my colleague, he used both "is" and "was" in relation to Janine, but you always say "was".'

The older woman nodded. 'That's very observant of you.' She ran a finger lightly over the computer keyboard. 'We both knew that if Janine was still alive she would have been found by now. I was the one who more easily accepted it. Now both Paul and I know she's never coming home again. At least, not in the way we had hoped. But now we can start to make plans.'

She glanced at Kate, then back to the keyboard. 'So many years since she went. When we started all of this, we were thinking that any publicity was useful to keep Janine's name and face in people's minds. We got a sense of purpose from it. Now our purpose has changed.' She looked briefly at Kate again. 'What our family wants now, Dr Hanson, is to take Janine back into her family, celebrate her life and mark its end.'

Thinking of the remains she had seen in the Rose Road post-mortem suite, Kate searched for something appropriate to say, without success.

Mrs Walker gave her a small smile. 'It's okay, you know,' she said softly. 'There's something to be gained from finally *knowing* that Janine isn't alive any longer.'

She paused, glancing down at the computer. 'Janine got her own email address in the couple of months before she went. It's still there. The Net was a complete mystery to us at the time. We've had to catch up quickly since then.' No trace of bitterness. 'Even now, I occasionally go into the office and type a little message to her.

Nothing elaborate. Just a couple of lines usually, telling her what we've done, what kind of day it's been . . . that we love her.'

She transferred her gaze to Kate. 'When I've pressed "Send", for those few seconds I've felt reconnected to her. She had to be out there somewhere. Now she's on her way back to us. She's coming home.'

Kate nodded, throat aching, not trusting herself to speak. She quickly turned her attention to the photograph on the desk. Janine and a small white Westie.

Mrs Walker noticed and picked up the photograph, running her fingers lightly over it. 'Ah, Josh! They went *everywhere* together when Janine wasn't busy.'

She returned the photograph gently to its place. 'Do you know, when he died, in 2004, it was like the last physical link with Janine had gone. Believe it or not, *that* was one of my worst moments.'

Kate believed it. She understood.

That was when it came.

'We'd like to have the diary back some time. We did ask for it a couple of years ago, but when it didn't materialise we decided we wanted the police to keep it in case they took another look at the case. Now that things have changed, we'd like it back when you've finished with it.'

Kate nodded, managing an 'of course', feeling complicit in Furman's neglect of this family.

As they left the room, Mrs Walker gently pushed closed the door of the wardrobe. It resisted. She opened the door fully and Kate saw inside a few items of clothing, seemingly unworn, one or two still bearing price tags. As the older woman tucked the sleeve of a sweat-shirt away from the door, she looked over her shoulder at Kate.

'Janine's new outfits. For university. We don't have her other clothes any more, but we couldn't dispose of these. They represented our golden girl's hopes for her future.' She ended, matter-of-fact: 'Another decision to make now, I suppose.'

As Kate walked from the room with the older woman, she kept her tone as even as possible.

'As far as you know or remember, did Janine ever mention any of these names to you – John, Jason, Alan?' Mrs Walker shook her head to each. 'I know they're not unusual names, but they would have belonged to adult males, men in their mid to late twenties at the time.'

'No. Sorry.'

'Did she ever refer to a young woman by the name of Molly James?'

'No.'

Kate had a sudden thought. 'Why was Janine going to the local shop?'

Mrs Walker smiled. 'To buy a card. She and all of her friends were scattering to various universities around the country in a matter of weeks. It was probably a good-luck card for one of them.'

Kate was silent on the journey back to Birmingham, thinking about the Walker family, about their ability to remain positive in a situation of such deep sadness. She gazed out of the window, thinking about police work. A little humour and a lot of horror. Coexisting.

Joe gave her a sidelong glance as he drove them back to Harborne. Kate's face was turned to the passenger window. A minute later he looked again, saw her take out a tissue and a small mirror. Returning both to her bag, she took out her notebook. Joe transferred his attention back to the road. Neither looked at the bypass site as it flashed past.

For the rest of the brief journey, Kate gave her complete attention to the information supplied by the Walker family. There was one key question, among others, to which she kept returning.

Janine set out for a short local walk on the day she disappeared.

According to Mrs Walker, Josh, Janine's little dog, went every-where with her. The fact that he ran after her that day, anticipating an outing, and had to be brought back supported it.

Josh expected to go with Janine the short distance to the postbox and the shop.

Why didn't Janine want to take the dog with her?

Further questions surfaced in Kate's mind, hard on the heels of that one.

Was Josh 'inconvenient' for her that day? In a way he wouldn't have been if she was simply anticipating a journey on foot?

Did Janine make a decision about someone that day that cost her her life?

Kate considered what Joe had said earlier, about the possibility of some sort of stun gun being used on Janine. There was another option.

Janine accepted a lift in a car belonging to someone she knew.

Or thought she knew.

Later that evening, Kate was in the sitting room reviewing the questions she'd written in her notebook, the headache she'd had on arriving home now almost gone. Just as well. She had a full university day tomorrow. Tutorials, a lecture, preparation, followed by a welcome weekend. She and Maisie were going shopping together on Saturday and having lunch in town. Kate was looking forward to it. Maisie hadn't yet reached the stage where she was reluctant to be seen with her mother. And if they could come home with purchases of clothes for Maisie that both of them agreed on, thought Kate, it would be a gratifying first.

Kate was now relaxed in the welcome quiet of the old house, checking her notes, thoughts beginning to drift. To the time when she and Kevin had moved from their first house to this one, bought with some of the money Kate had inherited from her mother months before. Kate had initially put Maisie in her crib in the room designated as a nursery, then promptly moved her back to the main bedroom, over Kevin's objections, because she was afraid of not hearing Maisie through the thick walls. She rested her head against the sofa, thinking about loss. The loss of a child.

Mugger put his head around the sitting-room door, giving Kate a speculative look and his version of a miaow. Kate looked at him and smiled.

'Okay, Mugsy. I'm coming.'

She got up and went to him, lifted him gently and carried him into the kitchen along with her notebook.

As Mugger crunched his meal, she stared at her questions. She riffled pages, back to the notes she'd made about what Connie had told them. Janine's hair was cut. He went to the trouble, made the effort, to do that. She frowned. Molly's hair wasn't cut. Was hair in itself of particular significance for the killer? Long blonde hair was one of the characteristics Molly and Janine shared with the other young women whose names had surfaced from the PNC MisPer database.

Why cut Janine's hair?

To defeminise her?

Or just because he could?
Why not cut Molly's?
Because he'd changed between 1998 and 2002?
He didn't feel the need.
So he changed his behaviour.
Change.
Graduation.

CHAPTER TWENTY-THREE

Joe was at Kate's house early on Monday morning to give her a lift into UCU. In the car, Kate gazed absently through the window, thinking of the worrying issue that had been in her head since the visit to the Walker home. And she was thinking of her own status at Rose Road. She breathed deeply. Civilian or not, it had to be raised.

'We *must* find Janine's diary, Joe. Even if it's only to give it back to the Walkers. They entrusted it to the police. Now I'm worried that Furman lost it.' She pushed her sunglasses to the top of her head and turned to him, her thoughts on the parents in UCU's cases. 'I'm also thinking about how it is that different people meet the same experience but respond so differently. If you get my meaning.'

'I get it,' said Joe quietly. 'Maybe it's not the same experience, though. Because they're not the same people.'

A few minutes later, they were inside UCU. Kate went directly to the glass screen, picked up a marker and wrote a single five-letter word in large letters: 'diary'. As Bernie and Julian arrived, she was adding a large exclamation mark. Satisfied for now, she removed her notebook from her bag and scanned what she'd written the previous evening.

Ten minutes later, she was sitting on the edge of the team table, having delivered her theory to her colleagues. She glanced at Joe, who looked laid-back, as always. Julian as usual had scribbled notes while she talked. A glance at Bernie confirmed what she'd expected from that department. He was clearly vexed, face heavy and stubborn, his bulldog-with-an-attitude look firmly in place. Kate sighed and pointed to words she'd written on the glass screen.

'What I'm saying is that if we accept the premise that our repeater didn't start out with murder, then we need to think about what he was doing *before* that.' She gave a small shrug. 'Example: he could have started with relatively minor sexual assaults. Or possibly rape.'

Bernie leaned his great forearms on the table, prodding the wood with a thick forefinger. 'We've got two, no, *three* linked cases already and hardly any time to do *them*, plus three other names of missing women. How's it going to help to widen our investigation? Give ourselves even more work?'

Joe responded quietly: 'Because, Ber-*nard*, sexual assault, rape, leaves a potential witness. Murder generally doesn't.'

Kate nodded. 'By widening our search to include, say, unsolved rapes prior to 1998, we could increase our chances of success with the abduction-murders. We might find there aren't any that fit, in which case we're no worse off, are we?'

Bernie looked even more aggrieved. 'Yes we are! Because of the time it would've took us to find the info and check it out.'

Julian looked up at Kate from his notes. 'Fit how?'

Kate slid off the table and pointed to another area of the glass screen.

'This involves you, Julian. We need a search for incidents of un-solved sexual assault or rape in . . .' She gazed upwards. 'Let's say we search up to five years prior to the bypass murders, so that's from 1993 to 1998.'

Bernie scoffed. 'There'll be flippin' loads of 'em and we'll—'

Kate shook her head, tapping the glass screen 'No, no, Bernie. Think about it. We can narrow the field if Julian trawls only for unsolved rapes between those two dates in the Greater Birmingham area in which the victims were young women aged, let's say, seventeen to twenty-one, blonde, slender, five-six-plus, educated.' She raised her shoulders. 'If our search was too wide, we would be inundated, like you said. We need to limit it.'

'But isn't that contrary to what you were saying in the intro lecture, Kate? That they don't follow the same routines.'

She looked at Julian, gratified by his ability to make links.

'It's the only place we can start right now. We know what he was doing during his murderous years. We need to retrace his behaviour. You're right, Julian, but what I was saying at the lecture was that we need to be wary of myths. The killer of Janine, Molly and whoever the femur belonged to is both an individual *and* flexible. So we need to be flexible in our investigation.' She glanced in Bernie's direction. 'Part of that flexibility is about the direction we take our investi-gation.'

126

Julian nodded, turning to the computer, but after barely a minute he swung back to Kate. 'I've got a lecture starting in half an hour. How about I begin the search when I come back later?'

Bernie still looked irritable. 'If *anybody's* interested in what I've got to say, I'd like to know how we're going to find the time for all of this trawling and messing?' Arms folded, he sighed heavily as he watched Julian pushing textbooks into his backpack. 'Throw us a rock, Jules.'

Kate grinned as Joe looked at her, eyebrows climbing.

'Thought you said you were on a diet?' said Julian, passing the M&Ms, and pushing more textbooks into the backpack.

Kate glanced at Joe, mouthing, 'Diary?' He responded with a silent 'Records' and finger-pointed the floor.

She looked at Bernie, the doer's offence history still on her mind. 'There are prior cases waiting for us, Bernie . . .'

'Sez you.'

The door swung open and a tired-looking face appeared around it. Harry.

'Connie said to let you know – we're still searching the bypass site, looking for more remains to go with the femur.' With that he was gone.

'He's earning his bread at the minute,' Bernie said. 'Down at the bypass all hours. I was in their offices the other day. They was having a meeting and it was all go, and—'

'What're you saying? Harry *always* works hard,' said Julian hotly, face annoyed.

Bernie craned to look at him, eyebrows up. 'Okay, okay, Devenish. Simmer down. I ain't criticising your playmate. Why do people *always* think I'm makin' a point?'

'Complete mystery to me,' murmured Kate.

The phone rang and Bernie snatched it up and listened.

'*Hallo*, bab! Yes, she is. Hold on.' To Kate, 'Maisie. For you.'

Kate took the phone and listened to Maisie, enthusing as she had done over the weekend about the orienteering trip and the sponsorship money raised, finishing with her being invited to have dinner at Chelsey's house.

Kate put the phone down, feeling a further layer of guilt settle on her shoulders. How many times had Maisie eaten at Chelsey's in the last week or two? She cast her mind back, trying to identify instances of Chelsey coming to eat with Maisie and her. She sighed. Yet another activity for which she needed to devise some kind of rota with Candice.

As she prepared to leave for the university, Kate's thoughts drifted back to the evening she and Maisie had made cupcakes. To Maisie's question about Mugger and her own response. Nature versus nurture. Whoever their doer was so monumentally angry towards, that person was obviously female. A powerful female? Or one he perceived as powerful? One he *had* to control?

CHAPTER TWENTY-FOUR

By late afternoon, Kate had returned to UCU from the university and was in Rose Road's basement, inside its vast evidence storage room. She had never been down here, although she knew it was the repository for Headquarters case files, plus a good proportion of those from lesser stations in the city and surrounding areas. To one side of the basement were the heavy metal doors of the cold room, where forensic evidence was kept at low temperature to prevent degradation.

Due to the unusually hot late-September weather, the basement was stifling, even at this hour. Kate glanced at her watch. She'd been down here ten minutes, and her hands were covered in dust and perspiration was sliding from under her hair.

Initially working on the theory that if an item from the Walker case had been misfiled, it might be inside a nearby box, she had examined the contents of four boxes bearing names beginning with the same letter. Nothing. She pushed the last of those back on to its shelf and moved on, to the fifth. Watkinson. After a couple of minutes of leafing through the contents the result was as before. Nothing.

Kate pressed on. When she'd run out of Ws, she started on the next letter. Halfway through a box labelled 'Yelland', she sat back on her heels and gazed at the surrounding shelves. *This is hopeless. I can't do it on my own.* Another thought occurred, hard on the previous one: *Maybe I'm looking in the wrong place?*

She pulled herself to standing, brushing the knees of her wheat-coloured trousers. At least that was how the assistant in Selfridges had described them.

Why the hell did you choose to wear light-coloured trousers to come here today?

'Because I didn't know what it was like down here!' Kate answered herself snappily, pushing her hair from her face, adding to the dust

129

already there. She sighed and moved forward a few feet, looking down at the files on the lowest shelf. *Not even in alphabetical order.*

Arriving at the end of the section of shelving, Kate slowly straightened, gazing between the metal shelf supports at the huge door of the cold room. She walked slowly towards it and stood, hands on hips. If the diary had been misfiled, it was as likely to be in there as anywhere else. Reaching into a trouser pocket, she pulled out the keys she'd been given for the evidence storage room and examined them. Within seconds she knew that the kind of key that opened the cold room was likely to have a very particular shape and wasn't among them.

Kate headed for the stairs and a now deserted UCU, straight to the cupboard where spare keys were kept. She examined them all. Nothing seemed likely to fit. She guessed that the key she needed was large, long and probably *sans* teeth.

Closing the cupboard, she left UCU, heading for Reception. Even at that hour it was a scrum, as Whittaker fielded queries from a number of members of the public bringing reports of stolen or damaged belongings and pet disappearances. Matt Prentiss was also there, delivering precise instructions to Whittaker on how he wanted him to dispose of the several envelopes he was waving at the young constable.

As Kate reached the desk, Prentiss, red-faced and clearly at the end of his short tether, was tapping an insistent finger on the envelopes he'd now placed on the counter. Kate stood on her toes and caught Whittaker's eye. He smiled at her and, interpreting her quick mime, left the desk, returning in seconds with what she'd requested. Conscious of Prentiss's malevolent gaze on her, Kate felt obliged to acknowledge him.

'Sorry, Matt, but I urgently need this key – it's very important.'

'And *this* is urgent forensic business. I'm not laying myself open to criticism for the way I do my job because *you* can't wait,' he snapped, waving the envelopes in her face before turning back to Whittaker. 'Right. Let's try it again. I want *you* . . .'

Kate escaped down the corridor, thinking that Joe was right. Prentiss *was* a tight-ass. She'd heard the odd comment about his unpopularity within the forensics scenes team. She'd never seen him smile or behave informally with anyone. *Pain in the tail.*

Running quickly down the steps inside the evidence storage room, she unlocked the cold room with the long, featureless key Whittaker had given her. Heaving open the massive door, she stepped inside and glanced around her, curious. It wasn't a refrigerator. Just very cold. Again she was faced with rows of heavy boxes, though this time there appeared to be no particular order at all. She walked slowly past rows of boxes and envelopes tied together. *Ah. Date order.*

Moving further inside, away from the door, Kate studied dates. Towards the back of the room she found what at first looked to be gold dust, in the form of two boxes labelled not just with relevant dates but with a 'W'. Five minutes later, however, they'd proved to be fool's gold. No 'Walker'. Dispirited, Kate wandered along the shelves, tracing the boxes and packets with her hand.

She stopped. She was in the 1996–2000 section. There were large envelopes and a number of cardboard cartons at eye level. She frowned at the gaps on some of the shelves, then recalled what Bernie had told her and what she knew from her own experience of the criminal justice system: that police case files were routinely sent to the Crown Prosecution Service at various stages of their progress through the justice system.

Lifting down one, then another of the envelopes, Kate peered inside them. Nothing relevant to Janine Walker. Replacing them, she pulled one of the cartons off the shelf and placed it on the floor. Flipping the lid, she riffled the contents. Nothing. Idly she looked at the name. Jarrett. No relevance at all. She replaced the carton and lifted down a second one, labelled 'Dijon', and knelt beside it.

Opening the box, Kate studied the top sheet. The name written on it was not Dijon but Kenton-Smith. Surprised by the disorder of the case files and boxes, she dug deeper among this one's contents, lifting out sheets of A4 and envelopes and— She stopped, holding her breath.

It was here. At the bottom of the box. Smaller than she'd anticipated. Ten centimetres by twelve. Thick. Still-vibrant red leather. A small inset on the front cover announced the name of its owner: 'Janine Mary Walker'.

Sitting back on her heels, Kate slowly took the diary out of the box and opened it. Turning the small pages, she gazed at words written in a uniform neat hand, tracing them gently with a fingertip, when without warning the cold room was plunged into darkness.

Startled, Kate remained motionless for a few seconds, her capacity for thought on hold. She put down the diary and got to her feet, feeling her way forward in implacable blackness. Edging along, steps small, she noticed the chill air for the first time. And the enveloping silence. She felt for her pockets, despite knowing that she didn't have her phone with her. *Damn!*

Moving slowly forward, arms outstretched, her hands made contact with cold metal. Kate's afternoon had just become infinitely worse. The door of the cold room was closed. With her on the inside. She stood there for some seconds, incapable of any thought beyond that of processing the immediate physical experience. The silence was suffocating. Like being inside a black velvet bag. Thick, chilly black velvet.

She extended her arms. Again her hands made contact with cold steel. She pushed on it. Totally unyielding. She slid trembling fingers over the hard surface, forcing her mind to envisage the features of the door, trying to recall if there was a keyhole on this side. She shook her head. She hadn't noticed.

Her arms dropped to her sides, and as they did so, dense blackness folded round her. She felt a first stirring of panic, followed by a floating sensation. She knew why. Apart from the floor under her feet, she had no other sensory cues. Quickly she reached out and touched the surface of the door again. She had to have a sense of her spatial position within the cold, dense blackness. Without it she was adrift. Panic surfaced again and she forced herself to breathe slowly.

After some deep breaths amid the blackness, Kate's ability to think logically had more or less returned. She glanced at the luminous dial of her watch. Five p.m. Who knew she was down here? She reviewed her earlier activities. She'd asked Bernie about the evidence store. He'd work out where she was. If he was still at Rose Road. If he hadn't left already.

She shook her head in the blackness, precipitating a third small wave of panic. She tried to recall everything she'd ever learned in her professional history as a psychologist about panic and self-control. What you didn't do was think about the immediate situation. Hands still on the steel door, Kate got control of her breathing.

Easy . . . Easy. Breathe in . . . and out.

Following her own instructions, pulling air into her chest, she felt her heart rate drop slightly.

Okay. You need to attract attention.

Come on.

Who else knows you're down here and might hear you?

Two names came to her. Whittaker, and the objectionable Matt Prentiss. Would they hear her in Reception? Were they still there? Probably not. Panic stirred yet again.

She tried a couple of tentative calls. 'Hey? . . . Hello?' The result was puny and muffled.

'Anyone?' She listened. Nothing.

Oh for God's sake. Even someone immediately the other side of the door wouldn't hear that.

All you've got is your voice. Get shouting!

Kate yelled: 'Hey! Come on. Whoever's out there? Anyone? Open the—'

A sudden click, and a seam of light appeared at the top and to one side of the door.

Kate stared at the light, eyes wide, mouth open, then gave the door a small push. It yielded. She pushed it again. It moved further. Shoving it hard, she pivoted from the cold room into the light, dust and heat of the evidence store.

Gasping, a sensation of nausea now kicking in, she took a few faltering steps to the nearby shelving and leaned against it, one hand clutching the metal support, eyes closed.

Hearing a small sound behind her, Kate whirled in its direction.

CHAPTER TWENTY-FIVE

'**R**ed? What're you up to? Ah . . . have you seen your hair and face recently?'

Kate stared at him, mind a desert, mouth open. She found her voice. 'What're *you* doing here! How long have you been hanging around? Did you see who was in here?'

'Looking for you. I just arrived. Nobody. Next?'

Kate was wired. She gestured wildly with both hands, blitzing Joe with more words. 'I was in here searching for Janine's diary, and the light went and I felt my way to the door and it was closed and . . .' She looked up at him, eyes narrowed. 'Someone locked me in. You *must* have seen who closed the door. Who *was* it?' she demanded.

Joe hooked a finger at her and led her to a panel at the side of the cold room door. Kate, hair on end, dust on her nose, glared at what he was indicating.

'Time switch. See? Releases the door after six minutes if the mechanism detects movement inside. Whoever locked you in there did it several minutes before I got here.'

Kate looked at it, arms hanging. 'Only *six* minutes?'

Joe gazed down at her and spoke soothingly. 'Somebody closed the door with you inside, yeah? But the safety device sprung you.'

Reviving somewhat, Kate huffed, rubbing at her face, spreading more dust, as she looked up at him.

'Do you believe me when I say that someone *purposely* closed it – with me inside?'

'You say it and I believe it.'

Kate gave the vast metal doors a confused glare as Joe continued.

'When the cold room was installed, couple of years back, I heard that a Health and Safety guy gave a talk Upstairs. He warned all personnel against closing and locking the door without first checking that no one was inside. That led to Gander deciding to pay up for the safety device – motion detector and override mechanism.'

He glanced down at Kate, who still looked hot and annoyed.

'Who knew you were down here?'

'I've been through that,' she snapped. 'Whittaker. That horrible Matt Prentiss. Bernie, Julian, possibly, and . . . you.'

'I mean apart from UCU, you little idiot. We're not likely to lock you in a cold store, are we? Although now that I think of it, it's given me some interesting ideas— *Ow*! Hey, remember who it was who came looking for you. I'm the hero here. It was destiny.'

'Huh! Hero-zero. More like *density*,' snapped Kate, annoyed with herself, aware that she looked a mess.

Joe waited. When nothing further was forthcoming, he leaned towards her, arms folded, speaking slowly and conspiratorially. 'What did you find?'

Kate's face changed. 'I *found* it. I found the *diary*.'

Walking around him, she went back to the cold room and stepped inside. The little red volume was still lying where she'd put it down, not far from the door. Quickly, she retrieved it and stepped back out.

'It was hidden, Joe, in an unrelated evidence box.'

'Misfiled? Misplaced?'

'I know it might sound crazy to attribute my experience just now to a deliberate act by *somebody*, but I've been thinking.' She looked up at him, face earnest, tapping the diary with a finger. 'What if the answer to Janine's disappearance, the *how*, even the *who*, is in here?'

Joe nodded, returning her look. 'Now you put it like that, I'm really glad I found you,' he said, blue eyes crinkling as he grinned down at her.

Kate's heart gave a sudden lurch.

Don't do that.

Don't give me that blue look, straight into my soul . . .

She turned quickly, headed for the stairs and disappeared, Joe following her. As they entered UCU, the phone was ringing. Kate was at the mirror in the refreshment area. Joe answered it as Kate sat down with the diary.

Putting down the phone as Bernie came through the door, he glanced across at Kate.

'Connie has some more information for us.'

Joe watched as she pushed Janine Walker's diary into her bag. 'Hey? What are you doing now?'

'Taking this home to read.'

'Uh-uh. Don't do that, Red. If somebody locked you in the cold room to hamper your search for the diary, it's remotely possible that having it in your possession could be risky. It's evidence. It should stay here overnight.'

With bad grace, Kate went to the small security cupboard in the corner of the room and placed the diary inside it. Only UCU personnel had a key.

In the quiet of the PM suite, they silently watched and listened as Connie imparted information about the remains, pointing first to one and then the other set and finally to a single long, slim bone lying in isolation.

'I asked Harry to go over personally and collect familial DNA samples from the Walker family. We now know for certain that these are the complete remains of Janine Walker.' She took a few paces to the other remains. 'We've already established that this is Molly James. Found within a couple of metres of each other.' Connie was silent for some seconds. 'I'm a practical kind of person. I do the science. But I like the idea of them being together in that place.'

Bernie pursed his lips as Connie walked the few steps away from them to stand by the table on which lay the single bone, stark in its solitariness.

'And now, I've got a little information to give you about this item, which is helpfully somewhat beyond the norm.' They waited. 'It belonged to a very tall young woman. My estimate is she was around five-ten.'

Connie looked up from the femur, voice low. 'So, UCU. Three victims, each killed at a different time. Your case just went big-time. You have a repeater.'

Kate felt tension rise as a little pain immediately behind her eyes lashed its tail.

CHAPTER TWENTY-SIX

At two o'clock the following afternoon, the phone shrilled in UCU as Kate arrived. The only one present, she lifted it.

'Unsolved Crime Unit. Dr Hanson speaking. How can I—'

'It's what I can do for *you*, actually, Dr Hanson.'

Kate frowned. The voice. She searched her memory. The photographer.

'Hello, Mr Brannigan.' She heard a rustling sound, then he was back on the line.

'Remember I told you I took only photographs of the models? Well, that's true, but I captured a bit more than that, apparently. Don't know if you're busy, but I'm calling from Harborne High Street. I'm doing some publicity work for *Doctors*.'

Kate nodded at the reference to the Birmingham-based daytime television soap, which used a number of locations in the area.

Brannigan continued, 'I'm happy to drop off what I've found at Rose Road later.'

Kate was reaching for her bag. 'I can come to you right now, Mr Brannigan. How about Café Rouge in ten minutes?'

She ended the call and scribbled a quick note to the others.

Within ten minutes Kate was sitting at a window table inside the small High Street café, sipping an Americano and watching a clutch of people on the opposite side of the road. She could see a shoulder-held camera and furry microphone focused on two bronze-faced actors who were pacing and talking. She'd watched them go through it three times so far. This kind of location work was no longer an event here. More an inconvenience at times.

The chair on the other side of the table moved suddenly, startling her, and she looked up quickly. It was Brannigan. She hadn't seen him come in. He sat down opposite her, looking amiable in a denim shirt, sunglasses pushed up into his thick hair. With a flourish he placed a slim folder on the table between them.

'After your visit, I did some searching in my files. Don't know whether these are of any help, but I think it *might* be her, the girl who disappeared, although she doesn't look like they . . . Here, take a look. See what you think.'

Kate felt her pulse quicken as she took the folder and slowly opened it. Inside were three photographs. Two were very clear. After looking at them for some seconds, she knew what she thought. She also understood Brannigan's expressed doubt.

Kate's thoughts raced as she drove through the afternoon traffic. Johann Pachelbel's *Canon* had spiralled several times before she reached her destination. She parked in front of the modern glass-and-concrete building and cut the engine, then picked up her phone and dialled a number from information she'd previously added to her notebook. A male voice came on the line. Kate was direct.

'This is Dr Hanson of the Unsolved Crime Unit, West Midlands Police Headquarters. I need to see you right now. There's something I want you to look at.'

Within a minute she entered the reception area, and after a phone call he appeared, looking calm and welcoming.

'Hello, Dr Hanson! Nice to see you. Come to my office. We can talk there.'

She followed him, noting the white teeth, smart business suit and neat hair. He led her into his office and they sat on opposite sides of the large desk.

'I was expecting to come to Rose Road.'

Saying nothing, but keeping her eyes on him, Kate flipped open the folder, slowly extracted two of the photographs and laid them in front of him. His eyes flicked from one to the other, then to Kate, then back to the photographs, a frown deepening between his brows.

She waited. Nothing came from him.

Kate leaned forward and pointed. 'These are photographs of Molly James. Taken on the day she disappeared. We know it's the day she disappeared because they were taken by the official photographer at a fashion show organised at the mall that day. Both of these are shots of the show's runway, but they capture Molly well. Wouldn't you agree?'

He made no response to that either, though Kate could almost hear his thought processes.

'Particularly this one.' She tapped the photograph of Molly showing her turning to her left, her companion equally well defined. She reached a mental count of thirty. Still silent.

'Do you have any comment to make?'

He had paled in the last minute and looked worried. 'I . . . let me think for a minute. It's a long time ago. I can hardly—'

She didn't give him an opportunity to finish. She tapped the picture again.

'At a rough guess, this photograph was taken within an hour, probably less, of Molly James disappearing and never being seen again. My understanding is that you didn't see Molly that day. Would you like to explain your presence in it?'

His face had drained of its last vestige of colour. He looked from the photograph to Kate, then back, silent.

Watching him closely, Kate heard her phone ring. Reaching into her bag, she pulled it out and listened, then, 'I'll be back in the office in around fifteen minutes. I'm going to suggest that within the next half-hour Mr Jason Fairley presents himself at Rose Road for a talk with us.'

She ended the call, picked up the photographs and replaced them in their folder, a sudden thought occurring to her. 'By the way, have you ever known a young woman by the name of Janine Walker?'

He looked at her, his face a total blank.

Kate walked into UCU, went directly to the table and slid the photographs Brannigan had given her from their folder. Her colleagues pressed closely around the table. Bernie gave a small air-punch.

'How *about* that?' murmured Joe quietly, examining the photographs closely.

'How'd he take it when you showed him these, Doc?'

'"Poleaxed" about covers it. And I doubt he knows about what's been recovered from the bypass site.'

Kate looked down at one of the photographs in particular, then fetched her notebook and riffled its pages. Finding what she was looking for, she glanced up at the glass screen, seeking further confirmation.

Bernie scanned her face. 'I know that look. It usually means that something we got that looks good's no bloody good, or there's some other snag.'

Kate shook her head. 'I was checking that Brannigan's initial confirmation to me of Molly's appearance on the day she disappeared fitted with what we already knew from the previous investigation. That she was wearing a pale-blue polo shirt.'

The three colleagues gazed down at the photograph. Molly James in life, glowing with health, lips slightly parted, eyes bright, Jason Fairley's hand on the sleeve of her white shirt.

Thinking ahead as to how the imminent interview with Fairley might proceed, Kate picked up her phone and tapped in the mobile number on the business card Brannigan had given her during their first meeting. She had a request to make. One she hoped he could fulfil in the next hour.

CHAPTER TWENTY-SEVEN

They now knew that Molly James had changed her appearance on the day she was abducted.

'Might it have been a different day?' asked Julian.

Kate shook her head. 'I trust Brannigan's information. He was at the mall because he had a contract. He took those photographs at that fashion show and he's already told me that it was the only one ever staged there, as far as he's aware. I've asked him if he can look out his records of the job, to confirm it and counter any doubts Fairley might raise about when the photographs were taken.'

She ran a finger lightly over the photograph, voice low. 'So. Here she is. Molly. On the day she disappeared, wearing different clothes to those she left home in. From what I recall, it also looks as though she changed her hairstyle. See? It's smoothed back. Secured at the back of her head in some way.'

Kate looked from Bernie to Joe. 'Jessica Barnes told you that Molly had a backpack that day at the mall?' They each nodded. 'Maybe it contained the change of clothes. We don't know what became of her belongings. But the big question right now is about Molly's own behaviour. *Why* did she change?' She checked her watch. 'He should *be* here by now.'

As if on cue, the phone rang. Joe lifted the receiver, nodded and hung up.

'Jason Fairley is in the building. And he's not alone.'

Kate and Joe walked into the interview room as Bernie diverted to the next room to observe. They found Fairley seated beside a formally dressed older man who had a briefcase at his feet.

Kate took the chair next to Joe. Glancing across the small table at Fairley, she saw that he was in slightly better shape than when she'd left him earlier. He didn't look thrilled to be at Rose Road, but neither was he still in shock. He nodded at her, face serious but now showing some colour.

Joe started the proceedings.

'Thanks for coming in, Mr Fairley. Lieutenant Joe Corrigan, Unsolved Crime Unit. We met recently at your place of work. This is Dr Kate Hanson, my colleague, whom you met earlier today.'

Fairley didn't speak.

Joe transferred his attention to the soberly dressed man sitting next to Fairley. 'And you are . . . ?'

'Alan Whitehead, of Whitehead and Graham, Mr Fairley's solicitor.'

Joe nodded genially, then looked back to Fairley, speaking quickly. 'Mind telling us why you thought it necessary to bring a lawyer to an informal interview aimed at helping the police learn more about Molly James's disappearance, Mr Fairley?'

Fairley stayed mute. Whitehead cleared his throat.

'Perhaps you're not familiar with the rules of law in the United Kingdom, Lieutenant Corrigan. Mr Fairley is entirely within his rights to bring legal representation to any meeting with the police, informal or otherwise. I'm here to advise him about any contribution he may wish to make to your inquiries.'

Whitehead glanced at Fairley, who gave a brief nod of agreement. Joe chose to ignore the doubt expressed about his knowledge of the British criminal justice system.

'Mr Fairley, Dr Hanson met with you earlier today and showed you two photographs. Is that correct?'

Fairley nodded at Whitehead, who responded on his behalf. 'Yes.'

'And you would agree that depicted in both of those photographs is a young woman known and easily identifiable as Molly James, who disappeared from Touchwood shopping mall in July 2002? Here. Let me refresh your memory.'

Joe took the two photographs from Kate and placed them on the table in front of Fairley.

'Yes,' said Fairley, with permission from Whitehead.

'In both photographs there is a male person clearly identifiable as you, Mr Fairley. What's your response to that?'

Fairley sat back in his chair, leaving Whitehead to reply.

'My client acknowledges that the male person in the photograph

142

bears some fleeting resemblance to himself, but it is not a sharp likeness, and with the passage of time . . .'

Kate felt a wave of irritation rising within her. Joe looked from Whitehead to Fairley, tone insistent. 'Yes or no, Mr Fairley? Do you acknowledge that this is a photograph of you with Molly James, taken on the day she disappeared?'

Once again, Fairley did not respond directly. Whitehead spoke for him.

'What my client is saying . . .'

'Your *client* has hardly said anything yet,' intervened Kate, unable to stop herself.

'. . . is that he cannot be positively identified in the photographs, given the limitation I have just described. He also says that it cannot be established without doubt that those pictures were taken on a specific day.'

Kate was furious. Mainly with herself for giving Fairley sufficient thinking time to consult his solicitor. She glared from Fairley to Whitehead.

'That fashion show wasn't a regular event for the department store—'

'Ah, but that's the point, isn't it?' Whitehead cut in unctuously. 'You don't have proof that these photographs were taken on that specific day and not on some other occasion.'

Joe looked from Whitehead to Fairley. 'We're making further inquiries on that, Mr Fairley. In the meantime, would you care to describe the nature of your relationship with Molly James at the time she disappeared?'

It was evident that Fairley did not care to do so. He sat staring at the table between Joe and himself.

Kate's eyes were on Fairley's face. The interview was Fairley's opportunity to give a credible account of the incident. So far his reluctance had done nothing to establish his trustworthiness. With a slight nod from Joe, she got to a key question:

'Witnesses in the original investigation said that Molly James left home wearing a pale-blue polo shirt and cream trousers. During this reinvestigation, a witness has confirmed that that same description was given to him by investigating officers who spoke to him shortly after Molly's disappearance.' She tapped the photographs. 'Take another look, Mr Fairley. *No* polo shirt. *No* cream trousers. Molly changed her clothes.' She transferred her focus to the lawyer, Whitehead. 'Your client was there. The question we'd like him to answer is "Why?"'

Whitehead adopted a patient air. 'And as I've already made plain to you, there's no proof that—'

There was a soft tapping at the door. Glancing from Whitehead to Fairley, Kate left the table and went to open it. It was Whittaker. With a brief message. She quickly read it. Brannigan had come through with the information she'd asked for. He'd looked through his records and even gone further – he'd checked with the editor of the *Solihull News* about the fashion event under discussion.

Kate returned to the table, her eyes briefly meeting Joe's, then sat, all of her attention on Fairley. 'Mr Fairley, we now have confirmation of the date of the fashion show.' She paused. '*And* that it was the only one ever staged by John Lewis at Touchwood.' Whitehead and Fairley were silent. 'So, these photographs *were* taken on the day Molly disappeared. We also know that they were taken some time after two p.m. Prior to that, Molly was casually dressed. Afterwards, her appearance changed . . .' Kate looked down at the photographs, as did everyone else in the room. 'To what I would term "formal". A white shirt, black trousers, and her hair smoothed back from her face. Can you explain that change of appearance, Mr Fairley?'

Kate waited. So did Joe, beside her. Fairley didn't move for thirty seconds, then he leaned towards Whitehead and whispered. Kate studied the ceiling.

Whitehead shifted in his chair. 'I need a moment alone with my client, please.'

Outside in the corridor, Kate and Joe were joined by Bernie. After a brief pause, Bernie spoke. 'What's your thinking about him?'

Kate stood against the wall, arms folded. 'He hasn't said enough yet for me to come to a conclusion about any involvement he might have had with Molly's disappearance, but his demeanour doesn't inspire confidence.'

She took one or two steps, then turned to her colleagues. 'Right now, I'm thinking about a very short note I saw on Molly's desk in her room, when I visited her mother, remember? I didn't appreciate its significance at the time. Now I think it could be key.'

'Remind me,' said Bernie.

'Someone signing himself – or herself – "J", suggesting that Molly goes over to "see what's available". Or words to that effect.'

Joe looked dubious. 'Any date?'

Kate shook her head.

'Any ideas?'

She nodded. 'Oh *yes*.'

Joe glanced at Bernie, then back to Kate. 'Okay. You continue when we go back in.' He looked down at his watch. 'They've had enough time. Let's get to it.'

Joe and Kate returned to the room, where Whitehead was wearing an inscrutable expression. Fairley looked cautious. And nervous.

Kate began. 'Okay, Mr Fairley. Have you anything to say to us?'

Fairley glanced at Whitehead, then nodded. 'I've just told Alan. I did see Molly that day, because she phoned and asked me to meet her.'

Kate studied him for some seconds, brows high. 'Leaving aside your reluctance to tell *us* about this, you didn't think to mention it to the original investigation?'

Fairley made no response.

'So, where were you when she rang?'

'At my office. Five Ways. So I popped over, just to have a coffee with her.'

Kate gave Fairley a level look. His use of the word 'just', a small hint at an attempt to rationalise his activities that day.

'Quite a distance to "pop", from Five Ways to Solihull. Why?'

Fairley shrugged. 'Just to . . . see her, you know.'

'Were you in a relationship with Molly James at that time?' asked Kate, studying him closely.

This provoked a vehement shake of the head. '*No*. We went out for about a year, but we'd finished a few months before . . . Her mother didn't approve. I'm . . . I was a few years older than Molly. Her mother didn't like me.'

Kate nodded. 'Okay. Molly wasn't your girlfriend at that time. Did she have another boyfriend?'

Fairley shook his head again. 'Mol wasn't up for another relationship.'

Mol. Kate thought back to the little message on Molly James's desk. 'Could she have had a boyfriend that she kept secret?'

Fairley shook his head once more, this time with obvious assurance. 'No. Mol was a very open kind of person. She'd have told me if she was seeing anybody. She told me everything. She even told me about

145

some bloke she saw fairly often in some coffee shop in the mall – I don't mean she was *seeing* him. She told me they never even spoke.' He shrugged. 'They just kind of . . . acknowledged each other, I suppose. It was nothing. What I'm saying is, she even mentioned *him*. A nobody.' He stared at Kate, then looked down at his hands.

'And you remained friends with Molly after your relationship with her ended?'

It was now Fairley's turn to nod.

Kate's eyes were on his face. 'Okay, how about this for a scenario? You went to meet Molly at her request because she'd phoned and asked you for some kind of encouragement, maybe a little moral support?'

Fairley's face reddened slightly, and his eyes slid towards White-head.

'Mr Fairley, I think Molly had an arrangement to meet someone that afternoon. Someone other than you. She clearly considered that arrangement important, because she changed her appearance. Which means she had to have left home taking additional clothes with her. We think she was carrying them in her Ellesse backpack. But for some reason she didn't tell anyone, not the friends she was with, nor her mother. She didn't want anyone to know about the arrangement. Except maybe *you*.'

Still no response from Fairley, who was now looking pressured.

Kate gazed speculatively at him.

'Let's think about this,' she invited with a quick smile. 'What circumstances would lead Molly to go shopping with friends, taking a change of clothes, and at some point ring you?'

More silence.

'Do you know what I think, Mr Fairley?'

He looked as though he'd much prefer that Kate didn't share her thoughts with him.

'More than one person who knew Molly at the time has referred to her being short of money.' Fairley looked quickly at Kate, then away. 'I think the arrangement Molly had that day was a job interview.'

There was a frown on Whitehead's brow as Fairley swallowed and leaned forward. 'It was *nothing* to do with me.'

Kate regarded him coolly. 'I think that's probably true, Mr Fairley, insofar as you weren't her interviewer. She wouldn't have needed to dress up for an interview with you. You and Molly knew each other well.' She studied his face. 'I saw a note in her bedroom, which I think *you* wrote.'

Whitehead's head jerked involuntarily to Fairley, whose face darkened.

Kate continued: 'I think that when Molly rang you, you already *knew* about the interview and also who it was with. But unfortunately for you, Mr Fairley, as things stand, you appear to be the last person to have spent time with Molly prior to her disappearance. Unless you know otherwise?'

Fairley was pale as he looked towards his solicitor.

Kate caught a glance from Joe and nodded. He looked Fairley in the eye.

'You need to tell us who it was that Molly was seeing, Mr Fairley. Right now.'

They watched as Fairley and Whitehead had a brief whispered exchange, at the conclusion of which Whitehead nodded briskly. Fairley looked from Joe to Kate.

'Mol's mom was dead against her having a job. She wanted her to concentrate on her college work. But Mol wanted to make some money.' He looked anxiously at Joe and Kate again, then down at his hands.

Kate watched him. 'While you're giving some thought to the rest of what you're going to tell us, Mr Fairley, can you confirm if you have ever met or known a young woman by the name of Janine Walker?'

Whitehead looked ready to intervene, but Fairley ignored him, conscious of Joe and Kate's eyes on him.

'No. Never. I haven't.'

Kate studied him. 'Okay. So – how about the big question we're still waiting for you to answer, Mr Fairley?' The atmosphere in the room was electric. 'Who was it that Molly James had an appointment with that day?'

Still looking down at his hands, Fairley gave them a name.

CHAPTER TWENTY-EIGHT

It was five forty-five p.m. when the call came from Reception to UCU. Bernie answered the phone, then hung up.

'He's here.' Walking heavily to the door, Joe and Kate in his wake, Bernie looked back over his shoulder at them, face animated. 'All in one day. We've got Fairley as a person of interest, a possible suspect, even. And now *this*. It'll be my pleasure to lead this one.'

Their interviewee was waiting for them in the informal interview room near to Reception. All three colleagues entered, Joe and Bernie taking seats opposite him, Kate to one side of the room. John Cranham looked coolly at each of them and said nothing. He evidently hadn't felt the need to bring any legal representation with him in response to UCU's request. Bernie started straight in.

'You had an appointment with Molly James the day she disappeared. We know that you got back from your business trip early that same morning. Tell us about Molly.'

Kate watched Cranham closely. No sign of discomfort. The well-dressed man gave Bernie a disdainful look, then glanced at Joe and across at Kate. He smiled at her. 'I can't tell you anything. Because she never arrived.'

He crossed one elegant leg over the other. Kate's peripheral vision picked up shiny black loafers with leather soles.

She asked: 'Why didn't you mention this before, Mr Cranham?'

As he gazed from her to her colleagues, Kate speculated that of all the occupants of the room, including Joe, Cranham was probably the most relaxed. He shrugged, giving a smile that, in different circumstances, might have been considered disarming.

'Because I'd completely forgotten. Look here, we're talking about nearly a decade ago. It just slipped from my mind. Surely you can understand that?'

Bernie looked at him, face hard. 'At the time of the original investigation, you was saying you wasn't even in the country. You recently told us the same. Until you had a "rethink".'

Cranham's focus was on the removal of an almost imperceptible fibre from the sleeve of his immaculate suit.

'Yes. And then I corrected my error,' he said quietly, unperturbed.

There followed a short silence, during which Kate heard only Bernie's breathing.

Joe broke the silence. 'What's with the game-playing, Mr Cranham? Why didn't you tell us when you confirmed *that* information that Molly had an appointment with you that same day?'

Cranham looked irritated. 'There was no "game-playing". I already told you. I'd forgotten all about it. Plus, it *didn't* happen. It was a non-event. She never arrived.'

'So when did you suddenly "remember" this arrangement you had with her?' asked Bernie.

Cranham gave a rueful grin. 'After Dr Hanson's visit to the showroom.' He glanced at each of their faces. 'Am I about to be charged for neglecting to mention an appointment I made years ago with a young woman to whom I might have offered employment but who apparently couldn't be bothered to attend or cancel?' He glanced at his hands, face haughty.

Kate's own face heated up. She wanted to slap him.

Joe leaned towards Cranham. 'The point is, when you did recall it, you didn't tell us,' he emphasised.

Again their interviewee looked irritated. 'I have too many demands on my time to chase after the police with snippets of non-information. What use would it have been to you?'

'That's for *us* to judge,' snapped Bernie.

'I had no contact with this girl. I didn't know her. I never met her. Ever. She was – is – irrelevant to me.'

Irrelevant. The discordance hit Kate. She glanced at her colleagues. They had also felt it.

Kate studied Cranham as he sat: the set of his shoulders, the relaxed hands, his head set high and slightly to one side as he favoured Bernie with a supercilious look. She recognised the self-assurance and sense of entitlement his wealthy background had bought. She delved into her notebook and took out the photograph of Molly James she'd removed from the glass screen prior to leaving UCU.

'Mr Cranham,' she said quietly. 'Would you take a look at this photograph, please?'

He glanced at her then held out a well-manicured hand for the photograph she passed to him. He stared at it briefly and Kate fancied that some of the haughtiness in his manner lessened. He pushed it back across the table.

'I remember it from the press coverage when she was missing. Very sad. But I never met her in my life.'

Kate took back the photograph.

'Thank you. Last question. Do you know, or have you ever known, a young woman named Janine Walker?' She felt Joe's and Bernie's eyes on her.

'No,' he said without any hesitation.

This time Kate merely nodded her thanks.

Cranham looked at each of them in turn, then got up from his chair. 'If there's nothing further, I'm leaving. It's late and I'm going to hit the rush-hour traffic. If you wish to speak with me again, I'll make sure it doesn't involve me in any further inconvenience. It will be prearranged. *You* will come to *me*. And I'll have my legal representative present throughout.'

He walked towards the door.

'Why did your family offer thousands of pounds as a reward for information about Molly, if she was so "irrelevant" to you?' asked Joe to Cranham's back.

Cranham turned, his eyes on Bernie and Joe. Cool. Controlled.

'Call it my father's public-spiritedness. My family's willingness to assist at a time of need in the community.' He paused. 'Which West Midlands Police should *not* rely on in future.'

With that as a parting shot, he was gone.

Back in UCU, Bernie was almost apoplectic with rage.

'Funny how he remembers some stuff and forgets other stuff, yeah? I still say his father could have offered that reward because he thought Sonny Jim was somehow involved with Molly. And who does he think he is?' Bernie stormed. 'Him with his "you come to me" attitude. He stops at the top of my list, the posh *git* . . .'

He was silent for some seconds, still simmering, eyes on the glass screen. 'Still, it's not all bad news. Fairley and him are still POIs. Now we work to move one or other of 'em up to being a suspect.

Whoever's killed these girls, he's a real piece of work. Once we've got one of them in the frame and start leaning on him, he'll show himself for what he is. We'll see it. This doer ain't just "somebody's husband, somebody's son".'

Kate's head jerked upwards. She looked at Bernie, surprised. 'Who said he was?'

'Julian.'

CHAPTER TWENTY-NINE

Mid-morning on Wednesday, Furman was in UCU, the vein in one temple pulsing. Kate gazed at it as Furman glared at her, Joe and Bernie.

'I'm the manager of this unit. As the manager, I –' he pointed to himself – 'tell you three –' he pointed to them – 'what you do and what you don't do.'

He paced, clearly seething, then wheeled on them, addressing Kate specifically as he waved a sheet of A4.

'What's this?' he demanded.

Kate glanced at it. 'That's a time sheet,' she said, tone helpful.

His colour heightened. 'I know *that*. What I want to know is, what makes you think you can spend one-point-seven-five hours with the James girl's mother?'

Kate looked him firmly in the eye. 'UCU needs information. Mrs James needed to talk. She's had to live through some very difficult years since her daughter disappeared. I felt that the least the Force could do was give one-point-seven-five hours to the visit, listening to what she had to say.'

He narrowed his eyes, hands on hips. 'Did you hear yourself? All that "feeling" and "listening". You're not her bloody therapist! This woman doesn't expect us to go over there for—'

Kate had had enough. 'Dianne James expects *nothing* from us at all,' she snapped, glaring back at him. 'Because *that's* what she learned to expect from the previous investigation.'

Furman's eyes narrowed, face pale with rage. He switched his focus from Kate to the others.

'Guess what I received this morning.' No one bothered to reply. 'An email. From Rutgers.' They all recognised the name of the top-class

Midlands legal firm. 'And what do I find out? That *you* three had Cranham in here. For an interview!'

Kate focused on keeping her breathing even. Cranham had followed up on his veiled threat. In the silence of the room, she heard sounds from the world beyond the windows of UCU. She saw Bernie and then Joe glance in that direction.

Furman ranted on: 'We've been over this. I said *no* interviewing of Cranham unless I sanction it. What do you lot do? You get him in.' He resumed pacing, one hand raking his short fair hair, the other loosening his tie, his face changing from pale to a dull red, the vein hyperactive.

Kate spoke. 'John Cranham had an arrangement with Molly to interview her for a job on the day she disappeared. He never divulged that, either to *you* years ago, or to us. He fits the type of person we're looking for. Someone with the ability to charm. Someone who could present as plausible and smooth to a young woman. Plus, he's mobile and—'

'*Who isn't?*' bawled Furman.

Kate monitored her breathing, holding on to her patience. 'We're looking for a *combination* of factors in our persons of interest. He has some of the attributes we're seeking. The fact that he had an appointment with Molly on the day she disappeared makes him relevant to this investigation.'

'*I* say when there's a legitimate investigative reason for any kind of interviewing of the likes of Cranham. His father's well in with the Chief Constable so he's a potential source of trouble, and you're seeing connections that don't exist.'

Kate felt her control slipping. 'Which is better than not looking for any connections at all,' she said, voice rising. 'What's the matter with you? Don't you *want* these cases solved?'

The last question reverberated around the room as she and Furman faced each other, Furman glaring at each of them in turn, finger pointing.

'I hold the three of you responsible for this business with Cranham. But you –' he jabbed the finger at Kate – '*you* won't be managed. You won't be guided. You won't be told. It's always your way or no way. This unit needs people who can work as a team. You *can't* do that. And these two let you carry on doing whatever you want!' He directed the finger towards Joe and Bernie.

Furman paused for breath. When he spoke again, his voice was low. 'What happens in UCU is in accordance with what I say. I'll deal with these two as police officers. But you're different. No way is *this* unit being led by some control freak with mad theories that could put *this* Force at risk of being criticised by the media and possibly sued for thousands.'

He took a breath, glaring at Kate. 'Everybody remembers the Wimbledon Common case. *That's* what happens when psychological *theory*,' he sneered the word at Kate, 'gets mixed up with police investigation. Well, I'm not having it, d'you hear? I'm not having you link these girls' deaths on flimsy evidence, then try to pin them on somebody with serious financial clout, solely on the basis of psychological mumbo-jumbo.'

He stopped for a few seconds, getting control of his breathing. 'The Cranham family's a strong force to be reckoned with.'

Kate's face switched from suppressed anger to disgust. 'And here am I thinking that *that's* what the police are supposed to be.'

The area around Furman's lips turned white. He took another A4 sheet from his file and waved it.

'See this?'

Kate stayed silent.

'*This* is a letter to your professional body.' He scanned it quickly. 'The British Psychological Society. It's addressed to their complaints and procedures department, reporting you for gross lack of professionalism, flouting orders and ignoring Force management decisions. It says—'

Red-faced, Kate leapt to her feet, squaring up to him, anger ignited by his attitude as well as his words. 'Don't you dare threaten me! Don't you *dare* lecture me about professionalism. *You*, of all people. We're only here now, working on these cases, because *you* didn't do your damned *job*!'

Seeing Julian standing white-faced in the doorway, Kate fought to bring her anger under control. 'You can't make an official complaint unless you give me a detailed explanation and an opportunity to—'

'*Watch* me.'

Bernie and Joe started to speak at the same time. Furman turned his rage on Bernie.

'You'll keep out of this, Watts, if you know what's good for you. There's real cutbacks on the way, and I can see the day coming when you're out of this Force altogether.' He looked sideways at Joe, his voice dropping. 'I'm putting in a request for *you* to be full-time Armed Response.'

Joe eyed Furman coldly, rising slowly from his chair. He topped the inspector by a good six centimetres.

'We'll see about that. In the meantime, Furman, you really need to watch your mouth when you talk to *any* member of UCU. That clear?'

The two men faced each other as the wall clock ticked. Amid the thick tension inside UCU, Kate's watch suddenly fell off her wrist and hit the carpet. It had happened before. Caused by her galvanic skin response. Her stress response. She recovered the watch, getting a grip on her temper and her voice.

'If you send that letter—' she started.

'Got *one* good reason why I shouldn't?'

'How about, if you'd done even a half-reasonable job on these two cases at the time, they wouldn't need reinvestigating now.' Kate paused, then, 'If you send that letter, I shall immediately request legal advice from the Society, and also from the company that provides me with five million pounds' worth of professional insurance cover. That'll buy me a few lawyers.'

She glared at Furman. He glared back. She could see him thinking his way around what she'd just said.

'You're on notice,' he snapped. 'One more step out of line, one more disregard of an order – this letter goes.'

He shoved the sheet back into his folder and stormed past Julian and out. In the aftermath of his rage, the room felt like a vacuum. Julian walked quietly to the computer station and sat, face pale, shoulders rigid.

Bernie broke the silence first, looking at each of them in turn. 'Furman's barmy. You do realise that, don't you? Barking. I always thought it. Now I can *see* it. He should see somebody. He's the one who's the control freak. He's—'

'—professionally dangerous for you, Bernie. And you, Joe.'

'Don't matter,' said Bernie, pointing in the direction Furman had gone. 'I'm not about to kowtow to the likes of *him*. He's looking for any excuse to fill UCU with some hand-picked lackeys.'

Kate suddenly became aware of more sounds from outside. 'What's going on out there?'

Joe walked to the window. 'Press vans with antennae have just arrived.'

As he returned to the table, the phone rang and he picked up. 'Hi, Connie.' He listened without speaking further.

Kate checked her watch and thought of Maisie, who would be in the university this afternoon, at a maths lecture. She was taking A-level maths soon. Years early.

Joe hung up and looked from Kate to Bernie.

'Connie wants to see us. The media know that Molly James and Janine Walker have been found.'

CHAPTER THIRTY

Igor let them into the quietness of the post-mortem suite. Connie was sitting under a powerful light examining a small item gripped by tweezers. Her fitted pale green tee and knee-length black linen skirt were visible between the open edges of her white lab coat. Pushing her glasses up into her short black hair, she hooked a finger at the arrivals, shaking her head as Bernie went for coveralls. 'Just gloves, Bernard.'

They walked towards her, pulling on latex.

'Well, UCU. Want to see what I've found on the remains of Janine Walker?'

Kate gave her head a small shake to focus, the scene with Furman still reverberating.

Connie placed the item gently on the examination table, under stark white light, and released it from the tweezer grip. They gathered round. Yet another puzzle.

Connie looked up at the three serious faces opposite her. 'The card's of similar construction to the one found on Molly James's remains, but this time there's a little more to say about it. Have a look.'

They followed her directive.

'There's some kind of pattern, or marks.' Kate pointed to a specific area. 'There. A round mark and another side by side. And a long stroke. All three in black.'

Putting on his glasses, Bernie pored over the fragment. 'Makes no sense to me. How about you, Corrigan?'

Joe bent close to the item. After a few seconds, 'Looks like letters. A word.'

Connie looked from one to the other. 'I've got some information about the card found with Molly James's remains. Forensics took a look at it and reported back.'

157

She walked quickly to her desk and returned with a single sheet of paper.

'It's pasteboard. Nothing to get excited about. Fairly common-place. Wes Jacobs describes its construction as follows.' Connie read quickly from the printed report: ' "Layers of paper pasted together. A common commercial process . . . extra-robust quality . . . extra paper layers." He's confirmed indications of it having been thickly laminated at one time. If it hadn't been heavy duty *and* laminated, it's unlikely it would have survived. Wes also confirms that there's the remains of colour, the kind you get from a permanent marker. Colour confirmed to be –' she turned over the sheet – 'red.'

Connie pointed to the small item now before them. 'This one looks very similar to me, in terms of its construction.'

'So, what's heavy-duty pasteboard generally used for?' asked Kate.

Connie pointed to the report still in her hand.

'According to Wes, extra-sturdy rigid pasteboard is often used for the construction of signs. Temporary signs. He also says that in this weight it would be strong enough to provide very temporary repair for, say, damage to the interior fabric of a building that might require more robust attention in the near future.'

She looked at Joe.

'I agree with you about the features on this one being a word. This time it's black ink.' She considered the item again, adding, 'It looks to me like Os followed by a heavy downstroke. Whatever other letters were there are long since gone.'

'Anyone have any idea what it might mean? Its significance?' asked Kate.

'Darned if I know. What're you doing?' asked Joe.

'Copying it into my notebook.'

As they prepared to leave, Connie followed them to the door, arms folded. 'I heard about the row.'

'*Already?*' asked Kate.

Connie looked at her, head on one side. 'Kate, the *whole* of your floor heard it first-hand. Harry phoned and told me.' She looked concerned. 'I have a high regard for UCU and I'm worried that it's made a bad enemy in Furman. You also need to be careful with the media, now that it knows about these two young women and the reinvestigations.'

CHAPTER THIRTY-ONE

Kate arrived home on Wednesday afternoon feeling a mix of emotions. The impact of her row with Furman was still with her, tempered now by a feeling that progress on UCU's cases was being made. She moved through the hot, silent house, from front to back, pushing open the folding doors to let in air.

Mugger was sitting patiently outside on the patio. She called to him. He didn't come towards the house, merely wafted his tail from side to side.

'Now who's put *you* in a mood?'

The phone in the hall clamoured and Kate went to answer it.

'*Hello*, sweetie,' said a husky female voice.

'Celia!' cried Kate with pleasure. 'I was going to ring you.' Kate and Celia had been friends since they were children. That friendship had survived their leaving their childhood homes, Kate's years at Oxford, Celia's in London, their respective relocations, marriages, Kate's divorce and several pregnancies, all of them Celia's, bar one.

'Of course you were,' responded Celia. 'We haven't met up since last month and I need a friendship fix. Seeing four kids through puberty is above and beyond. I need wine and laughs.'

Kate listened, grinning at the nearby wall. This was what she needed. Normal life. Sanity. 'Sounds good to me.'

They agreed on an imminent arrangement and Kate hung up the phone, still smiling to herself.

Running lightly upstairs to change, she noticed a pile of Maisie's clothes, neatly ironed and folded by Phyllis, lying on the chest on the landing. They'd been there for two days, despite Kate asking Maisie to put them away. Sighing, she hefted them and walked across the landing to Maisie's room, which was reasonably tidy compared to the bedrooms of friends' children that Kate had viewed on occasion.

Making her way to the wardrobe, she pulled open one of the large drawers beneath it. No space. She closed it and pulled open the other drawer. Space. Placing the pile on the floor, she began moving items aside so that she could add the ironed clothing.

She stopped and, frowning, picked up the two small items together between her thumb and index finger. She studied them closely, heart picking up speed a little. She sniffed them. Placing them on the carpet beside her, she pushed more of the drawer's contents aside. And saw an infinitely more troubling item.

Kate's heart hurled itself against her breastbone, perspiration prickling her forehead. Shocked to her essence, she carefully removed the small transparent envelope, hand quivering, to study the contents. Three small, shiny blue tablets.

No. Not Maisie. Surely to G—

She heard a car door close, followed by the front door opening. Shaking, she quickly rearranged the contents of the drawer, minus her finds, and quietly closed it. Walking on to the landing, she dropped the ironed clothes where she'd found them. She wasn't up to tackling Maisie right now. Maybe later that evening. She needed time to absorb what she'd discovered, and think about how she was going to respond.

Maisie's foot hit the sitting-room floor with a sharp thump. Shocked out of his catnap, Mugger leapt up, ears flattened, and raced under the low table in front of where Kate was sitting, textbook on her lap. He sat, fur puffed, tail flicking from side to side, giving Maisie a baleful look.

'Careful, Maisie.'

Maisie was perched on the pink Swiss ball they shared. 'Mom, how'd you do these? They're impossible!'

'Practice,' said Kate quietly.

Another thump. 'I *am* practising. And getting *worse*. Oh, for—'

Kate gave Maisie her attention. 'To sustain your balance what you need to do is sit very straight on the ball and hold your torso really taut,' she said, echoing Phil, her gym trainer.

Maisie's back was ramrod straight as she raised one foot, then promptly lost stability again.

'See? It doesn't *work*!'

'It takes time. Try some cognitive imagery. Imagine your body is a core of steel.'

'Hey, cool! I-am-a-core-of-steel,' intoned Maisie, Dalek-like.

'It does work. Imagine yourself having a core of steel and you'll be able to carry on for as long as you want. Nothing will unbalance you.'

Kate watched her daughter as she dwelled on the events of the day. The row with Furman. The way she'd challenged him. Not her finest hour, professionally. The 'finds' in Maisie's room. What advice had she offered Maisie just now? Core of steel . . . and balance.

Stuff bounces off steel.

Maybe she should try imagery in future contacts with Furman.

Despite the pleasant atmosphere between Maisie and her, Kate knew that she could no longer avoid what was on her mind.

'Maisie?'

'. . . six, seven, eight-nine-ten.' Maisie raised one small, tanned fist in the air. '*Yeah!* What?'

'You and I need to talk.'

'Okay . . . One, two, three—'

'Leave that, Maisie, and come here, please.'

Catching Kate's tone, Maisie looked at her mother. Her eyes dropped to the two items lying on Kate's outstretched palm. She didn't move, but Kate saw shock and guilt in equal parts in her daughter's face.

'Tell me.'

Maisie hesitated for a second, before deciding that counter-accusation was her best option.

'You've been in my *room*? You've been through my *stuff*! How—'

'Listen to me, Maisie—'

'—could you!'

'I said, *listen*.'

At the tone of Kate's voice, Maisie slumped on the ball, looking sulky. Kate forced herself to wait a few seconds before she expressed her thoughts. Any display of anger and Maisie would respond in kind, and then Kate would get nowhere.

'Are you smoking?'

No response.

'Maisie, I need to know. I would have thought you more intelligent than . . .' Kate reverted to basics. 'These haven't been smoked at all. Have there been others?'

161

Maisie looked up at her, then away. 'No.'

'Are you sure?'

Maisie flared. 'I said no, didn't I! You're checking up on me, going through my personal stuff, and now you don't believe what I say!'

Kate looked at her daughter's flushed, angry face. She did believe Maisie. She'd examined one of the cigarettes, its tip smeared with lip gloss. She'd sniffed it. Sherbet.

Looking at it now, Kate imagined the little scenario that had probably played itself out in Maisie's room: Maisie wearing cosmetics, fingernails painted as they had been last week, posing in front of her dressing-table mirror with an unlit cigarette. Her child-woman daughter.

The cigarettes had not pleased Kate. The other item she'd found in Maisie's drawer made them pale into insignificance.

'Care to tell me about these, too?'

Maisie flicked a sideways glance at her mother's hand, then stopped, lips parted. Silent. Kate saw surprise and shock in her face, quickly replaced by something else. Hectic thinking.

'In your own time, Maisie, but I want an answer.'

Dear God, this cannot be happening to us. That I should be having a conversation with my twelve-year-old daughter about—

'They're not mine!'

Kate looked at her daughter. Despite the furtive quality of Maisie's face, Kate sensed that the tablets were indeed not hers. But it couldn't be the whole truth. She thought over what Maisie had just said.

'So whose are they, Maisie?'

'I don't know. I *told* you . . . they're not mine.'

'Well they were in your room. No one else goes in there except you and your friends.' Kate was fighting to keep her tone even. 'What are they? I'm guessing they're not aspirin.' She instantly chided herself. She'd sworn she would not get sarcastic.

'How should I know?' Maisie scowled.

'Did one of your friends – Chelsey or . . . ?'

Maisie jumped up, giving the Swiss ball a little kick as she headed for the door of the sitting room, then turned, face flushed, arms rigid at her sides, small hands fisted.

'You are *so* unfair, Mom. I don't say stuff about your friends. You know Daddy doesn't like Joe coming here, but I don't—'

'Maisie, don't say another *word*. Go.'

'I'm *going*, I'm going to phone Daddy! I'm going to ask him if I can stay with *him*!'

The sitting-room door slammed.

Well done. You handled that really well.

CHAPTER THIRTY-TWO

Julian was busily processing the statements and notes accumulated by UCU's investigations, following an earlier visit by Furman demanding them. Mercifully, Kate had missed this.

Cool in a gauzy white shirt and dark grey linen trousers, she paused and looked solemnly from Bernie to Joe sitting opposite her, both in short-sleeved shirts against the rising mid-morning heat beyond the windows of UCU.

'What was done to Molly and Janine, and possibly the other as-yet-unidentified young woman, took him time and effort and may have put him at risk of discovery and arrest. That suggests he had an intense need to do those things. It was all a *fantastic* experience for him. Literally. He'd done it many times already. In his head. This was clearly no angry or jealous boyfriend.'

She glanced at Bernie, who was chewing his pen, and experienced a surge of frustration with her efforts to convey the psychological imperative of the doer. Bernie caught the glance and stopped chewing.

'Wha'? Okay, Hanson. Get on with it. I know it was impersonal stuff – that instrumental whatsit you was on about before. I'm no dummy.'

Sitting at the computer, Julian tittered.

Bernie turned and glared at him. 'Is that kettle on yet? Half an hour ago you said you'd do it in ten minutes. All you've done so far is sit there tapping and looking moody.'

Muttering, Julian left the computer station, taking pen and notepad with him. He continued listening as water boiled.

Kate went on: 'Impersonal as it was, each victim was pre-selected, on the basis of her physical characteristics. Only the doer knows why those are relevant.'

She stood and began pacing, turning as she reached the glass screen to look at her colleagues.

'It appears he blocked out the faces of two of his victims, and I admit I'm struggling with the meaning, the purpose of that.' Distracted, she removed the tortoiseshell clip from her hair, dropped it on the table and ran a hand through the weighty dark auburn mass.

Julian approached with mugs of coffee, handing one to Kate. 'Is it possible that the doer did what he did and then, when he'd calmed down, looked at what he'd done and felt . . . remorseful?' He sat, resting his face on his forearms.

Kate listened as he processed his own view further.

'But that progression doesn't fit, does it, Kate? Because he's got no emotional commitment to the victims at all. So why would he feel remorseful?' He looked up at her. 'He wouldn't. Would he?'

Kate smiled at him. 'Well done, Julian,' she said encouragingly. 'You interrogated your theory until it ran out on you.'

She looked to Bernie and Joe. 'Covering the face of a victim is typically the action of a murderer wanting to protect *himself*. From his victim's emotions. Her anger, disappointment, pain. It also protects him from his own shame, guilt, regret and, yes, his remorse. He covers her face because he feels bad about what he's done to her. The reason he feels bad is because of the emotional connection there was between them.'

Kate walked to the glass screen, wrote two words, which she underlined, and turned to face them. 'And *that's* the problem. Because I'm convinced that our doer is an instrumental psychopath.' She paced some more, this time away from the screen.

'Victim-focused emotions like shame and guilt don't apply to him. What our doer probably does feel is monumental rage towards one person, which he is generalising towards his victims through his behaviour. It's not about the victim in front of him. She's nothing to him.'

A phrase heard a day or so ago slipped into her consciousness: *irrelevant to me.*

She sat on a nearby chair and kicked off her low heels, wriggling her toes. 'He doesn't *care* about her emotions. He *wants* to see her fear. Her *needs* to see the pain. Because she's now paying for whatever situations, slights, insults and who knows what else he believes have been perpetrated against him by this one person towards whom he is so vastly angry. Each of his victims is merely a vehicle for all of that.'

Joe watched her, listening intently. 'So why *is* he covering their faces?' he asked quietly.

Kate had been down to the post-mortem suite to look again at the face coverings. All she had seen the second time were the same discolorations, patchy grey areas and yellowish-green to brown decomposition stains.

She shook her head. 'I don't know, Joe.'

Bernie took a mouthful of coffee. 'Given what you've just said, any name we got that you think we can push up to suspect?' he asked.

'Not Colley. The destroyer of these young women is capable of enticement, with an effective con, followed by total mastery over his victim. Colley can only achieve that with a female who is less than ten years old.' Kate glanced at each of them in turn. 'Our doer *is* a master. There's a kind of professionalism in what we know he's done. It's practised. He has the ability to plan. He has the skills needed to carry out his plan, and he's sufficiently personable to inveigle intelligent, sophisticated young women into the situations he orchestrates.'

'How about he just picked 'em because they was young and that's all there was to it?'

Kate nodded. 'You're right, Bernie. Repeaters often do choose smaller people, women, teenagers merely because they're easier to control. But in our cases, based on what we know of their general appearance, his victims were special to him in some way only he understands. It could be that there's something about them that is . . . reminiscent of someone else?'

Kate placed both hands over her face momentarily, then let them drop on to her lap, feeling beleaguered. 'He's a very confident killer. He's demonstrated that by his ability to con and snare tall, healthy young women and dominate them physically.'

Joe looked to Bernie, then back to Kate. 'Maybe *he's* tall. Well built. Fit. How about somebody who works out? A bodybuilder?'

'Remember I went to see Malins? He looks as though he's been a weightlifter in his time,' suggested Bernie.

Kate looked at each of them and shrugged. 'Possible. But he could also be your average male. Bodybuilding isn't a necessary characteristic. Think about it. *Most* men are able to take physical control of *most* women, simply on the basis of greater muscle power. In certain situations *I* might be wise to fear *you* three as individuals – you are very unlikely to fear me.'

Bernie gave her a sideways glance. 'Yeah? You sure about that?'

He dropped his pen on the table and started massaging each forearm with a heavy hand, a sure indicator of frustration.

'What I really want you to do is tell me what this doer is like, as a *person* – say, when he's going about his normal life, if he ever has one. You've said "psychopath" and all that's in my head is that bloke in that film. The one where the FBI woman goes and sees him in his cell, and he's going on to her about beans and wine and stuff.'

Kate moved to sit on the edge of the table, ordering her thoughts. 'Okay. Our doer's got the same murderously antisocial personality. But he's no Hollywood-style Lecter. We won't identify him by visible characteristics, such as a penchant for tight clothes, slicked hair and *bon vivant* interests.' She heard Bernie mutter as she continued. 'All roads lead us back to his *behaviour*. His capacity to blend. To appear ordinary. That's all we have to work with.'

She thought for some seconds, then stood and went to the front of the room again.

'Okay, Bernie. Here's my best answer to your query about what he's *like* as a person. He operates behind a workaday charade he's created for himself of "Mr Normal". But psychological theory can tell us something of his *underlying* personality.' Bernie sighed, looking impatient, as Kate considered how best to convey the individual behind the theory.

She took a deep breath. 'To understand the essential "him" behind the normal presentation, picture the average eighteen-month- to two-year-old child of your acquaintance or past experience.' Her colleagues looked at her, listening keenly. 'The psychopath has that same total self-focus, the same determination to get what he, or she, wants. In *some* ways they share the same world view – the two year old and the psychopath – which can be summed up as "I want! I need! Give it to me! And I want it now! I don't care if you are tired or ill or whatever else you might be feeling. Fill my need! Gimme what I *want*!"'

Bernie's frown faded as Kate continued. 'Neither the toddler nor the psychopath has innate curbs on his behaviour. He just does what he wants. But there's an essential difference between them. Most two year olds already have a degree of awareness of other people as separate entities, with emotions and needs. That's because, mercifully for the majority of little kids, there's at least one person in their lives who's shown them nurture, kindness and care.'

Memories of a two-year-old Maisie stole into Kate's head.

'That's why the toddler may pat your arm if you have a headache, or hide a broken toy, due to feelings of guilt.' She stood, aware of Joe's eyes on her. 'The adult psychopath, our doer, missed out on that developmental stage. Right now, he's *masquerading* as a fully developed individual. He's developed a false self. Because –' she emphasised with an index finger tapping the table – 'he has to conceal from others that he has no empathy, he has no guilt, and *therefore* he has no shame.'

In the following silence, Kate returned to her seat at the table before continuing.

'He's an adult who has not developed beyond the "gimme it or I hit you on the head" stage. But –' she looked at each one of them in turn – 'stupid he is *not*. He knows that to openly be what he is and do what he wants would bring him only censure, punishment.'

Kate was aware of the common assumption, particularly within the Force, that certain types of offenders were insane. She glanced around the table. 'He isn't mad. Not if he can delay his antisocial behaviour in order to avoid trouble for himself. Psychopaths can appear to follow the rules operating around them for much of the time, say at work, or in their relationships with others.'

'This is a guy who works pretty hard to fit in socially? He's a kind of chameleon, right?' said Joe.

Kate nodded. 'He's grown up closely observing other people and how they operate. The reason he's able to conceal his real self is because he can *act* what he's observed. He's a good *mimic*.'

Julian broke into the discussion. 'So that means he could be anywhere? Undetected? Acting and being "normal"?'

Kate smiled at him. 'Yes, though fortunately not all psychopaths are sexually deviant. However, sexual deviant or not, they still cause problems wherever they are. Think about it,' she invited. 'If you're a non-sexual psychopath, where might you choose a job in which you're actively *encouraged* to be ruthless, selfish and arrogant?'

'Canary Wharf. House of Commons,' Bernie huffed.

'Wall Street,' added Joe.

Kate nodded. 'Those professional areas provide the ideal habitat for the regular kind of psychopath, who wants what he wants, wants it all, and whose take on life is "I, me, myself and I", just like the toddler, but no longer two feet tall. He favours sharp tailoring, and he has his hands on your pension and investments. "Snakes in suits", as one eminent researcher has named them.'

'You're saying they live their lives cheating other people and nobody catches on to what they're up to? All this conning and people fall for it?'

Kate shook her head. 'Not always, Bernie. The trick is to fit the con to the person, in order to be successful.'

She looked across the table. 'Julian's right. They can be found anywhere they can push their own agendas, bend the rules, make everybody else's life miserable. Everyone has experienced a psycho-path at some point, most often in the work environment.'

'Furman,' murmured Joe.

Kate studied the names on the glass screen. 'The *sexual* psychopath is a whole other problem,' she said softly. 'Because throughout the time he's masquerading as normal in terms of emotions and under-standing of social rules, he's gratifying his sexual deviance. Leaving a trail of destruction and traumatised families.'

Bernie shook his head, one thick index finger raised. 'Don't tell us he had problems in his childhood, Doc. That's what gets right on my ti— nerves. Nothing's nobody's fault no more. They've all got an "ism" or a disorder or seen something nasty in the woodshed when they was four.'

He felt Kate's eyes on him and folded his arms, jowls reddening. 'My family never had nothing when we was growing up, with all of us kids to look after. But *we* never cheated people or done cruel stuff.' He stopped, eyebrows slammed together. 'Any road up, just don't tell me it's not his fault, okay?'

'Wouldn't dream of it, Bernie,' said Kate gently.

Julian suddenly spoke. 'So . . . to catch him, would it help to try to think like him, Kate?'

'Dr Hanson to you, lad! Get that kettle on again. All this theory stuff's giving me the 'eadaches.'

Kate nodded at Julian's question. 'We could try. But, as I said earlier, I think our best chance is to study his behaviour, what he's actually done, *really* closely.'

Furman had appeared silently at the open door of UCU during this exchange. Ignoring him, Kate glanced at Bernie, who was now looking downcast, and guessed that the discussion about small children was the cause.

'How's your daughter Janice getting on, Bernie?'

'Expecting again. Number four. She's coming over with 'em this Christmas. It'll be hard for her, being on her own, but she said she don't care about that.'

Hearing this, Furman gave Bernie a contemptuous glance. Kate saw it.

'Janice has done really well, hasn't she, Bernie,' she said, now following her own agenda, an eye still on Furman.

Bernie nodded. 'Yeah. I'm very proud of her, as you know. I mean, I never had an education really. Adderley Street Mixed, then secondary modern. But our Janice went as far as she could.'

Kate observed more contempt from the half-listening Furman. What she knew and he didn't was that Bernie Watts's daughter had indeed gone as far as she could. To Oxford on a scholarship. Since then, she'd worked at Hamburg University of Technology, her partner also an academic there.

'Yep, she's a good girl. She liked it at Balliol. Still doing well for herself now. A lot of that was due to her mother's influence, while she was alive.' He fell silent.

Furman's facial expression had faltered as he tracked the exchanges more closely. Now he flicked a searching glance at each of them, seemed about to speak, gave a final glare and exited the room.

Watching him go, Julian turned on his senior colleagues, incensed. 'Oh great! Now he thinks we're winding him up! Man, I'm *history*.'

'What's up with you now, Devenish?'

'It's obvious! He was thinking your daughter was a real—' Julian reddened and fell silent.

Bernie lounged against his chair, looking across the room at him. 'Yeah? What did he think about my daughter? Spit it out.'

Julian turned on Bernie, hot-faced. 'You can bet he'd got the idea your daughter was a bit of a waste of space. Council flat, benefits and all that. Next thing he hears, you're going on about her being at Oxford . . . Oh, *forget* it!' Julian threw down his pen and subsided, lounging sulkily on his chair.

Joe looked across the room. 'You think we should save Furman-the-Idiot from himself, Jules?'

Julian shrugged, saying nothing, clearly still annoyed.

Bernie glanced at Julian, then at Kate. 'What's up with *him*?' Without waiting for a response, he asked, 'Any of our persons of interest bear even a *passing* resemblance to what you've said?'

She nodded very reluctantly. 'Cranham.'

'So some in-depth interviewing of him might show his real side?'

'Possibly,' said Kate, thinking of Cranham's arrogance and apparent low empathy. 'But a problematic personality isn't sufficient evidence, is it, no matter what he might say? I think it's best we don't make early assumptions about anybody or target the investigation too soon. We need to keep it wide-ranging and see if it leads us to facts that could become solid evidence.'

Kate looked at each of them, again pushing the argument she'd previously made. 'We need to explore the possibility of this same doer having an offence history prior to these murders. If he has, then as Joe said, it could be a prime source of information, which might move us forward. Living victims are also witnesses.'

She glanced across the room. 'Julian? Would you try again to search for unsolved rapes?'

Looking morose and clearly still nettled, Julian jabbed the keyboard.

Kate had something else on her mind. Janine's diary. She'd had no real opportunity to read it. Going to the security cupboard, she unlocked and opened it, took out the diary and began the task, as Julian moodily tapped computer keys.

Fifteen minutes later, Kate gave Joe an evaluative glance as he studied the printouts of Julian's search, then walked to the secure cupboard and placed the diary back inside. Regardless of what he'd said about its potential risk, she had made up her mind. When she got an opportunity later today, not only was she was going to read it thoroughly, she was also taking it home. She wanted another pair of eyes on it, and she had someone very specific in mind.

After giving ten minutes of her full attention to her copy of the printouts, Kate knew that there were just four unsolved cases of stranger-rape against females in the West Midlands in the five-year period prior to the murders of Janine Walker and Molly James that met the criteria she'd specified – age range: seventeen to twenty-one years; physical characteristics: tall, blonde; plus 'educated', as defined by college, university acceptance or actual attendance.

Joe looked to Julian and made a writing motion with his hand. Julian went to the glass screen and picked up a marker.

'Just list the names and dates, Jules, for quick reference,' Joe advised as he read them out. 'Four rape victims identified as Josie Kenton-Smith, attacked in February 1995; Amelie Dijon in June 1996; Suzie Luckman in April 1997; and Tracey Thomas in December 1997. That's three potential living witnesses for us. It says here that Tracey Thomas died in a road traffic accident in ninety-eight. Her boyfriend was subsequently convicted for dangerous driving.'

Kate nodded absently. Suddenly her head shot up. 'Wait a minute! I've seen a couple of those names already. Definitely the first one, Kenton-Smith.' She thought for a few seconds, then smacked the table with a palm. 'In the cold room. It was written on something inside the box in which I found Janine Walker's diary.'

Kate watched Julian as he wrote up the details, thinking that another trip to the evidence store was needed.

Why that particular box?

Surely it wasn't coincidental?

She thought about the difficulties UCU had had in locating adequate information on the two abduction cases so far. That wasn't usual, even allowing for one of them being more than a decade old.

Kate felt tired. She glanced at her watch and sighed, wishing she could go home. No chance of that. She had to be at the university later that afternoon.

172

CHAPTER THIRTY-THREE

Bernie had UCU's phone in one massive hand, listening to the voice in his ear. Julian's concentration was on the computer screen. Kate quickly crossed to the secure cupboard and removed Janine's diary. She returned to the table as Bernie said a few more words into the phone and ended the call, and Joe appeared through the door with a Caffè Nero carrier bag.

Kate watched Joe as he walked across the room and took the chair next to her. She described what they'd been doing since he'd left over an hour before. 'We've gone through as many boxes as we could for any actual statements made by Kenton-Smith, the French student and Suzie Luckman. We even included Tracey Thomas. Nothing.'

Joe nodded, offering her a Danish pastry from the blue carrier bag. She shook her head.

Bernie looked across the table at her. 'Don't worry, Doc. I couldn't find no phone numbers either, but Julian's done some digging in the computer files and got a couple for us. For Kenton-Smith and Luckman.'

Julian transferred his attention from the computer. 'There's a separate file for victims of crime that includes their private phone numbers, so I—'

'Sounds like the type of database that's confidential and needs clearance,' murmured Joe, passing the pastry bag to Bernie.

Grasping it, Bernie lowered his brows. 'You never told me *that* bit, Devenish!'

'I got around the password because *you* told me to do whatever I could to get hold of the numbers!'

Kate looked impatiently from one to the other. 'Oh, stop it, both of you. We need that information. Sometimes rules have to be . . . put to one side. Anyway, it's done now.'

'Careers guidance courtesy of the Doc, Devenish. Follow what she says and your career in the Force will be over before it's started,' muttered Bernie.

'Ignore that!' directed Kate, seeing the expression on Julian's face.

'So, what've we got?' asked Joe.

Bernie answered. 'We got two current numbers. One for Luckman's mother. No reply so far. The other one's for this Kenton-Smith. I just finished speaking to her sister. Kenton-Smith works in London. Comes back to Birmingham late on Fridays and stops with her sister until the following Tuesday morning. The sister lives in F-F-F-Far-Qua-Har Road, Edgbaston,' he enunciated in a plummy voice, eyebrows working.

'Toney real estate,' commented Joe, recalling the occasions on which he'd driven along that particular road, past impressively individual homes in spacious settings.

Kate watched as Bernie slurped coffee and demolished half a Danish with one bite, crumbs cascading onto his shirt.

'I've fixed up to have a chat with Kenton-Smith next Monday. Wish all our witnesses was as willing,' he said indistinctly.

Kate frowned at him. 'Bernie, *that* needs a female interviewer.'

The bulldog-with-a-gripe face was suddenly back. 'What you on about now? This woman's educated. Up for a chat. Her sister said so.'

'I'm coming with you,' Kate insisted. 'I ask the questions. Kenton-Smith is a victim of rape.'

Bernie looked ceilingwards. 'So what you're saying is, I can't show no empathy to females, right?' He glared at her. 'Look, Doc, what happened to her was – how long ago? Plus, the Force has had a lot of training over the years. I know what to say and what not to say. All this sisters-under-the-fur PC crap gets right on my t—'

'*I* go with you to see her! *I* do the talking.'

Bernie looked seriously aggrieved. 'No change there, then.'

Kate picked up her bag and turned to Julian. 'Can I give you a lift to the university?'

He looked up at her. 'Thanks, but I'm cycling.'

Nodding in response, she glanced briefly at Joe reading through the information on Kenton-Smith, and left UCU for her university tutorials.

*

Later, Julian was gazing around Kate's room at the university, taking in the leaded window and the floor-to-ceiling bookshelves, finally settling on the large carved desk she'd told him her PhD supervisor had given her when he retired.

Sitting in the elderly but comfortable armchair, he nodded as Kate held out a book, open at the reference she'd just found for him.

'I like this room,' he said, looking up as he took the book, then bowing his head over it.

Kate smiled. In some ways the tutor–student relationship between herself and Julian felt more natural here. At Rose Road, she often felt distracted by issues such as a wish to protect Julian from some of the grim realities of forensic work, alongside the need to treat him as just another colleague.

Without looking up again, he continued, 'It's calm. Like, you can be . . . peaceful here. You can think.'

Kate crossed to her desk and sat down. She waited, knowing he had something on his mind. She also knew that with Julian it worked best if she let him come to her.

'Kate? Do you think I could . . . that I can . . . make it here? I mean, get a job here in Birmingham after I graduate?'

She looked at the earnest young face. 'Julian, I think you could do pretty much anything you put your mind to, wherever you choose to go.'

He flushed and looked down at the book again.

A few minutes of further discussion and the tutorial was at an end. As Kate made notes on his study plan, Julian put textbooks into his backpack, thanked her and walked to the door, pausing before he left.

'Maisie was in our stats class last week, with two other kids from across the road. D'you know, one or two of the students in my year ask her to explain stuff to them? She's *really* sharp, Kate.'

Kate nodded. 'Yes, she is. Academically.'

Too sharp, sometimes.

And nowhere near as grown-up as she thinks she is.

CHAPTER THIRTY-FOUR

At Kate's house some hours later, Celia was well into her stride.

'. . . and the nun in the bath puts her hands to her chest and says to the man, "How *dare* you! You said you couldn't see!" and the man says, "No. I told you I was the blind man from the village . . ." Hang on! I'm not sure I got that right . . .'

Half lying on the sofa, wine glass in hand, Kate erupted with laughter as the tall, shapely woman relaxing in a nearby chair mock-frowned. She glanced at Kate with a grin. 'So what've you been up to recently?'

Their friendship had survived for many years and still flourished, despite their getting together monthly at the most, due to claims on their respective time. A major claim on Kate's was staying overnight with Chelsey, a plan Kate had agreed with Candice with some mis-givings. She hadn't yet fully explored with Maisie the small blue tablets she'd found in her bedroom.

'Up to my armpits in deviance. Teaching the theory, dah-de-dah. I've also just finished a report on a criminal case.'

'Spare me, please. When I phoned a few days ago, Maisie told me you're also working at Rose Road again.'

Kate confirmed with a nod.

'How's Ol' Blue Eyes?' Celia asked, raising one eyebrow.

Kate laughed again. 'He's very well.'

'I just bet he is!'

Kate shook her head. 'Cee, the only thing you missed out there was a *phwoar*.'

Her friend grinned. 'Actually, he's extremely high on my f-list—'

'*Cee!*'

'I meant f as in *phwoar*,' she said innocently.

Kate gave her a sideways look as she sipped her wine. 'Course you did.'

'Well, he does put me in mind of Jeff Bridges the younger. And he's back! When you were thinking he might not be.'

'There was a rumour at Rose Road that he was thinking of staying put in Boston. Now he's back here for one more year.' Kate took a sip of wine. 'Anyway . . .' She lapsed into silence.

'Anyway what?'

Kate shrugged her shoulders. 'Nothing. Here for another year. We're working together again. End of story.'

'Kate, I'm three months older than you. *That* means I've got a lot more sense. I'm *telling* you, when I met him here at your Christmas get-together last year, I could see he was smit.'

'We're friends and colleagues, Cee, and "smit" is *not* a word.'

'Pedant.' Celia sipped her wine, eking out the one glass because she was driving. She glanced briefly at Kate, gauging her receptivity.

'*What?*' demanded Kate.

Celia put down her glass and gazed at her. 'A word to the wise, Kate. I think this work you do is too sad, too sombre for you.'

'It's what I'm trained for, Celia,' protested Kate, as she struggled to sitting and helped herself to more wine. 'And what d'you mean, "for me"? *Nobody* likes it. Actually, that's not strictly true. I do love deviance, and – don't look at me like that. If the expertise I have can be helpful, I have to do it, Celia. If I don't try and nobody else does either, it means that victims and their families never get to see an end to what's happened to them.'

'I know, I know. But it doesn't *have* to be you, does it? When did you become Ms Indispensable Crusader? Leave the police and the rest of the justice system to get on with it. It often works out in the long run, you know. If *nobody* cared, then UCU wouldn't exist, would it? See?' she ended, pointing at Kate, triumphant. 'That proves there are a lot of people in the system besides you who want to see justice done.'

Kate leaned back on the sofa cushion. 'The system doesn't look out for the victims of crimes, the families. Its initial focus is on identifying whoever did whatever was done. Then all the energy and money is focused on proving it. Somewhere along the line victims and families get left out of the equation. You're right. There are people who care. But, like me, they struggle against the system.'

She lay back on the sofa, then squirmed to look at her friend.

'Did you know, Bernie Watts has been regularly visiting three families for years in his own time? The investigations he and they were part of never got as far as an arrest. So he goes to see them, tells them about any new developments, or just listens.' She settled back against the cushion. 'Don't let on to him that you know.'

'I won't, but my concern right now is *you*. Your life. You had a rough time with Flaky Kevin.'

Kate squirmed again, shooting a suspicious look at her friend.

'It's a quote from Blue Eyes,' confessed Celia.

'Joe spoke to you? About me?'

'Calm down. He said it at that Christmas do. He's right. Flaky is exactly what Kevin is. About as trustworthy and reliable as a box of foxes. Look –' Celia sat forward as Kate frowned – 'I've been wanting to say this to you for ages. Don't let one bad experience stop you finding a new relationship. You bury yourself in work—'

'Work never let me down, Celia,' said Kate quietly.

'But parts of what you do aren't pleasant, are they? And, well, I think it keeps another negative memory alive,' she finished quietly.

The room fell silent for a few seconds.

'We both know why you probably chose forensics – crime – as a line of work.'

Kate looked at Celia, then sat up, placing her glass carefully on the low table nearby. It had never, ever been mentioned between them in all the years since it happened. When they were much younger, they didn't have the words. Since then, there hadn't been the motivation.

'It isn't because of *that*, Celia. I'm not sure it figures at all.'

'Oh, come off it, Kate!' Celia looked irritated. 'You're a psychologist! It *has* to be a part of it. Yes, I know. You're doing what you see as the right thing. The point I'm making is, the focus on police work, the contact with people who are in such tragic situations, plus the ones who've done awful things – does that do *you* any good? Or does it maybe subconsciously keep the old memory alive. You – we – got lucky as a child. That doesn't make you *anybody's* protector and avenger.'

She glanced at her friend's face, before carefully expressing her next thought. 'Kate, you weren't to blame for what happened. You don't have to work yourself into the ground now to prove you're a "good girl", because you believe you did something wrong by going to him.

I don't feel guilty because I didn't stop you. We were *six*, for God's sake.'

Kate shook her head. 'It doesn't figure in my work choice, Cee, and I hardly ever think about it. Much. It's a back-of-the-head thing. It's not –' she pointed a finger at her own forehead – 'up front.'

'Okay,' sighed Celia. 'Have it your own way.'

Kate knew that what she had just said to her friend was not the absolute truth. What had happened when they were children had contributed to what she was.

An overachiever with a need to be in control, according to Kevin.

All those years ago, innocence had put both of them in severe danger. The second time they saw the man's face, he was featured in an item of television news. He'd murdered four little girls in Surrey. Close to where Kate and Celia grew up.

Kate was on her feet, looking down at her friend.

'Celia? I've got something from UCU I need help with. Will you take a look?'

Her friend nodded, looking resigned, and followed Kate in the direction of the kitchen.

Reaching the table, Kate dug into her bag and brought out the small red volume. They stood side by side, leaning against the granite, Kate looking up at Celia, her facial expression earnest.

'This diary belonged to one of the victims in our case.'

'The case that's just been on the news? The digging near the bypass?'

'Yes. I'd like you to look at some of the comments written in it so I can check if my thinking is on track, or way off.'

'How does the Dynamic Duo respond to your ideas on cases?'

'Joe listens to the theory I offer and considers it. Bernie struggles. His first response is to question the sanity of people who do things like this. He thinks they're maniacs.'

'I can almost see where he's coming from.'

They sat at the kitchen table, Celia with a small shake of her head.

'Here I am trying to advise you against the work you're doing and I end up aiding and abetting . . .' She glanced at Kate, who was leafing through the small volume, not listening, and sighed. 'Okay. Let's have it.'

Kate pointed to a section in Janine Walker's diary for March.

'See here? She's written, "There again today. V. nice. Soph." – that *must* mean sophisticated. What do you think?'

Celia shrugged. 'Sounds plausible.'

'And she goes on: "Raised his cup to me."' Kate looked at her friend. 'What do you think of that?' There was a small silence. 'Go on, Cee! Give me your impressions.'

Celia frowned, studying the words in the diary, then looked at Kate. 'Impressions? Of him? The situation? It's not much to go on, is it?' She shook her head. 'Okay, let's see. Mmm . . . this girl – well, she's met somebody, a man obviously, in a . . . a restaurant! Or maybe a coffee place. And he's way older than her – because of the cup-raising and being sophisticated. And she doesn't know him. Did I say "met"? No, no. He's a stranger, but they've kind of started noticing each other.'

'That's *exactly* what I was thinking,' said Kate, with a vigorous nod, flipping pages and pointing at another entry. 'Now, look at this. A month later she's written, "Coming to Sheffield when he finishes his sec.tr. course. Wishes we met in Feb. So sweet."'

Celia gazed intently for some seconds at the entry to which Kate was pointing. 'No. I don't have a clue why Sheffield is relevant.'

'Sorry, Cee. This young woman was planning to go to uni there.'

With a frown at her friend, Celia examined the diary entry some more. 'Right. Finished his what course? He's a student as well? Rats!' She'd recalled what she'd said about the man's age a moment earlier. 'Okay, how about he's a *mature* student? "Wishes . . . met . . . so sweet" – I don't have a clue about that. Something *he* wishes? What's special about February, when they hadn't even met?' Celia paused. 'Hang on. She's young, you said? February . . . what goes on in February . . . nothing. A lull after Christmas . . . Hang on! How about she's referring to Valentine's Day? No, no. *He* was the one doing the wishing.' Another pause. 'Ah-ha! How about he took a trip that month, and once they actually began the social stuff, he was telling her about it, and said something like, "Oh, it would've been great if we had gone together, the view from my *room* was lovely", you know how men do – a chat-up line, to get sex into the conversation. What else?'

Kate flipped a few pages. To the end of July. 'See here? She says, "I'm glad he told me about seeing me."' She pointed out the line to Celia.

Celia gazed at it, chin on hand. 'Mmm. He's told her he saw her . . . So what?'

A couple of seconds slipped by, then Celia looked at Kate, suddenly excited.

'Hey! At the beginning – he saw her way before she saw him? He was fancying her from afar. Maybe he thought he had no chance? Because he was older! Yes, that would do it. He's about . . . say, in his forties, and he's seen her somewhere before, in this restaurant or coffee place, and he thinks, "Oh, she's good-looking but she won't look at me, be interested in me. I'm old enough to be her father—" *Damn* it!'

'What?'

'I've already said he's a student . . .'

'Mature?' prompted Kate.

Celia lightly tapped her own forehead with a finger, glancing at Kate.

'You do this kind of thing very often? It's driving me nuts already.' She took the diary from Kate and leafed pages. After a few more seconds' consideration, 'Nope. That's the best I can do. He's older. Sophisticated. A man of the world *and* a student. He saw her before she saw him, fancied her from a distance and then they met and she likes him. A *lot*. And he wishes they'd met before February. He wanted to get into her pants, if you ask me.'

'Thanks, Cee. You've confirmed what I was thinking about a lot of it. Other bits I'm not certain about either.'

Kate took the diary from Celia and held it, running the fingers of one hand lightly over the smooth cover. 'I know it's all relevant, but I'm not sure how . . .' she said quietly.

After a moment's silence, she opened the diary again. 'Any ideas about the sec.tr. course?' She pointed to a place in the written text.

Her friend looked at her, shaking her head. 'You just *never* give up, do you?'

'No,' said Kate seriously.

Sighing, Celia looked at the words in the diary. 'It could mean anything! Secretarial . . . no, that's stupid . . .' She suddenly looked up at Kate, face animated. 'Hey-hey! *Secret*? How about he told her he was doing some kind of secret training! Ha! Now then!' She rubbed her hands together, grinning. 'Ho, *yes*! That would keep her from mentioning him to Mummy and Daddy. Or anybody else.'

It was almost eleven o'clock. Celia had gone home. Kate stared out of the kitchen's extensive windows into the dark garden beyond. If Janine Walker had been the kind of young woman Kate thought she was, the doer would have needed to convey significant credibility to convince her of anything. Especially anything about 'secret training'. An older male, or even one who merely presented as mature, would probably have the ability to do that, Kate mused.

Especially if he was an educated, professional person . . .

She glanced at the diary lying on the table, then out to the garden again. She recalled the books in the chest in Janine's room. What had Mrs Walker said Janine wanted to do? Work for the UN. Janine was a savvy young woman with an interest in international politics. And this man she'd met told her he was engaged in some kind of secret training?

Tell someone something that's unbelievable and they don't believe it.

Tell someone something unbelievable about something they're already interested in . . .

Like the financial con man in America who told wealthy, intelligent people he could multiply many times the significant money they already had. A too-good-to-be true pledge that sent some of them to penury.

All part of the con.

Kate walked across the kitchen, turning out lights. She continued into the hall and upstairs, deep in thought.

What did Janine want? A boyfriend with political affiliations and involvement?

What about Molly?

She reached her bathroom, deciding on a bath. Quicker. No hair-drying. She looked into the large wall mirror at her own reflection.

She knew what Molly wanted.

To earn a little money.

CHAPTER THIRTY-FIVE

The car sped smoothly through the darkness along the dual carriageway, heading out of the city. Pushing to seventy, he overtook a clutch of vehicles, then remembered that the stretch of road was a hotspot for cameras. He slowed to forty. Impossible to move these days without coming up against rules, regulations and officious police.

He glanced in the rear-view mirror, briefly looking at his own eyes. They felt bad and looked worse. Like he hadn't slept in days, which was true. Anger heated his face. Until the last couple of weeks, his had been an orderly existence, centred around his work. Mostly. There had been some unorthodox actions, but only very occasionally. When the need wouldn't be denied. It was how he'd stayed under the radar. By being patient, avoiding regularity. Resisting the need. Until he could contain it no longer. *That* was control.

During these last few days, he'd begun to feel his control over the situation slipping. Yes, he'd had this one in his sights, and another, whom he'd named 'Latte Girl'. Each progressing nicely and at a pace that suited him.

A surge of anger made his face tighten and his jaw muscles bunch as he thought of the constant voices that had recently started up. Despite the inane chatter, he'd held it together at work, although he didn't know how he'd managed it. He seethed. It was their fault that he was here now. Had to be here. When the stupid, prattling, *vapid* voices had first started up, he'd ignored them. But they'd persisted. Forcing him to relive what he'd done years ago, making him run the action in his head, plummeting him into a vortex. Memories. Hunger. Now they were forcing *this* urgency on to him. This wasn't his choice. It was *their* responsibility that he was here.

Cooling his internal raging, he purposely relaxed his grip on the steering wheel, the passing lights reflecting from the ring on the third finger of his left hand. He breathed deeply, eyes on the road. He had to calm down. Angst and compulsion led to mistakes. Anyone who'd read anything knew that. He began to reason with himself. Maybe it *was* time? He knew her quite well already. He frowned. But it should be his decision when to act.

His thoughts drifted to the previous evening, when he'd got the things out of the backpack, buried his face in the clothes. Then he'd traced his fingers gently across smooth leather, feeling the little bumps made by the coins still inside. Maybe it *was* his decision. He was ready for her. He knew her well enough.

The car sped on, and the uneven tarmac started up a quickening rhythm in his head, *too-soon, too-soon, t'soon-t'soon-t'soon*, sending his anxiety spiralling once more, causing his jaw muscles to ache. Summoning control, he reduced his speed and the car went smoothly onwards along the wide road.

Fifteen minutes later, he pulled into a space near an unlit building. Switching off the ignition, he glanced around, careful to keep his face in shadow. Still quiet. He peered at his watch. Nearly midnight.

Opening the glove compartment, he took out two items. One he tossed on to the dashboard. The other he unscrewed, then tilted back his head and blinked. Better. His eyes had felt like coals all day. He checked in the mirror again, then threw the little bottle into the glove compartment, slammed it shut and settled to wait.

Within half an hour, the wide rear exit door of the club swung open. After a minute or two he saw her, with a gaggle of other young females. Her Thursday night out with her work colleagues. He'd learned this from the information he'd gathered about her during the last two weeks. They went clubbing on a Thursday night because some of the gaggle had dim boyfriends whom they saw on Fridays. See? He *did* know her.

He smiled slightly, sitting well back in the driving seat, watching, head on one side, as the young women kissed and hugged each other. What *was* that about? He'd learned to do stuff like that over the years. By copying. Watching himself in the mirror: *Oh, how terrible! Oh, I am so sorry. Of course I love you, you bitch*. He was good at it now. But it was still a mystery. His lips curled again as he watched. Probably loathed each other in reality. Probably trying to get one over on each other any way they could.

He watched as she separated from the crowd and approached the kerb. Now she was scanning the street. He cautioned himself not to move too soon. After a minute of scanning during which he'd observed that she was becoming anxious, he edged the car forward slightly, although he knew there were no CCTV cameras at the rear of the building.

Here, kitty-kitty . . .

She'd noticed the movement of his car and began walking uncertainly in his direction. He activated the passenger window and waited as she bent slightly to look at him. He pressed his head back into shadow as the young, diffident voice floated inside.

'Excuse me. Are you a taxi?'

He hadn't had to work for it. He was almost disappointed. She had given him his role and he was more than happy to take it.

'Where d'you want to go?' he asked, adjusting his voice, adding 'love' to give his words authenticity.

'The train station. How much?'

He watched her face keenly as he suggested a very modest sum. She looked pleased and turned to her friends some distance away, to wave and call good night and see-you-in-the-morning. None of them appeared to take any interest in him or his car. It wouldn't have troubled him if they had. He doubted their ability to give a useful description in the poor light.

The girl climbed into the back of his car and he pulled smoothly into the flow of late-night traffic, watching her in the rear-view mirror. She looked in the mirror and their eyes met. She looked away. Silence. He resumed his covert watching. He was now confident in his decision to bring it forward to tonight. He'd never attracted any suspicion. There'd never been a useful witness, and as for the police – halfwits, most of them.

He checked the road in front, then glanced at her again. She'd put herself where she was now. In his car. She was responsible for what was going to happen to her. She had created the situation. Irrefutable logic. Her fault.

The girl leaned back in the rear seat, tired from her evening of dancing and drinking. Not too much drinking. A lot of dancing. She knew she couldn't have walked to the station in these shoes. She turned her head to one side and stroked the seat's smooth surface. Leather. A bit special for a—

'Nice evening?' His voice startled her and she lifted her head.

'What?'

He experienced a quick stab of irritation. He'd expected her to be different. Didn't any of them have even basic social graces? 'I was asking if you had had a pleasant evening's entertainment.' He enunciated each of the words, but she didn't pick up the sarcasm.

'Oh, yeah . . . thanks.'

Again she met his eyes in the mirror and immediately glanced away, gazing uneasily at the shops, restaurants and pubs speeding past.

'Have *you* been busy tonight?' she asked, wanting to fill the silence, her voice small inside the car. Her glance drifted around its interior again.

'Not so bad. Not half as busy as I will be later on, hopefully.' He was warming to his role. 'Then it's home to . . . the wife . . . and kids, cup of tea and bed.' He watched her in the mirror to see the impact of what he'd said. He saw her face relax.

'I thought you had children,' she responded with a small nod.

He looked at her with feigned surprise. 'You clairvoyant, love?' He smiled into the mirror. Nice touch! He *was* good at this.

'Oh, no,' she said seriously. 'The little toy you've got there.'

His gaze shifted to the dashboard. She saw his eyes crease at the corners as she settled back, relaxing into the soft leather. The car rolled forward almost silently into the darkness, towards its destination. He glanced at his watch, then down, to the holdall in the footwell of the passenger seat. His 'apparatus'.

'Clever girl,' he murmured.

Out of her line of vision, the corners of his mouth curled downwards as he continued to look at her, softly breathing a single word, his lips barely moving:

'*Gotchaaaahhh.*'

CHAPTER THIRTY-SIX

Joe arrived at Kate's house on Friday morning, casual in white short sleeves and black jeans, biker-style boots replacing the brown Fryes. After being allowed inside by a silently judgemental Phyllis, he found Kate in the kitchen with Maisie. They were both still in pyjamas.

Maisie was at the table, frowning into her cereal bowl. Joe looked from her to Kate, omitting his usual greetings. Pushing the bowl away, Maisie left the table and the kitchen without a word.

Joe waited. Kate sighed, eyes on Maisie as she disappeared upstairs. 'Kevin had offered to have her for a sleepover this weekend. He called half an hour ago to say he can't.'

'Ah,' said Joe quietly.

She sat, leaning on her forearms, still looking in the direction in which Maisie had disappeared. Compassion for her daughter was part of how Kate felt. The other part was sharp disappointment with Kevin, even after years of experiencing his self-interest and mercurial commitment. She bowed her head, running her fingers through her hair. When Joe didn't comment, she glanced up at his face.

'What's wrong?'

He sat opposite her. 'Rose Road's received a report. A young woman is missing,' he said.

Kate stared at him. 'What? You mean, a local girl like . . . our cases?'

He nodded briefly, looking directly at her. 'She bears similarities to Molly and Janine. Her age . . . hair colour. Her name's Jody Westbrooke.'

Kate was bolt upright. '*When?*' she asked, eyes rounded.

'Her mother reported her missing in the early hours of this morning. She'd waited up for her. She didn't return home from a night out.'

Kate stared at him, hand pressed to her mouth. Then, 'So what's happening at Rose Road? Who's involved? Do we—'

'Gander's asked me to brief Upstairs about our cases, because of the similar physical characteristics. He wants them on to it from the start if there is a connection. But Jody Westbrooke isn't ours; it's an Upstairs case. When I do meet with them, I'll hear what they have to say about her disappearance and we can discuss it in UCU. Now, go get dressed and I'll give you and Maisie a lift. You can tell me what you found in Janine Walker's diary after you brought it home last night.'

She glanced at him as she walked to the door. 'How did you know?'

He smiled briefly at her. 'I know *you*, Hanson.'

'Give me ten minutes to organise Maisie. Help yourself to coffee.'

Following Maisie being dropped at school, Kate forced her thoughts away from domestic worries. She briefly outlined what the diary had yielded, then looked at the changing scene beyond the car's window.

'Why are we taking the back way into Rose Road?'

'To avoid the media. It's now a scrum.'

The media. Kate bit her lip. Local and national attention. She thought of the prior rape cases they'd identified and which she suspected were a precursor to the abductions. Incidents separated by months and years. She went back to biting her lip. And now this young woman. Was it him? Was he back?

Inside UCU, Bernie and Julian were drinking coffee. The blinds were drawn.

'A bit early in the day to block out the sun,' Kate pointed out.

'Some smart-arse has told 'em this is UCU. We've had one joker put a camera to the window, just as I was lookin' out.'

'What a photograph that'll be,' murmured Kate as she helped herself to tea, then opened each of the rape evidence boxes, glancing at Julian, who was listlessly tapping computer keys.

'How's it going, Jules?' Joe asked as he passed him.

Julian shrugged a thin shoulder. Joe backed up, giving the youth a closer look.

'Hey, buddy, you okay? Work not getting too much?'

Julian shook his head. 'I still need more notes on visits made and interviews done so I can enter the information and analyse it for anomalies. Furman keeps asking me for it. He forgets I'm only here part—'

The door of UCU opened and Harry appeared, Matt Prentiss behind him.

'Julian, I'm on leave from midday, so you're with Matt this afternoon. He's going to demo grid-laying of a site, okay?'

Prentiss looked at Julian. 'Three o'clock. *Don't* be late. I'm gone at four.'

Julian nodded, and Harry and Prentiss disappeared as the door closed.

Kate studied Julian over her cup. Was his recent moodiness connected to Matt Prentiss? She felt defeated. Problems at home, problems with their cases, and she still hadn't tackled Julian on the issue of his experience of Prentiss. *Some supervisor you're turning out to be, Hanson.* She massaged her face with both hands. Why were the young always a concern? Even when they didn't belong to you.

The phone rang and Bernie snatched it up. 'Yes. Oh . . . hello.'

Kate caught the change in tone and eyed him as he smoothed his hair. Dollars to doughnuts it was Connie calling. She listened.

'Mmm . . . You don't say. Bl— Well, well. Has he now!' After a final pleasantry, Bernie replaced the phone.

'What's Connie have to say?' asked Kate. He gave her a sideways look as he and Joe headed for the window.

'Media's here with reinforcements. They've heard about the latest girl. Connie says Igor's just told her that Furman's outside, giving them the benefit of his views.'

'Which are?' asked Kate, getting up.

'According to Igor, despite last night's development, he's all but denying there's a repeater, but if it turns out to be one, although he doubts it, he can reassure the public, blah, everything will be done, et cetera, et cetera, until the person responsible is arrested as quickly as possible. Furman, as usual, hedging his bets.'

Kate joined them at the window. 'And fortunately for him, the public will have forgotten his reassurances by the time the worst, as he sees it, comes to pass.'

'What's that? More victims?' asked Julian.

'No, lad. To Furman, the worst always involves *finance*. More money having to be spent. Longer he waits, holds off from acknowledging the true situation and avoids launching a full-scale investigation, the more money he saves. That's the way the Arse thinks and operates.'

They watched from between the blinds as Furman, in a pale grey suit none of them had seen before, faced the cameras, head nodding.

Kate frowned. 'If I didn't know any better, I'd say—'

Bernie interrupted. 'The bastard's had his hair blow-dried!'

CHAPTER THIRTY-SEVEN

He was sitting on the floor in the day's failing light, eyes riveted, hand against his mouth, willing his breathing to settle. She was lying senseless on the other side of the workshop.

When he'd first seen it he'd lost all control. She was still in his car at that stage, gabbling, wanting her mother, wanting her dad, her sister, her best friend, *oh boo-bloody-hoo!* There she'd been, scrabbling for her phone, and as he tried to drag her out of the car, she'd kicked him. That was when he saw *them*.

The shoes.

To match the streetwalker's bag.

He hadn't noticed them in the artificial light outside the club. How could she do it? How could she ruin it?

What was worse, without the high heels, she was—

He'd felt as though he was suffocating, his chest gripped in iron bands, worried for just a second that he was having a heart attack. He'd told her, his face apoplectic, eyes congested, mouth wide, lips drawn back in a feral scream of rage an inch from hers, how disgusting she was.

She'd become hysterical as he raged. Then she'd fought him. Like an alley cat. Until he grabbed her by the neck and smashed her face with his fist. She hadn't marked him, though. Just as well. He wouldn't have been able to go to work.

He gazed at her some more, his voice a hoarse whisper.

'Hey. *Hey*, you. *Slut*. What's the matter with you? Wake up. I've got a surprise for you.'

Filled with resentment, he glared at the unconscious figure. This was a lesson. For *him*. He'd learned the hard way. Because he'd rushed it. Allowed the pressure he was under to put him in that place where he *had* to do it. The incessant voices had kept reminding him, *reminding* him, so he couldn't think straight until he did it again. Well, here endeth the lesson. He needed to watch for as long as it took, to make sure they measured up. That they really were . . . her.

As he stared at her, at the soiled, torn trousers, the matted hair, his thoughts drifted. To a film he'd watched years before. Not *a* film. *The* film. When was that? He gazed upwards, calculating the years. Nineteen eighty-one. He was ten years old. He'd watched it with *her*, squashed against her in the semi-darkness, her heavy scent filling his head. The film was called . . . Get it right. Ah, yes. *The Collector*.

It was an old film then. About this man who collected butterflies. He tutted to himself. How stupid was that? Why collect stuff most people stamp on? But that was what the man did. And then he captured this woman – *she* had red hair – and he put her in his cellar. Not for sex. No, no. To own and explore her beauty. But then, gradually, he noticed that she didn't look so good, because of being locked in the cellar. So he had to get another one that looked as good as she once did.

He gazed across the room, shaking his head at the senseless girl lying on the concrete. That man was the only person in his entire life he had ever truly understood. Except for the butterflies.

He looked at her again. This one wasn't looking so good now.

He needed another.

CHAPTER THIRTY-EIGHT

Joe was gone, to give firearms training. Julian was busy with visit and interview notes he'd been given by Bernie. Kate had had to translate the shorthand in her notebook for him so he could include the information she'd amassed.

All was outwardly quiet in UCU when Whittaker entered and smacked down some internal post. Without a word he powered back whence he came.

Bernie watched him go with a shake of his head. 'He'll never stay the course, that one, y'know. Too keen by half. Hyper. He'll self-destruct. What's he brought us?'

He reached for the envelope and there followed a few seconds of silence.

'Would you bloody credit it! Human bleeding Resources. They're fixing for me to have some health tests. What the— Blood pressure? Cholesterol? Weight check?' He looked at Kate. 'I get it. You know who's behind this, don't you?' Kate knew she wasn't expected to respond. 'Right! I'm going up there to tell 'em what they can do with their—'

The door hit the wall.

Kate absently watched him go. She had examined the meagre details relating to the rape victims, but her mind kept returning to Jody Westbrooke, the missing girl.

To distract herself, she went back to the rapes. UCU needed to talk to each of the victims if possible. But for Kate, mindful of the remains yielded by the bypass site, one of them stood out.

Suzie Luckman. Blonde hair, blue eyes, five foot ten. Connie had told them that the femur found near Janine's skeleton was from a tall female. Kate's thoughts drifted to the three missing young women the PNC search had yielded. None of them was described as so tall.

The pathologist had also said she would take a DNA sample from the femur, but in the absence of any pre-existing indicators to its identity there was little more that could be done at this stage.

Kate studied Suzie's details, which indicated that she had moved to London several years ago. Where was she now? How could they establish if she was still alive? A treacherous idea sidled into her head about personal privacy. But it was the only way she could think of to determine Suzie Luckman's current whereabouts.

She massaged her temples with her fingers, then sat, hand against her mouth, heartbeat up. As she often did when faced with the clamour of opposing plans, she began playing devil's advocate.

One of the reasons Julian was in UCU at all was because of his past form. The hacking. He was currently under Kate's direct supervision.

And now you're contemplating asking him to do something he shouldn't.

It has to be done.

But it's something similar to what he's done before, and for which he's already been in trouble.

There's no other way to get the information. We need it. Now.

If you ask him to do this, you're absolutely in the wrong – as his supervisor, colleague . . . friend.

Three young women have already died.

This could jeopardise Julian's whole future.

There are three young women who don't have futures at all.

You might be wrong. Suzie Luckman is probably alive and well. In London.

What if she isn't? What if he's still operating?

Jody Westbrooke?

Kate shook her head at the implications of what she was considering.

'Kate . . . ?'

Julian's troubled voice slipped into her consciousness and she realised she'd been gazing at him. She refocused, taking in the anxious young face, the thin shoulders.

Needs must. A case of 'the greater good'.

According to you.

The voice inside Kate's head was oddly reminiscent of her ex-husband.

'Julian? Are you busy?'

He stopped word-processing and glanced back at her. 'I've got half an hour before I go and see Matt.'

Kate phrased her query carefully. 'If I wanted to establish the whereabouts of a person living, say, in London, how would I go about it?'

He gazed moodily at her, but said nothing.

She paused. 'I was wondering about, for example, credit-card activity. People who are alive have to spend money, yes? That kind of information could help us to establish their location.'

And prove Suzie Luckman is alive. Or dead.

She watched as a deep frown settled on the youthful face. She stood and walked over to sit beside him.

'Julian, I'd like you show *me* how to get into the database for credit-card activity with just a name and a date of birth.'

He looked nervous. 'That's way beyond my clearance level.'

Kate was reluctant to use any persuasion that might appear manipulative. Her internal argument continued.

What I'm about to say to him is what I truly believe.

Enough.

Kate gave him a level look, ready to deliver facts. 'Julian, we already have three murdered young women. There are probably more waiting to be found. He has to be stopped. To do that we have to move UCU's investigation forward. I want you to tell me how to do what I've suggested. It will be *my* responsibility. Nobody will ever know from me that you had any involvement at all.'

After a brief pause he pointed to the relevant keys, giving simple instructions for Kate to follow.

Twenty minutes later, she was considering the information she'd found. Details of numerous credit-card transactions for one particular young woman in London in the late nineties, involving supermarkets and other providers of basic needs. And lastly, two for 2003, including a shop where a purchase of clothing was made. Nothing since.

Waiting until Bernie and then Joe returned, she spoke to both of them.

'Are you two ready for some news?'

Catching her tone, they stood looking at her.

'Connie told us that the femur belonged to a tall female, five-ten, yes?' Kate said. 'Guess who used her credit card in September 2003 at the Oxford Street branch of Long Tall Sally 'but never again, any-where, ever?'

Without waiting for a response, she answered her own question. 'One of the young women on our list of rape victims. Suzie Luckman.'

There was an air of tension inside UCU. The kind that comes from the beginnings of progress. All four colleagues were aware of it.

Sitting on the table was a pile of emails and their attachments. Information from the investigation of the 2003 disappearance of Suzanne Rachel Luckman, investigated by the Metropolitan Police at the time.

Joe looked up from what he was reading. 'According to this, she was in Birmingham the weekend before she was reported missing. Visiting her mom.'

Julian looked a question at Kate. 'So she went back to London and was then abducted and murdered, like these other girls?'

'*Think* about it, lad. The bypass remains,' said Bernie.

Kate nodded. 'Suzie was buried less than six miles from here. She never returned to London.'

Joe leaned towards Kate, pointing at one of the email attachments. 'Yet according to this, officers from the Met visited her London flat on the Wednesday following her being reported missing by her employer the previous Monday. Suzie's weekend case was found inside, which was taken as proof that she *had* returned. Plus, the neighbour in the flat beneath Suzie's said she heard her moving around in the late evening of the Sunday and early hours of Monday.'

Kate took the email from Joe. 'It doesn't make any sense that he would follow her to London, kill her, then transport her body back here. To the bypass.'

Julian's brows climbed. 'So what about her stuff? In the flat? Maybe the femur isn't hers?'

'So . . . where *is* Suzie Luckman?'

The ensuing silence was broken by Joe. 'How about this, Kate?' She looked at the email paragraph to which he was pointing. 'Says here, the same neighbour told Met officers she *saw* Suzie that Monday morning.'

They sat in silence as Julian quickly gathered his belongings.

Kate was busy thinking. 'How soon after the investigation into

Suzie's disappearance began were the neighbours talked to by the police?' she asked.

Joe read through the email. 'Wednesday was the day of their first visit to her flat . . . Friday they talked to the neighbours.'

Kate stood suddenly and began pulling together the emailed information. 'There's the answer. The neighbour was mistaken.'

Bernie stared at her. 'How can you be confident of that?'

'Because of the way memory works. Specific events in a life are encoded firmly in our memories because they are special. Daily events aren't – that neighbour had probably seen Suzie countless times prior to that weekend. That's the problem with autobiographical recall. We're not efficient at separating one memory of an often-occurring general event from another. It's likely that the neighbour was confusing her stated sighting of Suzie that weekend with another.'

'That's disposed of that witness, then,' said Bernie drily. 'You ever stop to think you might be wrong, Doc?'

'Only very occasionally,' said Kate truthfully, sliding the emails into their folder. 'I think the rapes, including that of Suzie Luckman, were perpetrated by our doer prior to his turning to murder.' She walked to the glass screen and picked up the marker.

'Suzie Luckman's path crossed that of her rapist twice. Here. In Birmingham.' She wrote on the glass, then stopped. 'How unlucky can one person be?' she mused quietly, shaking her head. 'But, if my thinking is right, how did he know whereabouts in London Suzie lived?' She moved away from the screen to sit on the edge of the table. 'By the time of that second encounter . . .'

'He'd graduated,' finished Joe.

CHAPTER THIRTY-NINE

Josie Kenton-Smith, one of UCU's identified rape victims, was sitting on a comfortable sofa in the parquet-floored sitting room, sorting paperwork, when her sister showed Kate and Bernie into the room. She put the sheets to one side and stood as they entered, looking eagerly from one to the other as they shook hands.

'I can't tell you how pleased I am that the police are taking a second look at my case. Please, sit down. Ask me anything.'

Kate took a quick once-over glance at Josie. Well into her thirties now, with smooth blonde hair bobbed to shoulder-length, casually but expensively dressed. Cashmere. Fine gold necklace. Very subtle. She looked what she probably was. A woman of some substance. A professional woman. And no one's victim. Kate wondered if this was how Molly and Janine would look now. If they'd lived.

Bernie was nodding at Josie's words, a 'told you' look on his face as he glanced at Kate. She ignored him, her attention on the other woman.

'I can remember some details, but there's lots of gaps. Mostly gaps, I'm afraid.'

Bernie smiled at her. 'Don't worry about it, love. You just tell us whatever you can. All of us can only do our best, can't we?'

Kate was already on a slow simmer. At least it wasn't 'bab'. She smiled encouragingly at Josie. 'We're grateful for any details you can remember.'

'He drugged me,' she said.

Kate's mood nose-dived. 'Just tell us whatever you do recall.'

Josie straightened and looked away from them, tugging the expensive-looking cream cardigan closer to her body.

'Okay . . . It was a cold night, about nine p.m. I'd worked late and I was waiting for a taxi outside my office in Bennett's Hill. That's where

I was working at the time. It was a Tuesday. Not too many people about. I suppose whoever was in town for the evening would already have been in a pub or restaurant by then. Anyway, while I was waiting, a light-coloured car pulled up and double-parked. I remember thinking he would get into trouble. The next thing is I'm inside a car and it's moving. I must have been in shock. I don't *know* that it was the same car but I believe it was. Because the two things happened so quickly.'

She shook her head, lost in the time she was describing. Kate noticed that as she refocused, she sought eye contact with Bernie, as she did whenever she became hesitant.

'Take your time, bab,' he encouraged.

'What happened then? Do you remember anything about him, any details about the inside of the car?' Kate prompted, annoyed with herself for asking several questions at once and silently blaming Bernie.

The other woman nodded.

'I'd say it was an expensive car, you know; the engine was quiet, the doors made that solid sound when they closed . . . and the seat felt cold. I'm sure it was leather . . . That's all I can tell you about it. I don't really have a clue how long he drove. I can't tell you much about him. He'd already put something over my face, so I couldn't see. I was *so* frightened.'

Kate glanced at Bernie as Josie fell silent. She looked back at the woman, noticing that her fingers were laced tightly together, just beyond the long sleeves of the cardigan.

Bernie spoke again, quietly. 'It's okay. In *your* time. This is really important.'

Josie rewarded him with a grateful smile. 'You're very kind. I'm grateful for your sensitivity.'

Sensitivity. Kate's eyes flicked sideways, to check that it was Detective Sergeant Nightmare sitting beside her.

'I'm not even certain of the progression of events. I know that at some point he grabbed hold of me from behind. He pulled my head back by the hair and this cold liquid – they said at the hospital that it was juice – just poured into my mouth. I couldn't do anything to avoid it. I had to swallow. I remember his hands. Very smooth. Very warm.' She stopped speaking for a few seconds, then, 'They said at the hospital that I'd been drugged.'

Silence for some seconds as Josie searched among the sheets on the sofa, then reached for a piece of folded paper on the small table next to her.

'This is what the hospital gave me,' she said. 'I kept it, just in case the police looked at my case again some day. It shows what was in the juice. I was told to take it to the police – when I went to make my statement.'

Glancing at Bernie, Kate took the folded sheet the other woman was offering and read the information on it. *Flunitrazepam*. More commonly known as Rohypnol. The known side effect for anyone ingesting it was that they would remember little, if anything, of what had occurred while they were under its influence.

Kate listened as Josie continued.

'My impression is that he was a very angry person. I could hear him talking to himself – that's how he sounded.'

'What did he say?' asked Kate.

Josie shook her head. 'I don't know. It was just a blur of words but the sound of them – I think he said something about "your mother", and all *I* could think was, "You don't know my mother." Sorry, that's it. I was really out of it.'

She clasped her hands together tightly, only the knuckles showing, pink and white, beyond the soft cream sleeves. 'I don't even know what he did to me physically, but I opted for regular AIDS tests afterwards.'

Kate looked sympathetically at the woman. 'You've no idea at all what happened to you after you were drugged?'

Josie shook her head, lips pressed together. 'I was examined at the hospital. Rape was . . . confirmed. They took my clothes for testing and told me afterwards that they didn't get any evidence off them. They thought it might have been rape with . . . something, an object.'

Kate felt the other woman sizing her up, and gave her an encouraging look.

'I can't describe how unnerving it is to know that something so . . . invasive might have happened to you and yet you can't remember anything about it. All I remember is this – thing on my face. Then, nothing.'

Kate glanced briefly at Bernie, then back to Josie Kenton-Smith.

'Did you go to hospital immediately afterwards?'

Josie nodded. 'I was left in one of the side roads near the cricket ground. Edgbaston. I . . . I had no clothes on from my waist down. I was told they were folded nearby.'

'Someone found you?'

Josie gave a small smile. 'A woman and her husband. They'd been to the MAC to see a film and then they'd come out again to walk their dog. It was very late . . . quiet. They put their coats round me, made the calls, and waited for the police and ambulance to come.'

'This thing over your face, love. What was it?' Bernie asked.

'Sorry. I don't know. The hospital didn't mention it. Maybe he took it with him.'

Kate looked from Bernie to Josie Kenton-Smith. 'Did you make a statement to the police?'

'Of course. But not straight away. I was in no fit state for about two days. The doctors wouldn't let the police in to see me. I went to the police station when I got out of hospital. That was about five days later. I took this drug report with me. Even then, I couldn't do it properly. I was too upset. I had to go back again, about three days afterwards, and finish it.'

'Which police station did you go to?' asked Kate.

'The big one. Rose Road. In Harborne.'

CHAPTER FORTY

Back in UCU, Kate had two questions.

'Where is Josie Kenton-Smith's statement?'

Bernie pointed. 'I've looked through the box again. There isn't one.'

Kate continued: 'Do we take photographs of rape victims?'

Julian had been listening to the exchange. He nodded. 'Forensics take them if the victim has injuries. Jake Brown has a female colleague who takes photos of the victim's facial and body injuries. Want me to ask?'

Kate noticed that Julian looked slightly more upbeat. 'Could you go down now, Julian? Ask him to let us have whatever photographs are available for all four rapes?'

Half an hour later, Harry and Jake arrived in UCU with what had been found. Harry did the talking, placing a small stack of photographs on the table as Julian sat watching.

'Here's what we've got for the rapes that Julian's mentioned. I'm finishing in half an hour, but when I get some spare time tomorrow I'll have another look.'

He winked at Kate and rubbed his hands together. 'I'm off early. Going to the Rep tonight.'

'What's on?'

'Noel Coward play. My favourite. *Present Laughter.*'

Kate nodded. 'I saw that a couple of years ago.'

Glowering, Bernie turned his attention to Jake, who was laying the photographs side by side on the table. 'Let's get on with it.'

Jake looked at Bernie as he spoke. 'A colleague of mine took these. Harry will go through them with you. There's printed details on the back summarising the content of each photograph. I'll leave you to it. I'd like them back some time. For the records.'

He got up and headed for the door. Kate watched him go. He hadn't looked at her once in the few minutes he was in UCU.

She went and stood next to Harry at the table, listening alongside Julian as Harry picked up each photograph in turn to read details from the labels on the reverse side.

'This one is Josie Kenton-Smith, the one Julian specifically mentioned. It says, "Contusions to shoulders". So, nothing too bad. Mmm . . . bit of bruising. They hardly show up at all on this frontal shot, see? And see that? Labelled "1 of 1". That means no other photographs were taken. So that's it. Just bruising. End of story.'

Kate studied the photograph. A younger version of the woman she and Bernie had met earlier. She could just make out a bruise to the left of Josie's chin. She sighed. The experience still hadn't ended for that poor woman.

Harry picked up another photograph and studied it for some seconds, then turned it over to read the details.

'This is of the French girl, Dijon. Again, nothing very problematic in terms of the face, apart from a bit of a bruise on her jaw, here. See?'

Kate took a look. Dijon's lower lip looked as if it was split and her jaw was swollen. She retuned to what Harry was saying.

'Seems doubtful either she or Kenton-Smith were injured elsewhere on their bodies, given the absence of other photographs. Now, Suzie Luckman. We couldn't find any photos at all in that name.'

Kate felt her mood slide as Harry continued.

'And this one—'

'Doesn't it bother you, Harry, the lack of photographs for Luckman? Surely that suggests that the forensic records are incomplete?'

He shook his head. 'Not really, Kate. What often happens is that a file is made up and sent to the CPS for evaluation. The files don't always find their way back.'

'But there's no indication that there was ever a suspect in the rape of Suzie Luckman. Why would it go—'

'I don't know, Kate. Now, this one is . . .' He looked at the back of the photograph, then returned to the front. 'Tracey Thomas. Bloody hell! She looks a bit rough, doesn't she? Mind you, it's probably the make-up. No body photographs for her either.'

Kate took the photograph of Tracey Thomas from Harry and studied it closely. A young woman with ragged blonde hair, eyes heavily outlined with black liner and mascara. She looked again, feeling sudden sympathy for the girl, killed in a subsequent car accident. Harry had moved on to another photograph.

'This last one was in Thomas's file but it isn't your rape victim. See? Same surname, but different first name. Don't know why Jake included it.'

Kate looked at it, curious. 'What happened to her?' she asked.

Harry turned the photograph over, read the details and shrugged. 'Nothing. It was just a domestic.'

Kate took the photograph from him. 'I wouldn't describe it as nothing, Harry,' she mused, frowning at it.

The woman's face was a mass of swellings and contusions and, if Kate was not mistaken, her nose was broken.

'I meant nothing in the sense that she isn't one of your rape victims, Kate.'

Harry took the photograph back from her and considered it again, briefly.

'Now I look at it properly, you're right. She's taken a beating. That's what years of forensic work does for you, Kate. We see so much damage, it blunts us, yeah?'

Kate gave a small nod. 'Harry, when you're next in, could you and Jake search again for anything relating to Suzie Luckman? Somewhere here we've got the date of her rape.'

'Don't worry. I've got the details from Julian. It'll be top of my list.'

He looked around the room. 'Okay, people, I'm off! Anything else you need, let me know or tell Julian and he'll pass it on. Jules, my man, see you for the forensic testing module next week, yes?'

He raised a hand and Julian, flushed, smacked it with one of his own. Harry reached the door, passing Joe coming through it.

Bernie slowly shook his head, catching sight of Kate glaring at him.

'*What!* It ain't my fault if he walks with a lisp.'

'Don't "what" me!' snapped Kate. 'I've been "whatted" by the best. You don't even come close. Comments like that are homophobic, and it's also—'

'All right, all right! What's getting up your frock all of a sudden? And what's up with him?' He pointed to Julian, who was looking sulky again.

Kate glanced at Julian and frowned.

Shaking his head again, Bernie sat down at the table. 'Let's have a proper look at what they brought us.'

Kate closed her eyes for a few seconds, then resumed her scanning of the photographs.

They had nothing for Luckman. Nothing at all.

Now that they had some of the rape-related photographs, an idea was taking shape in Kate's mind relating to one of their persons of interest. She looked cautiously at her colleagues. This was going to be like asking turkeys to vote for Christmas. Or Thanksgiving.

She glanced from Bernie to Joe. 'Okay. What I'm going to suggest – and I will truly understand if you say no after Furman's ranting – is that we make *one* more visit to John Cranham.' Julian's head shot up, eyes round, face worried. Kate continued. 'And we take these photographs for him to look at.'

Joe gave her a long look. 'What makes you think Cranham will even *agree*? He's lawyered up.'

'You got a death wish or what?' muttered Bernie. 'Furman'd have your suspenders just for suggesting it.'

Kate lifted the phone receiver. 'I'm happy to go alone,' she said quietly.

Within the next five minutes, Cranham had listened to Kate's persuasive pitch then agreed very civilly to meet with her at his firm's showroom later that afternoon, on one condition. No Bernie.

'Yes, well . . . he's not one of my favourites, neither,' said Bernie when told this. 'I've got an appointment anyway. Fitness test.'

205

CHAPTER FORTY-ONE

Joe drove through Birmingham's urban sprawl and on, as it gradually gave way to lower-density suburbia, and then to spacious roads of large homes surrounded by extensive well-tended gardens. They had reached Solihull.

During the journey Kate asked Joe about his visit Upstairs and what he'd learned about the abduction of Jody Westbrooke.

'Where did it take place?'

'From outside a club called Running Wild, in Wolverhampton.'

'Any witnesses? Anybody see it happen? See anything?'

'Nope. One of her pals mentioned a car but couldn't give any detail.'

'So . . . she got in a stranger's car?' Kate asked, noting the first commercial buildings of Solihull's centre coming into view. 'It *fits*, Joe. It fits with Janine and Molly. They look similar. It's likely they were abducted efficiently, quietly, then transported—'

'Need to wait and see, Red,' he said quietly, eyes on the road. 'Wait for more details.'

Kate gave him a sideways look, then subsided.

Arriving outside Cranham's place of business, Joe parked and remained behind the wheel for a few seconds, looking at the building, then at Kate.

'Do you think he's involved at all? I'd like to know what we're doing here, Kate.'

Kate's eyes were also on the showroom. 'It'll work best if I don't tell you right now, Joe.'

Joe slowly nodded. 'Whatever you say.'

They left the car and walked into the showroom to find Cranham already downstairs waiting for them. He greeted Kate cordially and nodded at Joe. He led them not to his office, but past it, to a formal meeting room. A man was already waiting inside. He stood as they entered. Tall and elegant, wearing a dark navy suit with a fine pin-stripe, he spoke directly to Kate without any preamble as he handed her and Joe tea in bone-china cups.

'Sheridan Granville of Rutgers. I shall remain throughout your visit.' He smiled at Kate without her noting any change to his eyes. 'And prior to the meeting I want to look at any notes or questions you have brought with you.'

Kate silently thanked the barrister who had hectored her in court some years before, physically taking her court file from her whilst she was in the witness box. Although he was roundly criticised by the judge and Kate had included nothing in the notes that was negative, inflammatory or directly useful to the barrister, she knew that she could easily have done so. Good training. As Joe had remarked during the two earlier murder cases they'd worked on together in UCU, both of which had involved a wealth of documentary detail that they'd had to absorb, Kate was a 'quick study'.

She opened her bag, took out the few written questions and the photographs she had brought with her and handed them to Granville, not entirely with good grace but feeling that she had no choice.

Granville looked at the questions then the photographs, handing them back to her in the same order they were offered, with the same mouth-only smile.

At a nod from him, they all took seats around the formal table. John Cranham began the meeting.

'How do you think I can help you, Dr Hanson? I've got another meeting in ten minutes and—'

'That's fine, Mr Cranham. Thank you for agreeing to see us again. I need you to look at some photographs, if you will. They're of young women who we believe were victimised by the same man who abducted Molly James.'

Cranham nodded at Kate, glanced at Granville, then looked at each photograph as she placed it in front of him. Her eyes never moved from his face as he did so. When the last one had been placed and he'd examined the array, Cranham looked at her questioningly.

Kate kept her attention on his face. 'To your knowledge have you ever met any of these women?'

He looked at them then back to Kate. 'No. Never.'

Kate nodded. 'Tell me what you think of these women, Mr Cranham.'

He looked at her for a few seconds, then at Granville, and finally down to the photographs again. She watched as he frowned, shaking his head.

'They're young women . . . probably attractive . . . but I can see that they've been badly used, shall we say? Clearly something . . .' His frown deepened. 'I'd guess it was *criminal* happened to them. It's obvious that someone has treated them very badly . . . shocking. But not this one. She doesn't look as though she's been harmed.' He tapped the last photograph Kate had included in the array and his eyes came up to meet hers. He looked puzzled and only slightly impatient. 'What do you want from me, Dr Hanson? I don't recognise a single one of them.'

'Thank you, Mr Cranham.' She turned to his lawyer, adding, 'I think we're finished here. Thank *you* for your cooperation.'

Taking her cue, Joe moved towards the door, opened it for Kate and followed her out of the room. Perplexed, Cranham and Granville watched them leave.

On the journey back to UCU, Kate glanced at Joe, who had said nothing for some minutes.

'Thanks for coming with me, Joe. I had doubts that Cranham was involved in Molly's murder. I just needed to check.' When Joe didn't answer, she added, 'I wasn't expecting him to recognise any of the photographs, not even the one of Molly, but I didn't tell you what I was doing because I didn't want you to inadvertently communicate anything to him. He showed the anticipated mix of minimal tension and curiosity that anyone would who was being shown data linked to a crime, but no more. He recognised physical abuse in some of the photographs and his comments about it were appropriate.'

'How come you're so sure about him?'

'Because people with guilty knowledge mostly can't avoid showing their cognitive processes in their faces and the rest of their physical presentation. Because they're working hard inside their heads, it isn't unusual for them to show a reduction in physical response as a way of offsetting the effort they're putting into thinking. There was no suggestion of frenetic mental wheels turning behind Cranham's face. No signs of hard thinking going on, which would have been present if he had guilty knowledge of the women in the photographs. There was no indication of his having to conceal anything. Nothing to suggest he was thinking ahead, to what we might know and how he was going to deal with that if we asked him questions.' Kate lifted her shoulders. 'He merely gave the photographs close consideration. Nothing more.'

'You sound confident.'

'I am.'

A few minutes of silence slid by.

'Do you have something on your mind, Joe?'

Joe finally spoke. 'Where'd you get that last photograph?'

Kate glanced at him, then out of the window at the scene racing by.

'I went Upstairs earlier and asked for a copy of the one Jody Westbrooke's parents have provided. As with the other photographs, it had no significance for John Cranham.'

She turned to him. 'You think I should have told you what I was going to do?'

Joe appraised her with a glance, then gave his attention to the road, speaking quietly. '*You* are one risk-taking broad, Red.' He shook his head. 'When you went into that meeting, you didn't actually know that Cranham would demonstrate he wasn't involved.'

'Yes I did,' said Kate.

Joe gave her another look. 'Anybody ever tell you that a person can come across as too smart? Too sure?'

'A few,' she replied.

'And?'

'I didn't listen to them.'

He looked at her, then back to the road, shaking his head, mouth open in a silent laugh.

'In that case, I'll be your psychology confederate any time.'

They arrived in UCU to find Bernie there, alone in the subdued light, blinds half-closed. Kate could hear muted activity elsewhere inside the large building. She dropped her bag on the floor and sat, feeling hot and jaded.

'How'd it go with Posh Git?'

Kate nodded. 'Fine, even though he had his solicitor with him. Sheridan Granville.'

Kate felt irritation rising as Bernie's forehead creased. Why had she

209

mentioned the damned name? Bernie was *so* predictable. *And you're tired and edgy.*

Bernie tutted. 'Don't tell me. Tall, blonde, big chest and a snotty attitude.'

'He was tall, grey-haired and I'm assuming had all the usual complement of male bits,' snapped Kate.

Joe laughed quietly on his way to the Refreshment Lounge.

Ignoring both of them, Kate kicked off her shoes. 'We can rule out John Cranham. He never faltered when he saw *any* of the photographs. Including the one of the domestic-violence victim. If he were the rapist, it would have registered on his face to some degree that she didn't belong in the series. Believe me, I was watching him *very* closely the whole time.'

'What about this recent girl, this Jody? He might not have done the others but he could've jumped on her.'

'I included her picture too,' said Kate, massaging her lower legs, then stretching them.

Need some exercise.

Bernie gave her a brows-down scowl. 'In that case, it's a bloody good job he's not involved, according to you. If he had've been, showing him her photo like that would've warned him that she'd been found and . . . You *listening*?'

'Yes, and he wasn't.'

'Anybody ever tell you that you carry on like you got an answer for everything? Smart alecs ain't the most popular of types, Doc, particularly with the Job.'

Giving Kate a sideways glare, Bernie left the table, went to the glass screen, picked up a cloth and erased Cranham's name.

'You did *that* with uncharacteristic calmness,' said Kate, eyeing him.

'Yeah, well, I'm trying to keep my stress levels down. I'm not giving Furman no ammunition in terms of health.'

Kate leaned back against her chair. 'No tea for me, thanks, Joe. I'm done in. I'm going home. For a glass of white and a cool shower.'

She glanced at both her colleagues. They looked as tired as she felt. Too tired even to engage in the usual banter in response to what she'd just said.

*

Kate had made dinner for Maisie and herself. Now it was ten p.m. and the old house was silent. Maisie had gone to bed early.

Kate slid open the kitchen doors and walked out into the still-warm garden. She hadn't spent much time out here since the case began. Maybe Celia was right. Perhaps it was too much. She sighed, thinking of the things she didn't get around to doing while she was involved with UCU. She felt a quick surge of tension. She was keeping up with her two tutorial groups, but only because they were willing to fit in with *her* availability.

Sighing, glass in hand, she walked slowly away from the house. A faint tinkling sound started up from somewhere nearby and a small black-and-white shape leapt from among thick bushes.

'Hi, li'l cat! Where've you been? Had a date?'

Mugger wove himself around Kate's legs.

'Nice of you to check in. Come on, let's go inside.' She walked towards the house, then turned. The cat was now sitting on the grass.

Sighing, dead on her feet, Kate waved a hand. 'Come on now. No messing around.' Mugger stayed exactly where he was; only the yellow eyes moved, from Kate to the house and back again.

Kate frowned at the small animal, steadfast on the grass. What *was* the matter with him? 'Okay. Suit yourself. But don't come crying to me at one o'clock in the morning.' She walked a few paces away from him, stepped inside and slid the doors closed, locking them. Then she checked on him again. He still hadn't moved. She shook her head. Crazy cat.

As she turned back into the kitchen, there was a sudden whirring sound, causing Kate to throw wine on to the ceramic tiles as her heart went into free-fall. 'For God's sake,' she muttered, fetching kitchen paper to blot the floor, glaring at the bean-to-cup coffee-maker she used only occasionally. It reciprocated with another whir.

Kate left the kitchen in darkness and made her way to the hall and upstairs, turning out lights as she went. As she reached the landing she heard a low creaking sound and saw Maisie's door slowly drifting closed.

Damn the doors in this old place.

She quietly opened her daughter's bedroom door and looked inside. Because of Maisie's current upset, caused by Kevin's reneging on the sleepover arrangement, Kate hadn't asked any further questions about what she'd found in her room the other day. She still needed to establish who the tablets belonged to, but she was confident they weren't Maisie's.

She walked to the bed and looked down on her sleeping daughter, at the profusion of curls spread over the pillow. Despite the warmth of the late evening, she crossed the room and closed both window and curtains. She stood listening to Maisie's rhythmic breathing, then walked quietly back to the bed to look again at her sleeping child. Soon-to-be teenager. Soon-to-be young woman. She smoothed the thick hair.

Don't be in too much of a hurry. Take your time.

She swallowed.

One glass of wine is enough for you, my girl.

Propping Maisie's door half-open with a book to give her some air, Kate quietly left the room en route to the main bathroom.

CHAPTER FORTY-TWO

At eight o'clock on Tuesday morning, Kate flew into the kitchen, silky yellow robe billowing, switched on the kettle, then returned to the hall.

'Maisie? *Maisie!* Get up. We're late!'

She returned to the kitchen, organising tea, juice and the making of toast. Catching sight of Mugger outside, his forepaws on the window, she slid open the doors and he rocketed into the kitchen.

'What's got into you *now*?'

Maisie sauntered through the door, half-asleep. 'Don't talk to the cat, Mom. It makes you sound like an old person.'

'Morning, light of my life.'

Within half an hour of eating a quick breakfast with Maisie, Kate was showered, moisturised and dressed in a deep blue silk shirt and slim black linen trousers. Feet thrust into black suede wedge sandals, she began securing her hair in a band. *Still damp.*

'Oh, for God's *sake*!' Dragging the band from her hair and bending forward from the waist, she applied the hairdryer again. The phone in her pocket vibrated. It was Bernie.

'Hey, Doc. Just a reminder that if you're planning to come in by the front entrance, forget it. You should see it. Keep to the back way. Looks like they never bought the rubbish Furman spouted at 'em after all.'

Thirty minutes later, Kate had dropped Maisie at school and was approaching the back entrance to Rose Road. She slowed, looking ahead beyond the parked cars. The press were there too. A beeping sound came from behind her. Too late. She couldn't reverse. She drove on slowly and began turning in to the rear gateway.

Immediately, four or five people appeared in front of her car, two with cameras pointed at her. Kate was horrified. She stood on her brakes, fearful of injuring somebody, pressed the car horn a few times and inched forward. They parted and she drove inside at speed, parking out of sight.

Inside UCU, Kate found her two colleagues in dim light, the blinds drawn.

'I got caught! Out the back. I think they took photographs. Is anything being done about it? Them?'

Joe passed her a mug of tea. 'No word from on high. They're feeling pissed out there because they know Furman was giving them the runaround on Friday. Nobody's supplying them with any solid information so they're falling back on what they can add together then multiply.' He nodded at a heap of dailies on the desk.

Kate looked across at Bernie, who was reading the *Sun*, his mouth a seam.

'According to this, I'm a "*sixty*-year-old veteran". Bloody cheek.'

Kate went to where Joe was sitting, to peer over his shoulder at the local newspaper. No need to search for the story. It was there. On the front page.

'Mmm . . . they obviously weren't impressed with Furman's denial. This is all so inaccurate. Oh, for God's sake! "Bypass Killer on the Loose." Idiotic, misleading, clichéd *rubbish*,' Kate muttered, then fell silent, reading to the end of the article. 'They haven't specifically mentioned the Westbrooke disappearance in the story.'

Joe looked up at her. 'No one knows yet if it's connected.'

Kate straightened. 'It is.' She looked at her two colleagues in silence for a few seconds, then decided to go with what was in her mind. 'Given all this inaccuracy, how about if we talked to the press, gave them some basic, limited information?'

'You mean, get them on side?'

Kate looked from Joe to Bernie. 'At least two murders and four prior rapes that we suspect are connected. I think there's a need to get an accurate story out there but carefully edited in terms of what we know so far. But there's another reason why we should do it. Women need to be alerted to what we believe is a risk. If our doer stopped for a while but now he's active again, they must be warned.' She hesitated. 'It might even produce some leads for us.'

'From?' asked Bernie.

'Who knows?' Kate raised her hands. 'Associates of the doer in the nineties, who read the information, think back, and make a connection to him. Or a family that's missing someone, or a young woman who was raped and something jogs her memory.' She paused, pushing a stray curl from her face. 'Where's Furman?'

'In London, at some Home Office shindig,' Bernie said.

Kate eyed Joe. 'What d'you think?'

He stood. 'I'll set it up.'

He returned in ten minutes.

'I've arranged for two journos to come in here tomorrow. We need some breathing space because it has to be on our terms, Kate. That means having a plan for the interview.'

She nodded agreement, then glanced at her two colleagues in turn.

'I've been thinking. I've got an idea.' She waited, eyes on her note-book. When she glanced up, they were looking back at her, waiting. No joshing from Joe or attitude from Bernie.

'Suzie Luckman,' she began. 'You know that I don't believe she reached London after her weekend visit home. It doesn't make sense for the doer to go to London, kill her there and then bring her back here.'

She leaned on her forearms, silent for a couple of seconds, then, 'If we're right, and the rapes *are* connected to the murders, then that indicates that she was victimised twice by the same doer. That wasn't by chance. Nobody's that unlucky.'

She shook her head. 'If he'd stalked Suzie before he raped her, he would have learned her routines while she was still living here in Birmingham: where she lived, where she worked. And then, when she relocated to London after the rape, he must have resumed his stalking at the times she was visiting her family. That's how he knew where to find her, once he'd graduated . . . and then he killed her.'

Bernie got up from the table. 'You're now about to tell us you want us to look for stalkers as well as rapists?'

Kate frowned, looking downwards, thinking of the information in Janine Walker's diary. Tectonic plates slid together.

Her eyes widened. 'How could I have been so *obtuse*?' she said quietly. 'Janine Walker's mystery man. Telling her he'd seen her before . . .'

'Thought you said they don't approach the victim, Red?'

Kate stared at the information on the glass screen. '. . . Maybe she was an exception . . . although we don't know what he routinely did with any other victim. All I can be certain of right now is that Janine

215

didn't regard him as a stalker, and the reason for that is probably that he took his *time*, learned all he could about her indirectly, and then began to present himself as disarmingly normal and honest.'

She seized her notebook from her bag and flipped pages, looking up at her two colleagues, face pink.

'That's it. He stalked Janine,' she whispered. 'Just like he did Suzie.'

'And then there's Molly,' Joe said quietly. 'The references to her often seeing a specific male in the mall coffee shop?'

The words hung on the still air.

Kate got up from the table and walked quickly to the file on Julian's computer desk. Finding what she was looking for, as Bernie jiggled keys in his pocket, she returned to the table, sat down and studied the data. After a couple of minutes she took a red Sharpie highlighter from her bag, looking from Joe to Bernie.

'Got an A to Z?'

Bernie looked at his watch, then stretched to shelving near Julian's workstation, handing her a large spiral-bound book. 'You still coming with me to see Mrs Luckman?'

Kate nodded, as she looked at the map of the Greater Birmingham area, making faint red marks on it. After a couple of minutes, she sat back and studied her handiwork, eyes to one side, unfocused.

Not a perfect pattern. One or two outliers.

She looked again at the marks she'd made.

If you thought of the pattern of rapes and murders as a wheel, the centre of it was clear.

It was Birmingham. Specifically the south-west suburbs of Edgbaston and Harborne.

He was operating in his comfort zone. At its centre the place he was most at ease.

Home? Work?

216

CHAPTER FORTY-THREE

Forty-five minutes later, Kate and Bernie were sitting in the front room of a small semi-detached house in Moor Green, a suburb of Birmingham scarcely three miles from Rose Road. Kate peered out of the window, at similar houses surrounded by tidy green lawns and bright flower beds.

Bernie had done the talking this time, but released few details to the older woman sitting opposite, beyond that they were investigating some unsolved assaults in the Birmingham area.

Mrs Luckman, widowed mother of Suzie, had then gone to make tea.

'What d'you think?' asked Bernie quietly.

'About what?'

Bernie nodded in the direction Mrs Luckman had disappeared.

Kate looked towards the door. 'A bit vague?'

Bernie nodded as Mrs Luckman quietly reappeared at the door of the sitting room. 'I wonder – would you mind helping me with the tray? It's a bit hard for me to manage.'

Moving surprisingly quickly, Bernie followed her to the back of the house, returning with a tea tray.

Within ten minutes they had confirmation of the attack on Suzie, which had taken place not far from the house, on a Thursday night in April 1997. Conversation stalled after Kate asked Mrs Luckman to tell them what happened subsequently: whether Suzie had given a statement to the police or not. It was slow work to get even a chronological account of anything relating to Suzie in the 1990s. About the only thing of which Mrs Luckman appeared sure was that two police officers had visited the house immediately after the attack on her daughter. She appeared not to recall anything of the subsequently reported disappearance of Suzie in London and the ensuing investigation there, initiated by Suzie's employer when she didn't arrive for work. Julian had been unable to find any confirmation that Mrs Luckman or anyone else in Birmingham had ever reported Suzie missing.

Kate studied the elderly woman, sadly recognising the chaos and inconsistency about her daughter for what it truly was.

Mrs Luckman gazed back at them uncertainly. 'Well, the last I heard . . . she's working in London . . .'

Bernie glanced at Kate, clearly uncomfortable.

Kate spoke to Mrs Luckman gently, making her words as specific as possible. 'What did Suzie do after the attack?'

The old lady sat silent and still. After a long pause she looked at Kate.

'You think Suzie's dead,' she said, tone suddenly accusatory.

They waited, Kate becoming concerned that the conversational direction was causing the woman upset. Mrs Luckman stirred, re-focused, and she seemed more aware of her surroundings. Her eyes went to the clock on the mantelpiece: 11.45 a.m.

'Would either of you like a sweet sherry? Maybe . . . a *tiny* one?'

Both declined. More silence.

Then: 'A nice man has been here . . . Henry, I think his name was. He took Suzie's hairbrush.'

Kate knew of Connie's request to the Forensic Service that material be gathered from Suzie Luckman's family, after the pathologist had been told about UCU's theory that she might be connected to the femur recently found.

Mrs Luckman's eyes suddenly lost their vagueness. 'I know what you're thinking about Suzie. Sometimes I think it too. Something's happened to her. Something *really* bad. It's been so long, but . . . it's so hard to keep things *straight*.' She made a frustrated gesture towards her own head.

Kate and Bernie watched, disconcerted, as she suddenly dissolved before them, tears flowing. Then, in seconds, her mood changed again. 'Now I *remember*.' She beamed. 'Suzie's in London, having a lovely life.' She frowned. 'Maybe its a little game I play . . .'

Kate felt pressure forming in her own head. She could understand the self-deception, although she recognised that Mrs Luckman had a much more fundamental problem. She mentally calculated the other woman's likely age. Probably mid-sixties. The onset had clearly occurred somewhat early.

'Mrs Luckman. Can you talk to us about Suzie, because we never knew her.' Mrs Luckman's face softened. 'She's a bright girl. A clever girl.'

Bernie spoke next. 'Did she have a boyfriend, Mrs Luckman? At the time she was attacked?'

'No. She wasn't very settled living here. That's why she decided to move to London.' She looked at each of them. 'She *did* go. To London. She *did* go!'

Seeing Mrs Luckman's face about to disintegrate again, Kate hurriedly reassured her. 'We know she did,' she said softly, a hand on the older woman's arm.

No way would Kate divulge the result of the credit-card search. Or the reason for Harry collecting an item of Suzie's personal belongings. The poor woman appeared to have only a transient awareness that her daughter was almost certainly dead. Perhaps the kindest aspect of her condition was that it protected her from that reality.

Kate wanted to leave. Let the poor woman alone. But they had a pressing need to establish certain facts if at all possible.

'During the time Suzie was still in Birmingham, did she live here? With you?' Kate asked.

A quick nod of confirmation. 'Oh yes. Even though she was twenty-one, she hadn't sorted out her life. She didn't know what she wanted to do. Or be.'

'Had she any ideas?'

Mrs Luckman smiled. 'Funny you should ask. She was thinking of joining the police force. She was a tall girl, you know, but she told me, "Mom, they don't care about that any more."'

Kate made very brief notes. 'Before she left Birmingham to live in London, was Suzie working?'

'Yes. Sales assistant in Rackhams,' said Mrs Luckman, using the old name for the department store. 'She didn't want to carry on with that.' Her attention drifted as she gazed towards the window.

Bernie leaned forward. 'Listen, love, do you know if your daughter had any problems? You know – with men?'

Mrs Luckman shook her head. 'No. Suzie would have told me. She was a pretty girl. Could have had any number of boyfriends. She wanted to do something with her life before she met somebody and settled down. The only thing she ever really talked about was the customers she had at the department store. Her "regulars", she called them. Women, all ages. And a few men.'

Kate looked slowly upwards, her eyes meeting Bernie's.

'What did she say about the men, love?' Bernie's question seemed to have no impact on Mrs Luckman. Her eyes were vague. He leaned forward again, voice low, words careful. 'Did Suzie mention any man by name?'

Mrs Luckman's eyes had an unfocused quality. 'No. I don't think so. She met a lot of people in a day. She said they bought things for their wives. The men.'

'Did she mention anybody in particular?' prompted Bernie again.

A shake of the head, followed by encroaching vagueness. 'What about? What for?' her voice querulous.

Kate's gaze drifted round the small sitting room, the film of dust, the knick-knacks and photographs in frames. There was a photo of a young female on the sideboard.

'Is that a picture of Suzie, Mrs Luckman?'

The elderly woman turned to where Kate was pointing. 'Yes, that's Suzie.'

She got up to fetch it and handed it to Kate. Kate took a close look at the attractive young woman, at the perfect oval face framed by shoulder-length blonde hair, secured by what looked to be a black velvet band. She also saw the cream-coloured shirt and the fine gold necklace. She felt Bernie's tension as he absorbed the same detail.

'Mrs Luckman, would you mind if we took that photo with us?' he asked. When she didn't reply, he added: 'We'll be sure to bring it back.'

After a pause, the elderly lady nodded.

Kate looked from the photograph to Suzie's mother, doubting that she would get a clear response to her next question but knowing she had to try.

'When Suzie was settled in London, did she come home on a regular basis?'

'No. She would just ring me and say she was coming at the end of the week. Other times she would just arrive. She had her key.'

As they prepared to leave, Bernie turned to Mrs Luckman. 'Nice area, this. You got some good neighbours, Mrs L?'

The elderly woman shook her head slightly. 'Nice enough, but they're all young. At work all day.'

Now Kate didn't want to let the questioning go. 'Mrs Luckman? Can you remember Suzie ever going to a police station in Harborne?'

She felt a look of disapproval from Bernie. He probably thought she was pushing too hard.

The old lady nodded, seemingly a little more alert. 'I do. She went to the big one. She said she wanted to help other women who had had the same experience as she had, when she was . . . raped. She wanted to do some good. And she went to get information about joining the police.'

They left the house and returned to Bernie's vehicle.

'So there you are, Doc. She never made a formal statement.'

Kate shook her head. 'Given Mrs Luckman's vagueness, we can't be sure of that, although there's an indication Suzie did go to Rose Road.'

Without saying anything, Bernie dialled a number on his phone and waited for a response.

'Who're you calling?'

'Social Services' Emergency Duty Team. To ask if they know about Mrs L. I want somebody from the Access Service out to see her, pronto. The way things are going with the investigation, she's going to need some support anyway. And I'll phone 'em in a few days to check what they've done.'

Kate watched the suburban scene of neat semis, local shops and people flow past as they returned to Rose Road. Although Mrs Luckman had seemed sure that Suzie had visited Rose Road, they needed to keep in mind that she was not a reliable source of information. Kate frowned. Suzie wanted to help other young women, according to her mother. *Surely* she would have made an official complaint about what had happened to her? Kate had another worry. What about the irregularity of her visits home?

How does a stalker stalk when his quarry's availability is totally variable?

She sat back and stared through the window, thinking of Mrs Luckman, now alone in her house. *How vulnerable we all are.*

She glanced towards Bernie, who was occupied with driving. For all the irritation he caused her at times, for all his politically incorrect attitudes, it was Sergeant Nightmare who'd thought to make the call to Social Services.

CHAPTER FORTY-FOUR

Back at UCU Kate picked up a message left on the table. It was from Connie. She quickly read it, then showed it to Bernie: *Femur confirmed as belonging to Suzanne Rachel Luckman.*

Although it was what she'd anticipated, Kate felt suddenly weary. She leant against the edge of the table, thinking of Mrs Luckman, already in a difficult situation; now she would have this news to contend with.

Suddenly Bernie's voice was low in her ear. 'Come on, Doc. Buck up. We're on the move now. We've got a job to finish.'

As Kate contemplated this, the door opened and Joe walked into UCU.

He looked at them both. 'You've seen the note?'

Kate straightened, pushing back her hair. 'Yes. We need to get on with what we have to do,' she said quietly.

Kate and Joe had completed their plan for meeting with the media. They'd decided not to refer to the rape cases specifically, but would acknowledge three murder victims and their belief that the same person was responsible for all of them. Kate would give them her theory of the doer's likely background and personality. Joe, a more seasoned media communicator back in the US, indicated that he was comfortable to add anything else he thought relevant. Lastly, they'd make a specific appeal for the public's help. They'd decided that they would deal with Furman's response as and when he got to know about the interview.

An hour later they were still in UCU, but now facing two representatives of the press: the crime correspondent for *The Times*, Mark Belding, a tall, thin man with a lugubrious facial expression and a stoop; and an overweight, smiling antithesis to Belding named Colin

West, from the *Birmingham Mail*. Kate had borrowed a large sheet from the post-mortem suite and this now covered the glass screen.

Joe had outlined their investigation of the cold cases for the two journalists, giving limited details. Belding had scribbled during this, while West sat eyeing them, nodding occasionally, arms folded, the small audio recorder he'd earlier pulled from his pocket absorbing Joe's words. Kate felt disconcerted by the recorder and the fact that it was the jovial West who'd produced it, rather than the mournful Belding.

West looked at Kate, his plump face smiling and curiously inviting.

'So what's been your contribution so far, Dr Hanson?'

Sticking to the plan, Kate outlined her analysis of the nature of the abduction-murders and the kind of person they were seeking.

'We know a little about him,' she said. 'The nature of the information we have is delicate, and we're appealing to anyone who can link it to someone they know or have known, perhaps even intimately.'

She was quiet for a few seconds as Belding's pencil flew across his notepad. He stopped and nodded, waiting for her to continue. West looked encouragingly at her and she took a deep breath, still wary despite the planning she and Joe had done.

'We believe that the man responsible for the murders of these young women has very specific needs within his intimate relationships. He requires his sexual partners to be compliant. He would be the one to direct sexual activity. A wife or girlfriend would experience him in that context as demanding and controlling, even violent. Sexual activity is likely to involve tying up and possibly the covering of his partner's face. He's almost certainly a keen user of pornography.'

The two journalists stared at Kate, waiting as she thought about what she'd said so far, and what she was about to say.

'We're asking anyone who has experienced or recognises those kinds of behaviours and can link them to a man who was around the Midlands area in the mid to late nineteen nineties to contact us.' She paused. 'We would like to extend our request for help to any associates or work colleagues he might have had during that time, anyone who became aware of this man's attitude towards women. Can anyone make a link from the details I've just given to someone they've known during the past, say, fifteen years?'

She glanced at Belding as the pencil which had been rapidly

covering paper, stopped. He looked up at her. 'A lot of what you've described might be viewed by many people as normal.'

Kate was nonplussed for a few seconds. 'I did say *violent*, and if you think about it—'

She stopped, aware that Belding's pencil was still poised. *Clever.* He wanted her talking off-plan. This was harder than she'd anticipated. She glanced at Joe, who raised one eyebrow and gave an almost imperceptible nod, which she interpreted as encouragement.

'The behaviour I've described would be experienced by a sexual partner as oppressive. It would *not* be consensual activity.'

West nodded genially. 'Care to say a few words about his background, Doctor? Abused as a child, that kind of thing?'

'Not necessarily,' said Kate, still wary. 'But his upbringing would have had its difficulties. His behaviour indicates that he feels entitled to treat females extremely badly. I suspect that he experienced significant confusion in his relationship with females in his family. He may have felt overshadowed by siblings, for example, believing them more physically attractive or intelligent than he. These are possibilities, you understand. Some may apply and some may not—'

Belding cut in. 'What if someone reading what you've told us thinks he or she has information but they feel uncomfortable about contacting the police? What would you say to that person, Dr Hanson?'

'Please do it. Please call us. We can reassure anyone who contacts the Unsolved Crime Unit that the source of the information would be kept confidential.' Kate hesitated. 'At the moment we're doing all we can, but we need the public's help. We're appealing to anyone who thinks they may have information to contact us.'

Belding again. 'Why the gap from the early 2000s to now? Where's he been?'

Joe responded to this. 'First, we don't know that there is a gap. It's possible he has continued. He could have relocated his criminal activities. We've initiated searches of abduction-murder cases with similar behaviours—'

West jumped in quickly. 'What kinds of behaviours?'

'Sorry, we're not able to divulge that information,' responded Joe, easily. 'The apparent halt to his offending that you just referred to – he may have been in prison. Moved elsewhere in the UK, even left the country. We don't know. To cover all possibilities, we want to extend this appeal to law enforcement workers, prison staff or probation officers – if the information we've made available today is reminiscent of anyone they've worked with or come into contact with over the last few years, give us a call.'

Both reporters looked to Kate and she restated her main message.

'If anyone reading the description I've given of this man's intimate behaviour thinks that it fits someone in their family or someone they've known in the past, we're asking that they please inform the police. We appreciate that it might be hard to do that. But he's already murdered three young women.'

Both reporters stared at her. 'Could be he's just stopped,' said West.

'We think it very unlikely that this man would have simply stopped his victimisation of young females. We just don't know what he's done since 2003.'

'Can you say anything about the victims, Dr Hanson?' asked Belding.

'The three young women shared some similar physical character-istics. All in their late teens to early twenties, long blonde hair. Tall, slim. Educated. Tastefully dressed.'

'Given that you think he might be a risk currently, do you have any advice for young women of that description?' asked West, with his deceptively encouraging smile.

'*All* women need to live cautiously,' said Kate simply.

'Any plans to talk directly to the media in general? News channels, for instance?'

'No. None,' said Kate flatly.

The journalists took their notebooks and recording equipment and left, Bernie giving them a wide berth as he passed them at the door of UCU.

'How'd you think it went?' asked Kate, head resting on one hand, feeling spent.

'We'll know when we see the papers tomorrow,' said Joe.

Bernie massaged his jowls. 'And then the doo-doo will really hit the fan. Let's hope it gets us some leads.'

Joe lifted his long legs on to the table, crossing them at the ankle. 'It could be a spur to the doer to communicate with us directly.'

Kate eyes widened. 'What makes you say that?'

'There was this big case back home. Publicised coast to coast. This guy killed a lot of people. About ten, far as I remember. Then he stopped and—'

'Accordin' to the Doc, what they never do is *stop*.'

Kate said nothing, and Joe continued.

'*He* stopped. After he got a job as a kind of warden in his neighbourhood. A bit like your Neighbourhood Watch here, but waged and more official. He'd actually wanted to be a cop but they wouldn't have him. Seems the warden job gave him what he wanted, or needed. A uniform and a licence to shove people around. He got on television a couple of times, describing his work as a warden.'

Bernie looked at Joe. 'Right. So he stopped because he got a job he liked. Then what happened?'

'A reporter on Wichita's main newspaper knew about the murders – this is when the doer had stopped – so he gets hold of the details of the cases from press records and . . .' Joe paused, looking at each of them. 'This reporter, he wrote a book. It got published. Suddenly, the reporter's top dollar. Featured on newscasts and on talk shows. *That's* when the killer started communicating.'

Kate looked from Joe to Bernie and back, suddenly fearful. 'Don't say it. Don't say he killed again.'

'Nope. Like I said, he started communicating.'

'Who with? How?' asked Kate.

Joe stretched his long arms, lacing his fingers behind his head. 'He started sending letters to the newspaper, addressed to the guy who wrote the book. About *his* murders – because that's how he viewed them.'

'Yeah, so . . . why'd he do that?' Bernie asked.

'Because he was pretty damn mad with the reporter. Regarded himself as the expert on "his" murders. And he wanted to put the reporter straight on a few aspects. So he started sending him information about what he'd done. Stuff no one knew about, except maybe the cops. He also started leaving all kinds of spooky stuff around the areas where the murders were committed. Not too far from where he lived, as it happens.'

Bernie perked up. 'Spooky, as in?'

'Barbie dolls with their heads chopped off, that kind of stuff. Messages inside cereal boxes. Yeah? Cereal–serial. Get it?'

Bernie's eyes narrowed under lowered brows. 'You're having us on!'

227

Joe leaned back, raising his arms behind his head, lacing his fingers together. 'Nope.'

Kate gazed at Joe intently, a small frown above her nose.

Bernie waited. 'So? *And!* Then what happened?'

'He got caught.'

'How? I still don't get why he did all the barmy stuff.'

'I do,' said Kate.

Joe grinned across at her. 'He did it because he didn't like the fact that the guy who wrote the book was getting all the attention. He thought *he* should be getting the attention . . .'

'Now I know you're having us on!' Bernie looked from Joe to Kate, monobrowed, as Joe continued.

' . . . and he got caught because he sent a floppy disk to the reporter guy, describing the murders in detail. Because he's still pissed at him getting all the buzz. But first he sends him an anonymous note saying "Hey, if I send you some info on a computer disk –" bearing in mind this was in the seventies or eighties – "you won't be able to trace it to me, will ya?" and the reporter says, "Nah. Give it up." And he *does*. And they trace the disk to the computer at a local church where the killer was a member, and—'

'Yeah, right. I didn't come down with the first shower, Corrigan. I got things to do.' Bernie got up from his chair, adjusting his trousers, and headed for the door.

Kate called after him: 'Where?'

'Human bleeding Resources. Going to see if they got any of my test results.'

She transferred her attention back to Joe. 'I know about that case.'

He grinned sideways at her. 'Thought you might.'

'I hope we don't stir up our doer, Joe.' Kate felt his eyes on her. 'What?'

'Just wondering whether you got plans this evening?'

Kate got busy with her notebook and highlighter. 'Yes.'

Kate had been at home for just a minute and was moodily surveying the breakfast dishes still on the table, it being Phyllis's day off. She glanced at her watch, mood deepening. Where was Maisie? She heard a key in the front door and the thud of book bag on wood. Maisie stomped into the kitchen and flopped on to one of the chairs, looking at Kate, face irritable.

228

'*Mom!* I waited an hour for you! Where were you? Why didn't you answer your phone?'

'I can't find it. What do you mean "waited"? You were coming home with—'

Maisie's eyes rolled in her flushed face. 'Mom, you texted me and said to go to the Stu U—'

'I did no such thing! I wouldn't tell you to go to the Student Union. It's licensed! I've mislaid my phone so I couldn't have—'

'I was waiting in the *hall* of the Union, like you *said*. Mom, you really arc losing it!'

Kate looked at her daughter's accusatory face.

'Maybe one of your friends sent the text as a joke? Check the number.'

'I zapped it,' snapped an irate Maisie as she pushed herself off the chair and plodded to the door. 'Another thing. I think Phyllis is on the take.'

Kate looked up quickly from organising china, horrified at Maisie's accusation.

'What? That's an awful thing to say, Maisie. Phyllis has been with us for . . . Why, what's missing?'

'My best lip gloss. You know, the sherbet-flavoured one.'

Of course she knew. On the cigarettes.

'So? That's hardly Phyllis's style. You think she ate it?'

'No need to get sarcastic,' grumped Maisie. 'It's nowhere. Gone.' Her voice faded as she climbed the stairs.

Kate shook her head as she sat at the table and pulled her notebook towards her. Her stalking theory was bothering her. They didn't know whether the girls who'd been raped years ago were stalked. But if she was right, if Suzie Luckman had been victimised twice by the same doer, the second encounter *had* to be as a result of the doer watching and following her.

Kate frowned. And *that* was the problem. Suzie didn't come home regularly, according to her mother. Which meant that the doer had to be willing to – what? Hang around, on the off-chance she was in Birmingham? Kate shook her head. Highly motivated he might be. Patient, possibly. But willing to give up so much of his time to chance? And what about the weekend case? If her theory was correct, the killer had gone to the trouble to return it to Suzie's flat, perhaps to slow

229

down the police investigation. Had he stalked her all the way to London? She threw down her pen.

Maybe Mrs Luckman's information to them was wrong.

Maybe Suzie had had a regular arrangement to come home.

But it was one of the few times during their conversation when she'd seemed sure.

Kate shook her head in irritation.

It didn't make any sense. Stalkers didn't wait around for weeks, hoping for a chance of seeing their quarry.

Did he find out somehow that she was coming home on a specific date?

If so, how?

Half an hour later, Kate was in the sitting room, still prodding the issue, when Mugger leapt on to the sofa and began an enthusiastic washing routine next to her. She looked down at him, absently scratching the fur on the top of his head, between his ears.

'Hi, Mugsy. What you been up to? Working hard at your job – terrorising small furry things? Meet any nice ladies?'

She went back to the list to try a different angle.

Why did he kill Suzie so long after he'd raped her?

Maybe he knew she could identify him as her rapist?

Or . . .

He thought she could?

Kate's head dropped back on to the sofa cushion.

Getting nowhere.

She lifted her head and gazed into the middle distance, smiling faintly.

He'd more or less asked for a date. Joe.

The smile changed to a frown.

And you avoided it.

What's the matter with you?

CHAPTER FORTY-FIVE

On Wednesday morning, Maisie was sitting on the step of the front porch, elbows on knees, watching her mother. The house phone began ringing but she made no effort to go to it. After four rings, Kate's patience had worn thin.

'Maisie, will you get that, *please*!'

Sighing, Maisie got up and went inside the house. From the driveway Kate could hear her daughter talking.

'Hello? Oh, hi, Joe. No, you can't . . . Because she's got a man changing a wheel and she's in a mood so she's ordering him about and—'

Kate walked briskly into the hall and took the receiver from Maisie. '*Thank* you. Hello, Joe.'

'Hi, Red. Got a flat?'

'Mmm, the mechanic's just told me it'll take him another couple of minutes. I've got to drop Maisie— Oh, hang on, Joe . . .' The mechanic came to the door, and at the same time, a sleek-looking vehicle arrived on the drive with a loud beep.

Maisie picked up her school bag and ran towards the open door. 'Chelsey's mom's here! I'm going with them! Bye!'

Kate looked out to check, then turned her attention back to the phone call.

'I can come in now Maisie's sorted.'

'Don't forget. Keep to . . .'

'. . . the back way.'

'Press is thinner on the ground back there. How long will you be?'

Some quality in Joe's voice made Kate ask, 'What's the urgency?'

After Joe's reply she hung up.

Furman wanted to see them. And so did Gander.

It felt crowded in the office with the inclusion of all from UCU. Gander was sitting at his desk, Furman standing to one side of him. Kate was trying to gauge Furman's mood and the reason for the meeting.

Arms folded at his chest, Joe's attention was on the many Force photographs arranged on the long wall of Gander's office. Kate followed his gaze. Anything was better than looking at Furman. A detail in one of the photographs snagged her attention. Wasn't that . . . ?

It was Gander who spoke first.

'It's been brought to my attention that an unauthorised entry was made from UCU into a confidential database relating to credit-card use within the last three days.' He looked uneasy, but pressed on, with a glance at Furman, who was staring stonily ahead. 'Naturally, because of the . . . history, suspicion inevitably falls on—'

Kate saw Bernie give Julian an encouraging wink. Her face heated up. Because of Julian's past, they were ready to blame him for what she had done.

'Chief Superintendent Gander,' she interrupted, 'it wasn't anything to do with Julian.'

Both Gander and Julian looked relieved.

Kate looked directly at the Chief Super. 'It was me. My responsibility entirely.'

Furman was working himself into a rage, the vein up and running, but Kate could detect something else beneath the surface. Satisfaction.

'I *knew* it!' he said, his voice barely a whisper. 'That letter. To your professional body. It's on its way. As of now, you no longer have a role here. You're finished.' He pointed a quivering finger towards the door. 'You can—'

Gander intervened, voice weary. 'Hang on, Roger. It's not that simple. Kate is a contracted civilian.'

'Sir! Dr Hanson went into financial data without clearance. She also interviewed the son of a prominent West Midlands business-man when expressly forbidden. These infringements demonstrate that she's totally unwilling or unable to work by the rules of police procedure and follow orders, both of which she treats with contempt.'

Kate had had a presentiment in the last couple of weeks that this scene would eventually play itself out. She was only surprised it was so soon and was almost relieved it was happening. She ignored Furman, speaking directly to Gander.

'I'm not contemptuous of police procedure and I'm not going anywhere as long as I believe we can make progress on these cases. I'm *not* quitting.'

Furman glared at her, coherent speech almost deserting him. 'It's not up to *you*,' he managed to hiss. 'That isn't your decision to make.'

As Gander opened his mouth to respond to Kate, Joe suddenly rose and stood in front of Furman, disgust on his face.

'Your management skills are lousy, Furman.' Eyes locked on Furman's, he addressed Gander. 'Sir, if Kate is suspended, I quit UCU—'

Alarmed at this rapid turn of events, Kate intervened. 'No, no! This is my problem. It's my—'

Furman broke in. 'Too right it is! The Force is run according to rules and—'

Kate whirled to face him. 'What rules would those be? Always do the least you can? Never commit to cases? Never, *ever* give a thought to the suffering and loss of victims and their families? Because *those* seem to be the rules you work to, Furman. You're a disgrace!'

The others stared from Kate to a now white-faced Furman, but she wasn't finished. '*Show* that it's not true, what I just said. Tell us the names of the three young women we know have died,' she challenged.

In the silence, all eyes were now on Furman. 'Who the *hell* do you think you are,' he whispered, seething. 'Rules are there for a reason. And they're for everybody. Including *you*. The credit-card data you interfered with, the Cranham family whom you harassed. It's about human rights! That's the system we operate within. That's the *law*!'

Kate hadn't thought she could get any angrier. She was wrong. Now incandescent, she took two steps closer to Furman, causing Joe to move closer.

'So you think that *those* kinds of human rights – not to have your data looked at, or a wealthy family legitimately talked to because it might 'upset' them – are what matters? What about Janine Walker's human rights? And Molly James's and Suzie Luckman's and the other rape victims'? What about the rights of their families, who are done in by what happened to their children and have to carry on as best they can?' Kate glared up at Furman. 'If that's the system, then it's no damn good!'

Furman's eyes flicked to Joe, then Gander, who had a grim look on his face.

'Dr Hanson is clearly beyond her own control, sir. I recommend that she's given some compassionate leave time.'

Kate eyed him, still furious. 'If there's any move to reduce my involvement in these cases, I go immediately to the media.' She pointed towards the window. 'And I give it to them straight how shoddy, how superficial your investigations were in 1998 and 2002, and how you're now blocking our efforts to put that right.'

She was also thinking: *He obviously doesn't know we've already spoken to the press.* She waited, frowning up at him. 'What's the matter with you?' she asked, voice low. 'Are you afraid of your previous investigations coming under scrutiny?'

He gazed down at her, his voice almost inaudible. 'You go anywhere near the press and I'll bury you. If—'

Joe's deep voice cut in. 'Hey, Furman! I don't give a rat's ass for you or your crazy priorities. Don't throw threats around, d'you hear!'

Kate headed for the door, pulled it open and walked out of the room. Straight into Harry. She guessed why he was there. His usual calm, light-hearted demeanour was absent. Instead he looked agitated, eyes strained. He'd heard about the meeting via the Headquarters vine.

'Julian told me about the credit-card data,' he said quickly. 'I'm worried about him. I have to speak up for—'

'It's okay, Harry. There's no need. I've told them it was me. Julian's not in any trouble.'

'Kate, as his forensic manager, I can't tell you how glad I am to hear that.'

Kate glanced at him as they walked together. He looked troubled. 'What is it, Harry?'

They'd arrived at UCU. 'I need a word with you, Kate. It's about Julian.'

They walked through the door of UCU and sat at the table, Kate wondering what was on Harry's mind. He got quickly to the point.

'Have you noticed any change in Julian recently?'

Kate nodded reluctantly. 'Now you mention it, yes. We all have. He seems moody, tense.' She stopped speaking, then decided it was the right time to say what was on her mind. 'Actually, Harry, I was going to say something – I'm concerned about Matt Prentiss's interactions with him. I think that's what might be at the bottom of—' She stopped speaking as Harry vigorously shook his head.

'No, Kate. It's nothing to do with Matt. I suspect Julian's taking drugs.'

Kate stared at him, horrified. 'What makes you think that?'

'Like you said, his moodiness and—'

'But – that isn't like Julian. He's been in trouble before and he's *desperate* to do well now. It just doesn't—'

'Kate, we've had some thefts of money Upstairs, and I'm afraid Julian's the main suspect. I didn't want to have to say all of this and I've tried to ensure that information about the thefts has stayed inside the forensic team, but you're his main supervisor. You need to know.'

Kate stared at him. ' "Thefts"?'

Harry shrugged. He looked at Kate, face worried, eyes candid. 'I'm not sure I did the right thing, Kate, but Furman's clearly heard about the missing money from somewhere. He asked me directly about it. I said nothing. Now I'm worried that that's leaving Julian to do whatever he's doing . . .'

Kate was resolute. 'Well, Gander has to know.'

Harry shook his head. 'I'm betting Furman's telling him right now, Kate. This is all confidential, but it seemed only fair to me that you do know.' He looked at her and sighed. 'Sorry to be the bearer of bad news, with everything else that's going on. And I'm sorry about Julian. He's got great aptitude for forensic work – what more can I say? It's all very sad.'

Kate watched as Harry got up slowly from the table, looking exhausted as he walked to the door and out. He knew as surely as Kate did that this meant the end of the line for Julian.

Five minutes later, Kate was still sitting at the table. Her own position was little better than Julian's. How had it come to this?

Elbows on the table, fingers to her mouth, she stared ahead, unseeing. Maisie's financial security and her own professional reputation and future were probably in the balance. Dark as these thoughts were, they darkened further as her eyes moved slowly to the glass screen and she reread the notes on it, although she now knew them by heart. He *was* out there. He *was* operating. Okay, Furman might follow up on his threat against her. He might even finish UCU in its current form. But other people would take over the cases. Good people. Upstairs at Rose Road.

Kate closed her eyes tight, steadying her mouth with her fingers.

What was it Bernie had said? *Not over till the fat woman . . .*

It wasn't over.

Yet.

CHAPTER FORTY-SIX

Half an hour later they were all in UCU. Nothing had been said between them about the scene in Gander's office, beyond Joe confirming that Gander had refused to take any action against Kate. For now. For her part, Kate had said nothing to anyone about Julian.

It had been unusually quiet in the past few minutes. The day's newspapers had arrived. Bernie refolded the *Birmingham Mail* and slapped it on the table. Joe had skimmed through *The Times*, given it to Kate and was now watching her get the gist.

'*Oh* my—' She'd got it. She continued reading. 'What it says here is that the doer's a sadistic bully who was spoiled by his mother and sexually attracted to his sister.' She peered over the newspaper at Joe, eyes wide. 'I didn't *say* that! And why's my age relevant? There's a photograph as well. God, what a *sight*!' she muttered.

'I thought you looked cute,' Joe soothed.

Kate's eyes met his and stayed there for a few seconds, then, 'What've you got there, Bernie?'

'Along the same lines, but less polite.' He reached for the paper again and unfolded it. 'Sadistic wife-beater, fancies his mother, hates his brothers, had sex with his sisters – oh, and you're a red-headed minx who strikes fear into sex offenders.'

Kate leaned sideways and snatched the newspaper off him.

Bernie continued: 'It's more or less what's there. I've just cut out the fluff. They've worked in the word "psycho" for good measure. Makes him sound like he's got his own motel.'

Kate threw down the newspaper in disgust.

Joe looked at them both. 'Hey, come on! It's not that bad. It gives the bottom line on him.'

Kate's eyebrows shot upwards. 'Not that *bad*? It's completely missed the point of what we were trying to do. It's got no *finesse*.

We wanted people to read about him and think, "Ah, now that I've read that and thought about it, it sounds just like old so-and-so who I knew ten, twenty years ago." Anybody reading that'll think, "Golly! What a nutter", and won't connect him to *anyone* they've experienced.'

Joe swivelled round to face Kate, grinning, eyebrows raised. 'Golly?'

Smiling despite her tension and upset, Kate picked up the newspaper and threw it at him, aware that he was trying to lift her mood. Joe retrieved the newspaper with the air of the long-sufferer, placed it on the table and, leaning forward, forearms on knees, looked at Kate from beneath lowered brows.

'Yo' wanna be finessed, Red? Yo' is just lookin' in da *wrong* place, hear what I'm sayin'?'

Head on one side, Kate held his gaze. 'There's about as much finesse in that Southern act as in the stuff I've just read. I'm now going to my other day job,' she said. 'While I still have it.'

Kate sat on the wrought-iron table in her garden, her feet on a similar chair. A few hours of concentrated effort at the university, following the events at Rose Road, had left her feeling wrung-out. A call from Joe in the late afternoon had helped, as had his offer to visit later.

Pachelbel's *Canon* continued to play from the kitchen, failing to achieve its usual effect on Kate. Too reminiscent of her circular thinking about Julian and also her own difficulties. She adjusted her position on the table, the tan on her legs illuminated by the lights attached to the back wall of the house.

Despite her efforts not to think about it, her thoughts kept returning to her current situation. *If* her professional integrity, her ethical values, were publicly questioned by Furman, it could impact on her future. If that happened, she might find it difficult to progress, or even remain in her current post at the university. Alternative positions at the same level of salary might be difficult to find. And if *that* happened, she might even have difficulty ultimately in supporting her and Maisie's current way of life. This house. She gazed at warm brick, wisteria and wide windows.

Kate resolutely quit the mental merry-go-round and slowly sipped wine until she heard the doorbell. She went to answer it, then she and Joe walked out into the garden together.

238

He sat forward, wine glass balanced on top of the work diary between his feet, and went to what was on his mind.

'Kate, hear me when I say that Furman's a moron. He's got no right talking to you or anybody the way he does. In the States it would lead to litigation. I've spelled out my position to Gander.'

Kate shook her head. 'I don't want to cause you problems, Joe. Or Bernie, or . . . Julian. Trouble is, although he's not popular, Furman's ingratiated himself with a few people in high places in the Force. People who don't have to put up with him on a daily basis. His views and opinions could carry weight.'

'Then this Force is dumber than he is.' He looked into his glass, then at Kate.

'Don't go nuts, but have you considered keeping a low profile, then showing good behaviour as a wily next step? Or maybe even a quick acknowledgement that you were in error, for effect only, and . . . No, I guessed not.'

'Joe, I know what I did wasn't exactly right. I know it's technically breaking the law. But I think sometimes there are things we *have* to do that are for – I don't know – a greater good.' She sipped, then glanced at him. 'And now I've played right into Furman's hands. Now he thinks he's got me. I suppose in a way he has, hasn't he?'

She went back to a previous train of thought. For Kate, her work had always been what she was. What she loved. A lifeline at times of stress. Like when Kevin left. It had provided an emotional refuge. Demanded that she think, fill her mind with the theoretical. Kept her from dwelling on the personal. But these cases were personal. The Walkers. Dianne James. Mrs Luckman. They didn't have the luxury of pursuing information in order to find out what happened to their daughters. And now, by taking on the task, her own professional future, even her personal future, could be in jeopardy. That wasn't right. Surely?

'You're one tough broad, Hanson,' Joe said, narrowing his eyes at her. She glared at him, mock-serious.

'Nobody talks like that any more. Not even Americans.'

'Raymond Chandler?'

'He's dead.'

'He'd be surprised and hurt to hear you say that.'

She grinned, recognising her liking of Joe's ability to defuse tension. Even in dark situations. Serious again, she gazed into her now empty wine glass.

'We know a lot about what happened to these young women, Joe. We can't ignore it. Forgetting it isn't an option. We've also got some emotional awareness – of what it was like for them, the fear they must have felt.' She paused. 'Nothing was done properly during those first investigations. Furman put no real effort into them. He directed the superficial stuff, ticked the boxes, had people interviewed, played the part of the investigator. But – he didn't *care*, Joe. He still doesn't. I doubt he's given any of those young women a passing thought in all the years they've been gone.'

She tugged at the band on her hair, released her curls and ran her fingers through them.

Joe had listened and waited. Now he offered some carefully chosen words. 'Kate, if things get difficult for you, I can help . . .'

Kate's heart squeezed, afraid of what he might be about to say, mortified with embarrassment.

'*No*! No, Joe, really. Thanks. We're colleagues . . . friends. Maisie and I aren't your responsibility. Kevin may be a selfish idiot with commitment issues, but he wouldn't see Maisie without whatever she needed. What I just said about my professional future – I have to be aware of it, for Maisie's sake. But we can't let these cases go the way they have in the past, can we? A cursory dabble, some half-hearted inquiries, then close them, shut the boxes, send them back to the evidence store. Neat, tidy, forgotten. We owe Janine, Molly, Suzie, their families – and God knows who else besides – more than that.'

'I'm with you.'

Kate nodded, recognising sincerity in the few words. 'Who else will make the effort, give it the best shot, if we don't? This is the girls' last chance, Joe. Their cases will never see daylight again if we don't do all we can to find him. And if we don't find him, what about his future victims?'

Joe was staring at the grass between his feet. He didn't look at her as he quietly asked his question: 'What makes you run, Kate?'

The air around her grew taut. No one had ever asked her so directly. She knew there were two reasons. Celia was right. Although Kate hardly thought of what had happened to them that day more than thirty years ago, it had contributed to who and what she was.

240

She looked up into Joe's face. To reveal it meant trusting him. Did she?

'You know Celia? Well, years ago, when we were small children . . . we got into a situation. There was a man.' Kate stopped, taking charge of her breathing. 'He saw us. He called us.' *Breathe.* 'He was masturbating, Joe.' She saw his facial expression tighten. 'Six months later, he was arrested. For murdering four children.' She stopped and closed her mouth.

Joe waited, his eyes on Kate's face. When nothing more came: 'You and Celia were two lucky young girls . . .'

'I went to him, Joe. He called and I *went*.' Kate bowed her head.

'Kate, you were a *kid*. I don't know how old—'

'Six. We were six,' she whispered.

He nodded slowly. 'You didn't do wrong, Kate. You acted in innocence.'

Kate brushed her face with her hands. 'Like the young women in our cases.'

Joe was waiting. 'There's something else.'

She hesitated again. The other experience that made her 'run', as Joe had phrased it, was to do with her criminal casework as a forensic psychologist.

Getting down from the table, she sat on the chair next to him.

'You know that I take on work instructed by the courts? Well, a few years ago I was involved in a case in Manchester. I won't go into all the details but it became more than just another criminal case. It was about a girl called Karina. She was found dead in her bed one morning.'

Kate felt Joe's eyes on her as she continued.

'And I was, am, convinced that she was killed. By someone inside the house at the time. Karina went to bed in excellent health, Joe. She died sometime during that night. Nobody admitted any responsibility or involvement. I was asked to provide a psychological opinion on the matter. The police in Manchester had investigated her death. If they had a suspicion or theory, they couldn't or wouldn't follow it up. The Crown Prosecution Service didn't support anyone being charged. They said there was insufficient evidence.'

Kate looked away, then back to Joe.

'You probably know by now, Joe, that the legal system we have here actively supports only those cases it knows it has a good chance of winning. My professional opinion of the mother's boyfriend – his personality traits, his dismissive attitude to what had befallen Karina, his capacity to view others as objects – was ignored. On the basis that it wasn't "hard" evidence. Even though *he* knew that *I* knew he was involved in her death.'

Joe shook his head as Kate continued.

'Karina was only three years old. Little children don't die suddenly in their beds unless something *happens* to them. But they still said "insufficient evidence". She got no justice, Joe. As you sometimes say, "Go figure". The opinions I provide for criminal cases are as balanced and as rigorous as I can make them – but I won't fudge or avoid issues if I think they need commenting on.' She placed her glass on the table. 'That doesn't win me many fans.'

The music had changed a minute before, sidelining Pachelbel for something more up-to-date.

Joe put down his glass, stood and reached down for Kate's hand.

'What're you doing?' Kate looked up uneasily as he gently pulled her to her feet and stood close, a hand round her waist, his voice low.

'I think we could use this music. In fact, I think it'd be a *really* good idea,' he said.

Kate glanced up at him as they stood together. 'You think this song's appropriate? I'd hardly call what I've had a "perfect day".' She felt Joe's arms around her, his quiet voice in her ear.

'It's just a dance, Red, and everything's got some good bits, alongside the crazy stuff. We're dancing for the good bits.'

The music faded and they walked slowly inside the house and out on to the front drive. They stood by Joe's car without talking for some seconds.

'See you at Rose Road tomorrow?' Joe asked.

She nodded. 'I'll be there.'

Ten minutes later, Kate stood in her bedroom, about to close the window blinds. She leaned on the sill, looking out at the quiet, still-warm avenue. Not a leaf stirring. What had somebody told her when she first arrived in the city years ago? More trees in Birmingham than people. A heartening ratio, if it were true. She gazed at the sky, wondering if the hot weather was likely to end soon.

'Mom?'

She turned. Maisie was in the doorway with a textbook. Their truce was holding. For maybe the hundredth time, Kate thought of the small blue tablets, then banished them resolutely from her mind.

'Still working?'

Maisie nodded. 'Eng lit. A poem. I'm fed up and bored of it.' She pouted. Maisie's academic strengths lay well towards the mathematical and the scientific.

'Show me.'

They sat on Kate's bed together, looking at the text.

'Why use rotten old Latin for a title? Why not use an English word?' groused Maisie, lying down at Kate's side, a small frown above her nose.

Kate leaned against the headboard, an arm around her daughter. 'The thing to remember is that when people write things, like stories or poems, they tend to look for ways to avoid laying everything out, or making meaning too easily available for the reader.'

'Yeah, right. It's certainly making my life hard!'

Kate smiled down at her. 'Maybe they feel that they've had some life-changing experience that was difficult for them. They want to share what they've learned, without trivialising it. So they find a way of making the reader *work* for meaning, strive for understanding. They think their experience is worth being worked for. I think they also do it because we tend to remember the things that are a struggle for us. Why didn't you Google it?'

Maisie huffed. 'Mom, I've just done three hours of projective and inversive geometry, although I know what I'm doing with that. But this! I can't be bothered and I don't like it and it's well depressing.'

Kate looked at her, eyebrows raised. 'Do you know the story behind it?'

'No. Dodders just gave it to my study group and said, "Here you are, gels, deconstruct this *wonderful* work. By tomorrow, ten sharp!"'

Maisie had just given a very passable impersonation of her headmistress, Miss Dodson. Kate laughed, brushing a stray curl from the frown. She took the textbook from Maisie's hand.

'It's about a man who was very ill and had to have his leg amputated.'

'*See*? I told you it was depressing.'

'This was over a hundred years ago, when they couldn't cure what he had. He wrote the poem when he was in hospital.'

Kate pointed to one of the printed lines. 'There. He's saying he wouldn't be beaten by what'd happened to him. And he wasn't.'

She gazed down, watching Maisie's eyes track words as she read.

'Mmm . . . So he was determined not to give in, right?'

'Exactly. He wouldn't be beaten by his situation. "Invictus." It means "Undefeated".'

'Okay. I get it. He was brave and stuck with it. Still a bit depressing.'

Maisie returned to her room and Kate stretched on the bed, reliving the earlier, relatively unfamiliar sensation of strong arms.

What do I know about you, Joe?

Quiet, easy-going, funny, a good foil for my moods.

'Cool', according to Maisie.

But you didn't tell me what makes you run.

CHAPTER FORTY-SEVEN

Early Thursday morning, Kate was back in UCU feeling uneasy, although nothing further had been said about yesterday. She'd decided to continue as if her clash with Furman had never happened. Glancing briefly at Julian's smooth face, she resolved to deal with the information she'd been given about him in similar fashion. She would do and say nothing. For now.

For the last ten minutes she had summarised her views of the doer to her three colleagues. She'd described his likely basic physical characteristics – probably white, around his late thirties, owner of a quality vehicle and as likely to be in a relationship as not. They wouldn't be lulled into the cliché of a sad loner whom neighbours later said 'kept himself to himself'. Kate had acknowledged that given the varying times of the abductions, including the most recent, it was not possible to be categorical about whether he was employed, although she thought he probably was. Given the quality of his car, as suggested by Josie Kenton-Smith, even though it was years ago, it was possible that he had a career that came with some responsibility and kudos and was therefore likely to involve a degree of freedom on a daily basis.

She had felt she was on more solid ground with some of the aspects of his actual behaviour as suggested by the rape-murders, which showed him to be capable of planning and maintaining focus. That meant he was intelligent and unlikely to have serious mental health issues. She saw Bernie fold his arms as she said this.

She had summarised the meaning of the doer's behaviour towards his victims – sexually sadistic, a need to render any victim totally defenceless, a need to denigrate and control, almost certainly a long-term user of hard-core pornography. She finished with a brief reference to his possible childhood experience.

'His behaviour towards young women indicates the possibility that during his childhood there was an adult figure who was in some way confusing for him, probably very imposing, even frightening.'

'I thought you said to the reporters that you didn't think he was abused.'

'Not necessarily in the ways that might be anticipated to mean, Bernie – physical, sexual, possibly not, although I can't categorically rule those out.'

'Course not,' Bernie said, sarcasm showing.

'It's more a case of him experiencing a key adult as *mystifying*, bewildering, in behaviour or presentation,' Kate continued. 'The way he appears to manipulate and handle his victims, it seems to me that he sees *their* presentation of themselves as somehow at odds with what he thinks they really are. I would anticipate that he had behavioural problems as a young person. Therefore, if he has a well-paid, responsible job now, he achieved it subsequent to his teenage years, through ambition, diligence and a notable willingness to fit in.'

What had Celia said of him? *He's a student, a mature student.* Around twelve years ago.

Kate looked at her colleagues, trying to judge their reception of the information she'd just given. She knew that Bernie was wondering where they went from here.

'I have confidence in what I've said because it's based on what we know of his behaviour.' She walked from the glass screen to sit on the team table. 'I think it might help to consider his likely behaviour during childhood.'

'Why?' This from Bernie.

'Because when we decide that we have a POI worth raising to suspect, we can ask questions about it in interview with him. As a suspect in very serious crimes he's believed to have committed as an adult, he might find it easier, less threatening, to talk about what he was doing many years ago. Especially if *you* ask him, rather than me,' she added. 'We can also request his medical records, educational records, if there are any, to get reliable data about his early years.'

'So what childhood behaviours would we expect?' asked Julian.

'Truancy, pilfering, lying, rule-breaking, bed-wetting, fire-setting.'

'We could arrest half the population on them grounds!'

'No, Bernie. What would be significant for us is the *number* of such behaviours occurring and their severity, *plus* indications of the

246

personal characteristics I've already outlined. It's all of these, coming *together*. In *one* person.' Kate shook her head slightly. 'We haven't exactly been inundated with leads.' A thought suddenly occurred. 'Anything from our newspaper appeal?'

'Gander's put Whittaker and an officer from Upstairs on to that. They're going to let us know if they get anything that looks solid. Or even hopeful.'

Kate nodded. 'The only potential witness to Janine's abduction, the neighbour, is dead. No witness information from the rape cases – in fact hardly anything at all. It's all so – frustrating. In the absence of any new leads, maybe we need to consider the persons of interest we already have in as much detail as possible.'

Bernie rubbed his jowls. 'So the next step is identifying a POI who might have had even a passing connection to all these girls?'

Kate looked at her notes. 'I'm sure that Suzie Luckman was stalked and killed by the same person who raped her, who somehow knew when she was visiting Birmingham from her home in London. Janine Walker's diary suggests she was subjected to a degree of stalking, although she didn't perceive it in that way. With Janine, and to some degree with Molly, he came out of the shadows and made his presence felt. That's unusual behaviour, but it's useful for us – it tells us that he's physically acceptable, attractive even, although older than both of them. Further characteristics to add to the others we suspect, and ones that would be easy to verify, once we have him.'

Bernie frowned. 'I thought stalkers hung about for years being a pain in the arse. We arrested a woman last year. Got a thing for her doctor.'

'That would have been a case of stalked victim as love object. What we've got is a *predatory* stalker whose ultimate goal is capture followed by physical harm. In our cases, destruction. They're always male. Average age mid-thirties and probably employed.'

'Nice to hear an "always" in the middle of a lot of "probablies",' groused Bernie.

Julian looked at Kate. 'Do they ever threaten the person they're stalking, prior to striking?'

Kate shook her head. 'Predators are the least likely of all stalkers to do that. Their sole aim is amassing information so they can prepare for the ultimate attack. I am surprised at his approach behaviour, particularly with Janine, the indication of familiarity, as suggested in her diary.'

She reran Julian's question in her head.

'Actually, Julian, you've made me think. Whilst they're intent on concealing themselves prior to attack, some stalkers do show themselves in a way, sometimes by entering their victims' homes. Obviously, they're well placed to do that. They know the living arrangements and routines of the person they're stalking. It's another way of gaining intimate information in order to abduct. They may even take small, insignificant items that are unlikely to be missed immediately.'

Lip gloss.

Kate pushed her hair off her face, chiding herself for her paranoia, knowing it was inevitable, given the job she did and her knowledge of the capabilities of certain types of people. 'If his personality is how I've described, we can expect other deviant behaviours. When we have someone who looks to be a likely suspect, we check police records, see whether he's already known – for pilfering, theft, deviant sexual activity.'

She stopped again, thinking how best to phrase her next offering whilst avoiding a knee-jerk response from Bernie.

'It's fairly usual for predators to exhibit sexual deviance in a number of ways. I've already mentioned hard-core pornography. We've extended our task to include prior rapes. If and when we identify someone worthy of closer attention, we'll look for indications of voyeurism – for example, peeping, or other nuisance behaviour towards females.'

She took a breath. 'We're back to the graduation of offenders. It's not unknown for stalkers to begin their offending career as either peeping Toms or exhibitionists . . .'

'Flashing? *Colley!*' Bernie said.

'*No.*'

Bernie looked irritable. 'We have to turn at least one POI into a suspect soon, Doc. We've already got three.' He itemised on his fingers: 'Cranham, Colley, Fairley. You've ruled out Cranham because he didn't show no signs of knowing the rape victims. I'm still not convinced. Maybe he was just clever at hiding what he was thinking, yeah?'

'No. Concealment takes significant effort. As I said before, he wasn't expending any.'

'Okay, have it your way. How about Colley, the sex pest? According to you, Doc, he ain't got no self-esteem. So how come he's able to jump out at women?'

Kate replied: 'The fact of his doing exactly that demonstrates how under-assertive and low in self-esteem he is. His goal was to shock the women, Bernie. To reassure himself that he was capable of having an impact and causing an emotional response in them. Julian got a printout of Colley's exhibitionist records . . .' Kate riffled the pages of A4 in front of her. 'Here. Of his seven victims, four were aged between seven and nine and three were in their mid to late fifties. He feels intimidated by females who aren't in those age brackets.'

Bernie wasn't finished. 'You're not keen on Fairley neither, are you?'

'We need to keep our focus on the big picture, Bernie. My worry is, we get the wrong person in and the case against him starts to create itself. Or we get the right person in, but there's no tangible evidence for arrest. We don't yet have grounds to suppose that Fairley or any of the others have the majority of the characteristics I've talked about.'

Bernie stood, coffee mug in hand. 'So I say, get 'em in here and find out. As far as I'm concerned, Cranham and Fairley fit what you just said. Both of them could be this psycho type. Cranham's an arrogant bastard. The James girl was going for an interview with him. Next thing? She's dropped off the planet. We've only got *his* word she never turned up. Everything you've said applies to Cranham. And what about Fairley? He was *there*. With Molly. Around the time she disappeared.'

He turned to walk away, then stopped. 'Or both of 'em, even. Ever considered it might be a *twosome*? I say we make some subtle inquiries – old school mates, neighbours, people who deal with each of them businesswise, and try and piece together what they've been up to in the past.'

Leaning her forearms on the table, Kate frowned up at him. 'I'm no expert on police procedure . . .'

'You got *that* right!'

'. . . but I thought there had to be *some* solid evidence to link an individual to a crime before he can be formally interrogated as a suspect with a view to arrest. And if Cranham discovered we were trawling for information about him . . .'

'Yeah, well, it ain't an ideal world, this. Sometimes we do whatever we have to to get a case together. *You* know that, Doc, better than anybody. You're no fan of rules. We do what I've said and we float what we find with the CPS and—'

'Have it thrown back at us?' Kate responded. 'Much of what I've said, you wouldn't be able to check out unless you have them in first. We've had those three in for informal discussion already. What's the likelihood they'd come on a cooperative basis again? Zero. Both Cranham and Fairley have already involved lawyers.'

Bernie turned and headed for the coffee makings. Kate sent her last comment after him.

'And I can imagine the scenario if you decided to arrest Cranham and can't make it stick.'

No reply.

Joe looked at Kate, then across the room to Bernie. 'Don't forget, we're still waiting to meet one of our POIs. Malins. The building contractor. Sounds pretty antisocial. You know him, Bernie. What's your take on him?'

Bernie was back, frowning at his coffee. 'You'll soon see. Another git, but a different kind of git to Cranham. Cranham's got that posh front. Anything could be lurking behind it. Malins is more your thug type. Bit of a hulk. History of working out. No scruff, mind you. He likes his clothes and his cars.'

Kate looked doubtful. 'From what I've read and heard from you, Malins is angry, antisocial and sexually impulsive. Sounds like a pretty unpleasant individual. By comparison, our doer's a social chameleon intent on concealing his true nature. Seems to me that with Malins, what you see is what you get.'

Bernie stood in the middle of the room, staring at Kate, incredulous.

'This just gets better, this does! Let's cut out the unnecessary work. Don't even bother getting him in here. Just nail together a couple of theories and, bingo! That's another possible suspect disposed of!'

Julian had been silent for a while, the only sound indicating his presence being the faint scratching of pen on paper and pages being turned. Now he looked up at Bernie.

'Kate's only saying that Malins's profile as we know it doesn't fit with the behaviours in the cases.'

'And who's rattled your bars, Devenish?' demanded Bernie, colour heightening. 'It's "Dr Hanson" to you, and while we're on the

250

subject, you ask her if she profiles! Go on. Ask her! She'll tell you she *don't*. And another thing. I thought you was going to Waitrose's for milk this morning. There's none left.'

Kate sighed and looked at her watch. Less than an hour since they'd started the discussion. It felt like a day. A year.

'Look, when we see Malins, we'll be able to judge how good an actor he might be. Meanwhile, you, Bernie, and you, Joe, know how this works. Right now, are you confident that there's enough to up-grade Cranham or Fairley to suspect?' asked Kate, dispensing with Colley as any kind of contender.

No one spoke.

Kate glanced up at the glass screen. Cranham. Fairley. Colley. Malins. She was sure of what she'd just said about them. As sure as it was possible to be.

A treacherous thought slipped into her head. Could she be wrong? About one or other of these men? *Surely not.* The theory was con-firmed in her observations. But still. What if she *were* wrong? Her eyes drifted to the windows of UCU. The four of them were out there. At this minute.

Quitting these thoughts but distracted by others, of covert entry into people's homes, of missing belongings, Kate wrote a brief ques-tion in her notebook, one to ask the close relatives of the victims at some point – *Do you have home security?* – then started rummaging in her bag.

'What you after now?' asked Bernie, drinking his coffee with a grimace.

'My phone. It's this bag. I can never find anything in it. I need to speak to Maisie. She's doing some revision at Chelsey's house later and she needs reminding to ring me when she wants to come home. Why can't she just do as she's told?'

Kate lifted the unit phone, watching Bernie and Julian as they engaged in some mock sparring, Bernie ruffling Julian's hair.

As Julian headed for the door with his backpack, Kate checked her watch. She put down the phone when her call went unanswered and began replacing items in her bag. She had thirty assignments to grade before tomorrow.

She left her remaining colleagues and UCU. Whittaker was on duty at Reception.

'Had enough, Dr H?'

'Yep. Bye.'

Kate Hanson, divorced, single mother, job on the line, slightly fed up, tired, a little pissed off.

And now departing to gainful employment.

While I still can.

CHAPTER FORTY-EIGHT

Dennis Jackson stood in the darkness, not knowing what else to do. He'd recorded what he'd seen, before the spectacle stopped a few minutes ago. The police had been called and were on their way. His only role in the situation was now one of waiting.

He hadn't even been sure whether to dial 999. It wasn't as if she was in dire need of – anything. He took a fearful glance to one side. Not any more. He'd doubted the local station capable of responding to this. So he'd rung home and his wife said she'd take care of it.

He walked slowly around it, feeling annoyed with himself for his own lack of certainty. Well, he reasoned, how many people would know what to do? Finding something like that?

He peered at his watch. Two thirty a.m. Ten minutes since his wife rang to tell him they were on their way. He'd told his wife how cold it – she – looked. He'd wanted to take his coat off and put it over her, but his wife put him right. *For goodness' sake, Dennis, don't do anything until they come!* So he hadn't. She still looked cold. Deathly cold. Merely looking at her made him feel . . . conniving.

He listened. A hum of vehicles. Lights flashing intermittently as they left the road on the outskirts of Romsley village, and wove their way through the trees towards where he was standing.

They're here! So many!

Six vehicles came to an abrupt halt, three to one side of the small triangle of land, three to the other. A heavyset man heaved himself out of the first and walked with a ponderous, authoritative air towards him, tracked by . . . five, six, seven – he lost count as the uniformed officers bore down on him.

'Mr Jackson? Dennis Jackson?' rasped the big man, glaring down at him, his fleshy face severe, eyes inquisitorial.

Jackson nodded, mouth agape, brain on hold.

'Chief Superintendent Gander. Police Headquarters, Rose Road, Harborne. Your wife phoned this through?'

Jackson nodded again, understanding for the first time in his fifty-four years how it felt to lose the power of speech. In the absence of anything else to do, he stared up at the large policeman, then at the ground to the left of him. It, she, was still there. He hadn't imagined it. Who could?

They stood, motionless, gazing at the body lying nearby on the grass. Gander's face reddened around the jowls as he stood, silent, thinking hard. About youthfulness, and what kind of maniac had done what he was now seeing.

He walked heavily to the other side of the body, snapping his fingers at one of the immobile officers nearby. 'Light!' Jerked into action, the officer ran, giving the body a wide berth. Gander's speculations moved on, closer to home. To the number of young officers at Rose Road. He shook his head, lips compressed, feeling suddenly old. Weary.

Jackson took a couple of steps, tentatively offering the big man his torch. Giving him a hard look, Gander took it and trained it on the body.

'What the devil . . .' he murmured. 'What the *hell's* that? On her face!'

More illumination arrived and Gander looked at her some more. In all his years in the Force, he'd seen nothing like it.

He looked quickly to each side of him. '*You* four. I want lights at the perimeter of the scene. Over there, there and –' he pointed – 'there. Keep well away from the body.' He frowned, looking beyond it. 'There's what looks to be clothes over there. Keep away from them as well. Don't want you wrecking any evidence. Dr Chong and the scenes team are on their way. Get to it. *Move!*'

They scattered.

Only Jackson remained. Standing there, arms hanging at his sides, watching the scene unfold. Gander moved towards him, nodding as Whittaker read the man's details to him from a notebook.

'Okay, Mr Jackson . . . Dennis. Tell us about it,' Gander said.

No response.

'Come *on*, Dennis. I need you to tell us what you know.'

Jackson gave his head a quick shake, then spoke. 'I . . . I was walking along this pathway. We live in that house over there.' He waved a vague hand in the direction of a distant double-fronted property, surrounded by fields, his voice sounding odd, strangled.

'Why?'

Again, no response.

Gander reverted to formality. 'Mr Jackson. *Why* were you walking out here? In the small hours of Thursday, no, Friday morning? PC Whittaker here is waiting to write down any information you can give us.'

'What? . . . Sorry, I see what you . . . I work for the BMS.'

Gander immediately and erroneously connected Jackson to a driving school, then dismissed it. He waited, increasingly impatient.

Jackson appeared to gather what was left of his wits. 'I do research work. For the British Mycological Society. Currently, I'm conducting a nocturnal study of fungi – some are bio-luminous you see, so I came out here . . .' He saw the young officer frown and pause in his writing. 'Mushrooms,' he added, wanting to assist.

'So you were out here, picking some mushrooms?' demanded Gander, eyes suspicious as they flicked towards his harassed scribe.

'Fungi. No, no. Not picking them. *Recording* them.' He dragged a spiral-bound book from one of the pockets of his Barbour. 'See? This has all the species. Here.' He pointed a finger at an illustration and waved his other hand in the direction of a group of trees nearby. 'Deadly webcap. *Cortinarius rubellus*. I found two clusters over there. I've put a mark by it on the page, plus date, time, location . . .' Whittaker hurriedly made notes, looking bemused.

Gander had had about as much as he could take of the witness. 'So you found her during your . . . search? For these . . . things,' he said, verbally prodding Jackson, at the same time delivering a scowl to Whittaker, who was standing, pen poised.

Jackson nodded but said no more.

Gander waited. He could see the man was in shock. When nothing else was forthcoming, he realised that a change of tactic was called for. He gestured quickly to a passing officer and whispered to him. The officer scooted off, returning quickly with a flask.

'Here, Mr Jackson. Take this,' he ordered, offering him a steaming plastic cup. 'Never without a hot cuppa in situations like this. My wife insists on it,' he added, running a warning eye over a smirking Whittaker.

Jackson gratefully drank the hot sweet tea.

'Now. In your own time, Mr Jackson,' said Gander.

Jackson nodded, his face showing some colour as he clasped the plastic cup. 'Sorry . . . I came out of the house at about . . . I don't know what time it was. My wife will know. She'd made me some soup. I had that and then I left the house. I thought all this was . . . some kind of sick joke at first. You know, like a student thing. But that didn't make sense. Nobody here, except me . . . and her.'

Gander frowned as he watched the man. He was thinking that Jackson was a strange character and might have some connection to what had happened to the young woman whose body was lying a mere couple of metres away from them.

'That's a powerful torch you've got there, Dennis. Maglite. Without it you might have gone straight past her—'

Gander's words were stopped by an eerie sound starting up from somewhere deep inside Jackson. It continued for some seconds, attracting a few wary looks from officers nearby. It ended with a gasp.

'No, no, no . . . There was no chance of me missing her.'

Gander was now extremely irritable. Their only witness, if that was all he was, and he was an hysteric.

'What I *meant*, Mr Jackson, was that it's very dark. If you were focused on your mushroom search . . .'

Jackson pulled himself together with an effort, mopping his face with a handkerchief and finishing off the tea. 'You need to know . . . it wasn't like this when I arrived.'

Gander glared at him, lips compressed, face suffused. 'What! You've interfered with a *crime* scene?'

Jackson shook his head, grateful now for his wife's good sense. 'No, *no*! I haven't touched anything. But I *couldn't* have missed it,' he said, windmilling his arms suddenly in an agitated fashion. 'The stars, the blooms. Surging, shooting, spraying! Yes . . . Stars and blooms. Arcing into the sky. All around her.' He stopped, a balloon out of air; his arms dropped to his sides, plastic cup dangling from one finger.

256

Made uneasy by Jackson's turns of phrase, Gander frowned sideways at him. He remembered the sixties, even if he wasn't there, in the sense of being involved. He reviewed what he knew of the witness, considering whether he might be under the influence of some substance. What were the hallucinogenic drug choices these days? Mushrooms!

'Whittaker!' he hissed to his scribe, shoving a call sheet at him. 'Phone this number. Get his wife here. Now!'

Jackson heard this and shook his head.

'Wait. Chief Superintendent . . . sorry. I can't seem to get my thoughts together.' He offered the plastic cup to Whittaker, then pushed his hands into various pockets and compartments of his coat. 'But I can show you.' He drew his hand from a pocket. 'Look. Look at this. Now you'll see why I couldn't have missed her.'

Gander clicked his fingers at Whittaker for an evidence bag and carefully took the small object from Jackson, placing it gently inside the clear plastic. Task completed, he examined the exhibit by torchlight.

'The Lumix, sir. Nice one. Good time delay on the flash. I've fancied one my—'

Giving Whittaker a discouraging glance Gander looked back at the small, silver digital camera.

'How do I view what's on it?' He directed the question to Jackson who gazed at his plastic-shrouded property and pointed to one of several small buttons with a shaking index finger.

Gander pressed it and the black screen surged into life.

'Press that one to view what I took tonight,' murmured Jackson.

He did as instructed, passing several shots of no relevance to where they were standing, then stopped. He gazed down at the small screen, up at Jackson, then back, running the shots forward, then back. Three of them. He walked the few steps to inspect the ground around the body. He looked up at Jackson, then back to the ground, thinking that he'd been summoned into a situation of madness. When he returned to Jackson's side, there was a hard glint in his eye.

'If I'm getting your drift, you arrived on the scene within seconds of—'

Jackson shook his head. 'There was nobody here.'

Suddenly aware of the presence of the pathologist and the full

257

forensic team, Gander looked among the arrivals, searching for any-body who might help. Seeing the face of someone he regarded as an efficient archive of information, he gestured to him and waited until he was near enough for low conversation.

'Do you have a phone number for Kate Hanson, Creed?'

Harry looked surprised, but kept his voice low, to match Gander's. 'No, sir, but I can get it from the communications centre.'

'Do that. Call her. Now. I want UCU here.'

'Will do, sir.' Creed hurried off.

Gander peered through plastic. Now he saw. Now he understood what Jackson had tried to tell him.

What he wanted now was for one particular member of UCU to see it.

CHAPTER FORTY-NINE

Bolt upright in bed, Kate tried to work out what was happening. Door bell? House phone? The bedside clock told her it was 2.59 a.m. Any phone call at this hour wasn't good news.

Disorientated, she felt her way in the darkness to the bedroom door, across the landing and down the stairs to the phone. *Kevin? Celia?*

'Kate?'

It took her some seconds to recognise the caller's voice. '*Harry?*'

'Sorry to ruin your sleep, Kate. Goosey asked me to get your number from Communications and call you.'

He quickly related what was happening near the village of Romsley, voice animated, sharpened by stress. 'You've *got* to see this, Kate. It's a dead girl. Just *wait* till you see. Goosey wants UCU here, but particularly you. Get Julian here as well. This could be really valuable for his professional development.'

Absorbing the words, Kate frowned. Both she and Harry knew that Julian probably didn't have a professional future to develop. She wouldn't include him anyway. From what Harry had said, she'd decided. Julian was too young for this.

Responding to Kate's questions, Harry gave details of the location of the scene and Kate ended the call, disturbed by what she'd heard.

A rumpled figure wearing Kate's Fit Couture exercise vest with pink pyjama bottoms, hair riotous, appeared at the top of the stairs.

'Mom?'

Kate ran upstairs, pulling off her own nightclothes. 'Maisie, I have to go out for a little while.' She rushed into her bedroom and began dragging items out of the wardrobe, Maisie slowly following.

'Out? Now! Where? Why?'

Kate was hurriedly pulling on garments and tying up her hair.

'No details, Maisie, but listen to me, please. When I leave, you go back to bed and you *stay* there. I'll double-lock the front door.' She dived into the bottom of the wardrobe, scattering shoes, looking for her trainers. 'Do *not* open the door.'

'As *if*!' Maisie was now fully awake, watching her mother's frenctic activity. 'If I woke you up like this, you'd go apeshit.'

Ignoring her daughter's last word, Kate hurried on: 'I'll be back as soon as I can. Damn! I have to call Joe to ring Bernie.'

Maisie watched her mother fly downstairs to the phone. With a head-shake she padded to the landing, scooping up the cat, who had emerged from one of the spare bedrooms, tiny bell tinkling.

'Come on, Mugsy. Let's leave the oldies to get on with it. Whatever it is.'

After looking in on Maisie with further admonishments, Kate left the house and sped through the deserted suburban roads, on to the dual carriageway. She reached Romsley village in twenty minutes. She hadn't needed Harry's precise directions. It was a scene of high activity, police vehicles parked randomly, flashing lights and large forensic tent in place. Some of the local populace from the area just beyond the photogenic village had left nearby cottages or more extensive homes and were standing obediently, many in nightclothes beneath belted dressing gowns, behind a hastily erected cordon some distance from the site, under the gaze of two local constables.

As she parked, Kate saw Bernie some way ahead, leaning against his vehicle, arms folded, talking to Joe.

Leaving her car, she walked towards her colleagues. 'What do we know?'

'Nobody's saying anything yet,' muttered Bernie. 'But Gander's been asking for you.'

Kate turned and headed directly for the chief super, who'd suddenly appeared near the forensic tent's entrance. Bernie and Joe followed her.

Gander's mouth was downturned, jowls mottled. He took Kate gently by the arm, moving her to one side, his tone gruff. 'Terrible business, Kate. *Terrible*. But I need you to take a look, once I've brought you up to speed.'

Kate listened as, in a low voice, he quickly described the scene currently obscured by the tent.

'Dr Chong's in there with her now. He –' he pointed to a pale-faced figure in a Barbour – 'found her somewhere between two and two thirty. Right now he's as much use as a chocolate fireguard. But we think it might be the girl who went missing from the Running Wild club in Wolverhampton a few days ago.'

Jody, thought Kate.

Gander gestured impatiently to the young officer nearby, who sprinted towards them.

'Whittaker's got some evidence from the witness.' He turned to the constable. 'Show it to Dr Hanson, then phone in a request for more forensic support and a catering wagon. They're going to need it.' With a terse nod, he headed back towards the forensic tent.

As her UCU colleagues joined her, Kate looked a question at Whittaker.

'Here, Dr Hanson. Take a look. Press that button there.' He handed over the camera in its plastic covering.

Kate did so, Joe and Bernie peering over her shoulders. 'Oh . . . my . . . God,' she said softly, as the shots taken by Jackson appeared on the screen.

Depicted in each was the prone body of a female. White, young, nude. Kate looked closely at the area of the young woman's face, slowly shaking her head. What particularly jarred, beyond the spectacle of the body and its starkness against the grass it lay on, was what surrounded her. Kate counted slowly.

'There's twelve,' said Joe quietly.

Twelve spouting, spewing fireworks. Laid out equidistant around the body, forming a ring of thrusting, surging sparks and billowing showers of coloured light.

Kate looked around, then up at Whittaker. 'The chief superintendent mentioned the witness who took these. Where is he?'

Whittaker gazed at the scene, frowning, then pointed at the man in the Barbour. 'That's him, there. He keeps wandering about.'

Kate and her colleagues walked quickly towards the man.

'Mr Jackson? Kate Hanson, Unsolved Crime Unit, Rose Road.' She introduced her colleagues, giving the man in the Barbour a speculative look.

'You took these?'

They studied his handiwork again, the figure depicted on the screen still as shocking as when they had first viewed it.

261

'We'll be taking this with us, Mr Jackson,' said Joe to the still-dazed man who merely nodded.

'Now we need a proper look,' said Bernie to his two colleagues, voice low.

They walked to the forensic tent. Bernie was the first into the protective suit offered by a gloved constable at the entrance, following which he pulled aside the tent's flap concealing the scene within.

Connie's voice drifted across. 'Hello, Bernard. Come inside. Ah! Your colleagues are with you.' The small crouching figure covered from head to toe in white gazed at them through clear plastic, a voice-activated recorder in one latexed hand.

'You can probably see why Gander wanted *you* here, Kate. Give me a minute while I make some preliminary observations.'

Kate stared down at the body, then looked back to Connie, who lifted the recorder as close to her mouth as the plastic shield allowed, to continue her task.

'White. Female. Age estimate: fifteen to twenty-five years. Approximately five-three. Weight approximately one-ten. Hair blonde, shoulder length. Body unclothed.' Connie switched her gaze to one side of the body. 'Items of clothing present. Displayed on ground in seeming depiction of body. White trousers, grey-and-white striped vest top. No shoes or handbag present at this time. Ditto under-garments.'

She lowered the recorder to take a breath, then continued: 'No rigor. Decomposition under way. No body piercing. No tattoos visible at this time.' Another pause and a glance at Kate, 'Duct tape on torso. Three bands cross-wise. Face obscured by white cloth. Fixed in place with cord. Cloth embellished with crude facial features. Visible injuries: severe extensive bruising around the area of the sternum, continuing over left and right rib area. Bruising also visible to both clavicles. Reminiscent of hand grip. Defence injuries to both hands. No visible injury to genital area at this time.'

Lowering the recorder again, Connie looked up at them. 'She fought for her life,' she said quietly, then continued with her description. 'No jewellery visible. Right hand is fisted. Three or four long fibres visible within closed fist. Appearance: man-made construction. Colour in artificial light: difficult to determine.'

Connie rose to direct forensic technicians to photograph the body and its surroundings. Wes Jacobs walked slowly inside the tent, gave Kate a brief glance, surveyed the body, then began his task.

Kate and her colleagues followed Connie to the far side of the tent. Connie lifted the recorder to add her final comments. 'Items of clothes previously mentioned situated directly west of body. Not yet confirmed to be victim's.' She glanced at her watch, then stated the time into the recorder.

Kate looked down at the clothes, instantly transported in time. To when she was about five years old and her grandmother had given her an old cherished plaything. A paper doll collection. A doll in outline complete with sets of clothes for all occasions, ready to cut out and attach to the doll with tiny paper tabs. The clothes here were laid out in similar fashion. To mimic a person. Any link to childhood ended there. What they were looking at was vicious destruction.

Connie returned to the body, directing her comments to UCU. 'I'm now going to remove the face covering, so I can do a quick comparison for identification.' She held up a plastic-covered photograph supplied by the Westbrooke family. 'Upstairs appear pretty certain it's her – her clothes fit the description they have – but I like to record my observations *in situ* where possible.'

Kate was standing next to Joe. They watched as Connie selected a fine twin-handled implement from her case. Whittaker and Bernie took a few steps in the direction of Jackson, who had gradually increased his proximity to the entrance of the tent. Connie released the thin ties either side of the victim's head, gripped the cloth with the surgical tweezers and began to lift it gently from the face.

Several things happened at once.

Those with a view of Connie's action took a breath, then gasped. Kate's hands flew to her mouth and Gander appeared at her side.

'What the *devil*?'

Connie gently released the three-quarters-lifted cloth and sat back on her heels. There would be no facial identification.

They left the tent in heavy silence, shrugged off the disposable protective suits and handed them to the constable, who thrust them into a black plastic bag.

Jackson had seen what they had seen, from where he'd been standing just within the mouth of the tent. He stumbled towards them, face putty-coloured and shiny with perspiration.

Whittaker glanced at Jackson, did a double-take, then grabbed him roughly by one arm, attempting to pull him sideways as the latter vomited massively on to the grass, his own stout walking shoes and Bernie's suede lace-ups.

Kate and her colleagues left the site, Gander having entrusted Jackson's camera to them. Connie would collect it later. As Kate drove to Rose Road, thoughts on the night's events thrummed inside her head.

The face.

Missing items. Shoes. Bag. Underwear. Jewellery.

Souvenirs?

It was planned. The ghastly tableau.

The face.

Is Bernie right? What if I'm allowing theory too much weight?

They already had two persons of interest they could upgrade. If it *was* either of them, upgrading could prevent this happening to any other woman.

That face.

Anxiety surged through Kate. The young woman she'd just seen was beyond practical or any other help.

But the next one?

He's back.

Does he have his next victim in his sights?

He has to be stopped.

Another thought occurred to Kate, hard on the last, heart constricting in her chest.

Had the meeting she and Joe had with the press precipitated what had befallen this young woman?

Was this his 'communication'?

CHAPTER FIFTY

Kate drove unhindered through Rose Road's main entrance in the stillness of the sleeping suburb. She checked her watch. Four thirty-five. Even media types had beds to go to, apparently. But when the news broke they'd be back. In droves. Twenty-four-hour coverage. That realisation sent a further shaft of anxiety through her head.

As Kate got out of her car, Bernie's four-by-four appeared between the faux-Victorian pillars. She walked on, into Headquarters, its lights a beacon, its mass a leviathan among the darkened terraced homes. She passed the deserted reception desk and continued on to UCU, aware of activity elsewhere in the extensive building.

Bernie looked distracted as he came into UCU wearing latex gloves and rubber boots, carrying his shoes. He went directly to the towel dispenser on the wall of the Refreshment Lounge, then turned to Kate.

'Are we agreed this is him? No sign he cut this one's hair. But then he didn't do that to the James girl.'

'No,' responded Kate, leaning on her elbows. 'But he's still duct-taping. Now we know about the face-covering behaviour. We know the kinds of embellishments he gives them.'

Extracting Jackson's camera in its evidence bag from her pocket, she activated its screen and scrolled through the shots.

The covering on the face was particularly clear on one of them. An oval of white cloth, a hole at each side through which was looped what appeared to be fine cord. Kate studied the features on the cloth. What did it remind her of? Almost immediately she had it.

'Like a pantomime dame. How . . . *derogatory*,' she murmured, getting a nod of agreement from Bernie.

Joe was looking at the photographs over her shoulder, saying nothing. He probably doesn't know about pantomime, thought Kate.

She continued to stare at the features on the oval. At the thick black poker-lashes radiating from the eye circles, wide-set vivid blue irises staring, sightless, one slightly off-centre. The semblance of a nose, represented by a small inverted U shape and two black dots, evoking an upturned snout. The mouth a rapacious gash of greasy red, the cheeks round, feverish splotches of scarlet. The hair hanks of acid-yellow wool. The whole mask a travesty. A mocking parody, a caricature of the female face.

They'd seen the oval base before, features absent, long degraded. Kate looked from one photograph to another, considering the possibility that the doer might have developed the parody since Molly and Janine died.

Chilled despite the warmth of the night, she put her hands round the mug of tea that Joe silently passed to her.

'We'll need hard copies of these. What do we know for sure about Jody?' she asked, her voice sounding loud in the still room.

'According to Gus Stirling Upstairs, she left the Running Wild nightclub in Wolverhampton just before midnight on Thursday last. Her friends said they saw her get into a taxi,' answered Joe.

Five days ago. Before we went to the press.

Kate felt some tension drain away.

'So where has she been since then?' she asked rhetorically.

Bernie looked from Kate to Joe.

'Her family lives in Warley Woods, couple of miles from here. Anybody know how she was planning to get home from Wolverhampton?'

'Train, according to the friends,' answered Joe.

Bernie looked thoughtful. 'If she stuck to that plan, and the report about a taxi is reliable, I say she was abducted from the station. Dodgy places, train stations. Attract all manner of vermin. And they've usually got CCTV.'

Joe shook his head. 'She never made it to the station. She was seen getting into a *vehicle* outside the club. Witness assumed it was a taxi. She wasn't able to give any detail, beyond "big" and "pale-coloured".'

Kate sat silent, her thoughts roaming. She doubted the girl they'd seen so shockingly laid out died as long ago as last Thursday. Where had he kept her? Surely not in any domestic environment?

She began a mental review of her theories of the cases to date and the possible meaning, or purpose, behind the killer's behaviour. She considered what this body had showed them.

She looked again at the camera shots. The shocking spread-eagle pose. The pristine duct tape. And forming a circle around her, the lighted fireworks.

Kate counted them again. Still twelve.

Bernie reached for the camera and looked down at the screen.

'He was taking a massive risk doing all this. He had to arrange the body – and the clothes – then stake it out with the fireworks. Get them going. Anybody could have come past and seen him.'

'It's a fairly rural area, and it *was* the early hours,' said Kate.

'Yeah, but I'm thinking these country types don't keep the same hours as us townies. Look at Jackson. He was roaming about. Then there's late or early dog-walkers who might have come past, or even a car. It's barmy.'

Kate looked at the photographs. Bernie was right, of course. It *was* high-risk. What it showed was that the need underlying and directing the doer's behaviour was so necessary, so pressing for him, that it eclipsed even the fear of discovery.

What need did it serve?

Why fireworks?

Shaking her head, Kate again examined what Jackson had captured, then looked up at her colleagues, voice low.

'It's a tableau. The face-covering represents ritualistic behaviour. Like the duct tape. It's elaborate and fantasy-driven. *This* is his signature.' She stared at the scene depicted. 'It was planned, so that anyone looking at it would be hit. Right between the eyes.'

Kate looked at her colleagues again. 'And there's the problem. It makes no sense. The tableau is so . . . brief. If Jackson hadn't come along when he did, the staging element, the fireworks, would have faded, unseen, shocking as the rest of it was.'

'How about like you said before, Doc . . . "recreational" activity?'

Kate pushed her hands through her hair, frowning at the little camera, then looked from Bernie to Joe. 'He went to such trouble. I can't believe it was just for him.'

'You just said it, Doc. He wanted to shock somebody like Jackson out of his socks. And us.'

Kate shook her head. 'It's just not . . . *Damn!*' She seized her notebook and opened it, searching for a blank page. 'It was all so . . .

risky. Why bother?' She propped her chin on one hand as she wrote down comments and questions.

Joe was deep in thought, half reclining on the chair, his arms folded high on his chest. He glanced down at his watch.

'It's five thirty. Connie will be wanting to see us later.'

Bernie's head snapped upwards. 'Us?'

'Sure. You've seen the duct tape. Maybe there'll be pasteboard, like with Molly and Janine.'

'No. No,' said Bernie, adamant. 'UCU is strictly *cold* case. Upstairs are on to this one and—'

'It belongs to us.' Kate stood, her voice a tired monotone. 'I have to get home. Let's wait to see what else Connie might have.' She glanced at Joe, frowning.

He raised his brows.

'I don't know about you, Joe, but I was worried that this was the "communication" you talked about. You know. The case you mentioned. But it can't be, can it? He took Jody before we met the press.' She looked from one to the other of her colleagues. 'Don't know about you two, but I'm so relieved about that.'

Arriving home ten minutes later, Kate checked on Maisie sleeping soundly, Mugger stretched across the duvet. She went to the kitchen, going through the motions of making tea, then returned upstairs and lay down, staring at the pattern of a small section of window pane on the ceiling.

At nine fifteen that same Friday morning, Furman strode into UCU, glaring at each of them. Kate saw a newspaper among his files.

'Dr Chong's initial findings seem to link the Romsley case to the murders you three are working on. I'm anticipating that Gander will want some liaison between this unit and Upstairs, so be prepared. What's this?' He pointed at the details of the four rapes on the glass screen.

Joe gave him a brief outline of their search of the sexual crime database and the reason for it. Impatient, Furman gave Kate a glance.

'As of now, you've got more than enough to do with the Romsley connection.'

Kate eyed Furman, aware that Julian had already given him the information she was about to offer. 'We know that the remains of one of those rape victims have been found near those of Molly James and Janine Walker. The rape cases on our list don't appear to have been progressed by the police at all. If we can speak to the other victims, we might establish more links and they might—'

Furman glared at her. '*Might-might-might*. Show me hard evidence to connect *all* of those rapes to the bypass murders.'

She deep-breathed and shook her head. 'I can't do that yet, but it's too coincidental that the rape victims all looked similar.'

'If you can't show me an evidential link between each of those rapes and the remains, then you can forget them. We're not wasting resources on tenuous connections. The one who was raped then found at the bypass was, well . . . born unlucky.' He swivelled on his heel and headed for the door, then turned back to the glass screen, looking at the details of the rape-victim list.

He pointed at them. 'I can tell you why none of those rape cases progressed. Because after initially reporting the assaults, none of these women was willing or could be bothered to come in here and make a statement about what they said happened to them. It was a waste of police time then. It's a waste now.'

He looked up at the clock. 'It's nearly nine thirty. Where's Devenish? He wasn't at Romsley all night . . .'

'He's at the university. At a seminar he prepared for in his own time,' said Kate coldly.

The university. Where I should be right now.

Julian. Care was needed when he was given information relating to Jody Westbrooke.

She tuned back in to Furman, who was speaking. He was waving a newspaper.

'See the risk of talking to the press? Inciting the disturbed to murder? Hope you're satisfied. We'll see what Gander thinks about it.' He shoved the newspaper back between his files, turned and left the room. Kate watched him go, confident now that UCU had not taken any action that had precipitated Jody Westbrooke's abduction and murder.

She stared at the glass screen. They couldn't know if the doer had stopped after he killed Janine, Molly and Suzie. But say if he *had* stopped then? That would suggest that something had precipitated his killing of Jody. Kate followed the thought, eyes unfocused. Was it the *discovery* of Molly and then Janine that was the prompt? If

269

that was the case, it suggested that he followed the newspapers very closely. The discoveries hadn't been front-page news until very recently.

Kate sighed, massaging her forehead. Of one thing she was clear. What had happened to Jody was the responsibility of only *one* person. He had to be identified as soon as possible.

CHAPTER FIFTY-ONE

Sliding open the kitchen doors later that same morning, Kate called to the cat, then listened. Nothing. She turned back to the kitchen. Putting the unopened tin to one side, she switched on the radio, in time to hear a psychologist being interviewed on the news. He was offering some theories about the murder of the girl found in the early hours. Now he was well into his stride on the likelihood of a serial killer being 'on the loose'.

Kate sighed, the beginnings of a headache flexing itself. She glared at the radio.

Why don't you use every bloody cliché you can?

The voice of the news presenter joined the discussion.

'The police have reassured us that no effort will be spared until this monster is off the streets.' Kate compressed her lips at the last few words.

Cliché set complete.

'Clichés don't keep people safe,' she muttered, plonking down the makings of a belated breakfast, then wheeled at a soft sound behind her.

'Maisie! You startled me.'

'You usually go on about me being too noisy.' Already dressed, Maisie dropped into a chair and studied her mother. Kate intuited that there was something on her daughter's mind.

'I've phoned school and told them why you'll be late this morning.'

Maisie nodded, eyeing Kate. 'I've said I'll go swimming with Chelsey and Lauren at the weekend.'

Kate frowned slightly. 'Maisie, I'm not sure about Lau—'

'Mom, don't be so unfair! Lauren didn't leave those . . . things!'

Kate was having doubts about her previous suspicions. How would friends of Maisie's have got hold of the pills?

Maisie attended maths lectures at the university.

Julian?

She rejected the idea as soon as it occurred. She'd known Julian for eighteen months. No way would he put Maisie in harm's way.

She glanced at the tin she'd put down earlier. 'Is Mugger upstairs?' she asked.

Maisie face was troubled.

'No . . . Mom? It was on television, early this morning, about this girl being found. Was that why you went out during the night?'

Kate glanced at her. 'Yes, but there were lots of people involved with it. Not just me.'

'I thought your stuff was all old, like historical gruesome stuff.' Maisie helped herself to cereal. 'Guess what? Chelsey's mom used to be a model.'

Dropping bread into the toaster, Kate fetched plates. 'UCU's cases *are* mostly historical. Some of them are . . . unpleasant, but they're also about people's lives—'

She stopped. She'd just broken her own rule. About sharing information about UCU's cases with Maisie, no matter how superficial. She ran a hand over her forehead. She was tired.

'Just . . . be careful, Maisie.'

'What about?'

'When you're out there. You know. Strangers, cars.'

Maisie got up from her chair. 'Mom, how old do you think I am? I'm not a baby!'

Blackened bread hurtled from the toaster as Kate watched her daughter flounce from the kitchen.

CHAPTER FIFTY-TWO

The body was lying in harsh light on the stainless-steel examination table, head supported by a Sani-Block. The powerful air-extraction system hummed. Jody Westbrooke's face was now exposed. What was left of it. Or, more accurately, where it had been.

Inside the white forensic suit, Kate was well beyond her comfort zone. So far she'd limited herself to brief, peripheral glances and had yet to take in the details. Her heart rate accelerated as Connie walked towards them.

'Hello, UCU,' she said quietly, looking tired. 'Ready for the full story? I'll give you what I know, and where that's not possible, what I think.'

Three heads nodded as Connie gestured towards the body.

'We have confirmation that this is Jody Westbrooke. Eighteen years old. No physical disease. Non-smoker. Stomach contents – undigested cheese-and-onion potato crisps and dry crackers. No doubt those were provided by her captor during the period she was missing. The stomach takes approximately two hours to empty. Presence of undigested food would routinely indicate that death occurred within an hour or two of eating those items. In Jody's case, being in a state of mortal fear would have delayed her digestive processes. Time of death can't be pinpointed with any certainty, but given the condition of the body, I'm guessing she died at the beginning of this week, although I won't be as categorical in my report.'

Connie glanced at Jody's body. 'Whoever's responsible for this took her underwear, jewellery, shoes and bag. That's based on information friends and family have provided as to what she was wearing that night.'

She glanced from the table to each of them, then back, indicating the torso. 'She's been dead a couple of days at least.' She pointed a finger at the swollen, discoloured abdomen and similar swelling of the face and neck. 'See that? The skin on her torso and thighs is unstable because of post-mortem fluid accumulation.'

Kate bit her lip. 'Is that why it's . . . coloured like that?' she asked.

Connie glanced from Jody's remains to Kate. 'You mean these marks? That's known as "marbling". Due to the growth of bacteria in her blood vessels.' She looked from Kate to Joe and Bernie. 'She's clearly part of your series. *If* he did take a break, he's back now.'

Kate and her colleagues remained silent.

Connie continued: 'What happened to this young woman was savage. She was beaten very severely.' She lifted one of the hands and pointed. 'Presence of defence wounds on her forearms and hands. See? A fine, very sharp blade caused those.' A small silence. 'She fought furiously for her life.' Connie's words hit them. 'But the beating isn't what killed her. Death was due to a single crushing blow to the back of the head.'

Connie turned. 'Come here, please, Kate.'

Kate complied and Connie stood square in front of her, placing warm, latexed hands on Kate's shoulders.

'She was shaken like this . . .' Connie started a gentle push-pull movement. 'But *very* hard. She was of small stature, like you and me, Kate. The final push placed her head in contact with something solid that fractured her skull. No DNA in the form of semen, no hairs that aren't hers.'

'Fingerprints?' ventured Kate.

'No. He's a careful killer. But he missed the fibres which were gripped by her fist. Here. Take a look.'

They pressed forward to look at the long fibres they'd glimpsed at the scene, now in the plastic envelope Connie was holding.

'Remember I mentioned defence wounds? Her hand was fisted before his final attack. See the wounds on her knuckles? The small but deep cuts? At the time she sustained those, she'd already grasped these fibres and was holding them. Tight. Either he didn't notice or he couldn't extract them.' Connie was silent for a few seconds. 'I doubt it was the latter. Given the ferocity of his attack, if he'd seen them and failed to remove them, I think he would have taken her hand off.'

Connie's last few words stopped Kate's breathing momentarily. The faces of her UCU colleagues were grim.

Connie looked at each of them in turn. 'Only my *subjective* opinion, of course.'

They stood without speaking as she continued.

'The remains at the bypass site couldn't show us in any detail what he did to Molly and Janine. But they confirmed that Molly James's face and that of Janine Walker were covered. That face-covering and the use of duct tape at Romsley indicates a clear link between Jody Westbrooke's death and the bypass remains. No pasteboard item this time, by the way and no hair-cutting.' A small pause. 'Despite that inconsistency, he appears to be a creature of habit, who knows what he likes when he kills.'

Kate listened intently to Connie, aware of the need to study the doer's work in order to understand his behaviour, know him. She looked briefly at Jody Westbrooke's upper body, then away, to where Connie had placed the envelope containing the fibres taken from the fist. She frowned at them, thought processes ponderous due to the events of the last twenty-four hours.

Connie watched Kate, then spoke quietly. 'Come on, Katie, favourite student. Ignore the context. You've seen long pink fibres like these before.'

Kate felt tumbleweed drifting across the vacant planes of her mind. She looked at Connie, confused, then returned to staring at the fibres, feeling slow, stupid and embarrassed by her own ineptitude.

'Your daughter . . .'

'My Little Pony,' Kate said quietly, matter-of-fact.

'Well done,' Connie whispered.

They had reached the door when Kate turned, getting up courage to ask: 'Connie? When her face was . . . ?'

'A small mercy. She was already dead.' Connie looked up at the wall clock.

'Meeting in twenty minutes. See you Upstairs.'

275

CHAPTER FIFTY-THREE

The big meeting room was full and silent. No greetings, no words of camaraderie. Gander was laying out the Force's response to the Romsley slaying.

'The connection to UCU's cases means there needs to be liaison between the investigative team up here and the Unsolved Case Unit. As of now, these deaths are all regarded as the work of one repeat offender. Consequently, it's top priority. I'm in overall command. Any useful information, all leads, I want to know about it.'

Kate flicked a glance at Furman. His face was expressionless. She moved her gaze to others around the table. Wes looked tired. Harry was clearly exhausted. Sitting next to Harry, Matt Prentiss looked morose and detached. Kate studied him covertly, wondering how he dealt with the occasional horror of forensic work when his usual frame of mind was clearly so low. Maybe he didn't fully engage. She flicked another glance at Furman. If he was so concerned about the health of personnel, he'd do well to leave Bernie alone and focus on Matt.

On impulse as the meeting broke up, Kate hurriedly picked up her notebook and bag and followed Matt out of the room as he headed in the direction of the cafeteria. Seeing him order coffee and take a seat some distance from other, busy tables, she followed and sat down opposite him, hardly knowing why she was there.

Prentiss ignored her.

'What do you think about it, Matt?' she asked quietly.

He looked her up and down. Slowly. 'About what?'

Kate was fazed. It was surely the topic of the whole of Rose Road.

'I'm talking about the Romsley case. You were there. What's your thinking about it? Its bizarre quality?'

Silence.

Kate persevered. 'I would describe it as an outrage. What's *your* view of it?'

Silence. She cast around for anything that might open him up.

'We've seen her. This morning. There was nothing else found except the pink fibres?' She saw his lips suddenly compress.

'Are you questioning my professionalism?' he spat, reddened eyes fixed on her face.

Kate was shocked at his response. 'No, of *course* not. I was simply asking for your view of what we've all seen. How you feel about it. If you have any ideas or—'

His voice was harsh as he answered. One or two people near enough to hear glanced across at them. 'Nobody pays me to have *views*! Or to *feel*, or have *ideas*.' He stopped for a couple of seconds, then continued: 'It's a forensic job. *I* get it right! You want *views*, you want *feelings* and *ideas*,' he added, making the words negative, 'you'd best talk to Harry Creed.'

With that he got up from the table, coffee unfinished, and walked towards the door of the cafeteria and out.

Kate stared after him, wondering exactly what in their brief exchange had caused such vitriol. Puzzled, she left the cafeteria, four of his words ringing in her head:

I get it right.

I.

In UCU, Joe was adding details to the glass screen: Jody West-brooke's family's confirmation that she was wearing high-heeled shoes and carrying a handbag when she left. Julian was entering these facts into a database he'd created. He spoke to them all.

'Okay, the facts I've got are – Employment: word-processing. Location: insurance company, Edmund Street. Next one – boyfriend?'

Bernie shook his head. Kate rested her chin on her hands, staring at the notes she'd made.

'I wonder where he first saw her?' she asked.

'Outside the club?' Bernie had another thought. 'Hang on. He could've been inside the club, saw her and left. To get his car. What I don't get is she's only five-three. All the victims so far have been five-six at least.'

'CCTV at the club?' she asked.

'Equipment, yes. Operational, no.'

'Any more facts I can add?' persisted Julian. No one responded.

Joe tossed his pen on to the table.

Kate was thinking about what they'd seen in the post-mortem suite. 'He seems to have evolved since the earlier killings, but the duct tape and face-covering are both consistent behaviours. He showed extreme violence towards Jody, but we can't be categorical that that didn't occur in the previous cases.'

She had a sudden thought. Pulling the phone towards her, she tapped the PM suite number.

'Hi, Igor. Is Connie there?'

Connie's voice drifted over the line. 'Hi, Katie. I'm guessing this is about Jody Westbrooke.'

'I have another question. The damage to her face – what did he use?'

'I can't be specific, but I suspect that it was different from the implement that caused her defence wounds. The facial damage was caused by a *very* fine, short blade. Also, extremely sharp.'

'Okay . . .' Kate paused. 'Was there much damage to the under-lying bone structure of the face?'

'There were no knife marks on the facial bones at all. I couldn't have done a more skilful job myself, and I've had plenty of training in dissection and how to avoid bone damage during forensic exam-ination, for obvious reasons. He knew what he was doing. It was finely carved.'

Kate made swift notes. 'Do you think it's possible he was somehow *trained* to be able to do that. Maybe . . . medically trained?'

'Beware, Katie. There have often been theories that one or other murderer had medical training or was a surgeon. It's rarely turned out to be the case. You might want to speculate on alternative jobs to explain his skill.'

'Like . . . what? Any suggestions?' Kate listened, eyes on her col-leagues, then wrote in her notebook. She replaced the phone.

'No knife marks on the underlying bone structure. So the same behaviour *could* have occurred towards Janine and Molly. The doer had to have been very skilled to do what he did to Jody's face.'

'Any psychological explanation for that?' asked Joe.

Kate shrugged. 'I've got my own theory. The actual behaviour towards the face fits with my earlier thinking about him and his perceptions of his victims – in Jody's case it could be that there was a . . . compulsion to unearth some quality in her. Perhaps some aspect he wished to *see* for himself, or *demonstrate* to others. Maybe he was trying to show that beneath the surface qualities of the victim she was . . . different to how she presented herself. A difference only he perceived and felt driven to reveal.' She paused. 'He's extremely competent with a knife.' She scanned her colleagues briefly. 'So handy that maybe his line of work, not necessarily now, but in the past, involved legitimate use of one.' Julian's pen flew across paper.

Bernie had been listening closely. 'So he might have worked in . . . say a butcher's or an abattoir. How about he's some kind of doctor?'

Kate raised her shoulders. 'I think it's more subtle skills than those required in the meat trade. Connie's clearly not keen on medical skills being attributed to doers. I can see why. Think about the theories surrounding the Ripper in Victorian London, creating mayhem in impoverished neighbourhoods. Easy to see the appeal of his being a doctor or surgeon. A nice social contrast, played up at the time by the media.'

'Still might've been right, Doc. They never got him.'

Kate got up, walked towards the window then turned.

'Think of some other jobs requiring knife skills.'

'He could have some . . . technical kind of job,' suggested Julian.

Bernie glanced at him. 'Yeah? Like what?'

Julian shrugged. 'Not sure . . .'

Bernie shook his head. 'Like I said before. Butcher.'

Julian sat up. 'Hey, how about he's a chef? He works with food?'

Nobody spoke for a few seconds.

'That didn't get us far, Doc.'

Kate was staring into the middle distance. 'How about it isn't a *job*? What if it's some kind of interest . . . or hobby?'

'Any ideas?' asked Joe.

Kate was silent momentarily. 'Woodworker?'

'Whatever we come up with, it don't help us now, does it?' said Bernie. 'We need to keep an eye on what he's done but . . . What you up to?' They watched as Kate walked in determined fashion to the glass screen, then turned.

'My head is chaos and I can't stand it.' She seized a marker and began writing. 'I need to get this stuff sorted. My basic idea, which you know already, is that he stalked all of his victims, agreed? That involved him in some decision-making; for example, Decision Number One, which victim to select? Two, when and where to stalk her? And finally, Three, when does he stop stalking and move to the abduction phase?' She finished the itemised list and turned to them. 'Anything to add?'

'He would've known for years the kind of victim he needed. Because of his fantasies,' said Julian. Kate confirmed with a nod.

Joe leaned forward, pointing to the words on the glass. 'So he's clear about his victim. All he has to do is find a female who fits his criteria, start the stalking process, bide his time until he's ready.' Another nod from Kate.

Silence, broken by Bernie. 'How about this toy she got hold of? Where was it? In his house – no, that don't work. He wouldn't take her to where he lives. How about it was already in his car when he picked her up?'

Kate gazed up at the glass for some seconds. 'That makes sense, Bernie. If you're right, it also means that the abduction phase fell apart quite quickly, while she was still inside his car.' She paused. 'Did the toy just happen to be there? Or was it there for a reason?'

Bernie and Joe exchanged glances.

'You mean, like it was a talking point, once he got her inside the car?' asked Bernie.

Joe looked from Bernie to Kate. 'How about it was more a device? To disarm her. "Hey, gimme a break here. Look, I got a kid. I'm a regular kinda guy." '

'I agree with both of you,' said Kate, adding comments quickly to the glass.

She looked up at the words for a few seconds, then at her colleagues.

'I'm thinking about the likelihood of Janine's being a quiet, calm abduction, Joe. She *knew* who she was going with. Or she *thought* she did. But Jody?' Kate shook her head. 'No. He knew her, in the sense that he'd seen her, watched her. But she didn't know *him*. So he had to use a con – he offered her an *impersonal* service. A taxi ride. *That's* why he anticipated needing to disarm her. He expected that at some point she would realise all was not right. But it happened more quickly than he anticipated. Whilst she was still inside the car.'

Kate walked from the glass screen to sit on the edge of the table. 'And all this still doesn't answer the question: if one of the criteria on which he selects his victims is height, why did he chose Jody

Westbrooke? She was a short woman. If he watched her, why didn't he know that?'

Julian sat, shoulders hunched. 'How about he only saw her sitting down, inside places. He never got to follow her, like along the street.'

Bernie looked at him. 'But he's the boss. He's calling the shots. He could do anything, be anywhere—'

Kate left the table, paced to the windows and back. 'I think Julian has a point,' she said quietly. 'He didn't stalk her in a range of situations. That raises another question: *Why* didn't he . . . ?'

'How about that was one of his decisions? To cut it short?'

Kate frowned. 'But why would he do that, Joe? Why would he cut short what is such a pleasurable activity for him? Stalking has almost as much pay-off as abduction.'

'You ask me, he's Looney Tunes. Yes, I *know* what you think, Doc, but hear me out. He's doing all this stalking and following and fantasising, and maybe he's reached the point where he can't hack it any longer. Maybe it's a full moon or he remembers his potty-training going wrong, who knows? But whatever it was, it got him going again and he had no choice but to grab her when he did. He's a head-case.'

Kate looked from Bernie to the glass and back. 'And I kind of agree and disagree with you there.'

'Miracles do happen, then.'

'I don't agree that he's mad, but I *do* think that something got him unhooked. Something happened while he had Jody in his sights and just for a brief time he lost his coolness and control. He cut short his stalking phase and brought forward the abduction.' She paced, then put her hands on the table, leaning forward.

'*And* that's when he found out he'd got it wrong. She wasn't his "ideal".' Kate hesitated. 'Is that why she got such a beating?'

The room was silent for over a minute. Kate put down the marker and regained her seat as Bernie broke the silence.

'Don't know about anybody else, but I'm worried. You don't like this, Doc, but we've got Cranham and Fairley both linked to Molly James at the time she went. We need to get procedures in place. Check them two out, make inquiries about them . . .'

Kate nodded, tired.

This isn't for me, this kind of work
Balancing theory against risk. Having to work within rules.
Too hard.

And if we – if I've got it wrong?

There'll be another Jody.

Sooner or later.

Kate's heart missed a couple of beats. Joe was speaking.

'Sorry, Joe?'

'I was wondering if you had any ideas as to why he might cut short the stalking phase?'

Kate raised both shoulders. 'Perhaps he just had too many pressures in his "normal" life? Or . . . maybe he felt *compelled* to act. Say he had a relationship which ended. Or something happened with his job. Maybe he'd been told about redundancy – there's a lot of it currently – or maybe he was dismissed. Whatever it was, there was some . . . disruption to his situation. Some pressure.'

Joe's voice broke into Kate's thoughts again.

'How about a visit to Jody's parents?' He lifted the phone. 'Before I contact them, I'll check with Upstairs. Make sure we don't overload the family.'

Kate nodded absently, flipping notebook pages.

Why?

Why reduce the pleasure of stalking?

She stared ahead at the glass screen, unseeing.

'Joe?'

'Red?'

'Can I borrow your diary?'

He handed it over with a light 'My life is yours.'

She took the black Filofax and quickly found the day on which she and Joe had met the media, here inside Rose Road. Before any meeting with Jody's parents, she had to be absolutely certain of her facts. She examined dates, setting her mind at rest. As she'd thought, Jody had been abducted days before they met the press.

Kate was now back to the puzzle: why the rush to murder?

CHAPTER FIFTY-FOUR

Joe walked into UCU that afternoon miming 'Drink?' to his three colleagues. Just arrived herself, Kate nodded, then returned her attention to Julian, who was looking agitated.

'I was in the forensic lab and all I said to him was, "Weren't there any clues found at the scene?" and he went—'

Bernie interrupted. 'Look, Sherlock, they're under pressure up there. Yeah, yeah, I know he's a—'

'Tight-ass,' finished Joe, guessing the subject of the conversation.

Kate already knew the object of discussion. Matt Prentiss. Her primary concern was for Julian in her role as his senior supervisor, a concern she hadn't yet mentioned to her colleagues. Surely Prentiss couldn't be the source of any drugs Julian might be involved with? Could he? She reviewed what she'd heard about the man. Nothing to indicate drugs, although she'd heard whispers about alcohol.

'Do you two know why Matt Prentiss is so unsociable, so negative and . . . surly?' she asked, looking mainly to Bernie, on the basis that he'd been at Rose Road the longest.

Joe shrugged. 'I heard he stopped being Mr Congeniality a while ago, which is why Harry got the job of managing the forensic scenes team over him. Even though he's been here longer than Harry.'

'But what's his surliness *about*?'

Bernie responded: 'It started well before your time, Corrigan, and you, Doc. Must be four years back. He had an older sister.'

They all looked at him. 'And?' prompted Kate.

'Overdose. Died.'

They exchanged glances. 'So . . . what? How? Was it recreational use that went wrong?' asked Kate, her concern for Julian surging as she picked up the drug inference.

Bernie gave her a look. 'No, no. She weren't a *user*. I've never known anybody like you for looking on the criminal side.' He shook his head. 'She was suffering with depression is what I heard and took a load of her medication, but that isn't all the story. Pain-in-the-Arse Prentiss was a real perfectionist in his work here. Acted like *nobody* could work a scene better than him. That is, until he made a mess of one and got an official warning.'

Kate glanced at Julian, then on to Bernie. 'When was this?'

'About six months after the sister died.'

'What did he do?' This from Julian, eyes large.

Bernie rubbed his jowls and pointed a blunt finger. 'Listen, lad, you don't mention this—'

'He won't,' said Kate quickly.

Bernie nodded. 'What Prentiss did was compromise evidence in a sex assault case.'

'How?' asked Kate, eyebrows shooting up, aware that both Joe and Julian were listening intently.

'Bagged up the evidence, labelled it, all nice and according to protocol – then stuck it in his pocket. Connie nearly had his innards for garters. He denied it at first, then said it was an oversight. Didn't make any difference. The chain of evidence-handling was broke and it cost us a conviction. CPS was livid. Gander managed to limit the damage, on the grounds that Prentiss was under family stress, and he was put on compassionate for about a month. After that, Creed had to double-check Prentiss's work for months, which obviously didn't please Creed. Him and Prentiss got on all right before that. Not any more.'

Kate was thinking over what Bernie had said. 'Was there ever any suggestion at all that Prentiss knew something about the sexual assault case and actually tampered with the evidence?'

'Blimey, how'd you *get* to be so suspicious? *Nothing* like that. He was distracted and that caused a slip-up. He's recovered now and he's like a Rottweiler. You've seen how he gets on everybody's case at scenes.'

'Hypervigilance,' said Kate quietly, thinking of the paranoia and delusional thinking that often went with it.

The discussion was interrupted by the phone ringing. Joe answered. He murmured a few words, then hung up.

'Crete's loss is our gain. Malins has just arrived for his interview. And he's not a happy guy.'

284

CHAPTER FIFTY-FIVE

Five minutes later, Joe and Kate were seated in an interview room. It had been decided that Bernie would be a close observer from the room next door, given his prior knowledge of Malins.

Kate studied their visitor as he entered the room. Malins was wearing a polo shirt, startlingly white against his tan, and pressed chinos. She observed the thick neck, heavy shoulders and splay-legged walk. Also the stomach over his belt. He looked like an ex-weightlifter.

He pulled out the indicated chair abruptly and sat, wordless, crossing thick forearms. In the forest of gingery hairs Kate observed a selection of prison art, plus other tattoos of better quality. Among them, scrollwork enclosing 'Mum'; another, 'Kim-4-Evva'. A heart pierced with an arrow encircled the name 'Maz', casting doubt on the wearer's eternal declaration to Kim. Looked like for ever had a time-scale.

Maybe I have the chronology wrong.

Kate sighed inwardly at the banality.

Malins's attitude was one of glowering detachment. Joe started the process with introductions, coolly waiting for several seconds until Malins made eye contact.

'Thank you for agreeing to come into Rose Road, Mr Malins. The Unsolved Crime Unit here is reinvestigating the disappearance of a young woman named Molly James.'

Joe and Kate waited.

Malins transferred his gaze from Joe to the wall beyond.

Joe continued: 'When an officer from UCU talked with you recently, you didn't mention that you have a conviction for rape.'

Malins shifted his gaze to the rectangle of one-way glass on one side of the room, then turned his attention, very slowly, to Kate and Joe, casually insolent. Only two minutes in, and Kate wanted to smack him.

Malins's attention was on the wall ahead. 'That's right. I didn't.'

'Why not?'

'Didn't do it.'

Heat prickled in Kate's hair and on her neck. Joe leaned forward.

'A conviction is a *fact*, Mr Malins. It's where we start from with you.'

'Still didn't do it,' he repeated, his eyes on Kate, or more specifically on the top button of her cream silk shirt.

'Tell us about it.'

'Got nothing to tell you lot.'

Within five minutes, having been informed by Joe that he risked arrest if he continued to be uncooperative, Malins had provided a truncated version of his sexual offence, couched in the usual denials, self-serving distortions and rationalisations Kate had heard numerous times from offenders she'd worked with.

According to him, he and the young woman were part of a crowd drinking at a Broad Street bar in 2000. Malins described her as having 'tagged along' when he left. According to his account, on reaching an area of open ground, part-fenced for redevelopment, she had spontaneously indicated no objection to having sex with him.

Kate looked him in the eye, keeping control of her voice. 'The young woman you raped stated that you offered her a lift before you left the club, that you told her your car was parked on that area of open ground. That as you passed it you pushed her—'

'Didn't have no car with me that night.'

'That doesn't mean you didn't say it!' snapped Kate, control slipping. She saw Malins's face tighten as he looked at, then away from her.

'Tell us about the girl,' invited Joe.

Within a further five minutes Malins had sabotaged the young woman's character, describing her as 'well known' in the Broad Street bars for her 'friendliness' and willingness to drink. Kate and her colleagues had read all the statements made during the investigation of the rape. None of it fitted with what Malins was telling them. He was now busily attributing his conviction to misfortune and an inept barrister.

'She had a good brief. I had a muppet!' He compressed his lips and Kate saw in his face, the eyes, his capacity for anger. 'She got six women on the jury bawling and sobbing along with her when she was in the box.'

'Who was your barrister?' asked Kate.

'Idiot called Summers. I think he read up on the case while he was on the train coming to court. Waste of space.'

Not Osbourne. No. Kevin would have gotten you off.

Kate watched as Malins examined his own hands. She glanced at them. Well-kempt. Unexpected for a builder? The boss. A rapist with an alias. Julian had had to search offence records twice with a variation on the spelling of Malins's name, 'Malin', before they picked up the rape conviction.

'You got six years for the rape. Heavy for a first offence. You'd been in trouble before that.' Joe's last comment was a statement as fact.

Malins shrugged and folded his arms, adopting a bored expression.

'You probably know already. If you don't, why should I help you do your job? Look at your records.'

Again Kate felt her temper rising. 'We *have*. GBH and benefit fraud.'

Malins grinned at the ceiling, then at Kate. 'Get real, love. *Everybody's* on the take. That GBH was a fit-up. That was my missus at the time and the Job, working together to get me done.'

Joe looked steadily at Malins. 'You beat you wife almost senseless. Gave her a broken jaw. She needed reconstructive surgery after you'd finished with her.'

Malins yawned widely, ignoring what Joe had said. 'I told your mate, the fat bloke, I was in Henley-in-Arden on a job when that girl, what's-her-name, went missing.'

'Molly James. But you *knew* her,' said Kate, watching his face. 'You were working at her family home.'

'Supervising, sweetheart. I don't graft. I've got *employees* to do that.' He glanced casually at the steel and gold Rolex on his wrist, and blew air through his teeth. 'I seen her no more than a couple of times, max. I was interviewed after she disappeared. So were my lads. I told the police I never saw her the day she went missing. Like I said, I was in Henley.'

Joe returned to an earlier theme. 'Your rape victim, the "woman" you've told us about, was just sixteen. That week. That's why she was at the bar. Celebrating her birthday.'

Malins glared at him. 'You deaf? Or is there a language barrier here? I told you what happened. She looked at least twenty-five.' He transferred his gaze to Kate, smirking. 'Perhaps I give her something to remember her birthday by.'

Kate held his gaze, memory spooling to a photograph she'd seen of Malins's victim, looking young and dazed.

'It's your responsibility to reliably identify the age of any female with whom you initiate sexual contact,' said Kate without hesitation.

She got up from the table and went to stand against the wall, putting distance between herself and him.

Malins grinned at her across the room. 'Sixteen, love! That means legal.'

'It also means young and vulnerable. You were several years older. How old is your current partner, Mr Malins?'

Malins instantly lost the grin. His eyes narrowed and his bottom lip became dominant. 'None of your fucking business.'

'That's enough, Malins,' warned Joe.

'*Mr* Malins to you! I've had it here!' He got up, face full of animosity. 'That one in Broad Street was a slag!'

Kate recalled one of his tattoos. *Mum.*

'Did you have problems with the police when you were a teenager, Mr Malins?'

He looked confused at the sudden change of direction. 'Who doesn't?'

'Would you tell us about that, please?'

He sat, stared at her briefly, then grinned. 'You're just like *every* shrink I've ever met. *Tell me about your childhood, Alan, Tell us about your friends, Alan, your girlfriends, Alan.* What's so interesting about all that? If you want my opinion, all you shrinks get off on it – got no life of your own!' His eyes travelled from Kate's feet, slowly upwards. 'Might be an exception or two . . .'

'Keep it civil, *Mr* Malins, unless you want to be here a while.'

Malins glanced at Joe, then back to Kate. He smirked.

'What was the question, darling?'

'In trouble as a teenager?' replied Kate.

He nodded. 'I was a bit of a young tearaway. Got into a few scrapes. Long time ago.'

'Tell us about the scrapes.'

He shrugged, looking wary. Kate guessed he was editing his history.

'I pinched this kid's bike – well, he said I did. I was sent to a private boarding school after that.'

So many euphemisms, thought Kate, recognising the 'private board-ing school' reference, knowing its reality. Special residential education for difficult-to-manage youngsters beyond parental control. Malins's incidental reference to the 'shrinks' he'd met during his early years had already confirmed for Kate a childhood of emotional and behavioural problems.

'How did your mom and dad feel about that? Your being sent away?' She saw Malins move instantly to surliness.

'You ever find my old man, you can ask him yourself. Don't bother to let me know what he says. I don't talk about my mum, not to the likes of you.' He looked from Kate to Joe. 'I'm finished with this.'

Kate watched him as he got up and rolled towards the door, several scars visible through the gingery velvet nap of close-cut hair. She glanced at Joe, who shook his head slightly. They couldn't keep him. Kate addressed the broad back, angered by Malins's callousness to-wards his young victim.

'You've made some comments about women to us, Mr Malins. Is that how you judge them? Slag, slapper, whore; decent, pure.'

The back of the thick neck reddened. He half turned, speaking over one muscled shoulder, hostile. 'You missed one out, love. How about "stuck-up mouthy bitch"?'

Joe started to rise. Kate quickly shook her head at him. She had one final question. About an issue that had been nudging the edges of her consciousness.

'What was she wearing, Mr Malins? The girl in Broad Street?'

He turned fully, clearly thrown by the change in direction of Kate's question. 'Who d'you think I am, Tommy Hilfiger? Can't remember.'

'Try,' advised Joe.

'Jeans. A top. Shoes.'

Kate guessed that they were probably nudging the limits of Malins's descriptive powers.

'What were the colours of her clothes? Was she wearing any jewel-lery?'

'Can't remember. Don't give a f—'

Joe stood and Malins clearly thought better of it, offering a limited response.

'Black jeans. Orange low-cut top. A charm bracelet thing. Hang on! You saying I pinched her stuff?'

'Just answer the question, Malins,' directed Joe.

'Fuck *you*!' He switched his gaze to Kate, the smirk back in place. 'Ah! I get it. You're still on about her not looking her age. Well, let me tell *you*, the get-up she had on, if I had a sixteen-year-old kid I wouldn't let her out like that, showing her—'

'Thank you, Mr Malins. You've told me all I need to know,' said Kate quietly.

He gave each of them a hostile look, then turned, pulled open the door and walked through it.

As Malins disappeared from view, Kate intuited a childhood experience of a physically chastising then absent father, an inadequate, probably fearful mother and a brood of children who had never experienced consistent, sensitive care from anyone.

None of which made him a repeat killer.

Kate was keeping to an arrangement she'd made. A fairly regular one. She was stressed and her body was rigid with tension. She needed a physical challenge. She'd come to the right place.

A half-stifled gasp forced its way from her mouth as she lowered both legs very slowly to the mat, perspiration coursing from her forehead in spite of the air conditioning.

'Come *on*, Kate! Another set.'

Sitting up, Kate drank water from a plastic bottle, then lay down on the mat again. 'Easy for you to say, *and* I know how I'm going to feel . . . uh . . . tomorrow . . . uhh . . . morning. It won't include anything flattering about *you*, Phil.'

Phil the trainer took this calmly. 'My ears *always* burn around nine a.m.'

He supervised Kate's movements closely, then nodded. 'That's good. Your quadriceps and adductors are *really* strong now. Give me one more set.'

Kate gasped, giving him a sideways glare. 'This is *hard*.'

He glanced at her, then pointed at the mat. 'One day, Kate, you'll thank me for it.'

An hour later, Kate was at home in the wide walk-in shower, thinking of the weekend. The weather was predicted to be holding and she'd made a decision. No work. She wouldn't even open the door of the study. She was going to spend much of the next two days in the garden, doing a little weeding, leg muscles permitting, and a small amount of sun-soaking. Maisie had requested Pizza Express on Saturday evening, this time for pasta, and she wanted Chelsey to come with them. Which was fine, thought Kate, stepping out of the shower, because it was a way for Kate to repay Candice for feeding Maisie on several school nights recently.

The gym session had worked. She felt relaxed. In need of down time.

CHAPTER FIFTY-SIX

On Monday morning Kate parked her car and went to the boot to get her bag. She'd considered a cool dress this morning but decided against it. You never knew with police work where you might end up during the day. She'd settled on black trousers teamed with a pale blue short-sleeved shirt that showed off the subtle tan she'd acquired in the last day or two. Her hair was in a ponytail, tied with a narrow dark-blue ribbon.

Bring it on. She was ready.

'You look sun-buffed, Red,' commented Joe with a grin as he walked across the car park towards her, Bernie following. They made their way into Rose Road and then UCU, where Julian was in the middle of writing up an assignment as part of his forensic module.

'I need to be out of here in half an hour,' murmured Joe.

Kate raised a questioning eyebrow to him.

'Jody's parents. Still want to come?'

She nodded, pulling her notebook and pen from her bag. 'Before we leave, what do we think of Malins?' she asked.

Julian stopped writing and gave Bernie his attention as he crossed the room to underline Malins's name on the glass screen.

'For my money, he has to stay on our list of POIs.' He turned and gave each of them an eyebrows-up glance. 'He's got form for sex. On the list, yes?'

Joe nodded, looking across the table to Kate. 'I'm with Bernie at the minute. Malins is an angry type; he's victimised women before, including one he'd be expected to have *some* positive feeling for – his wife. It didn't protect her from his anger. Plus, he raped a young girl who was a stranger to him. Victimisation of known and unknown females. Doesn't seem to make a whole lot of difference to Malins. Suggests to me that he could have a real issue with females in general.

Look how he reacted when you mentioned his mom, Kate.' He looked across at Kate, palms up. 'How'd you feel about meeting Malins on a dark night?'

Perched on the edge of the table, Kate looked from Joe to Bernie and slowly shook her head.

'He's not the one,' she said, before switching her gaze to the floor, waiting for an eruption. It didn't come. She looked up.

Bernie was staring at her, waiting.

'So?' he said after a heavy silence. 'I'm stood here being careful of my blood pressure and cholesterol level. How about you tell us what's on your mind *this* time?'

Kate got down from the table and started to pace, because it helped her think. It helped her explain.

'Think about the situation when Malins raped the young girl . . .' She came to the table and searched the papers on it. 'That was in 2003. Since then, nothing sexual known. *Yes*, I know, Bernie. Just because he hasn't been apprehended since then for sexual offences, it doesn't mean he hasn't done anything else.' She spread her hands, palms up. 'But the *situation* he and his victim were in is relevant for us. They shared a context for a short time.'

She heard a brief snort from Bernie's direction, then silence. Blood pressure and cholesterol control were more or less winning.

'He was in the bar. She was in the bar. He noticed her. He invited her to leave with him.'

'You ain't suggesting that that tells us anything about what he done after?'

'No, Bernie. I'm merely identifying facts. The girl said in her statement that she went with Malins after socialising with him. She got it wrong. He also made a judgement of her – yes, I *know*, a very self-interested judgement. What he did was awful but also opportunistic. It indicates how thoroughly irresponsible he is. And antisocial, too. But what he did had none of the "planful" characteristics of our doer.'

Joe watched her as she paced. 'Can you be sure of that, Kate?'

She shook her head, feeling much more on top of things than she had on Friday. 'No, I can't. Theories don't come with guarantees. Malins was in that crowded bar, in full view of other customers, who probably saw him leave with the young woman. No stealth involved. To me the rape was an unplanned act.' She looked at them sideways.

'I know he has a history of behavioural problems and violence, but neither of those leads me to suspect he's our doer. Those factors merely confirm his—'

'Impulsivity!'

They all looked at Julian.

He blinked at them nervously. 'I'm just saying what Kate told us in our lecture last week.'

Bernie glared at him and he fell silent.

'Julian's right.' said Kate. 'Malins's rape was an unplanned attack by a male who has a history of impulsive behaviour. There's no indication of forethought, planning. There's no indication from what he did that he indulged in elaborate fantasy *prior* to his attack, which he then felt compelled to act out during the rape. The young woman said it was quick and brutal . . . Malins is thoroughly reprehensible, but he's not our doer.'

'You *know* that, do you?' Bernie said.

Kate ignored him. 'Malins is an antisocial thug and no, Joe, I wouldn't be exactly happy to meet him on a dark night, but then neither would I assume that he would victimise me. It'd depend on the *context* we were in, and his *perception* of that situation at that time.' She paused. 'But I acknowledge that his rape was a predatory act.'

'*A-ha!*'

'An unplanned predatory act.' Kate paced some more, then turned to face them. 'Whereas our doer plans *everything*. He has a mind full of carefully crafted fantasies. There is no impulsivity in what he does. Malins could be characterised as the "wham-bam" type of sexual victimiser of females. Compare that to what we know of our doer's stalking, his preparation, what he does to his victims.'

Silence.

Kate sat and pulled her notebook closer, frowning to herself.

What about his cutting short his stalking of Jody Westbrooke?

Wasn't that an indication of impuls—

The door opened and Connie appeared.

'Meant to tell you, Katie – analysis of the drinks cans by the remains of the small fire at the bypass? Several samples but no DNA matches on the national database.'

Kate distractedly nodded her thanks. 'I thought it was worth a try, as repeaters can revisit sites as a leisure activity.'

Bernie looked from Connie to Kate and scowled. 'And the less I hear about that, the happier I am.'

As Connie disappeared, he gazed towards the window for several seconds, then quickly walked across the room and peered out. Looking back at the table, he beckoned to his colleagues.

'Hey! Come and have a look!'

They went to the window.

'Take a look at *that*.' Bernie pointed at a pale metallic-blue BMW that was reversing out of a space, its driver clearly deliberating whether to leave by the front or rear entrance. 'That's Malins's car. I phoned him on Friday after he left here to come back in and make a witness statement about his contact with the James family.'

They gazed at the car in question, then back to Bernie.

'*Look* at it! Have a good look.'

Kate and Joe each gave the car a searching examination. They both saw it. Kate's eyes narrowed at the number plate: *GHB 4*.

Bernie nodded through the glass. '*That*'s a special registration. When I first seen it just now, I thought it was Malins the crim putting two fingers up at the police – about his violence. Then it clicked. He ain't dyslexic. It means what he wants it to mean. And it's *still* two fingers to us – Malins the rapist.'

'You think he's having a private joke?' asked Kate. 'GHB – gamma-hydroxybutyrate. Liquid ecstasy? Familiar as a club or date-rape drug.'

Bernie left the window, went to the glass screen and underlined Malins's name again.

Joe returned to the table shaking his head. 'Bernie, my friend, you can't make a case against a guy because he's got a lousy sense of humour.'

'Watch me. *That* fits with the Kenton-Smith case.'

Joe sat facing Kate. 'What was your interest in Malins's victim's clothes? Come on, Red. Give.'

'I was thinking about our victims' physical presentation. Not just height and hair, but the overall style they projected.' Kate pointed to the glass screen and the photographs on it. Janine. Molly. Suzie. Augmented by additional photographs from their families, including two from the Westbrookes. 'Look at them,' she invited.

They looked at the young women who'd never known each other. Janine with a heavy blonde plait. Molly with her blonde-brown hair smoothed into a ponytail. Suzie wearing her blonde hair in a long bob

295

to her shoulders. Jody almost in profile, a hairband holding back hair like liquid gold, an open expression on her sweet face. Kate looked away from the photos quickly, to her colleagues.

'Malins's description of the girl he raped has crystallised what it is about *these* girls that I believe set them apart from her and just maybe piqued their killer's initial interest.'

Kate walked rapidly to the screen and pointed. 'Look at their general *style*. It's not just about their hair. They all *dressed* in a similar way. It applies to the earlier victims as much as it does to Jody. Forget fashion. I'm talking about taste and style. It's about looking expensive. Classic. Which is quite unusual for this age group. I'm guessing that someone like Malins would describe it as "classy". It wasn't just the fact that they were blonde that snagged the killer's interest. It was much more subtle and pervasive than that.'

Kate stood close to the screen, indicating the line of photographs as she looked at each of her colleagues. 'See? The colours they wore, the *kinds* of clothes they chose?' The photos she was indicating were varied, some full-length studies, showing the girls' appearance in detail. 'Look. White shirt. Seed-pearl necklace. Cream sweater. Pale-blue polo shirt, brown loafers. No sharp-end fashion.' She stopped, gazing up at Molly's photograph, her name in gold just below her neck. She pointed to it and looked at them. 'Although *that* bothers me . . . it doesn't fit the style I'm trying to describe to you.'

'Fairley bought it for her, remember?'

'Mmm . . . but if it's not your style, why wear it if he's not your boyfriend any more?'

'I bet she still had strong feelings for him,' said Julian, nodding sagely.

Bernie rolled his eyes. 'Thanks, Marjorie Proops.'

'Who?' asked Julian and Joe in unison.

Kate looked intently at the clothes depicted in the photographs, running descriptive words in her head. 'I think their style of dressing is key, but I don't know how to define it—' She broke off, staring at the photographs, frustrated in her need to put a word to what she was saying.

Joe looked at the photographs, then at Kate.

'I do. We have a name for it back home.'

They all looked at him.

'In the States, it's called "preppy".'

CHAPTER FIFTY-SEVEN

They headed for Jody's family home through Monday's late-morning traffic. Despite the air conditioning inside the car, Kate felt perspiration ooze from her skin. She tugged restlessly at her lightweight trousers, wishing she'd worn something else. Not all of her agitation was attributable to the heat, however. Much of it related to what probably awaited them at the Westbrooke home.

To distract herself, she glanced out of the window as they neared the Warley Woods area. She recalled that its urban designation was either Smethwick or Sandwell, but to her eye it had the look of a village-like enclave. She watched as Warley Woods Golf Club slipped past, some way off the road, then looked ahead, knowing that somewhere over there, not too far away, was the dual carriageway of the Wolverhampton Road.

On arrival at Jody's parents' home, Joe and Kate were invited into the sitting room of the semi-detached house. It was as Kate had anticipated. A capsule of grief, the life, the spirit sucked from it.

Joe introduced himself and Kate to Jody's parents, a couple in their late forties, and a younger daughter, Anna, commiserating simply and genuinely with them on behalf of UCU and West Midlands Police. Jody's mother merely nodded as Mr Westbrooke quietly thanked Joe for his words. Jody's young sister watched them.

The family sat side by side on the sofa, looking as if they hadn't slept for days, which Kate assumed was probably the case. Almost a replica of Jody, Anna looked tired and stunned.

Kate gently pushed the conversation in the direction she wanted it to go.

'The night Jody left here to go to the Running Wild club, can you describe in detail everything she was wearing?'

Mrs Westbrooke stared down at her lap, making no response. Mr Westbrooke looked uncertainly at Kate.

She reassured him, her voice low: 'We wouldn't ask if we didn't think it important, Mr Westbrooke.'

He nodded, and described the clothes they had already seen. The white linen trousers, grey-and-white striped top.

Anna spoke suddenly into the silence. 'She had on a pearl necklace as well, and matching earrings.'

Both parents nodded, Jody's mother quietly offering her sole contribution to the entire exchange. 'Mine.'

Kate made quick notes on the tasteful items. As she did so, she reflected on the many media reports she'd seen over the years and the numerous times in her role as forensic psychologist that she'd heard of the sexual victimisation of young woman being attributed to the choices they'd made about their appearance. Dianne James had said the same.

But here were four young women dressed in a subtle, non-provocative style. They still died.

Joe turned to Anna. 'We need to know about her shoes and handbag. Can you tell us anything about them?'

Anna nodded and instantly sandbagged Kate with her reply. 'She was wearing red stilettos and she borrowed my bag.'

Rapidly reorganising her thoughts, Kate murmured, 'What was the bag like?'

The young woman sketched a shape and size with her hands. 'It was red too.'

'Was it made of leather . . . or suede?' asked Kate, still hoping for a response that might fit her theory.

'Plastic.'

Kate felt the theoretical rug jerking from beneath her. She wrote three words: *Shoes. Bag. No.*

'You haven't . . . got them?' asked Anna, looking from Kate to Joe, her face starting to crumple.

'No. It looks as though they were . . . taken,' ended Kate, avoiding certain words, but realising that those she *had* used sounded not only lame but ominous.

Mr Westbrooke had been watching them closely. He sat forward, face rigid with tension.

'Hang on a minute. You said you're from Rose Road? There was a chap from there interviewed on the television the other day. I watched it. It was reported in the papers as well. He was saying there was no serial killer on the loose!' He looked from one to the other of them. 'Is that what this is about? Is that what the police think?'

Joe leaned forward, hands open. 'We're looking at all possibilities, Mr Westbrooke,' he said quietly.

Jody's father looked shocked. 'If we'd known there was even a *suspicion* that there was somebody like that in the area, I'd have gone to the club to pick our daughter up. Why didn't anybody *say!*'

Mrs Westbrooke touched his arm and he slowly fell back against the sofa. She stroked his hand.

Kate looked at him, then away. Thank God their press involvement had happened after Jody went missing. Otherwise a ton of guilt, justified or not, would have been added to how she felt now.

She addressed her next question to Anna.

'How did Jody spend her time when she wasn't working?'

The young woman dabbed her eyes. 'She lived for dancing.' A few seconds of silence, then, 'She worked in town . . . she liked her job. She had some good friends there.'

'Where did she go, say for lunch, or to have coffee during the working week?'

Anna and her parents looked at each other. Anna responded for them. 'I . . . well, nowhere in particular. At least, she never said. They all had lunch in the office, but if she was on her own, Jody would sometimes go out, to a coffee shop, or get a—'

'Any particular place that you know of?'

Anna looked to her mother, then back to Kate. 'No.'

'A couple more questions and then we'll leave. Did Jody always wear very high-heeled shoes?'

Anna nodded. 'Yes. She had this thing about being shorter than all of her friends, so she thought it was a good way of getting noticed.'

Mrs Westbrooke sobbed.

They were back in UCU, having established that Jody had had no steady boyfriend and no history of difficulty with men, young or otherwise. Bernie now knew what had transpired at the Westbrooke home. Joe gave Kate a steady look. She saw it.

'What?'

'You're still convinced he stalked them?'

Kate nodded.

'Any doubts that Jody fits the series?' he asked.

'What do you mean?'

'Up to that night, he hadn't noticed she was short. He also hadn't noticed that her style . . .'

'I know what you're gonna say, Corrigan. The red shoes and bag. A bit, well, tarty, Doc. It don't fit your clothes theory.'

And Kate suddenly got it. Her own theorising earlier in the day burst into her consciousness with staggering clarity. Now she *knew*. She got up, strode to the glass screen, then turned to face her colleagues.

'Jody *did* fit. Until he curtailed the stalking phase. He didn't do it long enough to establish that she was short. Not long enough to check the consistency of her style.' Experiencing a need to sit, due to the suddenness with which the solution had crystallised for her, Kate went to her usual chair.

'I said before that something must have happened at the time he was stalking Jody. I suggested he might have become *distracted*, but that can't be the whole explanation. Whatever was happening to him at the time, it made his need to abduct and kill Jody supremely urgent.' She frowned ahead, voice quiet, then looked at each of them. 'Strong enough to make him reduce the time he spent stalking and watching her. Something got his fantasies rolling.' Kate looked down at the table. 'And I doubt it was merely the sight of her as would-be victim. It was something else. Something happening, something urgent, pressing, in some part of his life. And I *still* don't have a clue what it was.'

Silence.

'So – what's next?' asked Bernie, after a few seconds.

Kate spoke first. 'What Mr Westbrooke said, that if he'd realised the true situation, he would have acted to protect Jody. If someone had made him fully aware of the implications of what was being found at the bypass, his daughter might still be alive. But nobody *was* made aware. The police didn't alert the media. Then the media caught on to what was happening, but didn't have any details, following which Furman more or less denied any risk.'

Kate leaned on her elbows, fingers to her lips.

'We told the journalists we weren't going to do television news interviews, but I'm now thinking that an appeal should be made to alert young women and their families about the doer's activities.'

'You're right, Red. I think you should,' said Joe, voice quiet.

Kate's head came up, aghast. 'What? No! I was thinking of *you* doing it! Or Bernie.'

'I could be seen as an outsider, Kate.'

'Better coming from a female, Doc.'

CHAPTER FIFTY-EIGHT

Knowing that it had to be done, Kate went to Gander to deliver UCU's view that people living in the Greater Birmingham area needed a televised warning of the current risky situation in relation to females. Gander studied her for a few seconds, eyes sharp.

'Learn anything from your last contact with the media?'

She nodded. 'Keep to the points you want to make. Stick to them. Don't be drawn.'

He looked at his watch as he reached for the phone on his desk. 'Do it. I'll get on to the *Midlands Today* people. See if we can get it in tonight's programme.'

Kate returned to UCU and sat, staring at the glass screen.

The phone clamoured into the silence. Startled, Kate answered it, listened and hung up.

'It's fixed. I'm on tonight,' she said to the others, raising both hands. '*Don't* say anything.' They each looked at the small, tense figure and remained silent. Kate's thoughts were on Maisie. She should be home now. She'd had a lift from school.

Phyllis answered Kate's call and confirmed that Maisie was home. With Chelsey. Kate put her hand over her eyes, trying to think clearly. Or think at all. What day was it? Monday. Her housekeeper stayed later on Mondays and Fridays because she arrived later on both days. Phyllis confirmed she was able to stay until Kate got back. Kate said she would give her a lift home then.

'No, you're all right. I'll phone our Julie to come and pick me up,' said Phyllis, referring to her daughter.

Kate put down the phone without mentioning to Phyllis why she would be late. She felt strung out as it was. She didn't need Phyllis's or anyone else's reaction to the planned interview adding to her already anxious state.

Kate was inside the *Midlands Today* studio, on an upper floor of the Mailbox building. She'd mostly resisted the efforts of the make-up department, except for what she considered an over-application of lipstick.

Her heart was hammering as she sat on the red sofa, waiting as the newsreader summarised the several items at the beginning of the programme, aware that the announcement was routinely accompanied by an upbeat musical introduction not audible in the studio. She could see the faces of Molly, Janine, Suzie and Jody displayed on the nearby monitor's half-screen, the other half showing the facade of Headquarters at Rose Road.

Sitting there listening to the familiar format, Kate felt completely disorientated. Her heart ricocheted inside her chest as one of the presenters began the item, briefly outlining the latest details of UCU's involvement in the cases before turning to her.

'Thank you for agreeing to come on the programme, Dr Hanson. Everyone is now aware of West Midlands Police reinvestigating the unsolved cases dating back to 1998, and now the most recent killing, which is believed to be connected, despite a gap of over a decade. Do you have a message for women at this time, Dr Hanson? Presumably you would advise that they be especially vigilant until this person is caught?'

Kate nodded, hoping she looked cool and professional, feeling anything but.

'Yes, and I can be a little more informative about the risk.'

She looked to the relaxed presenter for guidance. He nodded encouragingly. Now, she was really 'on'.

'The man who murdered these three young women years ago, and Jody Westbrooke very recently, selects his victims first, then observes them for some time prior to his actual attack.' Kate had resolved not to use the word 'stalking'. It might create a picture that was misleading. She wanted to keep it simple. 'We believe this man's appearance is presentable, that he can appear sociable, even trustworthy. There's a possibility that whilst he is observing a female he may show her some low-level or friendly attention—'

The presenter interjected. 'Could you give viewers an example of what you mean by that, Dr Hanson?'

Kate nodded. 'Nothing elaborate. Possibly a simple hello, or a very small behaviour, like the wave of a hand, a smile in a café.' She thought back to Janine. 'Perhaps raising a drink to acknowledge her. If any female viewers, but particularly young women between the ages of say sixteen and twenty-one, blonde . . .'

Kate hesitated. She couldn't go into their 'preppy' theory. There wasn't time. She could see the studio floor manager making a 'wind-it-up' gesture with his hand to the presenter.

'. . . and well-dressed, have been approached or acknowledged by a man, a stranger, in the way I've described, or merely *suspect* a stranger of showing them that kind of interest, especially recently, we would be very grateful to hear from them.'

Kate gave the direct number for UCU, hoping there would be no more questions. Her mouth had dried up completely and her mind was a wilderness. The camera shifted from her and stayed on the presenter. At a nod from the floor manager, Kate fled, as the presenter repeated the telephone number.

CHAPTER FIFTY-NINE

Kate reached home feeling both exhausted and distracted and, after seeing Phyllis off, went straight to her study. Due to the increasing anxiety about possible future victims, she now felt forced to reconsider all-comers. Malins? Cranham? Fairley? She still murmured a subtle 'no' after each, yet knowing she was unable to reject them entirely as possible suspects. She thought of the three men and their various characteristics. They must be interviewed again. Questions asked about their personal histories. She made a note in her diary, imagining the likely emailed response from Rutgers. And Furman's response when he got wind of her plan.

Leaving the study, Kate went to the kitchen and switched on the kettle for tea. Maisie and Chelsey were still upstairs. She hadn't seen either of them since she came home. She listened. Nothing.

A sudden thought occurred to her, activated by a distant comment from Bernie. A murderous twosome? Maybe when they interviewed Malins, Cranham and Fairley separately, some link between one or the other would emerge? Furman's likely reaction to such a plan bore down on Kate. She massaged her forehead. Whether the negative response was from Cranham's legal representative or Furman, she knew she was perched on the edge of a professional abyss.

She thought of everyone currently involved in the cases, including Upstairs. If UCU continued to work on the basis of the doer's arrogance, they could add Furman himself to the list. Prentiss?

Or even an ex-husband. God, I'm tired.

As she drank tea, Kate's thoughts drifted to men she knew, socially and professionally. A couple of years before, a psychologist involved alongside her in criminal proceedings against an alleged paedophile had oiled his way over to her after they'd each given their evidence, to give her his views of the man on trial and why Kate's opinion of him was misguided. He'd gone on to suggest that she had a problem. With men. She'd responded that she would always have a problem with men who had sex with children, and that at that moment she had a real problem with *him*, for his unsolicited insights about her. Which of course nicely confirmed his view of her, given the no-win situation of making a response to him at all. The jury in the case eventually spoke and the judge sent the paedophile to prison.

Kate sighed once more. Did she have a problem with men? If so, did it cloud her judgement? She thought of Joe. No. She didn't have a problem with men.

She felt a sudden surge of anxiety and her headache flicked its long tail. While the days were slipping by, there was a very real possibility that the doer was frequenting coffee shops, checking his traplines, ready to close in again. Ready for another kill.

Kate left the kitchen table in search of medication, which she swallowed with the remains of the tea, realising she'd had no food for hours. As she placed her cup inside the DishDrawer, she heard the faint ring of a mobile phone somewhere on the upper floor, followed in a minute or so by two pairs of feet thudding down the stairs.

'Mom? *Mom!*' The feet crossed the hall and Maisie hurled open the kitchen door, followed closely by Chelsey,

'Why didn't you *tell* me? How could you! Mom, you are *so* unfair!'

Kate looked in alarm at her daughter's flushed face and accusing eyes, then at Chelsey, blonde-brown hair billowing around her face, grey-green eyes shining, looking excited and – *awed*? She and Maisie started jumping and clamouring together, giving little squeals.

Kate's hand flew to her head. 'What is it *now*, Maisie! I've got a head—'

'Lauren Downell just rang me! She's *told* me!' Maisie pointed an accusatory finger at her mother, the nail painted neon-orange, matching Chelsey's. 'You've just been on television! She was asking me about it and when she knew I didn't know she was, like, a total cow and— What's that *horrible* stuff on your mouth?'

The torrent of words stopped and both girls stared. Kate dragged the back of her hand across her mouth and looked. Lipstick. Bright. Red. She could see that Maisie was almost beside herself at not having been told earlier about Kate's televised interview. She was now glaring at her mother, breathless and mutely disapproving.

'Look, Maisie, I didn't know myself until earlier this afternoon that I would be doing the—'

'You rang Phyllis! You didn't tell her either, because if you had she would have told *me*!'

Chelsey's facial expression hadn't changed. Still awed. Kate rested against the granite, an ominous pulsing inside her head.

'Maisie, I'm sorry. Really. I should have told Phyllis to let you know.'

Kate didn't want to admit to the two young girls how nervous and disturbed she'd felt prior to the interview.

Seeing that Maisie was about to start up again, Kate pushed herself away from the work surface, voice firm. 'The cases UCU is working on at the moment – they're not the kind of thing I want you hearing about. Or you, Chelsey.'

'Yeah, right, Mom. So six o'clock's the new watershed? Ha! *Come on*, Chels.'

With that they darted from the kitchen into the hall, a whirl of tanned arms and legs, and disappeared upstairs. Kate waited for the familiar thud of the bedroom door, then left the kitchen and walked slowly to the sitting room, mentally reviewing the notes she'd made the previous evening. About the chaotic storage of records at Rose Road. In the last few minutes an idea had formulated.

Kate glanced at her watch. Eight thirty p.m. No time like right now. Given the current situation at Rose Road, she was sure they would still be there, and hopefully they would be willing to help her.

Still overwrought but now decisive, Kate walked quickly into the hall to locate her notebook and bag.

'Maisie? . . . *Maisie!*'

A muffled one-word response. 'What!'

'Come down here, please.'

Both girls appeared on the landing and hung over the banister. Kate looked up at them.

'I need to go back to Rose Road. I'm not sure how long for, so you will have to come with me and we can drop Chelsey on the way.'

'Why can't we stay here?'

'Because I don't like the idea of you two being alone in the house when I don't know how long—'

'Yeah, right. You don't trust us! We're not babies!'

Kate had had enough. She turned and snatched up the light jacket she'd left on the hall chair when she arrived home. 'Get whatever you need and come down! *Now!*'

The two girls disappeared briefly, then reappeared in the hall, ready to leave the house. Maisie's face was mutinous. A couple of minutes later, Kate watched Chelsey press the intercom button at the side of her drive and speak into the grille. One of the large black gates glided slowly open, and with a wave Chelsey slipped inside and started to run down the long drive towards the house.

'Mom?' said Maisie from the back seat of the Audi. 'Why can't I stay here with Chelsey?'

Fed up of debating with her, and realising it solved the problem of what to do with Maisie once they reached Rose Road, Kate got out of the car, walked to the grille and pressed the button.

'Hello?' Chelsey's mother.

'Oh, hi, Candice . . . Is it okay for me to leave Maisie with you for about an hour?'

'Of course. Send her in. See you later!'

Mercifully, it appeared that Candice didn't know about Kate's television appearance. Yet. As the large gate glided open once again, Kate released Maisie from the back of the Audi and watched her bound down the drive. She continued to watch as Maisie entered the house and she saw a wave from Candice.

Kate jumped quickly into the Audi, now free to put her plan into action.

CHAPTER SIXTY

Inside Rose Road, Kate was aware of the hum of activity beyond the quiet reception area. UCU lay to the left, but she walked past, straight Upstairs to the large incident room just beyond Gander's office, looking for two specific officers.

Walking into the huge room, she saw what was causing the hum. It was full of non-uniform officers, working at computers, reading documents, calling to each other, a small group having a discussion in front of a glass screen, the twin of the one in UCU. Kate bit her lip. She should have phoned first.

She caught sight of Gus 'the Kilt' Stirling getting up from his desk and heading towards a catering trolley. He waved to her as he went and she started towards him.

'Working overtime now, Kate?' he asked, grinning at her. 'Want some coffee? Something to eat? We've got—'

She shook her head. 'I was looking for you, actually. I need your help, Gus.'

He gave her a surprised sideways look.

She continued. 'Well, you and Al. Is he around?'

Gus shook his head and Kate's spirits dipped.

'He'll be here in –' he looked at his watch – 'about ten minutes. Tell me what you want, to save time when he arrives. Come on. Over here and have a seat. Just heard that you're a star, by the way.'

'*Don't.* I'm still recovering.'

Kate followed Gus to a table covered in paperwork and sat down with him. He eyed her quizzically as she launched her proposal, keeping it quick and simple to avoid wasting his time.

'It's about the abduction-murders starting from the nineties, which you know about. We extended our reinvestigation to include a number of rape cases prior to them. We've had some real problems tracking

309

down evidence and statements in those cases, Gus. In fact all of the evidence boxes for our cases seem incomplete. I need to know if that's at all typical of cases managed here.' She stopped, hoping that what she'd said didn't sound critical.

Gus gave a small head-shake.

'I doubt it, although case papers can end up at the CPS. But what do you want with me and Al . . . Hey, speak the Devil's name and he appears.'

Kate turned to see Al Bowen, Superintendent of Operations, coming through the door.

'Kate! Don't see you up here often. Fancying a change from the Brummie Bulldog?'

Kate's smile changed to a wide grin, recognising the reference to Bernie. Why did the police love nicknames? Despite the banter within Rose Road, she knew that Bernie was well regarded.

Gus outlined quickly for Al what Kate had told him so far. Al nodded, looking a question at her.

Kate chose her words. 'I can see you're very busy now, with the Westbrooke case, but I wonder if you'd have any objection to joining me in a small . . . experiment? It won't take long.'

Neither officer spoke. She pressed on. 'Just a few minutes. What I'd like you both to do is think of a case each of you has worked on separately here. The cases must be old, by the way. Dating between, say, 1995 and 2002. Oh, and I'd like one to be a solved case, the other unsolved.' She hoped that by specifying both it would test out the possibility that had been suggested to her, that the CPS held on to documents.

The two police officers exchanged glances.

Gus spoke first: 'And then what?'

Always the next question. *Police work and psychology. Well suited? Not convinced.*

'I want you to go down to the evidence store, find a victim statement, or similar, from the case you've chosen and bring it back up here. Before you do, I want you to identify the document you're going to search for.'

They exchanged another look, causing Kate to wonder if she'd overstepped some unspoken protocol.

'Okay,' said Gus. 'You want us to tell you the cases we've got in mind?'

Kate nodded.

'Mine's a 1998 stabbing,' said Gus. 'A brawl in Aston. A bloke was stabbed five times, including once in the chest, but he survived. That's why I remember it. Never got who did it. There should be a witness statement by one of his neighbours.'

Kate nodded again. She and Gus looked at Al.

'The case I'm thinking about is the murder of a woman in 1997. She was strangled and dumped in Sutton Park. Her husband's coming up for parole in a couple of years' time. It's his statement I'll be looking for.'

Kate looked from one to the other. 'Good,' she said quietly. Then she had a thought. 'Neither of the cases has been resurrected in any way to date? No appeals? No reinvestigation?'

Both heads shook

Kate took a deep breath. 'Okay. When you're ready . . .'

Al's eyes narrowed. 'Presumably you want to know how long it takes us, if we do find them?'

Kate nodded. 'You first, Gus, then Al.'

Kate glanced casually at the sweep hand of the Breitling on her wrist as Gus left the incident room at a good pace. He was back surprisingly quickly with the witness statement relating to his case. Kate checked the timing, wrote it down, then nodded to Al, who set off briskly. He also returned swiftly to the incident room, waving some A4 sheets. Kate wrote more figures.

Thanking the two men for their efforts, Kate left the room and ran quickly down the stairs and along the short corridor to UCU. Once inside, she switched on one of the lights and sat down at the table to consider the information she'd gathered.

Both officers had promptly located the statements they were seeking. Gus had taken six minutes ten seconds, Al five minutes fifty-seven seconds. She sat back and looked at the figures she'd written. Not an experiment in the true sense of the word. But a good enough demonstration for Kate that not all of Rose Road's records were as chaotic and incomplete as those for UCU's murder and rape cases appeared to be.

She stood, walked to the glass screen and added the two timings. Then she stepped back to consider them, wondering about the implications, if any.

She remained where she was for a few minutes, eyes narrowed on the glass screen, as relevant bits of information they'd acquired over the last several days began to stir and cluster inside her head, like filings to a magnet.

At home again, Kate rested her head against the back of the sofa. Maisie was upstairs in her room. Sulking. Kate was on a quest, unable to quit despite the hour.

Our cases are different.

Why?

Information is misfiled or missing.

Why?

Who managed the two abduction-murders in the nineties?

Furman.

Who appeared to have knowledge of the prior rapes?

Furman.

Kate reflected on gossip she'd heard about Furman's management style during her relatively brief experience of Rose Road. She could think of a few people there who might delight in doing him a 'bad turn', as Bernie would phrase it. Maybe they had. Maybe the missing and misfiled records were a product of professional mischief against him?

Her thoughts wafted and spun, tiny gossamer creatures riding thermals. Synapses fired and neurones connected. Her head jerked upright as items separated themselves from the clusters of information she was considering and became defined.

It cannot be.

That's madness.

Furman's a career officer. He couldn't be . . .

She thought of Bernie's response, next time she was in UCU and divulged what she was thinking. Before she allowed her suspicions daylight, she needed to explore them thoroughly.

CHAPTER SIXTY-ONE

Kate was in her room at the university when the call came.

'Hanson.'

'Hello, Doctor.'

Kate's brow creased, then: 'Hi,' she said, suddenly realising that she didn't know Whittaker's first name.

'Chief Superintendent Gander's asked me to ring and find out if you're in Rose Road today.'

'Yes. Around two p.m.'

'Hang on, Doctor.' There was a muffling of the phone, then Whittaker was back.

'Two o'clock's fine. The chief superintendent'd like to see you then.'

Kate replaced the receiver, wondering what was afoot.

Gander was sitting behind his desk, face stern, as Kate walked inside his office. He waved her to a chair.

'I've just come back from seeing Jody Westbrooke's parents. Tried to give them some reassurance that we're on top of this – this *lunacy*.' He shook his head, then looked directly at Kate.

'Lieutenant Corrigan and DS Watts tell me that you're convinced this animal's watching, following the young women he kills?'

Kate nodded. 'He's a stalker, yes.'

Gander heaved himself out of his chair, walked ponderously to the window and stood looking out of it. His back still to Kate, he spoke:

'We never had anything like this – this *palaver* – when I joined the Force, you know. The job was mostly about ordinary criminal activity. Burglaries, the occasional raid on a bank, domestics . . . Murders, yes, but we didn't have any of this . . . perverted activity.'

Yes you did. It just wasn't recognised for what it was.

313

Kate sat quietly. Waiting.

Gander turned to her, looking weary. 'Nowadays, your average police officer is expected to be a community "friend", social worker, diplomat . . .' He sat heavily. 'Don't misunderstand what I'm saying, Kate. They should be all of those things when they're called for.' He shook his head. 'But *now* they need to be psychologists as well. They need to understand what's going on in this . . . animal's head!'

Gander laced his fingers together, joined hands tapping rosewood. Kate waited some more.

'You're here all afternoon?' She nodded. 'Right. I need you to do something, if you will. I need you to talk to whoever's on duty. Tell them about stalking, stalkers – you know, what sort of people they are, why they do it, how to spot 'em. Help 'em understand what this animal's *about*.' He shot a look at her. 'Can you do that?'

'I can do that,' said Kate, quickly reviewing Gander's wish-list.

'Okay, then. Shall we say . . . three o'clock? A half-hour from you should do it.'

'Yes,' said Kate.

Gander looked both pleased and relieved. 'Good. *Good*. It'll help 'em get a . . . a handle on this . . . whoever he is. If they understand him, chances are they'll know him when they have him.' He stood, and Kate did likewise.

'Thank you, Kate. I appreciate your willingness, and at such short notice.'

An hour later, Kate entered the huge Upstairs office, where at least thirty officers, mostly male, were gathered waiting, no doubt in response to an edict from Gander. A glance around the suddenly silent room, at the folded arms and closed faces, told her all she needed to know. The Force wasn't renowned for the keenness with which it embraced psychology and its theories, especially around the issue of sex.

She walked to the front of the office, to stand before a wall-mounted whiteboard, as an incident from the year before slipped into her head. Joe teaching Maisie to play baseball in the garden. Maisie getting upset. Missing the ball more often than hitting it. Then, with Joe's encouragement, she got it. Maisie's jubilant words whisped through Kate's head.

I've got a great swing now, haven't I, Joe?

Sure have, Cat's-whiskers. Don't let anybody mess with it.

Kate smiled inwardly as she recalled the verse he'd recited for Maisie, which Maisie, no fan of poetry, had loved ever since.

She glanced across the room at the waiting officers

I've worked tougher crowds than you. And I've got a great swing.

'Sexual desire. Pleasure. Fantasy rehearsal. Satisfaction.'

Hearing the words, some of the officers looked surprised, some interested. Others slouched lower into their seats.

'*Those* are the elements of stalking.'

Kate turned, picked up a marker, wrote some words on the whiteboard, then turned back.

'Let's take a quick tour through the various types of stalkers. Knowing what he's about might help identify him.'

She pointed a finger at the whiteboard. 'Is he a rejected type, who had a prior relationship with the victim? Is he an intimacy-seeker with a strong need for closeness to salve feelings of loneliness? Or is he a social incompetent whose efforts to establish intimate relationships are blocked by his inability to engage in appropriate relationship foreplay – you know the type. Doesn't know how to talk to females, scares them off.'

She noted some grins within her audience, plus one or two glances at a burly officer, who glanced round, aware of the attention on him.

'*Hey!*' He frowned, then grinned as well.

'On the other hand, he might be the resentful type of stalker. Somebody who's been offended or upset, or so he believes, by the victim in the past, so he's pursuing her for revenge – he wants to get back at her.'

Kate returned the stares of her audience. 'The rejected and resentful types of stalker are relatively easy to identify, because there's usually a pre-existing link between them and their victim.' She glanced at the whiteboard. 'The intimacy-seekers and the incompetents aren't so easy to find.'

She made her voice low, deliberate. 'And we haven't even gotten to the fifth type.'

The silence in the room was intense. All eyes were now on Kate. She had them.

'The cases we're all working on involve the fifth type. The predatory stalker. This is what to expect of him. Multiple victims. Zero interest in intimacy as most people might define that. Definitely not a social

315

incompetent. No prior relationship with his victims.' She waited for them to digest what she'd said.

'What he does have is a problematic personality. He's likely to be psychopathic, which means he has the ability to socially connect, even charm, but is totally self-centred and lacking in feelings for anyone but himself. He's also likely to be somewhat intellectually smarter than the other types of stalker.' Kate paused.

'The key characteristic of stalking done by the predatory type is that it's always geared to destruction. He follows and watches because he has a plan. He's the least likely to reveal his presence, although he might make it felt in very minimal ways. His stalking period is the shortest of all. Around six months, on average. Predatory stalking is about information-gathering through watching, practising, rehearsing what he wants. His goal: power and devastation.'

'Thought it was about sex?' said a voice from somewhere at the back of the room.

Kate shook her head. 'He's a sexual sadist. We know this from what he left at the bypass and at Romsley. For the sexual sadist, sex is merely a *vehicle* for what he must have: the mastery, the total possession of his victim.'

The tension in the room was palpable as Kate itemised characteristics on her fingers.

'As likely as not to be employed. May have an intimate partner, but don't count on it. The majority have a criminal record. Don't count on that either. A proportion of predatory stalkers start their offending careers as serial rapists, although they can have committed less serious offences.'

'Anything we can count on? And why's it always "he"?' This from a different part of the room.

Kate nodded. 'There are instances of female stalkers. But the predatory type? Never. You can count on that. Until an exception occurs.'

She walked to the desk nearest the front, leaned her hands on it and surveyed the room. 'Look. What I'm saying *could* help identify our doer, once his name is part of the investigation. Without guidance, you could be relying on guesswork.'

She straightened and returned to the whiteboard, writing quickly, then faced them again.

'We're looking for someone with average to good intelligence.

Emotionally cool, possibly closed off. Socially alienated. Someone with little capacity for sympathising with others' pain, but never doubt his motivation to see and enjoy it. Someone who has difficulty with intimacy. A man who may appear laid-back, even passive. He's got a rich, rewarding fantasy life. He may appear 'absent' at times, because he's in his own head, daydreaming.'

Again there were some grins and quiet laughs at the expense of one of the officers in the room.

Kate waited for a couple of seconds, then, 'I think our doer is all of these things. During questioning you'll probably locate the foundation of his sadistic rage – in his childhood.' A few sighs and mutters drifted from the audience. 'I know. It's always back to childhood. That's often how it is. What he's done, is still doing, isn't about these young women. It's about a long-ago relationship that he found confusing or affectionless, possibly a relationship that was inconsistent or even absent at times.'

She waited a few more seconds for them to absorb what she'd said.

'Asking some subtle questions about his early years would probably pay off.' She looked around the room, seeing a few familiar faces near the back: Al, Gus, 'Sticky' Hemmings, Harry. Matt Prentiss. What she'd given them was probably enough. 'That's it,' she said quietly.

Kate stayed where she was as several of her audience drifted out. She returned their parting nods. Julian suddenly appeared at the end of the exiting group with Harry.

'Hi, Julian. Didn't see you just now. Hi, Harry.'

Harry didn't respond, looking preoccupied as he walked past and out. Julian saw Kate's eyes following him.

'Furman wants to see him.'

Kate nodded, wondering if the subject of that meeting was standing next to her. 'Going back to UCU?' she asked.

He nodded, and they walked together.

'What you just said, Kate, about a relationship in childhood that was inconsistent, lacking in affection – well . . . that's me and my dad.'

She looked up at him as they walked, reminding herself that, intellectually quick as he was, he was still young, constructing his own understanding of his true self. 'Yes, Julian, it probably is. But I don't observe in you any of the other qualities I mentioned.' She smiled at him. 'Remember, it's always about combinations of factors.'

She glanced up again at the young face, thinking that whatever suspicions Furman and Gander might hold about Julian, they were inaccurate or misinformed. Furman. Kate's suspicions blossomed anew.

There was silence between them until they neared UCU, when Julian spoke. 'I know somebody here whose father left before he ever got to have a relationship with him. Then his mother died.'

'That's a shame. Who's that?'

'I'd better not say. He told me in confidence.'

CHAPTER SIXTY-TWO

Early Friday morning, Maisie opened the door before the sound of the last ring had died. Hair centre-parted into thick bunches, she was dressed in regulation green school uniform, the skirt customised by neat rolling at the waistband, secured by a narrow red belt.

'Hi, Joe! Come in,' she said. 'Mom? It's Joe!'

'Good morning, Madeleine,' he said, mock-formal.

'Nobody calls me that,' said Maisie, matching his manner, plus a mock-pout.

'You're up with the dawn, Cat's-whiskers. Your mom busy?'

'She's got as far as going on about her busy day. We're expecting Daddy to call in for breakfast.'

Joe followed Maisie into the kitchen. Kate was laying the table with three places, and looked up as he came through the door. Having spent the last two days at the university, she and Joe hadn't seen each other since the middle of the week.

'Hi, Joe. Tea? Coffee? Maisie, for the *second* time, lose the belt and unroll the skirt to its proper length.'

He chose coffee. 'Hear you're expecting a breakfast guest.'

Kate grimaced, waiting for Maisie to reach the stairs before speaking, keeping her tone low.

'Kevin and I are going to discuss Maisie's contact. This time he sticks to whatever we agree to. And if he doesn't . . .' She left the sentence hanging.

Joe nodded. 'So. What're you up to today?'

'I'll see Maisie off to school, give a lecture at eleven and then I've got a tutorial with Julian. There's something on his mind, Joe.' Should she say anything about the suspicions circling around Julian to do with drugs? Or those around Maisie, for that matter? No. Maisie certainly wasn't Joe's problem. She sighed and continued.

319

'I need a quiet evening so I can get my thoughts on our cases ordered. I can't really do that if Maisie's around, so I'm hoping that Kevin will offer to have her at his house tonight, to make up for the weekends she's missed.'

'I was thinking, maybe you could use an outing. Nothing late. While we're carousing, you could tell me what you were up to the other night at Rose Road?'

Kate said nothing. Too soon. She had to sort out her own thinking.

'Okay, back to the outing.' He stood, stretching out one arm, other hand at his chest, to begin his pitch. 'I'm thinking a G 'n' T each, then Wongs, probably a couple more G 'n' Ts, followed by honey pepper chicken as an addition to the menu for two, then a tad more alcohol and a couple of my hot jazz CDs, maybe Vince Giordarno and the Nighthawks. Trust me on this, Red. You need some leisure time.'

Kate looked up at him, amused at his spiel. 'Idiot.' There was a short silence, during which they looked at each other. Kate's face had acquired a small frown above the nose.

'Joe . . . it sounds really . . . lovely. But, like I said, I need to work . . . on my ideas. Plus, I don't know if Kevin has other plans and won't be able to take Maisie. It's short notice.'

He nodded. 'Just an invitation between friends, Red. No expectations. No worries.'

Despite Joe's casual words, the air between them felt charged. She gazed up at him. 'Maybe . . . another time?' Another small silence. 'I need to talk to you and Bernie sometime, about Al and Gus and the—'

Maisie returned to the kitchen, unbelted.

'Don't take any notice of what Mom says, Joe. She's on edge because of Daddy.'

'*Maisie.*'

Maisie shrugged. 'Stay and have breakfast with us. Daddy will behave himself, won't he, Mom?'

Joe and Kate exchanged a glance as he placed his coffee mug on the table. Heading for the door, he gave Maisie a wink.

Kate followed him out. 'Joe, it's—'

'Not a problem, Kate.'

She watched him walk to his car, just as Kevin's low-slung vehicle purred on to the driveway. Damn! His timing always was hopeless.

'Mom! Where's my DS?'

'Stop shouting!'

Maisie appeared from behind Kate. 'Well *you* are— Hey! Daddy's here!'

She ran to the sleek silver Mercedes convertible that had just pulled up.

Kate walked slowly to where Joe was opening his car door. She gazed up at him. 'It's . . . awkward sometimes.'

A nod. 'I see it, and I'll take a rain check on that outing.'

She tried for light-hearted. 'I expect you're glad you didn't bother with children.'

He grinned down at her as he got into his car, then activated the window, looking up, eyes very blue, unreadable. 'Who says I didn't?'

He began pulling away from the house, then stopped to call back to her. 'By the way, Upstairs brought Malins in for interview about an hour ago, in connection with the murder of Jody Westbrooke.'

'*What?*'

Kate watched as Joe pulled out of the drive.

Maisie appeared at her side, face full of disapproval. 'Mom!' she hissed. 'Your mouth is hanging open again, like an old person. Get a grip! Chelsey will be here soon.'

Kate gazed in the direction Joe had disappeared, head teeming.

Back inside the house, she found Maisie and Kevin sitting at the kitchen table, laughing. She looked from father to daughter, recognising similarity in the shape of the mouth, the curve of a brow.

Unsettled, she went to the cafetiere, thoughts drifting back to when she and Kevin were first married. Both of them busy on weekdays, their weekends leisurely but focused. On each other. She switched on the kettle. Things changed. She changed. She got pregnant with Maisie. And Kevin remained himself. He never quite understood that Maisie needed her attention as much as he did; more, in the early months and years. He couldn't share Kate's attention. She stared at cool cream wall tiles.

'Mom! Listen to this! Daddy's *totally* mad. He says he's thinking of staying for a couple of weeks and he'll paint the house pink to give old Mrs Hetherington apoplexy and—'

Sounds from the direction of the front of the house distracted Maisie. She leapt from the table. 'Hey, there's my lift! It's early. *Quick*, Mom. Can I have some money?'

Kevin reached for his wallet. 'Here you go, Sweet Pea.'

'Wow! *Thanks*, Daddy! Mom, look what—'

'Yes, I can see.'

Kate followed Maisie to the door, to help her with her book bag and tennis racquet and see her off. She waved to Chelsey and her mother, then closed the door and walked back to the kitchen.

'Don't do that, Kevin,' she said quietly.

'What?' he said innocently.

'You know.'

'I gave my daughter a few pounds. What's the big deal now?'

'*Our* daughter. You know damn well that's not what I'm talking about, although I *would* prefer it if you consulted me first on money. I'm talking about giving Maisie mixed messages. About staying. It's immature.'

'It was a joke, Kate, for God's sake! She knows it's a joke. She's *smart*.'

'She's *twelve*, Kevin. Don't play with her emotions.'

Kate's thoughts slid away, to the time she'd discovered the first of Kevin's affairs.

Like you did mine. Bastard.

She took the coffee mug Joe had used from the table and placed it gently in the sink, tracing a finger around its rim. 'Look, all I'm saying is, think before you say things. You know she'd probably like to see—'

She stopped.

'What? What would she like to see, Kate?'

'Nothing.' She turned to find him gazing at her, a faint smile on his face. A face she knew so well. A face she'd thought at times she might still—

'Did I mention that Stella and I have been considering a reconciliation? It's no-go, though. It's definitely finished.' Kate looked away, feeling his eyes on her. 'Why do I always attract career women?'

Kate started clearing the table, ignoring his last question, recognising it as merely rhetorical. She'd suddenly decided she wanted Maisie at home this weekend. And she didn't have to jump at everything, or even anything, that Kevin said to her.

Core of steel, yeah!

Leaning now against the granite worktop, arms folded, Kevin gave her an appraising look. 'I see the boyfriend is still hanging around. Faithful to the end.'

'Joe's a colleague . . . A friend. A good friend. That's all.'

Kevin straightened, rubbing his hands together. 'Okay, what do you say to a moratorium? No mention of girlfriends, boyfriends or any other . . .'

Kate was no longer listening. She was staring out of the window, still thinking about what Joe had told her.

Kevin had left, having managed to avoid giving a firm commitment on his future contact with Maisie. Kate went straight to the house phone and dialled Rose Road. After a brief wait, Gander came on the line.

'Morning, Kate. Thanks for the talk to the officers. It's given them something to think about. I'm guessing your call is about developments with Malins?'

Kate walked with the phone into her study. 'Yes. Lieutenant Corrigan's just told me.' She hesitated. 'I've got doubts about Malins having had anything to do with Jody's abduction and murder. I also doubt his involvement with Molly's abduction. He doesn't fit the type we're looking for.'

'I already know what you think, Kate. Both your colleagues have given me a progress report.'

Kate waited.

'You can probably see the difficulty,' Gander went on. 'You more or less said it yourself in the television interview. We know this man's out there and we can't afford to take any chances – good work in that interview, by the way.'

So. That was it, thought Kate as she ended the call. She went into the hall, replaced the receiver, then walked slowly to the back of the house.

She pushed the kitchen doors wide and stepped out into early-morning sunshine. If Malins was arrested for Jody's murder, then it would be only a matter of time before he was also arrested for the earlier abductions. Tunnel vision. What she'd been afraid of from the beginning.

Carrying an opened tin of cat food in one hand, she walked down the garden, ears cued for a tiny bell. She reached the back fence, suspecting that the investigation was now out of UCU's control, and turned to look at the old house, mellow in the early sun, the ground floor of its back elevation covered in wisteria, a second show of violet and pale-blue flowers almost finished. And now she needed to get to the university.

She started back towards the house, calling the cat by name. *Where was he?* On reaching the patio, she suddenly stopped and looked down at a small wet patch on one of the slabs. Squatting on her heels, she examined it, heart constricting. Blood. Fresh blood. Standing, she quickly scanned the immediate area. Nothing. She put down the tin and began to search the flower beds and shrubs nearest the blood. Lifting the limb of an old rose bush, weighed almost to the ground with scarlet blooms, she peered into its shade.

There's something there. Something . . .

As Kate stretched out a hand and grasped the small item, the heavy limb slipped from her other hand, its vicious thorns raking the length of her forearm. She snatched her arm away, unaware of the twin scratches starting to ooze. She was looking at what she was holding. Blue velvet. Stained red. She gently shook it. A faint tinkle.

Kate pushed it into a pocket of her jeans and hurried to the water butt. Grabbing a bucket, she filled it, hurling water over the slabs. She didn't want Maisie to come home and see any sign of animal violence involving Mugger.

She chewed her bottom lip, thinking of what she might say to her daughter.

'So your next task is to check the data you have and do a draft write-up. Take, say, ten days, and let me have a look at it,' advised Kate, identifying the date and making a note in her diary as she drew the tutorial to an end.

She looked up at Julian as he stood in the middle of her room at the university, jeans low, another Grateful Dead T-shirt proclaiming his allegiance to a band formed years before he was born. He lifted his backpack on to the table and added a couple of Kate's own textbooks.

'Where are you off to now?' asked Kate, watching as he donned his baseball cap, peak to back.

'Day Three, Cadaver Camp,' he responded briefly, before finishing the juice Kate had provided.

Kate shuddered, although she'd heard other students use the same name for the Facility. Access strictly limited to those students judged to have shown particular skill, aptitude and application in their studies and who were regarded as emotionally robust. A thought occurred to her. Might Gander decide that Julian could no longer have that access, given that he suspected him of involvement with drugs? She watched as Julian hefted the backpack on to one shoulder. No cycling helmet today. He must be on foot.

Kate's thoughts went briefly to her own postgraduate days. When Winterton was laboratories, lecture rooms and a library. All changed now, its warren of high-ceilinged rooms given over to forensic laboratories, its wide swathe of grounds to post-mortem studies. The same grounds where she and other students had sunbathed a lifetime ago. She and Kevin . . .

'Hang on five minutes and I'll give you a lift.'

Without looking at Kate directly, Julian shook his head. 'No need. It only takes me a few minutes to walk.'

'Don't argue with your senior supervisor,' Kate replied, smiling but firm.

Maybe if she had a chance to talk to him without the pressures of Rose Road or the frenetic atmosphere around tutorials at the university, he might tell her what was bothering him. And about the drugs. He might know something about the general availability in the area of little blue tablets, although she was confident now that the ones she'd found in Maisie's drawer weren't hers. Still. The worry remained that someone in Maisie's social milieu appeared to have access to them.

As they walked to Kate's car, she thought of the most recent development in UCU's cases.

'Have you heard? About Alan Malins being brought in for interview about Jody Westbrooke?'

Julian's footsteps faltered then picked up again. 'No. I didn't know that,' he said after some seconds. Kate looked at him closely. She'd just caught surprise on his face. And something else beneath it. It looked to her like relief.

They walked on in silence, Kate puzzled, the theoretical argument she'd anticipated from him not materialising.

Ten minutes later, in Kate's car, she'd become aware of the shortness of the journey to Winterton. Her efforts to draw Julian out by talking about his work with the forensic scenes team had failed to produce any information. They'd almost reached the far side of the campus. She had another try.

'So, you're still enjoying your attachment to the team?'

Silence, then: 'Yeah.'

325

Raise it, thought Kate. It's been on your mind long enough. Julian clearly wasn't going to volunteer anything.

'Is Matt treating you okay?'

'Fine! *He's* . . . fine.'

More silence. Kate doubted that she would get anything out of Julian in his current mood. She could now see Winterton's bulk on the left-hand side of the road they were following. A small, silent wait for some traffic navigating the tiny bridge just ahead, then Kate drove on, slowing as she approached the wide entrance. She turned between the ornate brick pillars and drove steadily towards the house.

Even in bright sunlight, Winterton was indisputably gothic in the Victorian style, with its arched front door, massive mullioned windows and multi-pointed roof. The only features not included, as far as Kate could see, were gargoyle waterspouts. As they drew near to the building, she admired, as she had many times in the past, the handsome stone carving around the front door – a wolf-like animal perched on the keystone at the top of the arch, and on either side a line of small mice climbing inexorably upwards towards him.

What happens when the mice and the wolf meet?

She stopped the car in the shadow of the sombre building, glancing at her young passenger. Julian remained where he was, looking towards Winterton, not moving. Wherever he was right now, he wasn't with her.

'Okay?' Kate's voice sounded unexpectedly loud, given their close proximity in the small car.

It broke his reverie. He gave her a quick glance and reached for the door handle. Kate spoke quickly.

'Julian? If anyone is upsetting you or behaving in a way you don't like, or trying to involve you in . . . anything, just tell me and I can—'

'Bye, Kate.'

He was gone.

Kate watched him disappear, then drove slowly past the front of the house and back along the drive. She'd now got another pressing problem to deal with. What to say to Maisie when Mugger didn't return.

Well, she is twelve.

We've always had animals.

Maisie knows that there's a time to be born, to live and to . . .

326

Poor little Mugsy. Kate bit her lip as a childhood game slipped unbidden into her mind.

What's the time, Mr Wolf?

Time I ate you.

CHAPTER SIXTY-THREE

Kate arrived at Rose Road that Friday afternoon to find a note and a long list from Joe. There had been eighteen callers so far in response to the televised appeal, discounting incomplete or incomprehensible messages, plus numerous hang-ups.

She studied the information relating to the list of named callers. A number of them from females suggesting that their partners might be involved in UCU's cases. Joe and Bernie had checked each and dismissed them as likely candidates. Two calls from elderly women, each claiming to be the subject of male interest. One male was identified as the woman's postman, the other as a known conman whose way of gaining access to his victims' homes was to make unsolicited calls on the elderly, offering to do gardening. He'd been arrested. The other calls had been vetted. None fitted the criteria of a stranger making subtle contact with a female whose physical characteristics and appearance were similar to those of their victims.

Kate felt dispirited. Maybe they needed to give it more time. She thought again of the idea she'd arrived with.

Malins was still in custody in the basement of Rose Road. She knew that Furman had arranged for Joe to be part of an interview panel for five would-be armed-response officers this afternoon. She'd learned from Joe that Furman had sent Bernie to Solihull to make some neighbourhood enquiries about Malins.

Kate was glad of the emptiness and silence in UCU as she took her idea forward. She lifted the phone and dialled an internal number, hoping that the Kilt was there. He was.

'Hi! Gus.' Kate got straight to the point. 'Listen, how do you feel about me going down to speak to your guest, if there's still time?'

She waited as Gus turned the idea over. 'Okay by me, Kate, but it's up to Malins himself to say yea or nay, as he hasn't taken up our offer of a legal adviser. Given the seriousness of what we think he's involved in, we've applied for an extension, so we've got him for a bit longer. Leave it with me. I'll get back to you.'

He rang back almost immediately, to confirm that Malins was willing to meet with her.

Within five minutes Kate was inside the custody suite in the basement. She stood at the desk, waiting for the officer on duty to make arrangements and then come back for her. She'd never been down here. With previous UCU cases, the suspect had been brought to them in a formal interview room. She looked around. Featureless walls, and a large metal duty desk blocking the way to the cells and interview rooms beyond.

'Okay, Dr Hanson. Got him ready and waiting for you.'

She followed the custody sergeant's broad back to a small holding room. He opened the door and stood aside to allow her in. Another officer was already inside, standing to one side of the door. She knew both would remain throughout. Sitting at the interview table, PACE recording machine dormant, was Malins.

As Kate sat on one of the heavy chairs opposite him, Malins gave her rapid peripheral glances. He was clearly resentful, and also restless, boredom possibly at the root of his agreement to meet with her.

'Good afternoon, Mr Malins.' He transferred his gaze from the officers standing by the door, then flicked his eyes away, arms firmly folded across his barrel chest. Kate decided on the direct approach.

'You're being held as a possible suspect in Jody Westbrooke's murder—'

'Your handiwork!'

Kate shook her head. 'I doubt you had any involvement in it.'

He looked suspiciously at her for a few seconds. 'That's very interesting, love, but – ohh, *look*! I'm still in here!' He glared at the officers either side of the door.

'Why haven't you accepted legal representation, Mr Malins?'

He looked at Kate again, clearly irate but holding on to it. 'I thought I'd only be here for an hour or so. I haven't done anything and my usual brief's away. But I'm starting to reconsider.' He subsided into silence, turning from her, but Kate had already detected evasiveness in his face.

She fixed him with a look. 'Mr Malins, I need you to talk to me.'

'Yeah, right.' His eyes slid to the PACE machine at the end of the table, then to Kate.

She shook her head. 'No. No notes either. I ask you a few questions. You give me whatever answers you can.'

He looked sceptical. 'And I have to trust you're on the level? Will it get me out of here?'

'I am, and it might. No guarantee.'

Malins's mouth curled downwards. 'That the best you can . . . ?' He gave her a direct look, rotating his heavy shoulders, then sighed. 'Go on then. Fire away. I've got nothing better to do.'

Kate was direct. 'Your record shows that you hurt women, Mr Malins.' He compressed his lips as she continued. 'I need you to tell me about the women you've hurt.'

He looked from Kate to the officers and back. 'I've got no hang-ups about women, if that's what you're getting at. It was just my ex-wife . . .' He shook his head, as colour washed over his face. 'She was having it off with a mate of mine. She only done it because she found out I was . . . Anyway, I don't take that off any woman. So I just bopped her one.'

Kate nodded, keeping a neutral face. 'What about the young woman you raped?'

Malins unfolded his arms and leaned towards her, hands on his thighs. Kate heard restlessness from the area of the door as he answered her question in a hoarse whisper.

'I already told you. We were in the same group at the bar. She was cosying up to me. What'm I supposed to do? I . . . done the business. There wasn't any violence. Why would there be? She hadn't done anything to get me mad at her.' He gave Kate a keen look. 'From what I've read, that geezer you're looking for's a right nutter. It was in the *Sun*. A sicko! I'm not into that stuff. I'm just your normal bloke.'

Kate decided to go for broke. 'If I asked you whether you're attracted to women who dress in a certain style – tasteful, neat – what would you say?'

He looked at her, hands still on thighs, gingery eyebrows merged. 'What's with you and clothes? Looks to me like you haven't got enough to do.'

He stopped suddenly, eyes narrowing at Kate. 'Hang about. I've heard this lot talking about a shrink being on the telly. Was that you?'

Kate merely gazed at him.

330

'They said you were on about clothes then. *Look* . . .' He raised both hands, then, at more restlessness from the direction of the door, replaced them on his thighs. 'Should I know what you're on about? Because I'm telling you, I don't have a bloody clue.'

He was clearly irritated, but a glance at Kate told him that she was still waiting for a reply. He shrugged, expelling air from his mouth. 'I'm just your average bloke, yeah? A bit of leg, a bit of tit, and I'm happy.' He paused. 'Ask any bloke what he likes. Blokes like to see a woman who looks like a woman, know what I mean? But nothing too tarty, you get me?'

Kate thought she did.

Malins continued. 'The one at the club, like I told you, low-cut top, tight black jeans. Very nice.'

'Where were you at around midnight the Thursday before last?'

'They've already asked me that! About five bloody times. I told them the same thing each time. I was at A and E, Selly Oak Hospital. With this. They're checking it out.'

He waved his left hand and Kate noticed for the first time a flesh-coloured dressing on the palm. She looked at him, waiting.

The pale blue eyes fringed with ginger flicked away from her. 'I was doing some work at my old lady's house. The screwdriver slipped. I had to have stitches. Satisfied?' He folded his arms, gazing at the wall ahead.

'One last thing, Mr Malins. Where did you get your car?'

He stared at her for a few seconds, then shook his head.

'You ask me, I think you're all mad in here.' He sighed heavily. 'I bought it off a mate of mine. He's . . . living somewhere else right now and he doesn't need it.'

'What's your friend's name?'

Malins rolled his eyes. 'As if it matters, Gary Bennett.'

'And he has a middle name? Beginning with H?'

Malins stared at Kate. 'Yeah. Harvey. How'd you know that?'

Kate was back in UCU. Given the antisocial criteria by which Malins lived his life, he was probably telling the truth. Mostly. She recognised in him the capacity for over-assertiveness common to many sexual offenders. The violence against his ex-wife appeared to have been triggered by jealousy. It had an emotional meaning. Perched on the table, she gazed at the glass screen.

He did rape a very young woman. Which in itself is violent. But not sadistic.

Shaking her head, she transferred her attention to the phone, lifted it and pushed buttons. Gus answered immediately.

'How'd it go?' he asked.

Kate told him what Malins had said to her and her doubts about him as Jody's murderer. 'I know he has the capacity for violence, but not in the way we've seen in our investigation. By the way, how's his alibi holding up?'

A short silence, then Gus spoke.

'We're still waiting on that. We can keep him for a few more hours. Better to be safe than sorry.'

Finishing the call, Kate got down from the table and walked to the glass screen to draw a neat line through Malins's name.

The next time everyone was in UCU, she hoped to be ready to put forward her thoughts about the man for whom they were searching, and her theory of his possible proximity.

And wait for their reactions.

CHAPTER SIXTY-FOUR

In matching pink tennis skirts, white T-shirts and ankle-high white Converse trainers, Maisie and Chelsey walked side by side along the High Street.

'So, swear it wasn't you that left them,' demanded Maisie.

'No way, I *swear*! I don't mess with things like that and I don't know anybody else who does.'

Maisie sighed. 'Yeah, well, my mom is still on my case. She's a bit busy so she's not actually said anything else, but she *will*. You can count on it. If she asks you about some little blue tablets, just tell her—'

Chelsey grabbed her arm. 'Come on, Maisie. Let's cross here!'

Maisie looked up to see a break in the heavy Friday-afternoon traffic. One driver had stopped his large silver car for them and was waving them across.

As they raced to the other side of the road, Maisie was acutely aware, as always, of Chelsey's long legs and the capacity of her chest for bounce. She dwelled briefly on inheritance. No doubt she herself had short genes. *And* she was still in the trainer bra she'd been allowed six months before. Nothing much was happening in *that* department. Mom couldn't even get that right, she thought bitterly, reflecting on her mother's slim build.

As they reached their destination, Maisie's mood recovered. She loved the Fallen Angel, with its pretty pale-blue cupboards, the little cakes in their holders in the window. She was a favourite of the tall sophisticated twin sisters behind the counter. Now one of them came forward and smiled down into the heart-shaped face vibrant beneath the luxuriant curls.

'What's it going to be today, ladies?' she asked, including Chelsey.

The two friends pondered, pitting the Vanilla-Oreo against the Pink Dream. They selected one of each, and a juice.

For Maisie, the appeal of the cupcake shop lay in its having one foot in childhood – its sweet treats and baby-blue decor – and the other in the grown-up world, signified by the two stylish young women who ran it. It reflected Maisie's own situation. A foot in each world. All she knew was that she loved being inside the Fallen Angel, eating little cupcakes and laughing with her friends.

After a few minutes, Maisie put a hand to her flat stomach. 'Mmmm . . . that was de-*licious*!'

She glanced at Chelsey, who was gazing intently out of the window towards the nearby side street. Maisie's eyes followed her friend's.

'Who's that?' she asked, studying the car that had just parked there. 'Hey, wasn't that the car that stopped for us?'

'That's *him*! The one I told you about. The one who came into school,' whispered Chelsey. She turned back to Maisie, face animated.

Maisie looked from the car to Chelsey. 'The one who owns the acting school?'

'Mmm. He said he might be around here this Friday. You need to keep this quiet, Maisie, but he's considering giving me an audition for this play he's planning to stage at the Rep!' Chelsey took a last mouthful of Oreo cupcake.

Maisie frowned and drank juice, reviewing what she knew of Chelsey's keenness to go to acting school.

'If he was talent-spotting, how come he didn't ask anybody else at school if they wanted an audition? Dodders hasn't mentioned him, nor any of the other teachers.' She had a thought. 'Why don't you just stick with your dance and voice lessons for now, and—'

'I *told* you all I know. Dodders sent him to meet me in the entrance hall.'

Maisie gazed at her friend. 'If he's such a big talent scout, agent, whatever, how come—'

Chelsey suddenly got to her feet. 'You sound like your *mom*, Maisie. I'm going.'

'Where?' asked Maisie, looking up at her friend.

Face flushed, Chelsey gazed out of the door of the café, then back at Maisie. 'He's seen us.' She glanced at the car again. 'Come with me, Maisie,' she said suddenly. 'I know you're not interested in being part of it, but you could just . . . be there, yeah?'

Maisie glanced through the window of the little shop. 'I don't know . . . My mom . . .'

Chelsey picked up her backpack and moved towards the door. Turning in the doorway, she looked back at Maisie, who was still sitting at the table.

'Come *on*, Maisie. *Please*!'

Chelsey glanced out of the door towards the waiting car, its engine humming quietly, then back to Maisie, her long blonde-brown hair whirling. 'Are you coming or not? *Please*, Maisie.'

Tracking Chelsey as she headed out of the door, Maisie was torn. After a few seconds, loyalty won out. She grabbed her pink backpack and raced out of the café. Once outside on the pavement, however, she slowed, lowering the backpack to her feet. Chelsey was now at the car window, talking animatedly to the man and pointing back at Maisie, still lingering some distance away.

Chelsey turned to her. 'Come *on*, Maisie! It's *okay*!'

Maisie took a step forward, frowning at the driver. Eyes dazzled by the bright afternoon glare, she put up a hand to shield them, staring at the car. The talent scout, or whatever he was, was inside in shadow, sitting well back. With the harsh sunlight on her face, Maisie couldn't make out any details, yet there was something about him. Something familiar . . .

As she watched, her indecisiveness melted away. She'd decided that she wasn't interested in theatrical activities. Not if it meant going with this man. The car, now with Chelsey inside it, stayed where it was for some seconds, then slowly pulled out of the side road, slipped into a space amid the heavy High Street traffic and was gone.

Alone on the pavement, Maisie watched it disappear, confused, her loyalty to Chelsey and her mother's repeated cautions causing a dissonant clamour in her head. Mother had won out. She stared in the direction the car had gone, then back to the interior of the cupcake shop. She could see the two young women inside, serving customers. What if she went in and said – what? *My friend just got inside the car of someone she knows and it feels . . . weird.*

Yeah, right.

Feeling slightly nauseous, Maisie put on her backpack and started walking. She hadn't got a good look at him. She didn't think she'd seen him at school. But she'd seen him somewhere.

CHAPTER SIXTY-FIVE

As he arrived back in UCU late on Friday afternoon, Bernie eyed Kate, sitting in companiable silence with Julian, frowning at her notes.

'Got some news for you, Doc. Upstairs are charging Malins with Jody's murder.'

Even though Kate had anticipated it might happen, it was still a shock. She sat up, knocking over her tea. 'No! On what grounds? What evidence?'

Bernie itemised on his fingers: 'His past form, his connection to the James girl—'

'But that's not enough, surely!' she snapped, blotting the tabletop with tissues.

'Loosen your suspenders, Doc. His alibi fell to pieces. His mother said she never seen him. So wherever he was using his "screwdriver", it weren't at her place. I gotta say this. If it's walkin' and talkin' like a duck—'

As Julian watched, eyes wide, Kate slapped both palms on the table. 'We've been through this! Okay, yes, he's shown violence in the past. But he isn't angry towards women per se.'

'No, listen to this, Doc. There's something else you don't know. Upstairs spoke to his rape victim. Older now, of course. She told them how he was "really nice" to her, that she trusted him when he offered her a lift in his car. She says she never thought for a minute he was lying or that he would do what he done. That's obvious, else she wouldn't have gone with him, yeah?'

Silence.

He continued. 'So. There's the ability to charm that you're always on about. He put himself across to her in such a way that she felt safe.' He looked at Kate, tapping the table with a thick finger. 'Conned, Doc!'

'That's not *charm*,' she said, scornful. 'Not in the sense I mean. She was only sixteen at the time. She didn't have enough experience of males to make any judgement about him.'

'The James girl was older. Maybe he managed to come across to her as Prince Charming while he was working at the house. The boss! Kudos, see? If we'd moved earlier to raise him to suspect, like I wanted, we could have worked up to an arrest and UCU would've got the credit for the collar.'

'It isn't him!'

'You don't know *that*.'

Kate stared at Bernie, hot-faced, as she got to her feet. 'This is all *wrong*. It's a mistake. Everyone knows of cases where the police get so keen on a suspect that they ignore disconfirming evidence and end up with the wrong person in prison.'

Bernie's eyebrows rammed together. 'Oh yeah? And the prisons are full of innocent people, if you believe 'em! Look at what we've got. One, he was at her mother's place when Molly went missing. Two, he's a convicted rapist. Three, he's got a conviction for violence to another woman, his own wife. Four, he's got a short string, temperwise. Five, he's not accounting for his whereabouts when Jody Westbrooke went missing. Them's *facts*!'

'They're surely not sufficient to link him to the murders of Molly, Janine or Suzie. If he wasn't at his mother's house, where was he?' demanded Kate.

'Like I said, he's not saying, and that in itself makes him look dodgy. Look, Doc, I don't tell you psychological stuff. That's your turf. Mine's police procedure, right? And—'

'Where's the link to our four victims? I told you, Malins isn't angry at *all* women. Look at the duct-taping and other behaviours. There's no evidence Malins has sadistic inclinations.'

'He raped a sixteen-year-old girl!'

'Bernie, you *know* that isn't sadistic behaviour as defined by—'

Bernie snorted angrily, face suffused. 'Here we go! Up Theory Alley again. Definitions and airy-fairy experiments in ivory bleeding towers and stuff wrote up in journals by Dr Know-it-All, with pages of references and tables – Fig. one, fig. two – yeah? I've seen 'em. The stuff you got over there and what he –' Bernie jabbed a blunt finger at Julian, who was staring from one to the other – 'drags in here and has

337

his nose in for hours. Don't get the idea that because of the way we talk round here we know nothing—'

'*What?*' frowned Kate. 'Don't be so idiotic.' She glared at him and slowly shook her head. 'Bernie, you are the most incredible social and intellectual snob.'

He became still. 'You what? Listen, I'm Brum born and bred, me. I ain't ashamed of my roots. And I've been in the Force for—'

Julian watched anxiously as Kate threw down her pen.

'I didn't *say* anything about your background! I don't doubt your professional abilities, Bernie, but on this, you and Upstairs are *so* wrong. Trust me.'

'Bloody southerners!'

At that moment Joe came through the door, carrying a tray of machine coffees, UCU having run out of supplies.

'Okay, kids, gather round. I've just heard something of interest.'

They turned to look at him.

'Malins is no longer charged with murder. Solid alibi, plus consideration of Dr Hanson's views.'

'What?' seethed Bernie with the look of a bulldog watching a particularly meaty bone disappear out of reach. 'So where was he when Jody was abducted?'

'With two other guys, trying to break into a builders' merchants in Weoley Castle. Signs of tampering with the lock at the firm's storage facility and DNA that's his. He's been rearrested for that.'

In the ensuing silence, Kate and Bernie eyed each other. He took one of the cups.

'Okay. Maybe he never killed Jody—'

Kate stared at him. 'What do you mean, *maybe*?'

'He could still have killed the James girl. All I'll say, Doc, is I hope he's not let off for Jody and another woman goes missing then turns up dead.'

'If that does happen, it won't be because of Malins being released,' she snapped.

Joe looked at Kate. 'What happened to your arm? You been fighting again?'

Kate frowned. 'Rose bush. I was looking for Mugger. He's disappeared.'

Joe studied her for a couple of seconds, then with a nod he walked to the door. More armed-response interviews. Kate watched him leave. She hadn't told him she was staying home with Maisie tonight. She needed to work on her notes. And if her theory panned out, she would sell it to them.

She glanced at Bernie's face. Fat chance.

The phone shrilled. He lifted the receiver and barked into it.

'Watts! . . . Yep.' He looked across at Kate, brows climbing. 'Well, well. You don't say. We will.' He replaced the phone. 'We got ourselves a visitor.'

Kate quickly rang Phyllis to let her know she might be a little later than usual, then followed Bernie to the door.

CHAPTER SIXTY-SIX

Kate and Bernie walked to reception together. At the end of the short corridor, they found five people sitting waiting. Three men and two women. One of the women looked to be in her mid-thirties and had a magazine open on her lap; the other was a few years older, wearing a drab jacket, a bag of shopping near her feet.

'*That* must be her. The one reading,' Kate said quietly as they reached the desk.

Bernie looked with raised brows to Whittaker. Receiving a confirming nod, he walked to where the woman was sitting. Kate hung back slightly, aware of the uneasy truce between herself and Bernie. She listened as Bernie introduced himself to the woman, who put down her magazine and smiled up at him.

'Yes. I received a phone message from the Unsolved Crime Unit via the university a few days ago. My name now, it is Amelie Dijon-Masterson. Please call me Amelie. I was coming to Birmingham for a few days. I thought I would call in here, for someone to ask the questions.'

She agreed to talk with them in the nearby small interview room and stood to follow them. Tall, noted Kate. Once they'd settled inside, Kate continued to study the woman as she spoke.

Amelie Dijon-Masterson was slim and blonde, wearing narrow black trousers, flat black shoes and a cream-coloured top. Attractive. Not in-your-face sexy. No high fashion. But not necessarily her style in the nineties?

Within ten minutes, Mrs Dijon-Masterson, who now lived in Oxford, had confirmed in an easy manner and near-perfect English that she was attacked in June 1996. At the time, she was a student at Birmingham University. Bernie asked her for any impressions she had of her attacker. She responded with an eloquent shrug.

'Well, this is so many years ago. I do not think of it so much, you know? What can I say – I cannot describe him to you in any details. It was dark and it happened so quickly. He suddenly appeared as I walked and requested a light for his cigarette. He was not an older man. He was young. I say I did not see him well, but I think his hair was light in colour.'

'What makes you say that he was young, Amelie?' Kate asked.

The stylish woman raised her shoulders again. 'Well, he was slim and it was the hair. Long, you know? It was back here, like this.' She gestured with both hands to the back of her own head. 'Like, the tail. I felt it, yes? But I already told this. To the policeman.'

'Which policeman?' asked Kate quickly. 'As far as we're aware, you never made a statement.'

Amelie's eyes flashed. 'Oh, but yes! I did! You think I endure such outrage and go quietly away? No! I came here, to *this* place, to make the statement.'

As Kate and Bernie exchanged glances, Amelie lifted the black leather bag from the floor near her feet, placed it on her lap, searched its contents and produced a folded sheet of paper. 'I have brought it with me, the copy.'

She handed it to Kate, who stared down at the witness statement, complete with time and date – within days of Amelie's ordeal. It also included the name of the officer to whom she'd spoken.

Kate felt as if all her senses were on standby. Bernie rubbed his jowls, giving Kate a sideways looks. Amelie was obviously aware of their disconcertion.

'There is some problem?'

'You came into this building? Spoke to this officer?' Kate managed, pointing to the name.

'Yes.'

'Can you tell us what you remember of the interview, Amelie?'

'Of the *interview*?' The attractive woman opposite them looked from one to the other, confusion evident on her face. 'Let me think. It was in the early evening – see? The time is there, I think, yes? It was very quiet here, and I remember that I was glad it was so, because I did not think I would be able to do the statement if it was noisy and busy. You understand?'

They nodded.

341

'You didn't object to being interviewed by a male officer?' Kate asked.

Amelie gave another eloquent shrug. 'He told me that a female was not available because of the late hour . . . I didn't want to go away and return, so I agreed.'

'Tell us about him, the officer you spoke to. Whatever you can remember.'

Amelie looked from one to the other. 'Well, he was a young officer, about in the middle twenties. But I am guessing, because I did not look too closely at him, you know, because of how I was feeling? But he was tall, about – stand, please?' Bernie did as he was bid. Amelie stood too, almost as tall as Bernie, and nodded. 'Yes. About the same. But *slim*. And he had short hair, which was light- or mid-brown.' She frowned, looking down at her statement from years before. 'No. I cannot think of another thing to say about him. He was kind as far as I can remember – oh, he had not got the uniform, you know? Like you.'

They thanked Amelie for coming in to see them. As Bernie showed her out, she agreed that they could keep her copy of the statement.

Back in UCU, Kate scanned the single sheet carefully. What Amelie appeared not to have noticed was that there was no mention of her rapist wearing his hair in a ponytail. Kate glanced again at the top of the document, to the name of the officer who'd taken Amelie's statement. Bernie appeared and they both looked at the statement, then at each other.

'He told us the other day that none of the four rape victims bothered to make a statement,' said Bernie.

'Where is he?'

'Due back from London sometime today.'

Statement in hand, Kate walked slowly to the window and sat in the shadow of the half-open blinds, in time to see a car nosing its way out through the main gate, causing a commotion among the media representatives.

'Furman drives a Mercedes, doesn't he?'

Bernie confirmed it.

'What colour?'

'Like a pale gold. He was bragging about it a while back. Said it was "champagne", or some other poncey name.'

'Looks like he's back from London. And going again.' Kate looked down at the name on Amelie's witness statement.

Sergeant Roger Furman. Yet another item of information to add to her theory.

CHAPTER SIXTY-SEVEN

Neither Kate nor Bernie had spoken for the last five minutes. Kate got up from the table and went to the Refreshment Lounge, where he was boiling water for tea. She leaned against the tall cupboard, arms folded across her waist, one hand clutching the A4 sheet, watching him move to and fro.

'I need to talk to you, Bernie. I need you to listen to me – hear me out, yes?' He stopped momentarily and nodded. Kate took a deep breath. 'It's obvious that the rapes and the abduction-murders of Molly and Janine are linked. We've got a crossover victim, too – Suzie Luckman.' She looked down at her feet, then up at Bernie. 'Jody Westbrooke is a victim of the same doer, even though she was short and didn't fit his requirements.'

Kate paced a few feet from Bernie as he watched her, then turned.

'Bernie, I'm anticipating that you're going to call me either mad or paranoid – or possibly both – when I tell you what's on my mind. But because of this –' she waved the copy of Amelie's statement – 'it's time to say what I think.'

She paused. Bernie was listening, face receptive. Kate proceeded, careful not to overstate. 'I think somebody in *this* building is either directly involved in what happened to these young women, or at the very least has a personal interest in hampering our investigation. Whenever we've tried to follow up a lead, we've come up against chaotic or missing records. We're told that Suzie Luckman came to Rose Road to make a statement but we can't find it. We have no reason to believe that Tracey Thomas didn't make a statement, but can we find one? No. And Janine's diary. Put in the wrong place – but what a wrong place. In Josie Kenton-Smith's rape evidence box. Whoever did that probably didn't anticipate anyone making a connection between the abductions and the earlier rapes. It's like someone is deliberately working against our investigation.'

Bernie rasped a hand over his jowls. 'If you're right, why didn't whoever it was just . . . get rid of the diary?'

Kate gazed at him. 'Because he *thinks* like a policeman, Bernie. The diary was evidence, and if it was totally gone it would look very suspicious, draw attention too close to home. It had to remain available, so that it could be "found" if that ever became necessary.'

She glanced at the statement in her hand and slowly shook her head.

'When I asked Al and the Kilt to find statements from their old cases, they went *straight* to what they wanted. It's only *these* cases, *our* cases, that have such chaotic records. To me, that's too much coincidence.'

Kate's eyes drifted over specific words in the statement, aware of those that weren't there.

'And now look who we have taking Amelie's statement. When you wrote a progress report for Furman, did you include the rape cases?'

Bernie nodded.

'So Furman *knew* we were looking at them. Now I think about it, he even told us to ignore them. But he *never* mentioned that he was actually involved.' Kate held up Amelie's statement. 'Involved like this.'

'Perhaps he forgot? It's years ago.'

Kate tapped the statement in her hand. 'That's not all. I believe Amelie when she says that she told the officer who took her statement that her attacker had his hair in a ponytail. I *do* believe her. So why didn't Furman include it?'

Bernie's hand rasped stubble again, as he frowned at the statement.

'So what're you saying is that it's Furman who's covering up?'

'That's one possibility. All we can legitimately say right now is that Furman led both abduction-murder investigations and was involved in at least one rape investigation, but he sure as hell hasn't benefited us with information from his involvement. Plus, the statement he took from one rape victim didn't include key descriptive information.' Kate stared into the middle distance. 'Why not? What if . . . what if he knew the doer back then and was protecting him? You said it, Bernie. A twosome. The only way to sort this is to confront Furman when he comes back.'

She walked back to the table, Bernie following. Sitting down, she added a few words to her notebook, then looked at Bernie, who was sitting silently nearby. She knew he was thinking about what she'd said.

'Where's Joe? I thought the firearms interviews finished this afternoon?'

'Gone over to the Walkers' again, to tell 'em we'll release Janine's diary to them soon.'

Kate frowned. 'He could have phoned to tell them that.' She nodded at the table, to an additional photograph of Jody just received from her family. 'Could you put that up on the glass screen, please?'

Bernie walked to the screen and pressed the photo to the smooth display surface. In it, Jody's sleek pale hair was tied at the back of her head with a just-visible narrow pink ribbon.

Kate gazed at Bernie, conscious of her reliance on him or Joe to explain police procedure.

'All the rapes were investigated by Rose Road, weren't they?'

'This is Regional Headquarters,' he said with a brief nod.

'Before Suzie Luckman moved to London, I would have expected her to come in here and make a statement about her rape, wouldn't you?'

Bernie shrugged. 'It varies, Doc. If she was a cooperative witness and wanted to support the Force in getting him arrested and prosecuted, then yes. But she didn't report it straight away. Then she went off to live in London. Don't sound to me like she was committed to following through with it at the time. We can only do so much. Then it's up to victims to press their complaint.'

Kate wrote in her notebook and Bernie watched her.

Suzie came to Rose Road at least once. Her mother confirmed it. For information on a job.

Public-spirited young woman. Cooperative.

Makes no sense that she didn't come in for interview.

'Why d'you do that?' Bernie asked quietly.

'Every time I don't understand something or something doesn't fit, I write it as a question or a comment in this book.'

'Each to their own,' muttered Bernie, elbows on the table. 'If I done that, I'd be dragging it behind me on wheels. That's the difference between you and me, Doc. You sort and analyse. I'm more your

346

intuitive type. Which is why I'm saying Cranham or Fairley. Or Ma—Yeah, all right. Not Malins.'

More silence, then: 'You do know what I'm *really* thinking about Furman, don't you, Bernie?'

'Doc, there could be all kinds of reasons why he never mentioned taking the statement and not putting in the ponytail bit.'

'A pretty dire omission for an officer.'

'Maybe Amelie got it wrong. Maybe she *thought* she said it. It's a long time ago, Doc. Memory can play tricks.' He shook his large head. 'It's crazy, what you're saying.'

Kate looked up at him. 'Why are you suddenly supporting him?'

Days ago, she would have anticipated a stinging response. Now Bernie merely looked at her, eyebrows high. 'I ain't supporting the moron. It's just . . . what you're saying is . . .'

He eyed Kate as she leaned on her forearms, her hands clasped tightly together at her mouth, face set.

'Come on, Doc. We got enough problems without you losing it.'

When Joe returned, he found them sifting through the four rape evidence boxes. He came to stand by the table, hands in pockets.

'When I was at the Walkers', I remembered something we hadn't checked out.'

Kate looked up at him. 'What's that?'

'Malins's employees. So I went to see Molly's mom to get names.'

'How is she?' asked Kate.

Joe raised his shoulders. 'Like you said. She told me that Malins's employees were young local guys. She knows two of them. Happy family men now. No offending as far as she knows. They still live close by. The third one died in 2003. Auto accident.'

He continued, looking from one to the other: 'Well, it's nice to come back and find you two playing nicely together. Want some coffee?' he asked.

Kate nodded absently. She had spread all the documents from the Luckman box on the table in front of her and had gone through most of them already, finding no indication that Suzie was ever interviewed.

'Suzie would have *wanted* to talk to the police. She was thinking of joining the Force herself. Her mother said she came here to get details about career opportunities.'

'No disrespect to Mrs Luckman, Doc, but she's not the full ticket.'

'It just doesn't make sense that she didn't make a statement.' Kate turned to Bernie. 'The police do *actively* encourage women to report crimes against them, don't they?' she demanded.

Bernie gave her a sideways glance. 'You can't leave nothing alone, can you?'

He sighed, rubbing his large hands over his face, mustering what patience he had left on a Friday afternoon. 'Look. Try seeing it from a police viewpoint, Doc. What can *we* do if a woman don't want to talk to us? Insist she comes in? Try and force her to make a statement? After what she says she's been through? That'd go down well with the Women's Libbers.'

Kate frowned. 'It just seems—' She stopped dropping items into the evidence box and held up an almost blank A4 sheet with a printed heading: 'Witness Statement'. At the top of it was Suzie Luckman's name, address, a date and a reference number.

Her heart picked up rhythm. 'Look at *this*,' she said softly, waving the single sheet at her two colleagues. 'Suzie *did* come in. On Sunday, the twenty-fifth of May 1997. See?'

Joe and Bernie studied it.

'Why is there nothing written on it except for her details and the date?' asked Kate.

Bernie answered: 'She could've got cold feet. It happens. Women in sex cases come in saying they're up for making a statement, then after a few minutes they change their minds. They find they can't do it. They leave.'

Joe nodded his agreement. 'It's a big ask of any female victim of violence, sexual or otherwise.'

'You two have always got an answer for anything,' responded Kate, seeing the sense in what she'd just heard.

Bernie gave her a look. 'Now you know how it feels from this side.'

Still vexed, Kate thought of Suzie Luckman walking into the building, meeting with . . . She looked at the incomplete witness statement sheet – no officer name. She sipped coffee as Bernie hauled himself from his chair.

'It's time we wasn't here, Corrigan.'

Kate looked up as Joe stood and patted pockets for his keys and phone.

'Where?' Then she remembered. Earlier, Furman had asked both Joe and Bernie to assist at a police recruitment open day at West

Mercia Constabulary Headquarters in Worcester the following day. They were driving there this evening and staying overnight.

Joe smiled down at her. 'Listen up, Red. Keep your nose clean while we're away. Rest. Make notes, if you must. Do colouring. Stay inside the lines. Don't pass "Go". In short, behave yourself.'

She looked up at him. 'In other words, just look after the old homestead? Okay. Until I get a better idea.'

He shook a finger. 'No. No. *No* ideas.'

After they'd gone, Kate realised that she hadn't yet told Joe about her latest theory. About Rose Road. About Furman. Bernie would let him know.

She began replacing items one at a time into the Luckman box, preoccupied with thoughts about the cases. She now knew something was very wrong here. She lifted the phone. When she got a response she recognised the voice. Whittaker.

'Hello. What can I do for UCU, Dr Hanson?'

'Has Chief Inspector Furman returned yet?'

'Sorry, Doctor, but when he left, he told me he wouldn't be returning today.'

Kate put down the phone and decided to go home. She couldn't challenge Furman alone anyway. And if she was wrong, it would be all the ammunition he needed, given the state of their professional relationship.

Lifting the evidence box to the floor and pushing it under the table, Kate took Amelie's statement and Suzie's incomplete one to the secure cupboard. Squatting on her heels she unlocked it and placed both inside, Suzie's uppermost. About to close the door she stopped, heart constricting, eyes fixed on the scant details.

She'd found the answer to her question as to how whoever killed Suzie knew where to find her when she wasn't visiting her mother in Birmingham. She reached and lifted out the sheet, staring at the home address it bore: what appeared to be the number of a flat, then a road, and lastly an area. Camden. London.

Kate forced herself to breathe deeply as she slowly replaced the sheet and closed and locked the cupboard. Whoever murdered Suzie had to have known where in London she lived so he could return her weekend case and cause confusion as to where she was when she disappeared. He wanted to make that location geographically distant from himself. That way, he wouldn't be linked to it.

She stood but remained where she was, staring down at the small cupboard, its key tight within her fist. The presence of those few details suggested that, whoever it was, Suzie hadn't recognised him immediately. Recognition hadn't come until she'd started to make her statement. As soon as it did, she left.

This is mere conjecture. You've been accused of seeing links where none exist.

You don't know who interviewed Suzie. You can't know who she saw when she came here that day. Or even if it was here that she saw him.

And anyway, it's madness.

Air it as a theory and that'll be the end of you.

Kate gazed ahead, unseeing and shook her head. Madness or not, all lines of reasoning returned her to one location.

Rose Road.

CHAPTER SIXTY-EIGHT

He was inside the workshop. Sitting against the wall, his breathing under control, more or less. He hadn't expected her to be so strong. Or so wilful. Lucky he hadn't taken the little redhead as well, *her* daughter. He'd never have been able to control both.

He gazed ahead, across the workshop. That was another lesson. Too young. Although *this* was an anomaly. A purposeful change to his modus operandi. He grimaced at the police talk, experiencing a small jab of irritation. She wasn't going to rest until she got the answer. She just wouldn't leave it. He gave an imperceptible shrug. Fine. By the time she started working it out, he'd have her too.

He studied the anomaly, unconscious, three metres away from him, face down, blonde hair spread. A big girl. She looked way older than twelve, or however old she was. In fact, now he thought about it, there was little difference between her and other females of his acquaintance. He smiled. *Acquaintance.*

He looked at her again. Anomaly, acquaintance, and now an opportunity he wouldn't pass up. Need pulsed within him.

CHAPTER SIXTY-NINE

Kate hit Broad Street, which was seething with Friday home- and leisure-bound traffic. The lights changed and Kate came to a stop. She gazed through the windscreen, asking herself why she was here. The only answer she came up with was that George Brannigan had been at the scene of Molly's abduction. Another talk with him might dredge something from his memory of that day. She would also ask him where he himself was when Jody Westbrooke disappeared. For thoroughness.

As she drove on, Kate evaluated her progress in the cases thus far, including the friction she'd experienced. She came to a depressing but unavoidable conclusion.

Too wilful to be a team player.

And the constant insistence on police procedure. Rules.

Too frustrating.

And now she had a theory that even her UCU colleagues would consider bizarre.

Or mad. Maybe it – she – was?

Maybe she'd lost perspective?

Parking her car outside Symphony Court, she went inside and buzzed the intercom. Brannigan was at the door of his apartment dressed in baggy grey joggers and a black T-shirt when Kate exited the lift. He looked a little perplexed but immediately invited her inside. Kate took in the broadsheet newspapers spread over one of the coral sofas, and the coffee mug on the floor. He ran a hand through his hair, starting to fold newspapers.

'I worked late last night, so I've been relaxing a bit today. Here, have a seat.' He gestured to one of the sofas, then sat down on the other, facing Kate.

'I'm sorry to have to disturb you again, Mr Brannigan, and I hope you don't mind my dropping in, but I need to talk with you some more about the day Molly James disappeared.'

'Not at all. Ask me whatever questions you have. Fire away.'

Kate sighed. 'There's nothing specific. I was wondering if you'd thought of anything else, *anything* that might help us? Even the most trivial thing from that day?' she said, looking hopefully at him.

He looked back at her with a faint shake of his head. She could see that he appeared troubled by his inability to provide what she needed. She reviewed her thoughts of the doer. An actor, a mimic. She retuned to Brannigan, who was speaking.

'I'm really sorry. I want to help. Obviously I do. But there's nothing.'

'Would you mind telling me where you were late last Thursday night?'

He looked surprised, then got up from the sofa and walked from the room, returning almost immediately with a leather diary. He flicked pages, then nodded, showing it to Kate. She read the few words there: *Indoor Arena, Broad Street. 10.30 p.m.*, plus the name of a well-known band.

She nodded her thanks, recalling mention of the concert on television, and Maisie's enthusiasm.

'Their management booked me to do some after-show pictures. Here.' He handed Kate a card. 'That's their contact details. You can check. They know me. I was with them for a couple of hours, maybe a bit longer.'

Kate took down the details, then gave her attention to Brannigan, a possible way forward crystallising in her head. As a psychologist, she knew about memory function. She also knew that she needed to encourage him to search his episodic memory of that day, years ago, when Molly disappeared.

She leaned forward, voice low. 'Mr Brannigan, could you do something for me? Could you think back to the day of the mall fashion show?' He looked at her, uncertain. 'I want you to take your time. Put yourself right back there. It might help your concentration if you close your eyes for a minute or two.'

Brannigan gave her an evaluative look, then a quick nod. He could see she was serious. One hand supporting his head, he leaned against the sofa and closed his eyes.

Kate adjusted her voice to soft. 'Tell me exactly what happened that day, Mr Brannigan. From the time you arrived at Touchwood. You parked your car. Locked it. Walked inside the mall . . . What then?'

She watched, seeing his eyes move beneath their closed lids, voice as quiet as Kate's own. 'I had some aggravation getting inside the mall . . . I actually got there early . . . about one thirty p.m., but . . . I was stopped by this . . . security guard.'

'Why was that?' Kate asked, keeping her voice level low, her attention on Brannigan's face, his closed eyes.

'I had a couple of cameras in a bag I was carrying. Another one was on a strap round my neck. For some reason this security chap took exception to that . . . said I had to go to the office.' Brannigan's face registered irritation as he recalled the event. 'I showed them all the proofs of identity . . . they *still* phoned John Lewis's head office to confirm my reason for being there.' He shook his head slightly.

Kate's eyes were still on his face. 'So, you've been somewhat delayed but now you've arrived inside the mall, what happened next?'

Brannigan frowned. 'I was . . . under pressure to get started . . . find the best vantage point – the usual stuff. It was . . . crowded around the runway that had been set up for the show . . . Everybody milling about. I decided to wait it out . . . for people to get settled.'

'What did you do while you waited, Mr Brannigan? Where were you?' asked Kate.

He frowned, eyes continuing to move under their lids. 'I went and sat on the side of the runway where the models were due to come out. Sat there for . . . about five minutes, waiting . . .'

'Then what happened?' Kate pushed gently.

Brannigan looked annoyed. 'The security guard. The one I told you about . . . I saw *him* again.'

Kate nodded encouragement, although Brannigan wasn't looking at her. 'He was standing there . . . on the opposite side of the concourse . . .'

Kate remained silent, not wanting to disturb the flow.

Brannigan's brow creased and he lifted one hand. 'There was this shifty-looking scruffy chap over there . . . Forgotten about him . . . I'd watched him for about a minute because he looked so . . . out of place. Just hanging around. That's when the security guard came along. He had somebody with him.'

Brannigan opened his eyes and looked at Kate. 'I remember now. There was a police officer with him.'

'Can you describe the police officer?'

Brannigan shrugged. 'Quite tall, say five-ten. Fair-haired. Plain clothes.'

Kate looked at him sharply.

'So how did you know he was a police officer?'

'Because I saw him again when I called in at the mall a day or so later. By that time there were loads of them, police, uniformed and plain clothes. Everybody knew the girl was missing by then. They'd appealed for people who'd been in the mall on the day she went to come forward. So I did. I was in the area.' He grinned suddenly. 'Some of the officers were stopping people to ask questions and one or two others were taking photographs of the layout of the mall. He was with them, the officer I just told you about. I had a joke with him. I said, "I could've done that for you", and he laughed.'

A few seconds' silence.

'Funny what you remember when you really think about something, isn't it?'

Kate left Brannigan's apartment and drove home, thinking of Brannigan's recall.

A police officer, fair-haired. Plain clothes.

As she drove, her thoughts meandered.

Photographer. Photographs. Posing.

In the quietness and fading light, Abby Stevens's hesitant voice drifted around the room.

Hi . . . This is . . . my name is Abby Stevens. I saw you on TV, well, it was a lady, and she said . . . There was a long pause. *Anyway, I just wanted to say . . . there was a man. And he did what she said. Last week. In the Coffee Cup, near the cathedral in town. I know which day. It was the same day I got my new job. But listen, he didn't do anything weird. He was just there, looking at me . . . He smiled. Sorry for going on . . . I think I might be wasting your time. It's probably nothing . . . but I am the right age, like she said . . . and I'm blonde . . . My name is Abby—Sorry, I've said that already. My number is . . .*

As the call ended, a light on the answering machine suddenly glowed red, a tiny beacon in the dim quiet of UCU.

CHAPTER SEVENTY

Kate walked in on Phyllis laying the table for dinner and a pleasant smell of basil. Phyllis had made pasta, as she did routinely on Fridays. Summoning a taxi and thanking her housekeeper, Kate walked Phyllis out to the drive, waved, then went back inside. She could hear faint music from the upper floor.

She saw an untidy heap of papers beside a cardboard box on one of the granite surfaces. She went to it and looked through the small pile. Photographs. Family pictures and other mementos. Maisie had probably got them out. She'd just started a school project on family history.

Kate examined the items as she dropped them into the box. A photograph of Maisie as a toddler, astride a rocking horse, a dis-embodied hand supporting her. Another of Maisie in a tiny school uniform, complete with straw hat. A photograph of Kate and Kevin. She dropped it into the box with the rest.

The next item was the order of service for Kate's mother's funeral. Then a leftover invitation to Maisie's naming party, a picture of the plump, grinning infant on the front. A New Year's Eve menu for Simpson's restaurant. Kate shuddered. A wonderful evening and one of the few occasions when she was undeniably wrecked.

She glanced at the last item. A programme for a play. She'd seen the performance with Cee. She looked at the list of characters and the brief synopsis – 'for the character Garry, nothing matters but his ego . . . self-regarding infantilism . . . his view of life . . . to live and do as one pleases'. She dropped the programme into the box and replaced the lid.

Going to the end of the kitchen, Kate lifted the internal bolts of the folding doors and gave them a gentle push. As they drifted smoothly open, she listened, half expecting to hear the little bell, followed by

Mugger himself. Nothing. She turned away. Maisie would have to be told.

Crossing the hall to the stairs, she hung on to the curved handrail, her face upturned to ensure her voice carried upstairs.

'Maisie? Maisie! Dinner in a couple of minutes.'

The music stopped and she heard a door open. Returning to the kitchen, she finished laying the table and crossed to the wide hob. Within two minutes she was carrying plates of steaming pasta across the kitchen.

'*Mai*— Oh, there you are.' She deposited the plates on dinner mats and sat.

Maisie sat opposite her mother in silence. Kate forked pasta.

'How did your study afternoon go?'

More silence.

'Did you check with Professor Denton this morning about the calculus?'

'Didn't need to. I can do it.' Maisie sat back in her chair, poking listlessly at her pasta.

Kate looked at her daughter, then looked again. 'What's wrong?'

'Nothing,' muttered Maisie.

Kate gave Maisie's face closer scrutiny. 'You don't look very well.' She leaned towards her, placing fingers gently against her daughter's flushed cheek.

Maisie jerked her head away from the hand. 'For God's sake, Mom, just – leave me alone!'

Kate watched, surprised, as Maisie threw down her fork, pushed her chair back and darted towards the kitchen door, small face crumpling and dissolving. She sat, staring in the direction Maisie had gone, thinking of possibilities. Probably a row with Chelsey. She gave her attention to her pasta. She would choose her time to talk with her daughter.

The phone rang. Kate got up from the table and walked into the hall. Must get a phone in the kitchen, she mused as she answered the call.

'Hello?'

'Kate?'

Kate was about to open her mouth to respond, but her caller continued in a rush.

'It's Candice. Is Chelsey with you?' There was an urgent quality to the voice coming over the line.

'No, she isn't. Maisie's home and she's upstairs. Shall—'

'They weren't at school this afternoon. I rang earlier to check. It's gone six thirty now and Chelsey's not come home.'

Kate's face set. 'Candice, can I phone you back when I've spoken to Maisie?'

Hanging up, she started to call up the stairs, then had second thoughts. She walked quickly upstairs, crossed the landing and tapped on Maisie's door.

A subdued voice responded: 'What?'

'Maisie, I need to come in and talk to you.'

No reply.

Kate pushed open the door. Maisie was lying curled up on her bed. Kate detected small sounds of emotional upset. She walked to the bed and sat down next to her daughter, putting a hand lightly on her upper arm.

'I want you to tell me right now what's going on, Maisie.'

No response, except for a muffled sob.

'Come on, Maisie. Candice just rang. Chelsey hasn't arrived home.'

A series of quick sobs burst from Maisie as she sat up, followed by a torrent of words that froze Kate.

'We went to the . . . Fallen . . . Angel and . . . Chelsey saw him . . . he . . . came to the . . . school . . . he's a . . . drama coach . . . said she would . . . get a . . . part and then . . . she went in . . .' She paused, took a shuddering breath. 'In his car!'

Horrified, Kate stared at the hot face, glistening with tears. 'Chelsey got into a car? With a *man*?'

Maisie fell away from her, sobbing. Absently, Kate patted her daughter's arm, then got up off the bed.

'I'll be back as soon as I can, Maisie. I have to call Candice.'

Face against cold, hard cement, she wavered in and out of consciousness. Gradually, consciousness took over and she lifted her cheek from the floor, head hammering in the harsh light. The floor around her rose and fell. She lay down and more minutes slid by. Forcing open her eyes, her gaze fell on a low shelf nearby, contents just visible. Vision drifted, then focused: bits and pieces . . .

something . . . blue . . . little red heart . . . Her eyes slid over a small, familiar emblem: Ellesse . . . *Good Luck in Your New Job!*

Now fully conscious, she tried to rise, sliding her hands over the dusty cracked cement, feeling a light whisper against her palm from the little tongue of paper, almost invisible within one of the cracks. She grasped it involuntarily as two strong hands seized her ankles and began to drag her bodily, while her own voice screamed on and on.

CHAPTER SEVENTY-ONE

Chelsey's parents had arrived at the house shortly after Kate phoned to tell them what she knew so far. Kate had already called Rose Road, and WPC Rita Sharma had been dispatched on the orders of Gander to gather information. Whittaker was also with them now, having just come on duty.

Kate watched as Rita Sharma spoke quietly to Maisie, hoping that the youthful style of the young Asian police officer, lips lightly glossed, black hair streaked with vibrant red, would encourage her to talk. Kate herself had already tried asking questions, but each time Maisie had become incoherent. Kate guessed it was a combination of worry, loyalty and guilt. Guilt at their being out of school, as well as feeling responsible for not being able to do anything to halt the subsequent train of events, details of which were now slowly emerging.

Maisie looked exhausted. Kate went to the sofa and sat next to her. Chelsey's parents also looked exhausted.

It was 10 p.m. No word from or about Chelsey since she'd parted from Maisie more than seven hours before.

Sharma and Whittaker got to their feet. Sharma motioned Kate into the hall. Reassuring Maisie, Kate followed them.

'We've got all available officers at Rose Road on full alert,' said Sharma. 'We're going with Chelsey's parents to their house to see if the Kilt and his team have turned up anything from their search. Anything that might give us an idea of who was driving that car.' She lowered her voice, in case Maisie could hear. 'I checked with the head of the school. She's confirmed that the school has had no contact, direct or otherwise, with anyone presenting himself as a drama coach or owner of a stage school.'

There was a sudden harsh sound from the radio receiver attached to Whittaker's uniform. He spoke into it, then turned to Kate.

'Doctor? Lieutenant Corrigan and DS Watts are on their way back from Worcester.'

Kate watched, helpless, as the officers led Chelsey's dazed parents to the front door and out into the darkness. She walked back into the sitting room, where Maisie was sitting up, face pallid, dark smudges under her eyes, the eyes themselves bottomless.

Kate sat next to her and put her arm round her. 'You've done what you could, Maisie. You've told them all you could remember.'

'But it was no good,' whispered Maisie. 'I couldn't remember the car or *anything*.'

Kate hugged her, then encouraged her to lie down, tucking a light blanket around her. Time enough to tackle her about the truancy. Squeezing Maisie's hand, she went into the hall and phoned Phyllis, to ask if she was able to return to the house. Getting confirmation, Kate sent a taxi to collect her. Phyllis would be receiving a generous bonus for all she'd done for Kate in recent weeks.

Forty-five minutes later, Phyllis was at the house and Maisie was napping fitfully in the sitting room. In the hall, Kate looked at the time: 11.10 p.m. Without her mobile she felt reliant on the land line for information and wanted to be there to pick up as soon as she could. Realising that a call might not come for hours, she walked from the hall into the kitchen. Phyllis looked up as she came through the door but didn't speak. Her worried face said it all.

Kate took her notebook out of her bag and sat down at the now cleared table. Where to start? Until somebody told her otherwise, she would believe that Chelsey's disappearance was linked to UCU's investigation. Somewhat young, but Kate could see similarities. The blonde-brown hair, long and lush. Chelsey was tall for her age, topping Maisie by a good ten centimetres. But there had to be more to her abduction. Opening the notebook, Kate flipped pages.

The first line to catch her eye was the question as to whom Colley had seen at the mall when he cleared off 'sharpish'. Kate thought of her visit to Brannigan's apartment earlier. Finding his number, she walked into the hall and called it. He came on the line after four rings.

'Mr Brannigan? It's Kate Hanson again.' She bit her lip. 'Sorry, I've just realised how late it is . . .'

'No problem. I'm watching TV.'

'Remember you told me that you saw a tall, fair-haired police officer

361

with the security guard at the mall, and they were dealing with a scruffy man?'

'Yes.'

'Well, was the officer the same one you said came to see you at your premises some time after Molly James's abduction?'

'No. It wasn't him.'

Kate's mood went through the floor.

'The only time I saw the one with the security guard, was at the mall, like I told you.'

'Tell me again what he was doing there.'

'He was with a lot of other police officers, uniformed, plain clothes. He was with the ones taking photographs and taping off areas of the concourse—'

'Thank you, Mr Brannigan,' said Kate, faintly.

She put the phone down and stared at it for a few seconds, then went back into the kitchen. To her notebook. Her eyes skimmed over the written words. *The cold room*. She thought back to that day. Who knew she had gone down to the cold room? Bernie. Joe. Whittaker. Her head snapped upwards. Matt Prentiss. He was at the desk when she went to request the key. Tearing a page from the back of the notebook, Kate began to construct a list. Returning to her written notes, she read on.

One of the rape victims had described her attacker's hands as smooth and warm on a cold night. Kate lifted her eyes from the writing, staring to one side. Connie's hands on *her* shoulders, demonstrating the killer's grip on Jody Westbrooke. Connie's hands, smooth and warm. Was she attaching too much importance to such a small point? Could she assume from a mere suggestion that the killer had worn latex gloves that he had forensic awareness? She shook her head slightly. Who didn't have that kind of knowledge now? *CSI Land*.

She read on. The cards found with the remains of Janine and Molly. The photographs of the tableau created of Jody's body. They had meaning for the killer, else why would he bother? But what meaning? She tore another page from the back of the notebook and tore it again, into three little squares, writing words on each. Resting her chin on her arms, she looked at each one in turn. Nothing. She moved the little squares into a different order. If the cards and the display meant anything, they might mean something in relation to each other. She looked again at the words she'd written:

Red stain or pattern on white pasteboard.
Two black circles and a downstroke.
Fireworks.

She stared fixedly at the squares of paper, the words beginning a tattoo inside her head. How about:

Zero-Zero. Red. Fireworks.
Try the other way.
Fireworks. Zero-Zero. Red.
No!
Red. Zero-Zero. Fireworks.

Now it came so quickly that Kate's face heated up and perspiration appeared on her forehead. She'd had it the first time. Red stain. Valentine. February. February! In Janine's diary. Fireworks – November. It was about months of the year.

She looked at the zeros and the downstroke. Now it was obvious. Not really a word. An exclamation. A cultural usage she'd seen from her own visits to North America. In October, Americans sent greeting cards to each other for Halloween, the most often-used three letters an exclamation evoking cosy fright:

Boo!

Kate stared at what she'd written. Tableaux. Staging. Posing. She slowly shook her head. Why hadn't she realised? Why hadn't she guessed when she saw the pictures taken by Dennis Jackson at Romsley? Kate breathed in, then whispered the words.

'He's photographing what he loves – his life's work.'

She went back to her notebook. To her notes on the two rape victims who did go to Rose Road to make statements. But she knew now that there were three statements, the third never completed. Josie Kenton-Smith and Amelie Dijon gave statements and lived. Suzie stopped in the act of making her statement and left. She died.

Suzie did see someone.
Someone who looked familiar.
Someone who reminded her of her ordeal.
And maybe that person recognised her?
Much later, when Suzie went to Rose Road again, braver, wanting information, wanting to join the Force . . .
Maybe that time he saw her.
He feared she'd come to identify him.
He couldn't take the risk.

He knew where she lived both here and in London.
And Suzie Luckman had to die.

At that moment the phone rang and another piece of the puzzle slid into place. Communications Centre had *never* had Kate's home phone number. No one at Rose Road did. She went to the kitchen cupboard and pulled out the box of photos. It was where she'd left it. The topmost item. Crossing the kitchen, she went to the place where the paper recycling box was kept. She dragged it out and lifted out newspapers, scattering them on the floor. She had it. The *Evening Mail* for the previous Saturday. She went to the entertainment section and found it. It had finished its short run the day *before*.

It came into Kate's head like an express train. *Now* she knew why he cut short his stalking of Jody. He was at the bypass excavation. He *saw* his own historical handiwork. He heard his colleagues talking about it. A florid, intoxicating reminder of his own savagery. However many other women had or had not perished by his actions since that time, the discovery of all that remained of Molly James and Janine Walker which began UCU's reinvestigation had stimulated the all-consuming need. To do it again. He *couldn't* wait.

And Jody died.

The phone rang again.

Phyllis's voice called to her from the hallway.

'Kate? That American just called but the line went dead. Now *he's* on the line. Bernie Watts . . .'

Kate rushed to take the phone off Phyllis.

'Bernie! You've heard! Do you know—'

'Doc?' The line was poor. 'Your Maisie's not . . .'

'No, Maisie's fine. It's Chelsey. She's disappeared, but—'

'Bloody hell! Me . . . Corrigan are . . . our way . . . your place in about half an . . .'

'Listen, Bernie. I think I know who – hello? *Hello?*'

As the signal finally died, Kate hung up the phone and walked directly to the kitchen. She stared down at the list she'd just made. Heart beginning to pound, she spooled memory.

His cold dismissal of injuries. Julian's distraction and low mood. Everything about *him*, a lie. Kate brushed her damp forehead, staring ahead. It all slid neatly into place. Julian on drugs? Drugs in Maisie's drawer.

He's been in this house!

He *was* communicating with them, with her, all the time. Very subtle, but it was there. They – she – just kept missing it. There were still a couple of things she had to confirm. She had to be sure before she made the accusation.

Taking the stairs two at a time, and running to her bedroom, Kate changed into a black hooded top and jeans. He'd taken Chelsey so that he could do what he had to, but also to punish Kate. Maybe to teach her a lesson.

Back in the hall, she snatched up her keys, then went quietly to the door of the sitting room to check on Maisie. Sleeping now. Turning back into the hall, she went to the kitchen. Phyllis looked at her, her face a question.

Kate went to the work surface and the small notepad kept there for shopping needs. She began to write.

'Phyllis, I'm going out and I want you to call these two mobile phone numbers as soon as I leave, yes? *Keep* ringing them until you get an answer from one. Read whoever answers these three words.'

Phyllis nodded, reading the note. A place. And a name.

As the front door closed Maisie was on her feet almost before she was properly awake. His face. She'd seen it. In the line of traffic. As he stopped to let them cross. She *knew* him. She'd seen him only once before that, but she knew who he was.

She ran from the sitting room and out into the hall, voice shrill and desperate.

'Mom! *Mom!* Where are you? Mom—'

Phyllis appeared at the door of the kitchen. 'What's all this? You're supposed to be lying down—'

'Phyllis! Where's my mom?'

'She's gone out.'

Maisie stared wildly at the housekeeper. '*Where!* Where'd she go?'

'She didn't say. All she said was to phone these two, which I'm—'

Maisie seized the piece of paper and flew to the hall phone.

CHAPTER SEVENTY-TWO

Kate sped down the silent avenue and on to the main road. Exceeding the speed limit but not caring, she sent the car hurtling through the dark suburb. Thunder rolled and droplets of water hit the windscreen.

Minutes later she left the car and walked into Rose Road, past the officer on duty, who merely nodded at her as she continued on upstairs.

Opening Gander's office door, Kate walked quickly inside and closed it. Switching on the light, she stood in front of the wall of Force photographs. One of these held the key, but she had to be sure if she was going to help Chelsey. She walked a couple of paces forward, her eyes sliding from one photograph to another. So *many* faces in each one. She went directly to the middle of the array. Photographs of staff from 1994 to 2008.

And there he was. Still recognisable. Back then his fair hair was in a ponytail. In his area of work it was allowed.

Racing downstairs and into the admin offices on the ground floor, she pushed open one of the doors. She knew where to look, from when she'd been in here in the past to give staff details of her availability for UCU.

She went directly to a wooden cabinet with a series of wide, shallow drawers. An archive of Nobo wall charts. Staff leave. Furman had wanted Julian to create a database for the information when he'd first joined UCU. Kate had resisted, pointing out that Julian wasn't mere admin help. Pulling open a drawer dated 1995–8, she dragged out the large charts. She had to be certain she was right. She ran a finger down one of them. Two trips to America. Plus two days of leave: 22nd and 23rd May, 1997, the first a day after Suzie Luckman's neighbour said that Suzie had returned to her flat. The neighbour was wrong. It was

Suzie's killer she'd heard that Sunday. Leaving her weekend case. One name was written by each of the annotations.

Kate stilled, tension coursing throughout her body as the door of the office slowly opened.

'What the hell are you doing here?' asked Furman quietly, taking a few steps further into the room.

Not speaking, eyes on him, Kate swiftly chose her escape route, ran quickly behind the desk to the door and out. She hurtled down the stairs and out into the night, hearing footsteps coming after her and Furman's voice shouting her name. Running for her car, she threw it into reverse then aimed it at the exit.

It wasn't madness. Now she was sure. It all made horrific, disillusioning sense.

Within seven minutes, she'd left her car on the side of the road. Within a further minute she was in sight of the rear of the building's dark bulk, familiar even in full moonlight.

Thunder roiled and a few large raindrops fell on Kate's head as she reached the fencing. Solid. Eight feet high. She ran her hands over the smooth wood. No features. No hand- or footholds. A flutter of panic started up in her chest.

How long would he hold Chelsey, before . . . She quit the thought. She must focus.

She moved quickly, following the high fence in the direction of the road. It had to join the building somewhere. She recalled an item from a team meeting months back. These grounds used to be security patrolled. Not any longer. Cutbacks.

Reaching the point where the fence ended, she found it. A narrow infill of chain-link, joining fence to brick wall. Looking up, she could see a single strand of razor wire on top of the chain-link section. Without hesitation, she pushed the toe of one trainer into one of the lower links, legs powering as she pulled herself up by her hands. Repeating the process as the raindrops increased amid more thunder, she reached the top of the fence, then steadied herself, one hand on the brick wall, thigh muscles taut, torso rigid for balance.

Holding her position for seconds, she contemplated the drop on the other side, trying to judge the grassy covering's softness. Without warning the Chamberlain Tower clock split the silence and rent the air. Hyped and startled, Kate wavered then pitched forward, balance lost, razor wire snagging and tearing at her clothing, ripping into the flesh of one thigh. She landed heavily on the other side of the fence and lay for some seconds, air knocked out of her.

Struggling to her feet, she pressed herself into the shadow of the back wall, aware of sticky wetness sliding down her leg. Scanning ahead, she saw sheds and outbuildings, the most distant of which appeared to be a kind of workshop with a roller-shutter door. A seam of light showed under it. She crouched, listening.

Nothing.

Amid another roll of thunder, she headed silently for the workshop, avoiding the gravel path skirting it, ignoring the vicious pain now starting up in her thigh.

Reaching the workshop, she crouched against the wall, breath coming in gasps, a gaping sensation in her thigh making her queasy. She waited, struggling to bring her breathing under control as she listened for any sounds within. Ignoring the wetness now collecting inside one of her trainers, she crept slowly forward, keeping to the shadow of the wall. She reached a window and tried to peer inside. It was covered with what looked like a sheet of hefty cardboard.

That's when she heard a soft footfall immediately behind her, the low whispered words drifting into her ear:

'Boo! *Boooo!* Get it?'

Her heart hurled itself against her chest as she tried to look at him and more blood flowed. Before she could fully turn or form words, he had both of her arms pinned at her sides, her back tight against him.

'Uh-uh, don't do it,' he hissed, shoving her hard against the wall of the workshop, then crushing her mouth with one hand. 'Be a good girl, now, hmmm?'

She felt his breath on one side of her face as she strained her eyes to see his face. His body felt taut against hers. She guessed he was listening. For what? She jerked her head sideways, trying to escape the press of his hand.

His voice came again, whispering. 'No-ooo . . . Be still. We need to spend a little time together, don't we, hmmm? A little . . . date? Just you and me.'

Kate's mind was racing. What could she do? What should she say to stop him?

'I think we should go inside. How about it?' Roughly pushing the side of Kate's head against the brick wall of the workshop, he reached for and pressed a nearby button. The roller shutter slowly rose.

His lips were against her ear, voice a parody. 'What d'ya say, huh, *Red*?'

CHAPTER SEVENTY-THREE

Kate felt herself being slowly but firmly propelled forward as he held her, his arm tight across her chest.

His voice was low. 'I've got something I really need you to see, you interfering bitch. No-no-no, *stop* it! No pulling away. Come on, easy . . . easy . . . *There* you are. See? We're two colleagues being . . . cooperative.' He tightened his grip across Kate's chest. 'There you go . . . good girl . . . come on, *that's* right . . . A little further.'

Kate quickly took in the detail of the inside of the workshop, highly illuminated in the darkness of Winterton's grounds. He gave her leg a sudden vicious kick. It oozed, causing Kate's head to swim and the ground beneath her to heave.

Head dropping forward, she knew she had to stay conscious. Her one other thought was that, whatever happened, whatever he did, she must not allow herself to be taken inside that workshop. She tensed her body. Instantly he mirrored her movement, anticipating resistance.

And that was when Kate saw her. Lying face down on the concrete floor. Filthy pink tennis skirt, one hand flung beyond her head. The blonde-brown hair had spread like rays as it had fallen on to the dusty floor.

The sight of her, and the possibility of what the hair might be concealing, was too much for Kate. She arched her body, jerking her head against his chest. His hand momentarily loosened its grip on her mouth. As it smacked back into position, Kate sank her teeth hard into one of his fingers.

He cursed as he whipped both arms away from her. 'You crazy bitch! You're going to get my best, and that's a—'

Kate spun to face him, the ground once more heaving under her feet.

Face contorted with anger, he glared into her eyes. 'I'm going to give you an object lesson in—'

Letting out a sudden hoarse yelp, he was unaccountably propelled sideways, away from Kate. She staggered backwards and slid down the wall of the workshop, finding it difficult to focus, although she could hear his voice, now risen to a screech: 'My arms! Let go of my arms, you *bastard*.'

Slowly Kate raised her head. He was being held in a restraint position, legs splayed, both arms stretched upwards behind his back. Kate could swear she heard bone scrape bone.

He whimpered. 'You . . . you've broken my arm.' His voice became louder. 'I'll sue you for brutality, you madman! Let go of me! Get me some help, my fucking arm's coming apart!'

Her rescuer's voice drifted to Kate, low with a distinctive twang. 'Cry me a river, Creed. Keep on resisting and I'll shoot you in your damned head.'

At that moment Bernie and five other officers rushed forward, converging around Joe, his long legs braced, towering over his bowed prisoner, the harness of the shoulder holster stark against his white shirt.

Kate looked slowly from them into the open workshop. *Chelsey!* She hadn't moved.

Kate had never fainted in her life. Now she thought she might. Her trainer was awash, her foot slippery inside it. Ignoring it, eyes fixed on the girl lying nearby, she stood slowly, weaving forwards, head pounding, mind seized by the awful possibility that they were too late and what they might now have to confront.

Inside the workshop, she dropped unsteadily to one knee and placed a hand on Chelsey's shoulder. Warm. She looked at the girl's out-flung hand, something small between her fingers. She reached for it. Reaching again, hand shaking, she lifted the hair from the left side of Chelsey's face. The girl stirred and whimpered.

Kate felt strong hands on her arms. She was being lifted away bodily, leaving a dark red swathe on the concrete.

'Come on, Kate. Let it be. Come with me, bab – it's all right.'

She squirmed feebly, still clutching what she'd taken from Chelsey's hand, sluggish synapses firing a thready message. Bernie had called her by her name. Never before. Ever.

371

Another officer had appeared beside the girl stirring on the floor of the workshop.

'Face . . . *face?*' murmured Kate feebly, incapable of anything more.

She felt herself being carried away from the building into darkness. But not before she saw the girl being turned gently on to her back. Chelsey. One eye black, face swollen along the jawline. Still a beauty.

CHAPTER SEVENTY-FOUR

Late on Saturday afternoon, the little woman was brought into UCU, where she perched on the edge of one of the chairs. Joe studied the small figure wearing the too-big raincoat as Bernie went to make her some tea. In the silence the woman's eyes roamed nervously.

Suddenly aware of Joe's interest, she gave a tight smile. Bernie placed the tea on the table in front of her. They waited. Harry Creed's aunt broke the silence.

'He was such a nice boy. I can't believe this has happened!' She stopped and fumbled in her bag for a tissue. Looking up at each of them, she shook her head. 'It isn't his *fault*. They didn't handle it in the right way. She was my cousin. I was a couple of years younger but even *I* could see that it wasn't right.'

Bernie had taken a seat and was watching the woman intently. He glanced up at Joe. They both remained silent.

'She was *very* young when she had him, you see.'

She bit her lip.

'Why the charade?' asked Joe, frowning. 'This was the seventies. People didn't care about that kind of thing any more. Did they?' He looked at Bernie, eyebrows raised. Bernie shrugged his shoulders as she continued.

'You don't understand. She wasn't even fifteen when he was *born*! It was . . . kept in the family.' She shook her head. 'Look, I didn't come here to parade the family's . . . I brought this. I thought he might like to have it. Will you give it to him?'

She'd placed a photograph on the table. Both officers looked at it, saying nothing.

'Harry would have been about thirteen or so when that was taken.' She looked up at Joe, then to Bernie. 'You will see he gets it? *Please*?'

She scurried away, tea left to grow cold as Joe and Bernie passed the photograph between them. Speculating on who in the Creed family had fathered this woman's child when she was less than fifteen years old.

'My money's on her own dad,' were Bernie's final words on the issue.

CHAPTER SEVENTY-FIVE

On Monday morning, a tired, white-faced Kate was let into the custody suite. The Kilt was waiting. When he saw her, he came swiftly forward.

'You're sure about this, Kate?'

Kate nodded. 'I'm sure.'

Her manner didn't invite argument or reasoning. She'd been through that in UCU already. She'd insisted on coming down here alone. She walked carefully, notebook in hand, into the holding room. The one where she'd met Malins, a couple of centuries ago.

With the Kilt's help, she reached the waiting chair and slowly sat.

After being taken to Casualty late on Friday, she'd been transferred to the new Queen Elizabeth Hospital and a private room overnight. The stitches tracking down nine centimetres of the inside of one thigh pulled and pulsed.

Flinching inwardly, but determined to give him nothing, Kate slowly looked towards the opening door. The two officers bringing him inside still looked shocked. He'd been one of their own for years. Almost. She knew they would stay in the room with her. Kate hadn't argued.

He sauntered slowly across the room, an officer close on each side, and took the chair across the table from Kate. She looked at his hands. Palms together, almost prayerful. Held by two plastic ties. He was wearing a white forensic suit.

Seeing the irony of it, Kate smiled to herself, then looked him fully in the face. He stared back. Kate detected suppressed excitement. She broke the silence, voice low.

'Quite a performance. A little stereotypical, perhaps, but—'

'Fooled *you*,' he murmured indistinctly, staring into her face. Her eyes. 'Fooled ev'ryone.'

Kate met the stare head-on. 'What was the thinking?' she asked. 'That a gay man who loved Noël Coward plays wouldn't be a suspect in the murders of young women? I'm guessing that you got a lot of amusement from playing *that* part.'

He didn't respond, merely looked at her, and for the first time she noticed little flecks of green in the light brown eyes.

She waited. When he didn't speak, she continued: 'I *know* you now, Harry. I know that the very least of what you are is a liar and a manipulator.' Again she saw suppressed emotion and recognised it for what it was. Delight. 'You've been inside my house, took my phone and other things—' Kate stopped momentarily as anger surged. 'And you also left something. In my daughter's room. To cause a rift—'

He laughed. An odd, high-pitched little sound from somewhere deep inside his throat.

She ignored it, continuing: 'You caused a flat tyre on my car. I'm *telling* you that I know all this. You needed to show me – us – what you could do. But you couldn't get it right, could you, Harry?' His face was still, eyes watchful as Kate slowly shook her head. 'I remembered, you see. You just couldn't show enough humanity, empathy, when you saw those photographs of the beaten women. Because you don't know how.'

He smirked, mouth tightly closed.

'We know now that you were responsible for Matt Prentiss being blamed for a mistake *you* made. And then there was Julian. You manipulated him. You offered him drugs that he wouldn't take. You lied to me about alleged drug use because you sensed he was feeling increasingly nervous and confused about you.' She stared into his face. 'You were willing to ruin his life. All Julian has right now is opportunity and motivation. You would have seen him with *nothing*.' She ended, furious.

As she stared into Harry's face, the vacant orbs of his eyes, she saw his mouth move slightly and could have sworn she heard a mocking sound: *Boo-hoo.*

Harry sat, silent, his eyes unwavering, as Kate stared at him. 'Janine Walker. Molly James. Suzie Luckman. Jody Westbrooke.' As she went through the litany, something stirred behind the flat eyes. Unbounded avarice. He still had them. Inside his head. 'You photographed them. You photographed the horror of what you did to those young women.' She glared, still maintaining a calm matter-of-factness.

'We've trawled the records. We can't find you. You *must* have done something before . . . this.'

He responded with a hardly perceptible smirk. Secretive.

Kate kept her eyes on his face. 'That's all I have to say about what you've done. There'll be others who'll ask you questions about that. The reason I'm here is to—'

She broke off, staring at him. He was doing something. Something with his mouth. Easily unnerved in her weakened state, Kate watched his lower jaw move from side to side and his neck muscles bunch. She saw his rolled tongue emerge between his lips, saw within the roll a small white plastic item. Serrated.

Shocked, unable to process, Kate was taken completely unawares by the two burly officers suddenly appearing from behind her. They were on him in seconds, grabbing him on either side. One of them shot out a huge hand, clamping it around Creed's lower jaw.

'You *bastard*! Open! Open up!' He did so, slowly, and the small serrated item fell on to the table, where it lay, wet with bubbled saliva.

The cutting section of a plastic knife.

The officers remained frozen in position for several seconds, then, following an exchanged glance and a nod in unison, they let him go, each with a quick shoving movement. A latexed hand appeared from Kate's right, to pick up and remove the remains of the plastic knife, leaving only the little trail of bubbled saliva on the tabletop.

Kate looked at Creed. Still showing what he could do. Communicating his ability to manipulate any system of which he was a part.

Closely shadowed by his colleague, one of the massively built officers returned to the table and leaned on it, gloved hands supporting his muscular upper body, breathing heavily as he glared down at the prisoner.

'That was your one and only chance, Creed. From now on, while you're here, you get no utensils. If I had my way, you'd be sucking up your meals through a fucking straw. We'd be happy to watch you *starve*,' he murmured.

Creed grinned after their broad backs as they moved the few feet to the door, his joined hands in front of his mouth. He looked into Kate's face, green-brown eyes gleaming. Still grinning, and checking that her guards were sufficiently distant, he raised his tethered hands and in a minimal lightning-fast movement pointed both index fingers at her face, making tiny carving movements in the air between them.

377

Kate waited for a few seconds before she spoke, holding his gaze. She wanted him focused. She wanted him to know that she *knew*. Now she'd let him have it. 'I've got something for you, Harry,' she said softly, pausing so that his attention remained fully on her. 'I've also got a story. Would you like to hear it?'

He looked back at her, the grin still in place, but she could see he was curious, waiting. She could almost hear the whir of his thought processes.

'Well, this is a story about a man. A boy, really. And the boy didn't have a father, well, not one he could openly acknowledge. Which is sad and unfortunate, isn't it?' He was listening intently. She continued. 'But what he did have was a *sister*.'

His face was now a mask.

'The boy and his sister were close, as siblings often are. She was quite a bit older than him, you know,' continued Kate conversationally, 'and she had boyfriends *all* the time.' She skimmed a look Harry's way. His face and body were rigid. 'She was a very . . . striking woman, you see. Tall, with yellow-gold hair. What some men might describe as a good body. Well built, you know? She dressed to show it off. Tight skirts. Tight trousers.'

Perspiration beads had formed at Creed's hairline.

Kate continued her narrative. 'She wore her tight sweaters low, so that everyone was able to see what was inside.' She glanced across the table. 'Don't get the wrong impression. She was a good sister to him. Most of the time. But she needed to be out there. She had a life of her own, didn't she? She'd promise occasionally to stay in with the boy, but most nights he would watch her as she made her face up and got ready to leave him on his own with his grandfather.'

Kate frowned suddenly. 'Sorry, Harry. I forgot to tell you that this is a sad story.' She nodded, looking sombre, voice low. She could see that he was straining for every word. 'Oh yes. Very sad. Because the boy wanted his sister to stay with him. He didn't want to be with his grandfather. Grandad said funny things. Because Grandad had known something for years that the boy was just about to learn.' Kate leaned forward slightly, dropping her voice further. 'Grandad knew that the boy's sister wasn't his sister at all! What do you think of that?' She waited a few seconds. 'Have you guessed yet who she *really* was?'

She sat back and waited again. No response except for a reddening of Creed's eyes and a watchful quality to his face. 'No? Well, she was . . . his *mother*.' She saw his lips flatten into a thin line. 'I expected you to get that, Harry. Anyway, then the boy hated her, his mother. Because she was a sham. She'd lied to him for ten, eleven years. All of his life, in fact.'

Kate waited, looking into Creed's face, the skin stretched tight, the eyes riveted on hers. Seeing that he was not about to speak, she continued.

'And that's the end of the sad story . . . Oh, I forgot something else. I haven't told you what happened to the boy, have I?' She could hear him breathing into the brittle air between them. 'You see, the hatred the boy had for his sister who was really his mother just grew and grew. As he got older, he decided that no matter what they looked like, *every* woman was really like her. A sham. A lie. And he was *very* angry. But the women he was *most* angry towards were tall, slim young women who wore tasteful clothes and subtle cosmetics, whose hair was soft and blonde. He *really* hated them. Because he saw how good they were at concealing their true selves. He *had* to remove the masquerade. To expose the truth beneath.' Kate gazed at the rigid face, softening her voice. 'He had to find his mother.'

Silently, without taking her eyes off him, she felt for her notebook and drew something from between its pages. Holding it up so that he could see it clearly, she spoke softly again,

'Say hello to Mommy, Harry.'

That was when he lost all control. His eyes were almost completely white, face livid, flecks of saliva flying from his mouth, shocking the officers guarding Kate into action. They fell on him. An alarm sounded. Four additional officers rushed into the mayhem. It took them over a minute to haul him from the room.

Kate could still hear him, the high-pitched shriek now growing gradually fainter as they dragged him back to his cell. She looked down at the photograph lying on the table in front of her, studied the elaborately curled peroxide hair, the moon face heavily blushed, thick mascara around the eyes, sulky lips a downturned clot of slick red, thick neck pushing up from a sea of frills framing a deep cleavage to which a young boy was tightly clasped. Beyond the harsh cosmetics, Kate recognised something in the woman's face reminiscent of Harry Creed the adult. Rapaciousness.

Looking shaken, the Kilt walked slowly into the room and came to

379

where Kate was still sitting. He sat on the edge of the table, looking down at her, distractedly stroking a hand over his head.

'You okay, Kate?'

'I'm fine, Gus,' she said quietly.

He continued to stroke his head. 'How do you explain something like – *that*?'

She looked up at him. 'He needs to control and punish his mother.' She stood awkwardly and he put a hand under her arm to walk with her to the door. 'She died. Twelve years ago. But he keeps searching for and exposing her.'

CHAPTER SEVENTY-SIX

Kate was on leave from her work. All of it. For a month. Her leg was healing, the doctor who'd stitched it assuring her that his handiwork would leave nothing but an eventual faint scar.

She was now lying on the sofa, the cat curled awkwardly at her side. They were watching Morse, who was still grumpy.

A series of thumps down the stairs and across the hall and Maisie erupted through the door.

'Mom! Joe and Bernie are outside. And Joe's carrying this massive—'

Kate looked across at her and smiled. 'Homework finished?' Maisie nodded, curls chaotic.

Immediately after Chelsey's rescue, Maisie had sobbed, 'I'm sorry, I'm sorry' over and over again. Kate knew it was because she believed she was responsible for Chelsey's abduction. Because she'd allowed her friend to walk into danger alone. She'd had to explain to Maisie that she'd made a good judgement by not going too, that there was nothing she could have done to stop Chelsey from making the wrong choice. Chelsey had made her decision based on glib talk from Creed, starting when she saw him loitering near the entrance to the school, sufficiently plausible to snare the young and naïve. And some who were older and more worldly than Chelsey, who was now on the way to a full recovery. Maisie's own progress had been helped by a card from Chief Inspector Gander, thanking her for her contribution to the identification of Harry Creed.

Now Maisie squatted in front of Mugger, scratching him lightly between his ears.

'You silly cat. What you mustn't do in future is take on a fox! Don't *do* that!' She shook a finger at him, then laughed and stroked his head. 'See? That's another lesson you missed! Now, if you're very good, the

381

vet said your collar can come off tomorrow.' She turned to look at Kate.

'Mom?'

'Mm . . . ?'

'Do you think he's okay? He was in Mrs Hetherington's garden for ages before Bernie found him. He might have psychological problems.'

'Mugger or Bernie?'

Stroking the cat, Maisie looked sideways at her mother. 'As you're back to your normal self, can we talk about Facebook?'

The door of the sitting room swung open and Phyllis looked into the room. She'd had a quick discussion with their visitors about Kate's convalescence.

'Them two are here. Shall I let 'em in?'

'Of course, Phyllis.'

Phyllis disappeared, muttering, 'Suppose they'll be wanting coffee and . . .'

Kate and Maisie listened as Bernie's voice reverberated from the hall.

'How you doin', sweetheart?'

Phyllis's response was a series of unclear murmurings.

'Play hard to get. I won't give up!'

Maisie leaned against the sofa, giggling, as Bernie and Joe walked into the sitting room, Joe with a huge bouquet of roses and a card. Kate looked up at him.

'Somehow, Corrigan, I hadn't seen this as your style.'

He grinned. 'It's from all at Rose Road. *Including* Furman.'

'That I do *not* believe!'

'No? I'm cut to the fibre of my being, honey chil', that you should ever doubt me. Hi, Cat's-whiskers.'

Maisie grinned up at Joe. 'Hi yourself.'

A tray of coffee cups in one hand, Phyllis elbowed Bernie, but mainly for effect. She knew the role he and Joe had played in Kate's rescue. She took the roses from Joe.

Joe smiled down at Kate, then bent his long legs so that their faces were level. 'It's true. He spoke highly of you not an hour ago.' Kate looked at him, searching for sarcasm. 'Seriously, Red. We had a very pleasant team meeting. Furman paid tribute to your outstanding

382

intelligence, your beauty and my arrest technique. He also expressed his sincere relief that Ber-nard has been passed as fit.'

'He was thrilled all right,' said Bernie, eye-rolling.

Joe continued the story: 'Then he expounded for around ten minutes on the Force's duty to protect the young and the vulnerable in society, after which we followed him to the High Street for a celebratory team lunch, where he narrowly missed making roadkill of the *Big Issue* guy in the Waitrose car park.'

'What! Is he okay?' Kate thought of the courtly man who worked the pitch outside the supermarket.

'Yep. Leapt like a gazelle from Furman's wheels. We decided to skip lunch.'

'You idiots!' laughed Kate. Reminded of the young and vulnerable, she asked, 'How's Julian?'

'He's fine. Creed was doing a real number on him. And Julian was doing all *he* could to resist his influence. Creed thought that Julian was malleable, so he made a point of befriending him, slowly trying to groom him, offering him tabs. He was too worried and in awe of Creed to say anything.'

Kate looked concerned. 'But is he all right? Tell him he can come and stay here . . .'

'He's shaping up fine, Doc. I think he was shocked how Creed turned out, like we all was, but he's young and he's coming to terms. He's been stopping over at my place most of this week. Tell you what, that lad can cook!'

Kate's thoughts drifted to something Bernie had said about repeaters being people's sons and husbands, a phrase he'd attributed to Julian. Doubtless Julian *had* said it, but she now thought of its more likely source. Harry Creed. Quoting the words of the beleaguered police officer heading the hunt for the Yorkshire Ripper years before, the meaning of his reference being that repeaters were all but indistinguishable from anyone else.

Wrong.

If we're vigilant, we see them.

She also thought back to what she'd said about the psychopath as work colleague. It was true. Creed, the manipulator of Prentiss. She knew that it was Creed who'd compromised the evidence-gathering. Doubtless he had manipulated Prentiss into a position where he had no choice but to accept the blame. Prentiss's demeanour was now much more understandable. Who wouldn't be angry?

They'd read Creed's medical and educational records. After the references to his emotional and behavioural difficulties as a youngster, and his seemingly aimless teenage years, there was an indication of him appearing to settle down. He'd started an arts course. Kate would have staked money on it including some kind of sculpture. She rejoined the talk in the room.

Bernie slurped coffee. 'A real con man, Doc. An ac-tor. When Creed the late-starter done his forensic training in the early nineties, he was based at Bradford Street. That was Regional Headquarters then. I've now spoke with a couple of people who worked there at the time. They've got no recollection of him being gay.' He shook his head. 'He sabotaged all the records of our cases. He interviewed Amelie Dijon, posing as Furman. By the way, Goosey's torn a strip off Furman about his management style. Doubt it'll make any real difference to the Arse's underlying attitudes, mind you.'

Kate raised her brows and grinned. 'Bernie, you sounded quite psychologically minded when you said that.'

Bernie watched as Maisie walked to the sitting-room door and out, Mugger in her arms.

'Yeah, well . . . You was right about his other motive, by the way.'

Kate shook her head. 'Making sadism pay. Producing heavy-end pornography from it. That way he got to enjoy each of the murders for as long as he wished, and so did his paying clients, in their case, vicariously.'

Bernie looked disgusted. 'They're being visited by Upstairs. We've seen a calendar Creed was working on. He called it his "work in progress". Said he was waiting for the cold weather so he could finish it – 'December'. Some of the images are equivalent to the highest level on the Copine.'

Kate recognised the reference to the scale used to evaluate the level of deviance of child-abuse images. She looked away. She couldn't take too many reminders yet.

Joe perched on the sofa arm looking down at her.

'You done good, Red,' he said quietly. 'Connie and the team are working full-time at the bypass. And the Facility.'

Kate's thoughts spooled to what they now knew about Harry Creed and his towering rage towards his mother. How many dead girls would have been found to have paid for it with their lives by the time it was all finished? Creed was a vacuum. An emotionally empty vessel who wanted to render others empty by reducing them to nothing. He wasn't seeking retribution. He simply enjoyed doing what he did.

She thought of Creed inside her house. The locks had all been changed and an alarm system installed. The bill for three thousand pounds was modest for ensuring Maisie's safety and Kate's peace of mind, even if Creed was incarcerated.

'What a waste,' she said softly, then looked up at Joe. 'I can't do it any more. UCU. I'm not suited to it. I'm too impatient to follow rules or be in a team. But it's more than that. There were so many cues and clues that I missed—'

Bernie intervened: 'You never missed 'em. You wrote 'em down and—'

'Exactly. So much information and I *still* didn't see it. It's made me realise – I respond to our cases as if they're academic exercises. I got so caught up in solving the puzzle that I lost impetus.' She looked away. 'It could have resulted in Chelsey . . .'

Joe gazed down at her. 'Listen up, Kate. It's the same for all of us. When we first notice something, it's not always possible to see its relevance. Or even if it *is* relevant. When does a cue become a clue, huh? It takes time for all that stuff to form a pattern so we can recognise its meaning.'

'Yes, and by the time it did, Chelsey was in his hands and Maisie could have—'

'Hey, cut yourself some slack, Kate. You got the answer. You took days to solve cases that were ten-plus years old.'

Bernie leaned towards her. 'You'll get used to police work, Doc, as you do more of it.'

'No. Police work's about rules and procedures. I don't get on very well with either of those. And like *you* say, Bernie, I feel safe in Theory Alley. Non-emotional, contained. And that goes back to the first problem—'

'Blimey, that's ten minutes I'll never get back. Is there much more of this?'

'There's nothing to blame yourself for, Kate,' Joe said. 'Why would anybody think of it being an inside job? Nobody else did. You got the answer. It was the same for us. We knew what you knew. When we were in Gander's office last time, I was looking at the photographs on the wall to avoid listening to Furman and stop myself smacking him in the mouth. *I* saw the photograph of Creed and his hair but I didn't connect it with what Bernie said about the French student who was raped. See? With twenty-twenty vision it can seem obvious. It isn't.'

He paused, then said: 'What you did took real courage, Kate. You *strode* in there, for Maisie's friend – not an easy act to pull off when you're only five-three.' He grinned down at her. 'One tough broad. Nobody knew how tough.'

'Me included,' said Kate with a shudder.

Bernie heaved himself off the sofa, glancing out of the window. 'I got a few things to do back at Rose Road. Looks like summer's over. Sky's black over Bill's mother's.'

Joe looked at Kate, eyebrows up. She shook her head and grinned.

Kate was exhausted.

'Where's Maisie?' she asked.

'Making a cake with Phyllis,' said Joe, looking up from the chords he was practising quietly on the Gibson L5 guitar. He'd brought it to the house days before, when Kate began her convalescence, and had visited every day since, waiting patiently for her to recover.

'Joe?'

'Kate?'

'When I said to you ages ago about you being pleased you didn't have children. And you said . . .'

He stopped playing and looked at her for some seconds. 'Is it important that you know?'

Kate looked up at him. 'Yes . . . *No.*'

'Pity Bernie's gone. He'd have loved *that*, for sure.'

Seeing the small frown above Kate's nose, he went to sit next to her. She leaned her head on his shoulder as he spoke quietly. 'How's the leg?'

'Fine . . . Don't change the subject. Tell me.' She yawned.

'Okay. Well now, let's see. Once upon a hippy time, I was at university. And so was she. I was a real young kinda dude. We got married. Fast-forward about five years and we knew that all we shared was our . . .' He looked down at Kate, sleeping soundly.

'I guess it'll keep for another day,' he said quietly. He listened as Kate murmured something in her sleep and grinned down at her.

It sounded like 'density'.

EPILOGUE

Several weeks after the separate funeral services for Janine and Molly, all from UCU were invited to a combined memorial to celebrate the lives of the two young women. Invitations suggested that those attending did so in colourful clothes. Kate had been reluctant to go until it was confirmed that no press were to be allowed anywhere near.

She walked into the little church wearing a cream-coloured coat, the nearest to colourful that she owned. Maisie had lent her a long lapis-blue scarf with fringes and sequins. Alongside Kate were Joe, Bernie and Julian, wearing matching pale-blue ties embroidered with tiny dark-blue flowers.

Every surface inside the church was covered with informally arranged pink roses. 'In Paradisum' from Fauré's Requiem played as the guests assembled.

During the service, 'Nimrod' surged through the building. Kate had her jaws clamped together so hard her face ached. Then there were smiles as parents and other relatives and friends of the two young women related their memories of them.

At the conclusion of the service the congregation was informed that the music that would play them out of the church was the choice of both mothers. Gasps of surprise and more smiles appeared when the first familiar strains of 'Here Comes the Sun' were heard. The buoyant crowd surged out through the church doors, then clustered in smiling groups in the cold winter sun, some still singing.

Afterwards, Kate and her colleagues went back to the Walkers' house. She watched guests remove their bright coats and scarves, faces flushed by the early-December chill. The house was filled with flowers. One wall of the sitting room was given over to a display of photographs. Two smiling young women at various stages of their short lives.

Kate left Bernie and Joe and walked towards a spray of yellow roses in a tall vase at the centre of a table full of food. She touched them gently, recognising them as UCU's contribution.

Furman was hovering at the other side of the table. Their eyes met. As far as Kate was concerned, there was little he could say to defend his careless response to the destruction of all four young women. She knew he'd been officially admonished. After a few seconds he nodded at her. She acknowledged him. If she were him, she wouldn't have dared come today. She turned away and walked over to Joe, who was in conversation with Paul Walker.

Mr Walker turned to her. 'Dr Hanson, thank you so much for helping us celebrate Janine and Molly's lives. And for uncovering Janine's spirit, even when her situation was so bleak.'

Kate nodded, knowing he was referring to the little note she'd taken from Chelsey's hand as she was removed from the workshop at Winterton.

It had lain in a crack in the cement floor of that horrific place for all those years, a testament to Janine's knowledge of her killer and her determination to identify him: *Janine Harry LIAR help me.* The workshop had yielded other evidence. Jewellery. Clothing. Other items that Kate and her colleagues recognised, others as yet unidentified.

Kate opened her bag and took out a small red volume and handed it to Mr Walker. It could be returned now that the criminal case against Creed was prepared. He nodded his thanks. Seeing this, Mrs Walker came over to them, hugged Kate and kissed Joe.

'We're so pleased you're all here. We'll be posting photographs on the website in a few days. Look, there's our son, Nick, and his baby.'

Kate looked towards the door at a tall fair-haired man carrying a laughing infant in his arms, then turned back to find Dianne James standing next to her.

'Hi,' she began, unsure of what else to say. It suddenly occurred to her that Dianne looked different.

'I've taken myself in hand,' the other woman said in response to Kate's uncertain glance. 'After UCU became involved with Janine's case, Paul and Isobel got in touch with me.'

Kate glanced to where the Walkers were talking and laughing with various guests, and saw Bernie deep in conversation with Connie. She looked back at Dianne.

'So . . . you're feeling . . .'

'I don't get angry or fall apart at the slightest word any more. Molly's loss will always be there, but I'm learning to live with that. They –' she nodded towards the Walkers – 'helped me realise that we grieve because we love . . . and that I was letting Molly down by living as I was. She's up here.' Dianne tapped her forehead. 'And I had to start being different. To give her a better place to be.' She glanced around the room. 'There's quite a few of us in our group now. People who've lost children to violent crime.'

Kate looked at her, remembering how she herself had felt when they first met. 'Dianne . . . when I visited . . . I didn't know what to say to you. I hope I didn't appear uncaring . . .'

The other woman shook her head. 'You didn't. How are you now?'

'I'm back at work. The university.'

Dianne smiled. An attractive woman, Kate realised. A woman with a purpose. She thought of Suzie Luckman's mother, now in full-time care.

Is it better to struggle through grief or to be relieved of it through incapacity?

She breathed deeply.

Maybe just . . . different.

Dianne had something to ask Kate. 'I've been told he'll get life. What does that mean? Will they keep him in for . . . always?'

Kate answered truthfully. 'Harry Creed is dangerous. But he has human rights. His lawyers will probably want to get special hospital status for him. If they succeed and once he's there, he'll put on a show, manipulate his way around the system, volunteer for all the treatment programmes available, as a result of which, if he's ever released, he'll be even better at manipulating people than when he went inside.' She stopped, biting her lip. 'Sorry to sound bleak. And I seriously doubt he'll ever be released.'

Dianne nodded. 'I appreciate your honesty. What a waste there's been already. Who knows what he'll have cost other families before the investigation has run its course and we know the full extent of it.'

Kate knew that excavation of the bypass had been extended still further and was continuing. The grounds around Winterton were also being dug up. What better place to hide remains than in a location where they were legitimately kept? After it had been fully excavated, the plan was to demolish the house and related outbuildings.

Dianne glanced across the room, then back to Kate with a smile. 'I think somebody's looking for you.'

Kate looked in the same direction. Joe.

In the last days of the year, the four colleagues were back together at Rose Road. Boiler trouble had left the building without heat for the last two days and it was deathly cold inside UCU. The table was covered with boxes, each with a clear label. Gander had lent them Whittaker, who had worked tirelessly in scarf and fingerless gloves to help them sort and label the documents.

Kate was at the window, staring at the smart little terraced houses opposite. All quiet. Residents able to go about their business and park their cars, unhampered by media vehicles. What had begun in this room as a very cold case had become one of the biggest inquiries in the UK, certainly the biggest West Midlands Police had ever had. Still ongoing Upstairs. Only yesterday, Kate had driven along the bypass and seen bright yellow digging machines passing between leafless trees.

Kate had also seen Creed. A few weeks ago. When he was taken to court and remanded again. It had emerged that he intended to make a plea of diminished responsibility at his trial. He was now biding his time in the special hospital unit. Kate's responsibility at some future date would be to testify to the callous planning and heartless calculation of which he was capable.

'Kate?' Hearing Joe's voice, she turned back to the room and walked to the table. Each of them took a box and headed for the basement. To the 'solved' section. When the table was empty, they walked out of the room and stood together in the corridor. Joe looked at each of them as he closed the door of the Unsolved Crime Unit.

Till the next time.

He lay on his narrow bed and pressed the button on the remote control for recorded programmes. Up came the list. He went immediately to the one he wanted. A *Sky News* report. He watched himself come into view, his upper body concealed by a blanket. With compressed lips he watched as he was led from the prison van, scarcely visible, to a side door of the court building. The scene was ill-lit, the filming done from the road.

The location suddenly shifted. To the front of the same building. He slowed the recording. Here she was, in bright winter sunshine, highly visible in her tailored suit and high heels, as she slow-motion walked from right to left on the screen and the camera ate her up. He reran it. Right to left. Reran. Right to left. He stared at her image, at the dark-red hair bouncing and swaying around her shoulders.

His mouth formed a smile. He knew they would search all recorded programmes at the end of the week. They would delete this one. He'd lose tokens for being 'bad'. But he had a plan. To be really good in future. See where that got him during the long haul.

The smile stretched into a wide grin. He breathed out words as he watched her on the screen, vital, confident. Free.

'*Seee yooouuu!*'

ACKNOWLEDGEMENTS

My sincere thanks to the following for their valued professional advice and patient guidance: Chief Inspector Keith Fackrell, West Midlands Police (Retired); Lynne Hart, Assistant to H.M. Coroner, Birmingham and Solihull Districts; David C. Knight, PhD, Assistant Professor, Department of Psychology, University of Alabama at Birmingham; Sam Taylor, Fitness Trainer, Birmingham; and Dr Adrian Yoong, Consultant Pathologist, Birmingham.

Given the quality of their support, any technical mistakes are, needless to say, my own.